I0817875

TULL & EBBE

SEVEN WINTERS' TIME

THE SECOND NOVEL FROM

GRIFFIN WRAY

107|18

Tull & Ebbe

Seven Winters' Time

Hardback Edition ISBN-13: 978-0-9993776-1-1

Released by Uskoa Press on March 25, 2021.

Wrap cover design and illustrations created by
Yannick Bouchard at illusorydreams.com.

Visit **uskoamythos.com** to view a map of the isle and to learn trivia about this tale.

"The LORD will fight for you, and you have only to be silent."

Exodus 14:14

The Holy Bible, English Standard Version®

"Do not be unequally yoked together with unbelievers. For what fellowship has righteousness with lawlessness? And what communion has light with darkness?"

2 Corinthians 6:14

The Holy Bible, New King James Version®

The appearance of "LORD" in small caps is used in place of His true name.

The Second Creation of Yah—the characters in this and other Uskoa Press novels who do not exist in our time—abide by a varying translation of Scripture that does not deviate from the core meaning but is fitted to the language of their land.

CONTENTS

2 | Still

In a Time Afore

The 14th Eve beneath the Moon of the Old Embers
The 91st Gathering Season of the Accession
In the blessing of I'Esh, who tends the harvest.

Ebbe Demesne of the Shelby Territory
191 Taurog Roadway.
84 ticks of the clock since bedtime.

The Old Fathers wrote of a time when Yah heard their fathers' warring from the throne room of His supernal perch and wept for the unending wickedness of His Second Creation. His tears seared the veil that separated His realm from His creation's and fell upon them like fire. The embers burned with such ferocity that not even the seas extinguished them afore they reached the caverns of the Fallen First that rested beneath the seas and set loose His betrayers. Out of His promise to never rid the terrane of the secondkind again, He sent the purest of His warring ministers to defend those who broke His perfect heart.

The Last War of the Second Creation paled by comparison to the battles of the First Creation. As all that was once unseen became visible, the land that Yah prepared for the secondkind changed evermore. Continents overturned and became isles, and their many seas flowed as one whilst all that was recorded and established collapsed. The Old Fathers marked this time as the Accession of the First Creation; a coy dismissal of their own blasphemy—of their warring—against Yah's perfect plan.

Now, not far from the battlefield where the Last War ended, nor where the shadows flowed like streams unto wickedness, stood the oldest structure in the

Shelby Territory. Neither those who built in the timber-lush Jacoby Territory at their western border nor those who carved out their purposes in the ore-laden Carpenter Territory at their eastern border had a view of the forty-six-room plot called Ebbe Demesne in this time. The Shelbians, who settled near the territory's abundant streams and waterways, had less excuse than their neighbors. Then again, they learned of the well-told curse.

Afore the Accession, the castle-like ancestral home of a family no longer counted amid the territories was surrounded by orchards ripe for farming and hunting. The plot's owner served as benefactor of one hundred nineteen souls and was counted as a fair liege. He was reported as fair in rule, though stricter on his sons than his workers. History proved that those who loved him suffered a hasty end.

Both his adult sons saw their ends in hunting accidents; the first by beast, the second by his own father's hand, and joined the mother who died amid the fog when her sons were still blameless. Unhinged by grief and haunted by wailing voices without form, the name-stricken patriarch turned his hand against his heart. The workers fled, the fields turned fruitless, but the curse remained. After this, the family name and ancestral home withered.

As the place fell unto dereliction, a greater terror made histories vanish. Winds reshaped mighty nations and seas rerouted creation; but Ebbe Demesne withstood. The plot dared an unseen hand to strike. Her fields overturned and a new forest grew unto an entanglement with the former till they created a natural defense around the cursed ancestral home and as far as the foothills to the east. The secondkind called this entanglement the Behemót Woods.

In a place that gathered fog and shadows, new residents clustered. Their form matched no other, yet they were all the same. Their skin had the luster of stone and wood. Their eyes looked like flame-hollowed candles. Fire from the swords of their siblings burned their mouths, lest they speak rebukes against the Creator whose throne room they once kept. But their limbs, six in all, terrified the most; for they moved faster than other fallen creatures and were weightless, as though in flight.

Shelbians—many of whom worshiped the glebe—learned to keep their travels pointed away from Ebbe Demesne because of these swift and misshapen creatures. Oft did they hear the cries from the dark that turned a hearth cold, but seldom did they risk for those who dared to forge a new legacy amid the ruins. Those who invited suffering deserved wrath. True Shelbians did not sacrifice for other souls.

TULL & EBBE

The blameless soul never needed to fear the surrounding darkness of the eve; unlike those selfish Shelbians. The pure heart and the unpolluted mind stood as the greatest pieces of armor meant to defend against the most treacherous of weapons: the Liar's tongue. So near to the Behemót Woods, lie-filled fear took the form of tendrils of light, a chorus of disembodied shrieks, and the plucking of souls from their paths. These conditions mingled and shook an orphan from his blamelessness—seventy moons afore his intended time.

In Yah's displeasure for the hurrying of His sculpted plan, a gathering of Squires—none bigger than the bare-footed runner—descended. They sought those creatures who hid in the lush forest and dwelt between entangled branches as if in secret. Yah would not show them kindness in their preying or challenging. No Creator would.

The sharpness of thorns cut open tender soles and unleashed waves of heat that mingled with the fright that stirred the blameless heart. As he stood idle in pain and unsure of his next step, a path-leading light from above stopped too. He held no kettle lantern and the woods received none of the secondkind's abstruse progress. This light burned purer than fire, swifter than the eye, and as steady as a peace-filled soul. Even so, in his blamelessness, the runner did not yet perceive the source.

Cries from within the darkness urged him to flee, but the eve and a lack of sense toward his surroundings muddled his path. Still, against all that might crush his spirit, he took his next step as the light led him. He pushed onward and away from briars and Ebbe Demesne. The Behemót Woods that did not keep out harm worked in defense's stead to visit harm upon an unintended prey.

"Come this way!" A voice in the woods sought to lure.

A focused light pierced the entanglement of limbs and branches, then a shrill cry ascended. The soul who fled gasped even as his faultless eyes filled with the sky-fires' reflection. As a Squire rid the eve of the luring spirit, the runner remembered his plight when, beneath him, the terrane slithered as if he stood on a beast. He turned toward walls he could no longer see and observed the tendrils of emerald colors that scraped against the sky-fires' belly from the manor's glass atriums.

"This way!"

"'Yah, our perfect Creator, makes war in my name!'"

This second voice he recognized, but his ear deceived him afore. He knew also the words—a verse—of which the speaker made him memorize one half for a moment such as this. If they were separated, he would not be lost for the speaker would call out her half of the verse as proof that she sought him. Though he obeyed his unspoken words, he could not find the voice to call out to her. Another snap of branches from a different place in the darkness then confused him further.

"I say, 'Yah, our perfect Creator, makes war in my name!'"

Conflicting directions upset the blameless soul but the light above shone brighter. He then broke from his arrangement with she who called, and ran. As he raced harder, he sought a trail hammered upon the terrane by the hooves of Ligurus; a stallion with eyes that never rested and a reassuring step that eased a frightened soul. He trusted that any path made by the stallion would keep him from harm, though the light sought another path for him.

In a safe route's stead, he discovered a tree that captivated the imagination. Though humble in span and sparse in fruit, the trunk of this timeworn almond bore hatchet scars where the bark fell away. No blameless soul could imagine, let alone fear, a foe that deserved such harm. As trails of fire crisscrossed, silhouettes crept amid the twisted branches that grew downward and near to his crown. The exposed pulp of the almond tree shimmered like the low-slung moon and a sound like patient breathing grew surer in his ears, even as limbs creaked and bent.

Mesmerized by what stood afore, he paid no mind to what crept behind. A creature with an indistinct face borrowed more than a polite share of the eve's cloak and gained on the soul whose bare feet bled. Bulbous, misshapen hands squeezed the dagger-like end of a branch as two more arms extended from between shoulders and hips with the intention of the creature's heart. Whilst others suffered in their ceaseless attempts to overthrow the supernal, this fallen creature settled for the ease of delivering a blameless soul to his end.

Like that unsuspecting soul, the twisted figure—whose visage matched their soul in the moment of their turn against Yah—fixated too long on what kept from reach. By the time galloping hooves coursed through the glebe, the creature's time of prowess ended. The oblong head marred by extinguished sockets and a singed mouth took the brunt of a horse's unforgiving brow as a pair of lights converged near an opening in the overturned terrane above. Ligurus batted away the threat and kept low as his rider leaned so far to one side that a lesser horse might topple.

A smooth arm plucked the idle runner off his feet and made his eyes widen as he raced headlong toward the scarred tree. In the same moment, from high above them, a plume of white flame announced the departure of a creature whose form gleamed as burnished bronze. As for the bright-eyed runner, his entire body rolled backward and away from collision as a second hand seized his thigh and flipped him. His deepest gasp made his head swim in the powdery-sweet scent of clematis terniflora.

His memory responded by way of a searching hand and he felt both a racing heart and a leather rein. Ligurus, with his rear hoof, crushed the head of the creature who failed. Softness enveloped the runner like the dark. Then, from a proud breast, the purr of a trusted voice coaxed the rescued soul to settle.

"Worry not, beloved Nelson, for I have found you."

Squires dragged the Fallen First from their hiding places and still more cleared a path for the fearless stallion. Blameless Nelson James Tull's rescuers never turned from that path. In the dark of the Behemót Woods, though, even the most trusted course changed. Either the horse stepped amiss or his rider lost her perception for they ended up at a stopping point created by a steep hillside that offered no way out.

Sondrea Ebbe Conliffe, who spent her blamelessness on Ebbe Demesne, stayed aware of the dangers of the Behemót Woods. She kept reins in hand as she nestled the small body to hers and witnessed the rising from the terrane wall of creatures who stood as the secondkind stood. No Squire raced down in rescue. Her heart raced and matched that of he whom she held, that she might further shield him.

The whispers of spirits fell as the dust from those surrounding foes. Still, she did not cower. In point of fact, she sat prouder upon Ligurus than seemed responsible and drew the eye toward her pure-hued gown as a target. She found amid those foes the form that the other shapes looked toward and kept her copper-hued eyes fixed. Only her thumb moved as she stroked Nelson's neck and kept hidden the soft light of the identifier beacon that rested beneath his flesh.

"Keep as still as you can"—she drew him in—"and I will keep you as near as I can."

Afore the last syllable of her promise reached his ear, a rush of air produced a drum-like thud that took the strongest off his feet. Those who responded with sharp gasps and cautionary stances shared a similar fate; not one, but two at a time. Six fell afore the others coiled back unto the glebe in retreat. Footsteps as heavy as Ligurus's then produced a resonating voice that mimicked the reserved hush of fired arrows. "My granddaughter?"

"Here I wait."

TULL & EBBE

A hand larger than any other north of the Loy River settled atop Ligurus's crown and teased the stallion's right ear with a stroke that mimicked the sensation against the boy's neck. "You rode well, young friend."

The horse nodded in acceptance of the remark and struck the glebe with his front right hoof. His jostled rider chuckled and took another breath. As her chest swelled with relief, she kept her hold on Nelson but inspected his wounded feet.

"He misses his folk?"

"He misses the peace that Mim stole from him with tales of my father's parlor." When her eyes met with the blameless orphan's, she drummed his chin with her index finger. "You gave me such a fright. I believed I'd lost you."

Tears filled in their elder's eyes but did not fall across his age-creased cheeks.

"Evermore will I find you."

"You must give thanks to the Triune this eve," that booming voice demanded with all gentleness, "and teach the boy to pray as he ought."

"I will, as you say, Grandfather."

"I believed you would."

Nelson followed the hand atop Ligurus's crown toward a silhouette that made giants tremble. The darkness of the woods surrendered not one glimpse of his face but could not dim his crown of snowy hair. Still, the blameless soul imagined being watched by a soul so mighty.

"Use a sure hand when you pull the thorns from him."

"As you say. I will mend him well!" She hugged and kissed her passenger.

"Trust in my granddaughter, blameless soul. We will let no harm find you again."

Again. How oft promises clung to that setting point.

The mightiest of hands slipped from Ligurus's head and the silhouette moved nearer to the horse's ear. "Take them to see my Maia now."

"You'll travel with us?"

"No."

Ligurus kept Sondrea from arguing with a soul feared by many creatures, but never by her. To her, Beau Itzal Zeck was the gentlest, warmest, and most loving soul ever formed by their Creator. The misshapen retreated away from he of mighty legend, though bulbous hands swatted at blameless crowns and tugged at the hem of pure-hued gowns. As Ligurus put distance between them, his smallest rider listened for the sounds of heavy feet making little noise as he walked toward trouble alone.

TULL & EBBE

Screams then reached new heights of fear. Ligurus trotted faster but the sounds still reached their ears. Letting pass how his rescuers sought to shield him, the blameless soul learned ways to map strange surroundings with senses that went unchanged by the darkness. In this, Yah found a way to guide him in his purpose; letting pass what the Fallen First, Ebbe Demesne, or the Taotáva whom Zeck now terrified had planned.

Maia Espe Zeck, mother to the rider and daughter to the soul who faced harm alone, took Nelson with both hands and returned his feet to the glebe even though she saw his wounds. She had eyes as warm as embers and dimples that she kept from Sondrea's face. With an affectionate hand, she wiped Nelson's cheeks. "There are many frightening sounds, but you need not fear them. You may believe my word."

"Mama cannot lie." The fiery-headed rider claimed. "Papa saw to that."

"We've heard our fill of tales this eve, my daughter." Maia's tone heeded a threat that went unseen. "Take him unto the parlor, mend his feet well, and keep him warm now. I'll see to Ligurus."

Neither moved.

"Worry not, daughter. Your grandfather will return to us soon and I am in no danger. Do as I say now. I have told Mim to keep his tales within." She reached out and gave Sondrea's chin a gentle squeeze. "We cannot all suffer our imaginations."

Nelson felt a hand tug him from Maia Espe Zeck's warmth and through the doorway toward rooms where wood heat billowed, but the pair went no further. They stood like statues—as still as Sondrea requested of him afore—and watched as Maia tethered Ligurus's reins; though, they divided their interests for hope-filled glimpses of the soul who protected them but kept to the Behemót Woods rather than setting his heel upon Ebbe Demesne.

"You two!" Maia laughed as she returned, then turned her daughter's course toward the inner rooms. "Come! This is not our purpose."

As mother and daughter debated such claims, the blameless soul who belonged to neither felt a need to get one more look at Ligurus. The keen-witted horse, as if to reassure him, dipped his brow and struck the glebe a single time. His audience traded worries for a smile and waved to the stallion afore a gleam of light rolled along the slick crown of a soul with shadow-hidden eyes and a beard that concealed the throat. Ligurus huffed at Mim—storyteller and bully of blameless souls—who made a terrible face toward the child, as if a creature to be feared in the dark, then led the stallion away.

Though the soul who caused the commotion tried to watch over Ligurus, Maia closed the door between them. This motion, unbeknownst to him, also ceased her daughter's bickering. Neither fretted over the horse's safety, nor Mim's unsettling ways. Their reeve subsisted to disturb the soul in their care. As Maia claimed, his storytelling and agitation needled and, in peace's stead, made spirits of fear and doubt aware of whom he riled.

Whilst Maia stoked a wood fire, she who rode Ligurus crouched and inspected her rescue in the light. Though she sniffled, and tears amplified her copper-hued irises as she pulled thorns from between his toes, she offered a peace-filled smile and the scent of clematis terniflora that arose from her warmed skin. He offered a subdued grin; still, his pewter irises drifted above her head of brilliant tresses toward the opposite wall where a mural of four men offered courage; save one. Amid the bravery of other souls, he who fled found hope again.

"Letting pass what Mama says, would you like me to tell you how neither of us would be born lest the souls in your beloved mural took an interest?"

Even as he nodded, she took him beneath his arms and hoisted him toward a couch that let them lay and gaze together. She kept his ear close to her heart, that she might soothe him and train him to know her above any other in the Seven Territories. Her mother offered no objection but dimmed the light of the room and locked them in. Whilst the cries in the wind and the tendrils of unnatural light lasted till morn, no harm shook the walls that eve as the Countess of Ebbe Demesne began her tale.

"There were, in our past, four souls who were brave; almost as brave as I will see you become . . ."

Guardians & Foes

One

The 25th Eve beneath the Moon of the Weeping Stone
The 72nd Sowing Season of the Accession
In the Mercy of Yah, who gives the rain, the seed, and the bloom.

The Knotted Caves
The Carpenter Territory Limestone Lodes.
12.5 parasang east of the Behemót Woods.

The Last War of the Second Creation ended without a victor—this much, all souls amid the secondkind learned afore all other lessons. Those who survived the warring instructed their fruit and, with somewhat exaggerated tales, retold the events of their time to the era that followed. Ministers descended from the sky-fires and battled the Fallen First who clawed from the glebe and swam through the Forbidden Sea. These were the First Creation and the reason why the secondkind no longer warred and seldom ruled.

The secondkind lived by the *moon*. Their calendar counted one *span* of thirteen distinct *moons*, each of which cycled for twenty-eight risings and settings. The measure of time began with the moonrise—the *eve*—followed by moonset—the *morn*—and the highest point of warmth and light—the *peak*—when souls hid from the Fallen First and sought slumber. After a deep winter, the entirety of Yah's creation sought a fruitful return out of doors and beneath the span's first moon that marked the thaw of the seventy-second span since the Accession of the First Creation.

All experienced a moment when the unseen proved visible and marked an end in their time of blamelessness. Those who perceived and understood were called

Believers. Those who saw and denied were called Partakers. Each splintered into preferred sects, but at their core remained united: Believers lived in obedience to the Ministers and their shared Creator. Partakers lived against them and sympathized with the downcast Fallen First.

The Accession redefined creation's structure of might and prowess. The armies of the secondkind, their governments and their churches, fell as the sea rose and divided nations. Continents were reformed, divided by a single, unending sea, into what the psalmists called a multitude of isles; seventy-four isles cut off one from another. No communications, no weapons, and no hope of retaliation.

Those creatures of brass and fire who descended from the sky-fires, called Ministers, plucked putrid deformities from the darkness, and carried them unto Judgment. These mighty siblings warred till the fire of their battle blotted out the stars. The only light that rose vaulted from the shed forms of those who fell first and evermore. Those shed souls carved a new path in the skies that let the sun return, though less formidable in magnificence.

In the aftershock of their undoing, the secondkind lost much of their history. The count of souls was divided; first by one-fourth, then by one-third, again by one-fifth, and yet once more by one-eighth. Till the Era of the Reformers—second after the Accession—marked the Era of Despair's end and fear abbreviated the Era of the New Fathers. Then, a fruitful season bloomed and the secondkind's fold increased a centesimal. In this, the observers of the firstkind's warring agreed they must do more than survive.

~

In the forty-eighth gathering season of the Accession—after the Ministers born above and the Fallen First who fell beneath emended the land through their warring—the elders of Yah's Second Creation drew together four brave souls who stood in the darkness of the Era of the Reformers for all created souls. These four—called Guardians—held authority over the secondkind and took counsel amid a collective of judges who issued law upon law. None stood against them. None stood a chance.

TULL & EBBE

Their purpose—as commissioned by their judges—was to offer shelter for the Second Creation. They were never asked to hunt, but to corral. In their purpose, they interfered with the Fallen First and drew them away from the souls whose purposes strengthened the secondkind in other measures. Few saw them. In point of fact, few perceived of their existence, and credited the Ministers' adoration of the secondkind with the labor of the Guardians.

From the forests of the Jacoby Territory, the judges chose Beau Itzal Zeck, who had the girth and reach of the territory's proudest trees. Some believed him a specter after others told of attending his interment. No soul offered proof to their fables, and even he proved curious when pressed for an account. Still, a soul with his stature drew little dispute with his willingness to attract harm.

From the anthracite mines in the Weston Territory, the judges chose Buster Roderick King, who pulled from harm nineteen of his fellow laborers during the Peekskill Mine collapse. Though many souls campaigned to serve Buster as their judge, he towed a greater desire for their souls' defense than a mind for their laws. By the time he let his preferred scion succeed him, he held the distinction of serving the territories unto his fifty-sixth winter—older than any other in the territories on either side of the Loy River and the mountains that supplied fresh water.

~

North of the No. 9 Steam Tram, where the Shelby Territory's forests shared the terrane with the limestone lodes of the Carpenter Territory, a grove burned with unnatural flame and scalded the faces of once well-hidden caves that burrowed deep into the glebe. In rebellion against the rules of their judges and the demands of their elders, many novitiates—souls who were neither blameless nor in their purpose—took to the place called the Knotted Caves to prove their independence. They explored and dove against sense and decency. Here, many souls learned who they might be without the Triune's hand upon them.

TULL & EBBE

From the depths of caves without end, voices howled and cries haunted the surrounding fields like the first chill of winter. Misshapen creatures—as all are created—ran in dread, their blunt hands fanning smoke and burning light from their eyes. In the manner that insects and creatures erupt away from harm, so these souls appeared out in the open without regard for being seen because they could not see in the light. Though they kept no wickedness, their sounds made the secondkind fear-filled till they too cried for souls who would relieve their imaginations.

A barrel-chested man of massive build rode on a stallion that appeared more like a pony beneath him. Though smoke stung his eyes, too, he scooped helpless, pleading creatures off their feet by the armful in a figure-eight pattern, around burning trees and unto a thawed brook. His stallion wheezed from the constant, hurried pace but never failed him. The rescued numbers multiplied, but not faster than brilliant, yellow-green flames leapt from branch to branch.

A rider with dark skin sat atop a blonde horse and mimicked his fellow's routine. A green kerchief kept the smoke from his nostrils and mouth; though even those he rescued could not pin his tears on irritation or heartache. Not as gifted in reach as his fellow, he proved equal in strength. He loved his mount and pressed not as hard—but never did his dedication falter.

Till a foe bolted from the caves with a terrifying rage, their mercy never surrendered to their weariness. A soul with a complexion that matched the lode stones drove a blade into the stallion's hindquarter and let his rider topple. Saplings broke beneath him and his gelding tumbled across fire-heated rock. The creature who brought them down howled—as a wolf howls—as if a call to war.

Another team of horses—these unkempt and brutish in gait—rode through and swatted the rescuers with fiery spears. The soul with the stone complexion commandeered the startled blonde foal and howled a second time in an indiscernible tongue. Though none answered his rally cry, the sound of breaking wood announced the rising of the soul he upended and his target. Enraged by the sight of a Guardian, he charged when he ought to have rescued.

Guardian Beau Itzal Zeck possessed the strength to force a galloping horse sideways; not to frighten the animal, but to throw his rider. Guardian Buster Roderick King possessed the strength, and swiftness, to catch that rider and sling him back toward the soul who toppled trees. Zeck lifted their common foe overhead, jostled him till he dropped his fiery spear, and then flung him. He landed at the feet of another—

so close that his obscene countenance showed across a pair of well-oiled boots. As he looked up with murky, yellow irises, he saw a chiseled jaw crease with a smile afore a gleam of light delivered a fist.

~

The Archibald Territory offered their best in Randolph Hereford Wylie. He winked at Zeck and Buster, though they smiled because he rubbed the knuckles chafed by their foe's resolve. Astute at inventions and blessed with charm, Wylie rose as headship of the Guardians; as big in reputation as Zeck in stance. While this ascent pleased his simpler fellows, not all approved of Wylie's title—or his swagger.

~

Not every foe bore the appearance of creatures—though all foes were created. A lone soul who labored against the foursome evaded capture, defeat, and even identification. Imaginative souls accredited this foe for the identifier beacon that Randolph Hereford Wylie invented. The Archibaldian then convinced the judges to issue a decree that all souls born to the secondkind must bear his proudest creation, lest one soul go "uncounted and forgotten."

Chronicler Philip Clapham Tarry lavished the Guardians' foe with the name "Paladin" in articles of his news page, for crimes of theft, intimidation, abduction, and terror. Unlike reports that claimed Paladin wore a crimson-red sash and stood twelve heads high, he dressed in no memorable fashion and stood no higher than the most common soul. Theatric, to be certain, but far from supernal.

None who saw him denied his peculiar features. His jaw seemed hinged in a manner different than the secondkind's, and his nose more beak-shaped and obstructive of his deep-set eyes. Some imagined him deformed. Even Tarry suggested this as the reason Paladin hid his face. The imagination of others provided the Guardians' foe with additional unearned fright.

TULL & EBBE

While Buster steadied the horse and Wylie calmed the local onlookers, Zeck caught their foe trying to sneak away and raised him off the terrane by his ankle. For a moment, afore Zeck focused, their foe's face *changed.* The words for an accurate description escaped the Jacobian, but his complexion ran pale and his fists turned loose. What he saw disturbed him. Enough that he stood over the soul, uncertain whether he ought to end him or defend him.

Then, a swell of green light that shimmered with bursts of golden hues struck Paladin and upended mighty Zeck. An identical blast struck the hand of the fallen foe and revealed a gleaming dagger. Meant for Zeck? The tip of the blade turned as malleable as sap and scalded the wielder's hand. As Paladin favored the limb, Zeck turned toward he who saw the weapon that the towering Jacobian missed.

~

None proved more powerful than the Erori Territory's functionary, Theodore Reaume Conliffe, now the Count of Ebbe Demesne in the Shelby Territory. In point of fact, most cowered in the presence of the unrivaled magick-wielder. Known by his silhouette of slicked-back hair and a riding cape, the fire that burned from each gloved palm without source proved the fourth Guardian's identity. Those enamored by Wylie's ruggedness and charm turned disinterested in less time than the headship took to piece together what occurred while his back was turned.

~

Seen as a powerful soul who disarmed a frightening foe, as a friend who saved Zeck from harm, and as a protector who finished Wylie's work for him, the count stood as the eve's hero. But, in the brushwood, another watched. Like Paladin, his face changed as his rage swelled. For him, the title and name of the soul that the crowd celebrated sounded vulgar. He reached a misshapen hand toward the defeated soul but lacked the courage to stand and be seen by their foe.

TULL & EBBE

Then, an opportune moment arose. A shrill cry from an elder drew attention toward a frail creature whose form changed in the mist. On staggering footsteps, a soul of tremendous beauty marred in ash and blood staggered from harm. Afore she struck the terrane, the crowd gasped, then the count offered further spectacle when he soared from a perch high atop the lode stones and landed within reach of the harmed dove on a graceful descent.

"Cherished Maia!"

None esteemed the count more than Maia Espe Zeck, daughter of the Guardian from the Jacoby Territory, and hope-filled novitiate to a Reformer. In the height of their reign, the Guardians' kin aided them: Buster's youngest brother, Dion Reginald King, Wylie's nephew, Morey Blazkowicz Stensby, and Zeck's only fruit. Though her father tended to those he rescued, the count swept Maia up in his arms and found the reflection of sky-fires in her devout irises.

"We are but a simple leap from mending." Without a glance toward any other, he made a declaration. "I'll see that she's safe, old mate!"

Eldest of the trio, and of an age fitting to be wed, Maia found attentiveness from both eras; but coveted none—in recent moons—above the count's interest. She traveled along and offered the care of a nurse to those in need and was never unappreciated by her present rescuer. Even when he leapt again, she never looked away from his wedge-shaped face. His magick, which worried the other Guardians, let them travel in moments what the others would cross in three watches.

Those beneath their ascent swayed in fear and crouched nearer to the terrane while the count carried Maia over the tops of trees. The secondkind did not take to the air or sea since the Accession, so the act showed both his bravery and his regard for her—in her eyes, at least. He shrouded them in a false cloud, blotted out their position, and shed a single tear for her to see. As the droplet fell, the weight of a small, white moonstone struck her breast and stole her attention. His trickery, however magickal, boasted wealth and significance that the other Guardians oft denounced. From the look in her eyes, Maia believed him the grandest of any soul.

By the time the pair arrived at Ebbe Demesne, his magick had mended her wound. Even so, he held her in his arms and carried her indoors. His magick understood his mind and moved ahead of them, opening doors, and confusing those abstruse defenses that he allowed Wylie to implement there. No other greeted them nor stood in their path as he carried her along a familiar passageway.

TULL & EBBE

In the ways of her father and his fellows, Maia kept a nook in the great manor that was hers alone. There she slept, studied, and watched the sky-fires through marvelous oval windows that cast every detail in the orange hues embedded in the glass. While others skated on frozen millponds and sought their purpose at the tutelage of sturdy and upright elders, Maia, Morey, and Dion lived on the hem of tremendous wonders.

Petals of light bloomed outside her window and Squires the size of canaries roosted within her line of sight. Flecks of light like the shimmer of firelight vied for her attention and sought to lure her interest as the count delivered her to her door like a courted lover. A creature with the elegance of a butterfly spun and soared for her attention. Even so, the brighter the light burned, the darker the shadow turned behind Count Conliffe.

Now, though he went in gentleness to make amends for the suffering he caused, the count's intentions soon changed. The sight of fair Maia as she slipped her uninjured limb from the sleeve of her pullover and bared a faultless breast, stilled him. She saw his distinctive silhouette in the reflection of glass then turned toward his face and let him look upon her. In this, the sinful Believer proved a greater power over he who surrendered his soul to magick afore her birth.

His eyes crept along her body the way that ice thaws. Upon a second tour of her figure, he found a softened smile on her face. Maia did not cover, nor did he turn away with a gentle blush. She removed her clothing in his presence and let his magick shroud her till the entirety of the room glowed and suppressed the brilliance of those creatures who vied for her innocence.

Whereas other suitors offered her trinkets, Maia received another gift from the count. He spoke words in a tongue she interpreted as a novice. Light like ribbons unfurled between them and caressed her skin, well-pleased by her stark beauty. As his magick tore, magick also teased. The ribbons of light entwined around her torso and limbs till she drifted off her feet and went slack for the wielder like a subdued breeze.

~

TULL & EBBE

The exchange did not end with that display of temptation and dark wonder. The count set foot unto the nook contrary to a protector, and Maia Espe Zeck enticed her father's fellow till his want for her exceeded his regard for the great Guardian from the Jacoby Territory. Loyalties shifted with the first touch and Theodore Reaume Conliffe's desire consumed his heart in the manner that his magick seduced she who would become his devoted and secluded bride.

~

By the time the others arrived, Conliffe and his young lover had composed an elegant deception and borrowed upon the well-known adoration that Beau Itzal Zeck heaped upon his bride—Lea Christine Fabray—and their daughter. They rested in wait and separate chambers then listened to the heartsick actions of he who rushed through the manor, discarding the markings of his purpose, that he might be seen by her only as her proud and loving father—his most-cherished duty. Any wrath Zeck kept toward the reckless magick that his fellow boasted vanished when Maia greeted him with tenderness—as if her farewell from his provision.

"Maia!" The hulking soul wrapped her in his arms. "Forgive your father, my daughter. I never ought to have taken you near to harm."

"I am well, Father. All is well!"

"No, no, rest well." He hung his head as though the weight of Ebbe Demesne rested on his shoulders. "I set aside my sense, daughter. I was too proud to boast your interest in my purpose. I ought to have boasted how well I kept you safe."

"My recklessness harmed her, old mate"—the count peered through the doorway like light from another room, till a twinkle in his eye found Maia—"not your pride. Each of us have made promises to Maia—and to Morey and Dion—that they might join in our purpose. Truly! From this eve and every eve that follows, I will show greater regard for Maia's many . . . needs."

Zeck heard every word, but never turned toward the magick-wielder. "As you say, as will I."

"You don't have to protect me. Neither of you have to protect me."

"Now, now, Maia." The count crept further into the room as his lover stretched her foot toward him. "There shall be no more arguing. How can we proclaim that we are Guardians lest we keep safe those most precious to our souls?"

Zeck's hold proved more secure, in agreement with Conliffe's words, and Maia sighed till her head found her father's steep shoulder. Her gaze remained set, and the count's grin proved equal portions of delight and deviousness. By the look in her eyes, Zeck's daughter no longer sought the sheltering of her father. She craved another's interest, and the count's arrogant smirk announced his awareness of that desire.

~

Once the deception took root, Maia found reason upon reason to avoid her parents and their humble home. Few suspected when the count increased the time that he devoted to furthering his tutelage of her. Maia gained insight into the count's realm but did not sense the spell he set upon her. His magick ensured their many visits went uninterrupted, but even he overlooked another's affections for Maia.

~

Morey Blazkowicz Stensby and his overflow of suspicions found the ear of Maia's father in scorn toward Conliffe. By then, four moons had passed. When Zeck found the pair, there was no denying Maia's affections, or her gravidity; which he blamed on magick's deceptiveness. The Jacobian then struck his fellow Guardian so hard that the blow shook the Twelve Territories and, by some measure, the mind of Count Theodore Reaume Conliffe. Maia then cursed her father for the first time and defended his deceptive fellow.

The same soul who chose fear above helping Paladin—who bore the guise of a jilted scion and sowed discourse through the outfit that destroyed his kind—watched as the Guardians' reign ended like a fire doused in unclean water. Blooms of color wilted, and Maia Espe Zeck—secret bride to the count—wept over her father's actions and her husband's character-changing wound. The creature who lacked the courage to confront them in his true form observed—and relished—the aftershock of his meddling. Those who flaunted power oft behaved as fools—arrogant, pride-filled fools.

Thereafter, the first era of Guardians was no more. The foursome returned to the territories of their birth and Ebbe Demesne received few visitors again. Letting pass how Wylie and Buster tried, Zeck refused to see or speak to the count. Seven winters passed afore the two stood beneath the same roof again. By then, all had grown too old to serve the secondkind for Yah's glory.

TWO

THE 19TH EVE BENEATH THE MOON OF THE FRAIL DOVE

THE 83RD WINTER OF THE ACCESSION

IN THE CARE OF THE HELPER, WHO KEEPS SOULS FROM FRUITLESS WANDERING.

158 CHESWELL PATH

THE SCURLOCK CHAMBER HOUSE.

30 PARASANG WEST OF THE JACOBY-SHELBY BORDER.

Zeck the Guardian shunned his former fellow—his daughter, too—till the pair's fruit reached the age of seven. What a soul towed in bravery did not outmeasure his unforgiving ways. All souls warred inward. This soul, once mighty in stature, collapsed from within. He held onto the pain too long and feared—some accused—asking his daughter to forgive him for his own stubborn pride.

Which of them sought reconciliation went unrecorded, but once he felt the first embrace of Maia's daughter, his heart found restoration. The grand pair proved inseparable. Though a child lacked the understanding toward the ways their elders wounded and betrayed, blameless Sondrea Ebbe Conliffe proved keen-witted and strong-willed enough that she sensed her mother's woundedness as much as her own desire for a father figure amid the growing absence of the count. Afore her eighth winter, she had learned how to ride a horse and steer her grandfather's steam rig; both of which she commandeered back and forth across the Jacoby and Shelby territories.

On the same eve she turned eleven, whilst her mother believed her grandfather took her for another of their wandering rides upon Ligurus's proud back, she proved her driving skills and delivered the former Guardian to the Scurlock Chamber House in the Jacoby Territory. There awaited evidence—not for the celebrant—of all that Zeck believed and obeyed on the instruction of a fiery Warring Minister called

TULL & EBBE

Enke'loi. For the many battles, the heartache, and even the rumor of many resurrections, the Guardian brought with him his most-trusted fellow in the hopes that she would believe his heart till such a time that she could understand his word.

After she pledged not to tell how they arrived, he saddled her atop his shoulders and towed her to the doorway where a sliver of a woman met them and led them into the chamber house. Those who saw them rolled away from the corridors and toward the glass walls, but never took their eyes off her grandfather. Like them, she too found oddness as he hugged a soul with shimmering honey-and-crème-hued hair and a face she did not recognize, but curiosity soon turned her toward a different sight.

A newborn babe rested on the other side of a door that seemed to open as though she were expected there. The chamber house—where new births and peace-filled ends mingled—hosted devices unlike any other she had seen afore. This included a tall copper post in the corner of the room that echoed the rhythm of a mother's heartbeat and pacified her fruit. The entire room sounded like comfort, but a plume of coldness arose with the turning away of a pale frame and the fold of covered legs as the elder greeter reassured the curious soul.

"You're allowed to go nearer."

Less spans separated the bedded plume and wide-eyed visitor than visitor and babe, of which there were eleven down to the same eve. The plume had milky skin, hair the shade of chestnuts upon muddy terrane, and hid the left side of her face. Letting pass the chilly reception, the blameless Countess of Ebbe Demesne accepted their elder's offer to enter the room. She checked to see if her grandfather noticed, and then set her other foot unto the next lit floor panel in hopes of a clearer view of the distant babe.

"I believe he's going to be girl-happy, for all his first eve's visitors have been beautiful."

The newborn acknowledged such a claim and the visitor's presence with a kick of his legs and a stretch of long toes that scraped from beneath a blanket that matched his mother's. His visitor stood at breathless attention, as if afraid she had disturbed him and afraid of a scolding word that never came for her. Then, a warm hand slipped along her shoulder and a soft hip drew her eye. That same honey-and-crème-haired figure whom her grandfather hugged approached the babe and covered his feet after a soft sweep of her thumb to his toes.

"Have you held a babe afore?"

Tull & Ebbe

Sondrea's head turned with the might to rattle her full cheeks and disguised how oft her parents kept her from other souls. She had not even noticed how the plume—the babe's mother—had kept silent all along.

"No?"

She then felt the cold drift away as his mother turned away on the bed whilst their elder slipped her hands beneath the babe and raised him with effortlessness. A gown unfurled from his tiny form and boasted his first purpose: outgrowing his covering. He proved as malleable as a half-mashed potato and drew close to her breast afore he cooed again. This earned him a kiss, afore she who held him offered more attention to their fiery-haired observer.

"We must keep his head and neck supported, evermore and gentle"—she showed the technique with that same tenderness—"as I am."

Unbeknownst to the child, the shade of light in the panel beneath her small feet told of her wellbeing. The source burned bright and pure as an indicator that the countess remained in sterling health.

"Can you hold your arms out as I am?"

She studied the posture and proved able.

"I'll set him in your arms now so you can learn."

The wide-eyed soul corrected her posture as proof of her readiness, but had not counted the weight of him. In an instant, he was both lighter than air and mightier than all her fears. Her mouth shrank as the size of her eyes increased, but a calming word kept her from trembling.

"That's wonderful."

Bathed, dressed, and nursed, the babe proved less interested in how well she held him but raked a tiny hand through her thick plumage of fiery red hair. The sensation drew his eyes and made her rigid at the sudden shift of his form.

"I have him still. He'll not fall from our care."

As proof, the newborn settled.

"He must approve of you. What do you imagine?"

"His eyes are silver."

"*Pewter.*"

She looked toward her elder's lips and recited the word without sound. Her gaze then returned to his soft face. Every feature seemed so small and unflawed that she started to marvel over the creature.

Tull & Ebbe

"I see flecks of pale lavender too. Those colors remind me of the monkshood flowers that grow near to my home." His grandmother then squinted. "And yours are copper, like honey sat afore your great-grandmother's brightest kettle lantern."

She nodded and, as his eyes found her face, offered a grin. No other expression felt as justified.

"The color of the rarest Squires."

The Guardian's slow, churning voice caught his granddaughter unaware but she did not loosen her hold on the babe.

"He is fine?" The room's new elder drew a patient breath. "We heard he would suffer—"

"He struggles, as you say, Guardian Zeck."

"I am only grandfather to this beloved soul now"—he swept a proud hand along the crown of his granddaughter's head—"and that settles me like the Peace."

"Letting pass the needs of the territory," the new grandmother jabbed, but never lost her grin.

The Second Creation still learned of an illness called *si'el uni'epotus* by the Ministers and *drowning sickness* amid their kind. Immersion of those affected souls induced rapid heart palpitations that provoked full arrest, tunnel vision unto fleeting blindness, and breathing woes to asphyxiation's end. The newborn marked the fourth soul afflicted since the third era increased the secondkind's count and the first whose mother survived the birthing. What the blameless soul failed to see in the new mother, and the babe in her hold, was the rareness of their skeletal systems: broad shoulder blades that shielded the upper back, lengthened limbs, sturdier hips, and a spine that held two extra vertebrae.

"This bright-eyed traveler is as I imagined her, Beau." The honey-and-crème-haired soul reassured she who celebrated her own birth, "Your grandfather talks the ears off every creature within the sound of his voice at the slightest thought of you. Do I remember well? Do you dislike the purpose our old fathers gave to our fruit? Blameless Sondrea—"

"I am allowed to be called Countess."

The elder woman proved patient against the sound of a mighty inhalation from such a small torso. "As you say."

"You remember well." Zeck chuckled as he ran a coarse finger against his driver's cheek. "My fiery Sondrea Ebbe Conliffe."

"Our decisive countess. I, too, am counted as a decisive soul. I am Juanita Gene James, Sondrea. On the bed to your left side rests my son's bride, Kara Doe Nelson. This pewter-eyed bundle is her son; called Nelson James Tull."

Sondrea spoke the babe's name and his mother turned her head further from the sound.

"His father?"

Kara drew her knees toward her breast.

"Kara's brother fetches him from his purpose for his son's benefit."

"He's not yet seen his own—"

"I tell you"—Kara's husband's mother interrupted Zeck and redirected their attention onto the fiery-headed child—"I believe Sondrea has the assurance of a Guardian. She calms him so. Maybe we decided too soon on Perry!"

"This new lot is not fit to be called true Guardians." A second time, Sondrea corrected Tull's grandmother, whom she did not yet recognize or respect as the advocate of the Jacoby Territory. "Are they, my grandfather?"

~

Nine spans passed without Guardians afore a new era arose in the eighty-first sowing season. Representing all twelve of the isle's territories, they abandoned more than the traditions of their elders. The second era of Guardians heaped wrath upon the firstkind. They hunted and attacked without mercy—with a mindset unto making the isle so treacherous that every member of the First Creation would abandon them.

They were aerialists and bare-knuckle brawlers adorned with tempers and salty tongues. With every effort, the outfit of twelve proved their disregard for the ways of the former era and the rule of their judges. The Twelve Territories flowed with blood and ash as they littered the highest places with the bodies of their soulless foes. This was no longer the time of Beau Itzal Zeck, nor the Era of the Reformers, and the Triune alone could frighten Their creations.

Tull & Ebbe

~

277 Ely Yeary Way

In a time of reckless cruelty.

Beneath the watch of new Guardians.

That lurker who observed the aftershock of the count's betrayal stood now against a new threat. Twelve souls—three females—arrayed in vivid attire that showcased their figures proved heirs of Conliffe's selfishness and pride. None stood prouder than Cameron Lou Fenner from the Archibald Territory. He strutted and whipped his hair, challenged through insults, and betrayed fellows as oft as he defeated foes.

The two souls tangled to the point where stalemate kept either from victory. Matched in strength, height, breadth, and cunning, only one trick remained: underhandedness. The lurker—called Noeu by a since-captured accomplice—changed the shape of his arms and made the Guardian slip. He too brought up a knee and took the breath from the foe who wanted to end him.

He flung the current headship of the secondkind's protectors above his head and let him freefall onto the copper skin of a steam kettle that served the locale's travelers. The frame buckled, as did that Guardian's, and his body slithered headlong toward the cobblestone arena known to Gierigians as Patroon Avenue. The victory appeared obvious; still, Noeu leapt. When he landed, he would break the proudest back in the territories.

Cam sensed as much and rolled away afore Noeu struck. With what might remained in him, he marred his fists against the face and body of the lurker—still, he never broke bone or drew blood. In this, the Guardian found his anger kindled. Lividness followed with the nearness of his shadow. Wrath was as familiar to him as breath. The more his foe withstood, the viler his assaults became. Like Conliffe, he too sought to cleanse the terrane and to bury all that offended him.

This time, the lurker's crime was the targeting of a meat supply meant for the Gierig Territory. For all their advancements and privilege, there was not one reputable hunter amid the Gierigians or the Archibaldians. So, they traded mechanization for meat from the Creighton Territory. That another stole from the supply provoked the ire of those territories' Guardians.

TULL & EBBE

The Creighton Territory's Alison Brackett Nance, a temptress in tongue and figure, proved more wicked than cunning Gierigian Herb Atkins Benest. Nance coaxed their enemies, lulled them, and then delivered vicious ends. Even as her victims surrendered their last moments, she slapped their faces and taunted their ears with barbs that would heckle them unto the Judgment. Each time, she laughed.

In her confrontation, she let the atavistic ways of her territory guide her. The way she battled back and forth with Noeu and Cam mingled bloodlust and seduction and made Benest lose his desire for a strategic test of souls. Nance prowled against their foe, took his heftiest punches, and never once mopped the blood from her flesh. When her hands failed, she used her head and cheeks to deflect their advances.

Few stomached how the Creightonians fought. When limbs failed, they used teeth. Even in their affections, the most docile drew blood as a show of claim and loyalty. Cam, who bore marks that he hid from his Archibaldian bride, grew jealous when Nance sank her teeth into Noeu's exposed chest. When their rival howled, she drew her thighs around his midsection like a noose.

She and foul-minded Shelbian Barton Blinken Ganix sabotaged villages to defeat single souls. Neither showed regret. Worse, with every victory they demanded alms, parades, and recognition from their judges—as those they defended meant little to them. Even so, those *worthless* souls cheered and flattered their new heroes without regard for foes who never struck against the secondkind.

As Cam tore the biter from Noeu, Ganix thrust a push dagger between their foe's jutted shoulder blades. He pressed his face against Noeu's, smeared blood and sweat, and gasped vile words as he stabbed again and again. Then, when he ought to have fallen, Noeu shook his head and laughed. He rammed Ganix away with his crown, drove his boot into Cam's groin, and sank the dagger between the ribs of Nance's unprotected midsection.

What those three Guardians did not claim as their own fell beneath the destructive nature of Hector Geirolf Picadura, Guardian scion from the Creighton Territory. When others failed to please Nance, she invited her eventual replacement to do her bidding. Hector lusted and hungered till all stood as potential satisfaction. He raped whom he could not seduce and burned what he could not steal.

For Noeu, he reserved a bootheel. He stomped and stomped, as if he wagered that he could reduce the head to mash. Not once did he alter the shape. As his rage grew, so did his Creightonian habits. He tore at the flesh, ripped away an ear, and sliced

Noeu's lower lip. Afore he stepped back to admire his efforts, he watched his foe reform—unharmed in any way. Hector then fell to his knees and screamed out in blasphemous rage.

A Minister draped in fire descended and smattered Hector with a bladed mace. What tissue that suffered also cauterized afore his body landed—thirty heads from where he committed his sin. The Minister raised his mace a second time, and the wave of fire that formed a tail scorched Noeu. As he howled in agonizing pain, the soul who called down a Minister to handle his dirty work laughed. A stained smile formed across his face and blood dripped from the long ends of his mustache.

As the Minister realized Hector's deception, the fiery creature struck and fractured the cobblestones. Gas lampposts fell from their roosts and the pane-faces of nearby shops shattered to dust and pellets. Hector felt his fear and repented in his heart afore the Minister ascended back unto the sky-fires where the First Creation warred. The next sound the Guardians heard was that of Noeu's feet as he fled without the coveted supply of meat.

"Victory . . ." Hector coughed and spat a broken tooth.

Nance spewed vulgarities and silenced him. By the time she tore away a belt of pouches that covered her sternum, Hector was on his feet. She bent at the waist, set her weight against the overturned gas lamppost, and opened her torso as much as possible with an embedded dagger.

"You're braced then, vezér?"

"Worsen the scar and I'll take your head," she threatened through clenched teeth, and still thrilled him.

He clutched at her shoulder, pressed his thumb against her damp breast, and ignored her agitated glance as he plucked Ganix's dagger without pulling the skin. The fallen lamp reflected on the blade, showing little blood, and Hector smiled. As his mouth opened to let out some sound, he took a fist that cost him another tooth. He fell, struck his face, and then took the brunt of Nance's knee as she landed upon him. She howled in pain, clutched the dagger and her wound, but never counted how many more teeth she took from her scion.

"Nance?"

"Don't touch me!" She mopped Noeu's blood from her lips and slung droplets across Hector. As she stood, she kicked his hip. "None of you touch me!"

"I want only my dagger."

TULL & EBBE

She huffed till the air between them went up two degrees and then slapped the flat dagger into Ganix's moist palm. He licked the dagger clean and returned his favorite weapon to a sheath on his belt. "That shape-changer's blood won't mend your snake tongue, Ganix."

"Nor your falling curves." Silence followed his barb, then both Guardians laughed like howling wolves.

Four conquerors worked alongside as much as against eight defenders who upheld the works of Wylie, King, and Zeck. Those eight—Mick Curtis Whigham, Herb Atkins Benest, Harlan Bottin Vosburg, Kim Debney Byrne, Perry Wallace Rudat, Colborn Ziba Shelley, Ember Willows Martel, and Edmond Anson Elragadó—represented the Weston, Gierig, Carpenter, Othniel, Jacoby, Perlin, Damaris, and Larson territories. Though Mick and Perry had excessive tendencies, the rest proved true to their purpose in their time. Still another would not be named again.

But, on the hem of their vileness, even a sure-hearted soul suffered a moment of turning away in disgust. Edmond Anson Elragadó, the first Guardian from the Larson Territory, shunned the unclean, but could, for the good of the outfit, dole out an intensity of wrath that dizzied many souls. What set him apart was that he never reveled in his behavior. The Reformers and the Ministers rid the secondkind of every disease, but bloodletting still disgusted him.

Afore he voiced his disapproval, he frightened a smooth-faced man dressed in a gray, waist-length cape, black suit, and a white blouse with a banded collar. He looked as appalled by Edmond as Edmond felt toward Nance and Ganix. Both stepped backward from the other, blushed, and gauged the rivaling degrees of disapproval.

"You"—Edmond's intensity showed with spittle that leapt from his mouth—"are not to be here. This area is restricted, lest—"

"Guardian, I tell you, I am aware of my place. My presence was ordered by Judge Cyril Adair Mumus." He then reached into a loose satchel that hung from his wrist with a corded strap. "I'm to offer this."

The fog of Edmond's breath mingled with the steam that rose from his sweaty face. "You're a herald?"

"I could tell from your hat that you must be clever!" The herald's eyes fixed a moment too long.

Edmond snatched the folded parchment from the herald's gloved hand. "Get!"

TULL & EBBE

Arrogance changed the herald's face and he backed away three full strides afore he pivoted on a wooden heel and departed. Edmond glowered first at that heel and then at the way the herald's cape glided and skipped in time with the racket of his steps. He removed the glove from his hand, dusted his bare fingers against his trousers, and applied a ginger touch to the startling-white brim that kept his eyes from the sky-fires. In battle, his hat kept secure a wig and false brows that he donned.

"Cameron! Edmond brings us word!"

Cam rose too, nursed a sprain in his lower back, and hobbled as he kneaded the tenderness in his groin. "From the judges?"

"Well, Edmond?" Nance's authority rose as a proud breath lifted her chest.

His eyes fell flat and his lips stretched into a humorless frown over Nance's habit of repeating every word their headship spoke. Oft with a smarmy tone. "A herald of Judge Mumus."

"Well, if you can find the light beneath the brim of that hat, why not read for us, Eddie?" Cam's abrasive voice drew sneers from the cruelest Guardians.

By the perfumed scent on the paper, he gathered, "Could be our numbers rise."

"Not by my ways!" Hector retorted from all fours as he sought his teeth.

Nance drove the heel of her boot against the cleft in his backside.

"Tell us, where was this new and blameless soul born?"

Edmond turned toward the downed gas lamp. "Perry's territory."

The wiry Jacobian, oft seen with an exaggerated grin, lost his smile and turned solemn in posture. "Mine, you say?"

"Worried, are you?" Harlan Bottin Vosburg howled at the fears of the lot—minus the Larsonite eunuch.

"'On this eve, the nineteenth rising beneath the Moon of the Frail Dove"—his voice stilled—"Reckoner Kara Doe Nelson gave to her husband, Mechanician Patrick James Tull, a son; named Nelson James Tull. He is fit, watchful, and blameless. Present at the birth were the child's grandparents, Declan Patrick Tull and his bride—'"

Edmond looked away from the herald's note as Nance whispered in Cam's ear. Her sultry voice wafted like the fog till weighted syllables caught his ear. This child was the grandson of Juanita Gene James—first amid women to serve as judge-emeritus now four spans.

The reader unfurled the folded slip and read a final entry, jotted in haste. He then chuckled enough that Nance ended her words. "'Also present was first Guardian of the Jacoby Territory Beau Itzal Zeck and his granddaughter, Sondrea Ebbe Conliffe, who celebrated her eleventh span this same eve.'"

The mention of his predecessor caused Perry to shift an uncertain gaze toward his headship. "We ought to send alms, Cam."

The Archibaldian slapped Perry's shoulder and jostled him. "As you say. And, believe me this, we will! But, first, our judges will honor us."

"Declare a byway and let fall any who seek to hinder us!" Ganix shouted with a shrill howl that made a nearby pack squeal.

Nance felt a scrape on her cheek, lost beneath the pain from the dagger wound, but her intense, moss-brown irises never veered from the note in Edmond's hand. With a saber of her own, she sliced the paper in two and spat on the terrane. "Another who'll beg our protection and despise our ways! Like his grandmother!"

Cam risked much when he slapped her backside.

"I warned all not"—she spun, ready to turn the saber against him.

In harm's stead, he isolated her forearm and, without releasing either hand's hold, he drew her close enough to kiss her mouth and neck. Her body shook from the isolation and her brow dropped against his shoulder. She again whispered in a way that let her fellows hear words that Edmond preferred not to consider. In seeming knowledge, Cam kissed she whose taste for violence upset fearless men.

"Guardians!" Cam spun Nance then drew Hector to his feet. "Let the meek revel!"

As the Guardians departed and the territory's chief and deputy inspectors swarmed, Edmond, alone, retrieved the herald's fragmented note. He then recorded the blameless soul's name and the eve of his birth onto the pages of a well-kept journal. During his time as Guardian, he had learned to track the births—not the ends—of each soul who increased the secondkind's populace.

> *74. Nelson James Tull, b. 11.19.083; mother Kara Doe Nelson and his father Patrick James Tull. Jacoby Territory.*

THREE

THE 4TH EVE BENEATH THE MOON OF THE MOTHER'S SONG
THE 107TH WINTER SEASON OF THE ACCESSION
IN THE CARE OF THE HELPER, WHO KEEPS SOULS FROM FRUITLESS WANDERING.

OVERLOOKING A SHELBIAN RIVER CAMP
IN THE UPPER CARPENTER TERRITORY.
NEAR TO THE LODE REGION.

Now aged by another twenty-four spans—one-fourth of them spent as headship of Guardians, scions, and abettors—Edmond remembered well the eve when the secondkind celebrated a new birth. "Tull, are you in position?"

~

The Era of the Fallen Lands changed the count of territories and protectors. Nine Guardians fell away, four more rose, and shared their elders' purpose: to keep safe the fellow souls of the Second Creation from the many harms inflicted upon them by the warring of the First Creation. Edmond Anson Elragadó surrendered all for his purpose. As a soul put beneath the knife by Alixus Elam Katch, he defended a territory whose judge ensured he could never produce an heir. So, he took scions into his care. He never called them *sons*, yet oft showed the instruction and regard he believed a father ought to show.

~

TULL & EBBE

"Boy . . ."

"Forgive my intrusion, headship, but our Jacobian fellow cannot respond." The patient tone of Arthur George Green, third Guardian from the Weston Territory, softened the harsh wind but did not relax Edmond's heavy breath. "He proves ready, but stands in direct sight of that which we seek. To respond, he must risk showing the gleam of his beacon. Shall he declare his position?"

"Your word suffices, George."

Now, the Guardian who kept a pristine, white hat stood in silence and did not shiver as snow fell upon his bare forearms. This long winter changed him, as though he had let go of the aches and the fears many associated with the season and the frailty of eunuchs. He invited fear. He sought the root of such emotions and led others to do the same.

Edmond nodded toward Harlan Bottin Vosburg, his trusted friend of twenty-six spans, and cast not one flake of snow from the brim. Harlan, whose bellowing laugh and bear-like stature defined him, disheveled his lush beard as he raised his hands to his mouth and cawed into the darkness. A soft rustle from two unseen points responded.

Then, Barton Blinken Ganix rose. The first Guardian from the Shelby Territory—never exhausted of complaints or gassiness—crowed as shrill as any creature that they declared a huntable foe. This marked his greatest efforts. Two more rustles began, but a sharp fracture of wood stole the elegance of soundlessness.

All knew to watch and not distract. None of lesser authority than a chief inspector's deputy belonged out of doors whilst the curfew of the judges remained over them. Another thump produced a hollow thud, followed by the whine of a jarred plank once secured by screws. The sound then moved from out of doors and into a cottage stained by the grit of the region's anthracite mines and river muck. That same grit proved combustible when too near to the mire that the fallen members of the First Creation—or *firstkind*—used as a salve upon their blistered husks.

The visible Guardians held steady and awaited the next sound of trespass. As all turned breathless, a lone figure prowled with an ease of step that upheld the tension. Led by an ear trained for delicate sounds, he crouched along the stone hem of the cottage and dragged his lower half over the snow-blanketed glebe. If the humidity fell, his legs and boots would become matchsticks upon the volatile terrane.

TULL & EBBE

~

In the one hundredth Growing Season since the Accession, Sebastian Wredden Shaw stood as the third recognized Guardian from the Jacoby Territory. By the first moonset of his tenure, Shaw met his end. By the moonrise that followed, the fourth Guardian from the Jacoby Territory arose—Nelson James Tull.

As grandson of Judge Juanita Gene James, and approved of by the territory's first Guardian, a mighty reputation awaited. Then, all watched as he outshone forecast opinions and forged a reputation that dared loom with the elders who established the Jacoby Territory. Tull nudged the prestige of the outfit in a direction opposite their predecessors and caused his elders to change with those who joined him. Gone are the vivid costumes and sharpened tongues—replaced by colors that suited the elements and hand signals that served as a language recognized by only seven souls.

~

The soul who crawled thrust his rigid left hand in the direction adjacent to the cottage's hem. So crisp was the action that the sound within the house creaked. Above him, a deformed silhouette stood afore the gauze-like drapery that swayed as the picture window failed to hold back the wintry breeze. That same breeze cast the top layer of fresh-fallen snow across the Guardian who settled body and breath.

The creature in trespass stood ten heads high but boasted neither in width nor build. In ambit's lack, the saenn saet'ti'e increased in peculiarity, as this creature bore arms that reached the floor and diaphragms that once kept reserves of breath which allowed them to alert Yah's furthest armies with a single trumpet blast. A face with two small mouths and eyes like dull embers turned toward the breathing pane as if haunted by memories of an illustrious song no longer sung. So far from the court of the Most High had this traitor fallen!

TULL & EBBE

The prowling soul vaulted sideways, shoulder over shoulder, and landed upon his toes without a grunt. He then flung two daggers through glass, fabric, and the malformed husk of the saenn saet'ti'e. The creature's wail reduced the top half of the picture window to grit and made the Guardian shield his head. Foe identified foe, and the silence changed whilst his hands grasped matching knife handles.

Without compassion for the creature's wail, he spun at the waist and extended his arms outward. The tethers crimped onto the buttress of each dagger and bolted onto the manacles about his wrists, letting him attempt to pluck from the home the intruder. As the saenn saet'ti'e resisted, a film of mire mingled with the mining grit. Violet sparks ignited and consumed the creature. Afore the Guardian fell to the flame too, he leapt headlong through the remnants of the picture window and into the cottage.

~

In the eras that followed the Accession, the rarest of souls bore the purpose of defending the Triune's Second Creation. Every Guardian and their scion—down to their scion's scion—mastered the bow, the sword, the knife, darkness, and fire. None handled a weapon till they survived a complete moon cycle in a mix of locales: the forested bluffs of the Jacoby Territory, the ice-girded mountains of the Carpenter Territory, the ash fields of the Creighton Territory, and the brutal shores of the Forbidden Sea. They excelled in their purpose—that other souls might prove fruitful in theirs.

~

Inside the cottage now, the outfit's best sneak darted from room to room with serpent-like agility. A fast foot and keen eye aided in the dark and let him creep beneath the sight of remaining creatures without detection. Even to those who knew to watch, he appeared as no more than a breath of fog enticing the shadows. Still, a foe worthy of the Guardians understood both fog and shadow and discerned their true voice.

TULL & EBBE

Though the Guardian plucked a blameless soul from her bed with ease, the added strain changed the song from his lips. Her slight arms held to his neck, raised his breath one octave, and betrayed their position to the other saenn saet'ti'e who sought their disruption. But, she of ten blameless spans proved worthy of risk. In this, she proved a delectable find for the fallen.

Dark hair with a violet tinge spread like feathers atop her head as her rescuer pivoted on an untold footpath. Crimson fingers grabbed at her but never took hold. In a scream's stead, a higher-pitched, faster-paced weapon teased the ear and redefined the balance. The sharpened tip cut away a feather of hair and the polished shank offered less than a glimmer of a relay's false light. A hiss of air dislodged the clasp on the shaft's hind end and a copper wire as fine as the cut hair ensnared the beast's wrist.

As she in the Guardian's arms cried out, three identical, rapid-fire arrows secured the saenn saet'ti'e, with the fourth serving as a snare against the throat. The copper line sliced open a flame-hardened husk and tightened as the skeleton of the house became a resting place for all four tips. The bound creature sought their scream and the blameless soul covered her ears, unaware that the wire restricted sound.

The Guardian dipped, shoulder-first, and ran headlong out the door. He cradled his bounty against his torso, rolled, and then tumbled through fresh-fallen snow. A mist of ice crystals scattered, but a boundary of stacked wood stopped his body. The startled and blameless soul burst upright in tears whilst laughter arose from her successful protector's lips.

"Well-aimed, brother!" Guardian Asham Benjamin Gera patted the damp cheek of his haul and teased her clipped strand. "Close."

From a hilltop embankment, Guardian Nelson James Tull relaxed his bronze bow and offered neither an excuse nor apology for his aim as the rescued soul kicked Asham between his navel and groin afore she fled.

"Mama!"

Out of the copper-banded relay that each Guardian kept near their collar, the voice of Olley Hendrie Falk carried. "I've got a silver alms that guarantees the judge of your territory will remind you that Zeck would've skewered both wretches with one meandering shot."

"Cora! Come nearer, my daughter!"

TULL & EBBE

Tull looked to George, who kept sight of the ornery blameless soul, then nodded in agreement with Olley. "I can promise as much, and let you keep your alms. Asham suffered yet another disgruntled rejection."

"She might prove the youngest." Tull's spotter, Guardian Arthur George Green, concealed his relay and offered a smile as bright as the sky-fires for Tull to see. "I believe we have found our reason to rejoice this eve, my friend!"

The voice of the outfit then interrupted via their handheld devices. "Well run, Guardians. Do a head count, broom for strays, then meet me at the fork of Ellsberg Lode Trail. Ganix . . . see Gera to his feet."

~

Like Beau Itzal Zeck afore him, the Guardian from the noble Jacoby Territory did not boast. Never a soul who chased affection, his steadiness and resilience provided much to the outfit and to the territories. He is a gentle Guardian for an era gentler than those of his ancestors. Still, there are some who say he will bring great torment to our land. They who cower from the light are blind to true wonder.

~

Tull crouched toward the case of his bow and looked toward the evacuated home at the creature he pinned. The wires that bound his lode held till Squires descended from the sky-fires to reclaim their traitorous sibling. Whether he aimed askew, his purpose went fulfilled and his heart rested. Their brilliance captivated him, a testament of the blamelessness that still dwelled within him, and he watched over them afore he rested his bow.

All the while, the tears never stung his eyes and the smile never faded from his smooth face. Few were the souls who shunned the praise of others and sought the *smallness* found in the shadow of great creatures. On any other eve, he might have chased the flicker of their light through the deepest forest and the highest peak. This eve, he found a wonder he did not understand—as those from above consoled the creature who betrayed them too.

He buckled his weapon with tremendous care, and then showed the depth of his compassion. "I'eos tä älä eyksi si'el u ansai'tsee urmon, Yah, elmoi'ta urmoa kai'keelle si'el ui'l lemme; ne, i'eoi'ta mea raka stamme i'ea ni'itä, i'eoi'ta kutsumme vi'hol li'se ai'ksi. Olkoon ni'in."

When Tull lifted his head out of prayer for the Fallen First, he found a watchful figure—a familiar silhouette—who observed him from a distance. No admonishment followed. Still, the Jacobian understood the expectations of his purpose.

"'We mend, we train, we guard, and we make proud He who made us.'"

Guardian Olley Hendrie Falk laughed as he joined the pair and tossed a burning torch to George. As he offered his gruff impersonation of that familiar silhouette, he recited the rest of the words heard by Tull and the third era of Guardians when they received invitation into the outfit. "'If even the breath behind my rules is too difficult for you to bear, I'll give you leave.' I tell you, I would risk marring if such invited ten ticks with that well-formed sylph who watches us from the roots of those twin black gum trees."

"Three ticks to tie your ego to the tree she hides behind." George goosed Olley's rear with the snuffed torch and ducked his swats.

"Five ticks till she catches her breath"—Tull awaited and saw Olley's smug reaction—"spent on squirming and mockery of you."

George's laughter landed him one swat after all.

Tull counted off ticks of the clock with his fingers. "The remainder ought to suffice for an Archibaldian of your—"

"Measure." The Westonian smiled at his Jacobian fellow.

The Archibaldian between them remained unamused. "Two ticks? You be—"

"One tick. With the other spent on unwinding those trouser straps for the unscathed gear you tow with such pride. I accredit you with one tick."

"Truly!"—Olley offered a snarl in rebuttal of his friends—"I tell you one tick with me invites more joy than she'll get from an entire eve with the *hero*."

The trio observed as Asham hooked an arm around the watchful sylph.

"I tell you! I do not wish to spend the next two moonrises listening to him dream about the 'if and when' that invites the terror of his headship."

"Does that not still leave three hundred and sixty-two eves for you to boast your plans of 'if and when'?"

"Better me than Asham."

"Better Ganix than Asham."

Tull and Olley looked at George—who mastered his tongue. When he spoke, he spoke in truth.

"I believe I'd sooner let the Devourer feast on me than serve either soul."

"I imagine such a fate is *why* either would tow the mantle."

"'Tow the mantle'? Have you been staying up all morn reading again?" Olley patted his friend's chest and hooked an arm around him as though Tull needed protection or guidance. "You need a dove."

"I prefer to know their names, I thank you." He broke Olley's hold when he retrieved his case and quiver.

Not to be slighted, Olley withdrew two of the grappler arrows that let Tull restrain their foe from afar. "As you say!"

The crossness of Tull's rebuttal fell as short as his next step. In the last word's stead, he proved silent and still, which drew similar expressions and curiosity from his fellows. Then, too, Olley and George softened at the sight that he beheld. The boasting of victory faded when the Guardians witnessed twin sisters—one who kicked Asham and still wept—nestled in the arms of their father as their mother challenged Edmond with an enraged spirit. Even Asham, who spoke out of turn at record pace, backed away from the family who showed more regard for the Fallen First then those who risked for them.

Then, Olley cursed. "All that for Partakers!"

~

Honest souls suffered beneath the warring of the firstkind. The Guardians were their shield—the realization of whispers uttered in times of hopelessness and fear. Still, they held no candle to the protectiveness or worth of a loving family. What dreams they abandoned, what hopes they yielded, lived on in those they guarded. As they kept no families of their own, the Guardians oft lived *above* but seldom *amid*.

~

"You heard his prayer?" Soberness filled Olley and the confirmation of George's nod. "What were his words?"

"He asked for mercy."

"For that creature?"

"For us all—if only one of us deserves mercy."

"We do not."

"Is that not the definition of mercy, my friend?"

"Philosophy and theology rile me, George." Olley sidestepped down the hill and tucked the stolen arrows in with his gear.

"Be cautious, my friend, and do not seek what will not keep you from the pit."

Olley batted an eye and clucked at such advice, but neither bothered Tull. Afore the Archibaldian reached the valley, he found uncounted souls who vied for his attention and saddened his Westonian fellow. Tull noticed, too, and flicked his brow at George in shared disappointment. Neither possessed the energy to fail to sway their friend on an eve so cold.

Olley and Asham oft appeased those who sought a Guardian to warm them. George frightened and Tull evaded; each with ease. Those from the Weston Territory believed spirits haunted the Second Creation and influenced the will. Tull, from afore a time when he bore the title of scion, conveyed kindness but not warmth. The attention wearied him more than his purpose, and he went to work on the *lesser* of the Guardians' responsibilities and started mending the cottage's exterior for souls who cursed his purpose.

He showed kindness to those who lingered; as though they proved more than fickle. Those who offered him handmade trinkets or food from their own gardens received his gratitude and never his denial. That they devoted time, labor, or sacrifice to him as a show of appreciation deserved a similar show of his appreciation, but never his gluttony. His mind never forgot a name, a home territory, or the purpose handed them by their shared Creator.

TULL & EBBE

By now, all learned what gifts the Jacobian would accept—scarves, socks, a saddle duvet for his stallion, Blizzard—brother to Olley's stallion, Firefly—and foods created by labor that he would not dismiss as meaning less than his own labor. He proved willing to lend his ear and, to those who seemed susceptible to the Fallen First, he oft issued wisdom to guard their hearts from infestation—and their reputations from his fellows. Olley and Asham, as though in competition, left the compassion to Tull, but bedded more than their share of souls who brought offerings to the places where the Guardians earned alms.

On this wintry eve, against the judges' curfew, souls sought to reward and not refuse Asham. The youngest and less seasoned of all Guardians showed bravery. Now, a blameless soul who despised him would see the approach of morn because of him. Though the Guardians tired of his boasting, the proof of success eased the solemnness that settled in the aftershock.

FOUR

ELLSBERG LODE TRAIL

38 PARASANG SOUTH OF THE FORK.

NEAR THE DISPLACED MILL GEAR.

None appreciated the Guardians from the Creighton Territory. They—Alison Brackett Nance, Hector Geirolf Picadura, and Asham Benjamin Gera—were filthy in habit, character, and tactic. Nance grew disgusted with the secondkind and settled in the barren lowlands. Hector refused to follow the orders of a eunuch and left the outfit without a scion. A territory-wide lottery selected Asham as their third Guardian.

So, while the judges blamed Edmond for every complaint and failure, none could oust obnoxious Asham. He spoke and never listened. Played and seldom trained. He neither believed nor partook; which was to say, he lacked the wit for decisiveness. He wanted a portion of all—minus amity and obedience.

He bedded as many souls as he could and never bore guilt for those he stole from the beds of his fellows or strangers. He borrowed gear that he oft broke, swiped food and never replenished, and fell derelict in his duties. Asham behaved like Ganix. Despite the Shelbian Guardian's uncountable flaws, Ganix, in the era afore theirs, had proven as wicked in battle as he was toward those whom he counted inferior.

Early in his purpose, Tull watched Ganix reach into the throat of a beast that stood on six proud legs and ripped loose a spiny tongue that spewed rancid, ammonia-like bile. His hand and forearm swelled to the girth of his thigh thereafter. Asham had never risked in that manner. Hector, who frightened wolves, kept his former fellows from harm upon occasion and Nance once kept Tull from his end afore she thrashed him. Asham served his own interests—the worst of all the secondkind's traits.

As such, honor faded faster than the eve. The recent hero proved the bivouac's current chump, as evidenced by the way he awoke that morn—sideways and in restraints. The same grapplers that Tull fired from a bow ensnared the outfit's best sneak to an oblique silver maple tree with branches that covered all four tents and the fire that warmed the youngest Guardians. Unlike Tull, Olley did not rely on a weapon, for he embedded each head into the tree by hand. His anger set loose the wire, which he twisted around Asham's limbs.

The two oft bickered—like siblings who despised the other's birth—and ruined many moments with foolishness and barbs. Olley's treatment, not that Asham rose above a brutal taunt, held him back from his purpose. Worse, their headship's bitterness toward such behavior sowed a wickedness in Asham that none suspected. Neither proved wise enough or willing to avoid the other.

Tull oft returned from a patrol and discovered the aftershock of the pair's misdeeds. Olley's belongings weighted with rocks in the nearest brook. Asham wrapped and bound in his tent—and staked to the glebe. The pair never tired afore they wearied those who lived alongside them. Asham fitted to a tree provided no shock.

"I tell you, when I cut free—"

Olley pulled tighter, till the force stole Asham's threat and replaced the fruitless sound with gasping.

"Nelson . . ."

"Nelson slept through the storms that washed half the Larson Territory away this past growing season. Your breathless mewling won't stir him."

"Geo—George . . ."

Olley pulled tighter and opened the arm till a cleft in the tree pinned his foe's elbow. "Has calling for George ever benefitted you?"

"Nels—I say"—he gurgled as the muscles in his neck seized—"Nelson!"

"Leave him be. He took the last patrol."

Tull sighed from disturbed slumber. "I woke afore he finished his earlier plea."

"Ah! Nelson! A pleasant morn."

Tull's scarred toes retreated away from the snow that settled too near to his tent.

Olley voiced the motive behind his act. "This indwelling canard let the torches go to smoke; though we warned him the fog would creep from the mines and settle upon us. Check your wares. I tell you, the fog lingers worse than Ganix's—"

Tull groaned as he stretched and let a chorus of crackling joints resound.

"Lest you started dreaming and told none of us, your back could use the change in direction, old-timer."

TULL & EBBE

"I tell plenty."

"You tell little." George agreed with the agitated Archibaldian.

"How you thanked me not to tell Violet after you squirreled away her pearl-hued hair ribbon"—Tull emerged from his tent in time that a well-packed snowball burst across his shoulder, dusted his smooth face, and clung to his long lashes—"or tell her of your scathing temper."

Asham's voice gave Tull more of a chill than the snow as he sang out, "Ohhh, is George sweet on Violet?"

The bound Guardian made a deserving target for snow cast from the hands of the Archibaldian and the Jacobian on George's behalf.

"Stop!" Asham spat a cluster of dirty snow. "Apologies, George!"

Tull and Olley shared boastful grins over their results and the latter tossed a brass alms toward the former—the cost of spent tools that kept Asham lashed. "A ribbon from Violet Grey Pinney is a fine reminder, George."

"As you say."

Because George's soul proved the gentlest of the outfit, the duo withheld more than the mildest ribbing—afore Olley scathed every ear with a harsh curse as he searched through his gear.

"The fog does thieve."

"This time, I've lost my new lorgnette."

Now Tull traded glances with George, who saved all the possible alms for seed to use on his farm in the coming sowing season. Olley overpaid for trinkets and contraptions that belonged in cases, not in bivouacs, and not damaged on foes. He repeated bad habits as much as Asham; still, none restrained him to the nearest tree. Other than Harlan, none could wrangle the yob.

"And my caster has gone wandering!"

"The burnished caster?"

"I've no other."

"You three prattle like a pack of biddies."

The coils of gear fell from Olley's stone hands. "My ear deceives me."

"As you say."

"Mine too," Asham declared.

"Have you not yet learned of the trouble your tongue causes, Creightonian?"

"Vile." Olley flung away heaps of gear. "Vile!"

TULL & EBBE

An innocent chirp escaped too late to cover the self-pleased chuckle from Olley's tent. The agitating sound riveted Olley's knees, righted Tull's posture, and turned George's head. Even Asham risked further harm to his skin as he strained to see the source of the territories' most identifiable accent. Nothing bested an Archibaldian like wounded pride.

No other soul loathed the Shelbians to the profound depths in which Olley wallowed. He reveled in his hatred of every literal soul born in the centermost territory north of the Loy. His abhorrence toward Shelbians needled his temper but his mother's fine tutelage kept him from blaspheming. Still, he learned nothing of forgiveness.

"A moment's pause, my friends."

A rustle throughout the shell of his tent spoke to his refusal to let go of old wounds. After the outfit, the second wisest to his prejudice were the Shelbians. His brisk tone shed every hint of privilege, and true disdain lowered his voice to grumbling octaves. The back of his neck turned red and his knuckles pale when he clutched at a bare leg, then plucked from his tent the source of his outrage.

Her wideset eyes showed the fear of a trapped creature and skin dusted with freckles turned slick with worry. The arrogance of her tongue mingled with her racing heart and muddled her plea. She then recanted in a second tongue; common to those who lived along the waterways of the Shelby Territory. The harsh syllables sounded worse with coarse breaths and a shrill whine that foretold of her knowledge of the cruelty that the Archibaldian showed souls from her territory.

As he grated her bare thigh and arm upon the frozen glebe, ratcheting his grip as if to fling her toward the spent fire, he took his eye off his fellows. Ganix remained indifferent, even upon seeing a fellow Shelbian suffer. Tull rummaged for a bolt adorned with a sedating vial. George reacted with less discretion and gathered ashes from the firepit. These he flung toward Olley's eyes to subdue him with momentary blindness and breathlessness.

Even as the Archibaldian fell to his knees in a fit of coughing and groaning, George proved he was no easy savior. With a level head and stern tone, he accused the deceptive soul who remained on his other side. "Why would you seek this? Why would you invite such harm?"

TULL & EBBE

"I wanted a Guardian in my number." As she shrugged, the blanket fell away from a column of diminutive, crimson-red ribbons inked between her shoulder blades for each lover she took.

"I tell you"—Olley swelled like a boiling kettle—"she spoke with no such accent when she approached me."

His remark went unchallenged as stillness swept through the bivouac and a fretful look overcame even Ganix.

The Archibaldian faced his friends with a scowl caked in wet ash. "Tell me anyway."

"Odd turn."

"Unfortunate."

Ganix's uneasy laughter needled Olley, who washed his eyes with more fallen snow. "What?"

None volunteered their discovery, but Asham proved his dimness that landed him in trouble and started the ruckus in the first place. "Even I see her ribbons!"

"*Ribbons?*" He who washed away the ash seemed jovial at first, willing even to cast another barb toward George over Violet. Then, snow melted upon his brow. "She . . . is . . . not . . ."

"Most Partakers are Shelbian."

George muttered at the way Ganix's every word sounded like a boast.

"No."

"Then she is not a Partaker?" Blinded Olley appeared torn between his next dousing of snow and a relieved breath induced by Tull's previous remark.

Tull shook off the obvious. "I noticed that I have a blanket of an identical pattern to hers. That is the odd turn."

At long last, Olley's deceiver found her full, accent-enriched voice again. "I proved cold in the eve! I chose the wrong Guardian, the fire was out, and you were on patrol . . ."

No other sighed as a Jacobian sighed. That sound was as close to swearing as he neared. "Sister Elsa Cassaway gave that blanket to me when I was announced as Guardian."

"Then tell her Helena Diane Köcsma finds her cross-stitch needs tautness."

TULL & EBBE

Unmoved by thievery, yet too proud to wear shoddy coverings, she tossed the blanket back to the Jacobian and put to use the opportunity for the surrounding Guardians to admire her in form and fearlessness.

"I tell you, in the coldest watch, your tattered bedding warmed me more than your selfish friend."

"Selfish?"

Though the Partaker teased the Jacobian's chest with her fingers, Tull tilted backward to avoid her lips.

"Does a Shelbian call me selfish?"

"I displease you, do I?"

"You are selfish, Falk." Ganix spat as he turned in threefold disinterest.

"I am a Believer."

Helena's smile turned as perverse as her behavior. "In an eve, I could turn your heart, Jacobian."

Tull proved his disinterest, too, and adorned her again with the blanket that he would elsewise pitch unto the fire as Believers took nothing unclean into their beds. "This belongs to you now. If the cross-stitch displeases you, prove yourself able and re-hem your trinket. You'll receive nothing more from this lot except the confirmation that your territory rests to your left. Now get on your way."

The Jacobian and the Westonian remained solemn as she turned toward their friend's tent. Both kept the watch, for they understood the root of Olley's hatred. Tull gathered his tin of water and tossed as much to George, who saw that the subdued Archibaldian's hands felt the smooth flask. Olley unscrewed the cap and doused his eyes whilst the pair resumed their watch over Helena's departure.

The Shelbian Partaker reemerged from Olley's tent, adorned in her wares this time, but not without Tull's blanket in tow. She exited their camp toward the nearest road and cursed the Guardians with the smugness that most in the territories rejected. "Önel égült ro ha dék!"

"Oake i'en äkoi'ena!" He who understood the tongues of Ministers rebuked she who spoke the language of the Fallen First and smirked as his words made her flee. Then, as though a voice whispered in his ear, he sensed another presence. He turned toward the forested hillside opposite her path and found Edmond in silent observation again.

"How many ribbons did she gather?" Helena's agitated lover paled with disgust.

TULL & EBBE

"Three columns." George refrained from a lie.

"How many?"

"Two ribbons in each." Tull did not.

"Seven is a respectable number. I can abide by that." Olley's color returned with his boast, though he was further from seven than even Asham would admit.

"You prove your generosity, Nelson." Bound Asham took advantage of Tull's attention, unaware that their headship stood at his back. "That's your strength! Your ceaseless generosity."

"I'll not cut you loose."

"I tell you, that mean streak of yours is what keeps you alone. You have an ornery way about you." He shut one eye and sought George's nearness. "Does he not, George? He could learn much from you!"

George waved off the compliment and helped Olley to his feet. The Archibaldian understood the intervention and bore no dispute. All the while, Tull stood with as much restraint as the binds that kept Asham. When last the fog stole from them, the Jacobian lost a patch embroidered with his father's name that he carried in place of having no photograph of the departed soul.

"Ko vata ki'poa, koeri'a."

"What's that?" Asham hollered. "What's he whispering about, George?"

"His words were not meant for our ears."

"No more of that silver tongue. Down here, we speak common."

Imbued with the spirits of the Fallen First, the fog acted as a thief, yet never stole the pointless ramblings that abounded. Like the shadows that consumed, the fog stole trinkets and ought to have provoked the silence associated with fear. Had Asham fulfilled his duties to the outfit, the torches would have lifted the temperature and dispelled the mist upon which the fog spread wider; which ought to have produced regret, if not shame. His disregard cost him—but would cost another, too.

"Who's turn this time?" Harlan led Edmond, who walked a step ahead of Ganix, and who returned to the bivouac carrying a bitter air of delight over Asham's failings.

Tull's scowl proved which of the younger Guardians towed the burden of watching over Asham in his *troubles*. Where they traveled next proved a favorite locale for the Jacobian. Now, another's laxness delayed him. Olley was not wrong to punish Asham, but the agitation that Tull felt exceeded his due.

Harlan then faced the awarded. "Truly, you deserved the time in Parantua."

"The duty is mine."

"Stay with him"—Edmond tossed his own blanket to Tull—"but don't interfere."

"Ever?" Asham's nervous yelp pleased Olley.

"Offer him clues on the second eve, but don't put your hand to hilt for his sake afore the third." Edmond wound the lace of Asham's boot around a fox-shaped trinket molded from murky orange glass and patted his underling's calf. "The soul who returns this to me gains reward."

"Looks like you lose twice, Tull."

Olley heard Asham's barb and struck hard enough that the back of his mouthy fellow's crown struck the tree that kept him.

Tull offered back to Olley the alms he paid for binding Asham.

"Oh"—Olley refused his offering—"such efforts are my delight."

"Once you've settled at the inn, put your slyness to use and find time to tuck"—Tull showed and pushed the alms into the breast pocket of Olley's high-collared vest—"into the pocket of our favorite Keeper's daughter."

"I would delight—"

Tull seized Olley's shoulder. "In no pocket sewn upon what she wears in your presence."

"I would never—"

He tightened his grip. "And, you're not to see her as you introduced your last dove as an excuse to uphold our agreement."

Olley brushed away his friend's hold. "I do understand you."

"George?"

"I will help him keep his word to you."

"Truly, Nelson, if she means so much to you, you ought to take hold and—"

This time, Tull used a sound fist and his full weight to filch Asham's consciousness and invite peace to the camp—minus Ganix's uproarious delight.

As calmness visited in the fog's stead, Edmond gathered food for two Guardians and an anthracite cell that would avert further thievery. "We'll wait for you till the third morn."

Harlan gave to Tull a well-worn book and a pat to his back when they noticed that Ganix urinated on the root beneath Asham's head. Olley handed Tull his most expensive and most worthless tool. Ganix left him with a pocket of matchsticks; the cheapest tool in his stash. He abandoned camp afore the lot, and Tull stood the watch till the last—George—vanished from sight without his kettle lamp.

Tull surveyed the branches for signs of disturbed snow, set a narrow perimeter with the torches, and then gathered more wood for the fire. Though he listened for a change in Asham's breath, his eyes counted the empty footprints left by Olley's deceptive dove. Soon, the silence needled him. Inspired to fruitfulness, he set his fellows' alms in his tent and made better use of the coveted isolation.

He took from the pocket of his coat a journal, through which he leafed from back to front as his hind side found a perch. In the same moment that he sat, the deckle edge of a photograph aged sixteen spans fell astray from the binding. Olley exceeded the kindness of friendship when he presented Tull with the gift on the first eve of his twenty-fourth span. That which cost twelve copper alms and a signed handbill from Betty Kay Olley, the Archibaldian's thesp-mother, held the unattainable value in the distinction that no earlier photograph of the Jacobian existed amid his belongings.

The stripling soul beside him in the photograph was more radiant than the ornamental kettle lantern she held and as ageless as the sky-fires. Few souls cared about him then, but she oft ran to his side. He mattered to her when all he had was a grave marker adorned with his father's name and no other could tell why. By her example, he offered similar regard to a soul whose recent letters brimmed with doubt and discouragement. From a recess in the sheath of his boot he took a cedar pencil and wrote in soapstone what he intended for no other soul.

> *Each has discovered by now our purpose and, I believe, you are no different. What you will achieve exceeds my influence. I am the cloud that shields the moon. For a time, the light hides. Then, the cloud fades and all see the moon in her splendor. In time, all will see you and regret their former blindness, J. J.*

He felt a stirring in his heart but did not notice a lingering light that watched over him from on high. The burnished brass creature moved with more grace than the wind and stayed near long enough to encourage his heart. When he weighed his thoughts again, he composed a closing doxology.

How vast are Yah's mercies?
How uncounted are His offerings?
What have we done that we
—in our foolishness and pride—
See a portion of His glory?

He tucked his pencil behind his ear, then reclined on his right palm and admired the brilliant plumes of color that rolled through the sky-fires. "Who am I to You?"

"Well, I tell you this much"—Asham cleared his throat—"I believe you snuck that tap in on me in my temporary state of helplessness."

Tull's sigh rivaled the fire and he tucked safe the photograph, then crammed his journal underarm afore he rose and exited the camp. Though he would keep the restrained fool in sight, he had no desire to pother beneath Asham's listless ramblings. He prayed only for peace; though, in his mind, that might have included asking the Triune to freeze the Creightonian's tongue like the waters in winter. Then, in opening his eyes and reestablishing his focus, he looked a while longer upon that old photograph.

No Need of Rescue

An Interim

The 5th Eve beneath the Moon of the Mother's Song

The 107th Winter Season of the Accession

In the Care of the Helper, who keeps souls from fruitless wandering.

<u>Beacon 072.19.434 recognized at 41 Court of Learning . . .</u>

Identifier confirmed—Sondrea Ebbe Conliffe.

Observe at all times beneath Edict No. 112009-11B.

A collective emerged beneath the serenity of a brilliant eve, not two ticks after the exterior lights on the territory's last-built stone structure turned dim. The location changed at every meeting and, like those afore, this locale meant little. They who lacked access to an ever-traveling steam tram like the judges used, never went without a place to meet where even a judge's eyes could not see them. Such were the benefits of those souls deemed *above* other souls.

Even amid elitists, though, obstacles and clashes arose. One conniving soul sought influence at the expense of their purpose as an equal collective. Then this soul refused to meet with that soul due to a familial gripe or petty offense. Another favored comfort over risk. In the end, eight of twelve recognized souls gathered to debate the topic of the secondkind's convicted souls and the reform they experienced.

Society, or what stood as the societal rungs amid the secondkind, had no formal name for this collective, but those counted within the lot used the word *overseer* more oft than not to define their blood-appointed purpose. Each territory that remained after the Accession washed over them contained varying numbers of souls. From them, the eldest souls arose as headships in the absence of any government or law enforcing outfit. The elders of these twelve overseers were the souls who approached the firstkind for help in rebuilding amid the devastation.

Though five territories withered at the Era of the Falling Lands, the tradition remained set, and the nearest blood representative of those eldest lineages held an invitation. Their few critics accused them of working against judges or, worse, determining who would serve as judges, guardians, chiefs, abettors, and scions. In truth, and at various times throughout the eras, the overseers acted as each, and oft without accountability toward their fellows. And whilst they held select positions of power around the seven remaining territories, they no longer meddled in such decision-making.

Yet, communication failed long afore the noble word of their members. By their current roster, members included one advocate, one advocate scion, and one chief inspector, but also two of the northern territories' most notorious troublemakers. Feeble Gwilkoava of fallen Perlin wilted in the desert-like nub of a detached southern territory behind the mountains where she buried her successors.

Hamer of Creighton and Paiva of Weston shared a coach—no doubt to inflict madness upon their shared driver by way of debating their conflicting beliefs and love of foul cigars. Those from Shelby and Carpenter remained neglectful and absent. The same with the eldest of the former Gierig, Matox, who upheld a meager purpose that thrived in the dim-to-darkest watches of the eve and provided him much-needed alms. Salter of Archibald left alone and without farewell, in a hurry to travel though his proved the shortest trip of all. A law-writer from Damaris proceeded away in an opposite direction of the advocate of Larson; as most fled from that seated and crude judge.

Whilst most acted as though strangers, the elder souls whose blood ran the longest through Jacoby and Othniel embraced as sisters afore their farewells. Guild, of fallen Erori, who kept away Forgney the Carpenterian and Sówka the Shelbian, remained and addressed the fairer pair with a tip of a long-billed hat then left with a backward glance that spoke of paranoia as much as lust. An ambling departure of the coach that held the elder Larsonite blocked the paths of who selected which of the two coaches draped in equal shadow.

An outsider in every form emerged from another shadow and cursed—in glare alone—at the uncertainty that bloated the moment. The advancements the secondkind made toward their transportation mingled with their inability to offer an extravagance of designs. As such, their steam-drawn and horse-drawn coaches looked almost identical in shape. That both women traveled by way of horse-drawn coach muddied his ability to keep the two apart as they entered the false glow of gas lamps and further confused the eye.

In the Era of the Reformers and the Era of the Falling Lands, those *forgotten* by the secondkind remained comforted by the shadows and the lacking light. They—who proved older than the secondkind—dwelled in darkness, where the Triune's favored let belief falter and watched Partakers embolden their stance against their Creator. Their ears filled with the wailing of those souls when they invoked suffering and no salvation came, but the sound of wailing never ceased in their ears.

Without the benefit of sound or the clarity of sight, this observer used cowardice as his guide for the eve. He targeted neither the judge nor the chief inspector, for they were too powerful in name. In a similar way, he dismissed Hamer and Paiva, for their successes made them frightening to him. Salter offered no substance of mourning and Kind Hand—the law-writer—had not ripened, let alone rotted, enough to deserve a cruel end. So, he set his eye against two who were known throughout the northern territories for their power, their privilege, and their substance: Greer and Fabray.

The Taotáva were neither members of the First Creation nor the Second Creation, nor were they a mingling of those lines. In simplest terms, they were *between*. They were present afore the Last War, the War of the Conquered Sea, and the War of Souls, with a beginning that traced back to the fall of the Pillar of Lies but not afore the retreat of His Mighty Rains. When the sea of stars caught fire, they were beneath, looking up and gauging the depth of what once they called the *heavens*.

As with the view above them, the untouched place that they declared theirs soon became a nesting place for the Fallen First. Those creatures—Yah's betrayers—chased the Taotáva till they overtook the surface. So, the souls who went uncounted amid two creations retreated from the sky-fires' splendor. They congregated in caves and pits and lost their memory of the light. Then, the secondkind exceeded their number and advanced beyond them in every measure.

Those souls whom the firstkind doted over spread like a rash across the flesh of the isle that remained. Given their low numbers, they claimed plots in excess to their needs out of a belief that Yah might make them plentiful again. They sought the means to keep their fruit near to the vines. The Taotáva bore no such instinct. All elders were mother and father, all peers were sister and brother, and all the blameless souls were daughters and sons to them.

Though the uncounted elders demanded that all keep from the secondkind lest they anger Yah—who cast down those who displeased, struck the trees with fire, and froze the glebe—and provoke further mulct, better they leave to their warring the First Creation and let stumble the Second Creation. Better that they hide and remain uncounted. Better that they wither—*unremembered.*

One who bore no desire of forgottenness traveled further from the shadows and caves than elders dared. In the low light, he appeared as any common male soul who found favor from those drawn out of a fiery brass sea by Yah's mighty hand. Beneath the moon and the sky-fires, he ran the bulbous pads of long fingers across a false face and let his ravenous form resurface in the aftershock of his touch. Where tissue proved thinnest, the skin gave way to oily, necrotic webbing that held his eyes and jaw together with brittle strands.

The fog that scrubbed clean the season's latest snow provided cover for him. Where the mist failed, he tucked his slender shoulders into a worn nook between a pair of teetering silver maple trees and manipulated both posture and height till he took on the likeness of an uncounted branch. As a trait none explained, the Taotáva blended with their surroundings. Near the throat, his skin bore the texture of bark and disguised his ears from all but the cold as he rested in wait.

Called *Ming*, which meant *fox* on the Taotáva tongue, he abhorred the bitterness of winter less than the dark, the caves, and the rules of elders who bore no pride for all that they were. He would freeze, but he would not wither. He would not hide nor go uncounted any longer. Their fear, by his measure, should belong to another.

Charles Ralph Steinberg, whose purpose to those who did know the soul seemed minimal, was far more than a driver of lavish coaches, an opener of doors, or an announcer of arrivals. He traced his line back twelve eras afore the Accession and hailed from a sterling lineage. That same lineage scoffed at his title: Driver. They claimed he embarrassed the name and standing of all Steinbergs afore him and preferred he not be counted by those who followed.

TULL & EBBE

He enjoyed the stability of his purpose and the certainty of what his benefactor expected of him. Promptness, obedience, and a decisiveness that anticipated both the whims and demands cultivated a trusted servant into an unseen agent. Though he dared not face the creatures that turned souls into Guardians nor reason with an advocate's wit, he labored on behalf of she who towed the adoration of souls from each noble calling—and many others—with tremendous elegance.

What skills he possessed, like his understanding of setting and his keen recall for detail, served well. He mapped routes by the count of trees, the firmness of the terrane, and not by the interpretations of others. Not one burning light nor a single grove escaped his attention. So, when the mist off the Forbidden Sea obscured the plains that skirted Malachi's Vine, an uncertainty toward common, untainted travel drew a sense of wariness.

Despite an array of travel options, his renowned passenger requested the winter coach and a team of two twin, hickory-colored stallions. Much of the territories' travel relied on steam and an experimental, clean-burning fuel gum developed by a nervy inventor who caught fire to two laboratories and fourteen engines. Had he any say, beyond his benefactor's polite habit of seeking affirmation of the occasional whim, he still would have chosen the coach over the ethane gum-powered roadway cruiser or rig so many souls owned.

A corollary of the gum was dizziness unto intoxication and slumber in those exposed too long to the fumes. Even so, with only the scent of the horses afore him and an anthracite kettle beneath his seat, the driver's eyes teased him. He had no other source of blame for what he believed he saw. So, he rubbed his eyelids, batted his lashes, and strained to see what the low light defended, for he swore he identified the most powerful soul in the Archibald Territory perched beneath the branch of a silver maple tree.

"My honor!" Given the cries of the abrasive wind, Charles Ralph Steinberg's voice never reached the passenger cabin. Once he grasped what was about to happen, fear stole his voice in full.

Not one soul in the seven territories—nor the five that the Forbidden Sea claimed in the Era of the Falling Lands—observed Judge Cyril Adair Mumus running afore. A soul who towed as much influence as he lacked the need and his stout build intensified such activity. So, at the sight of the oncomer's sprint, Charles ratcheted his hold of the reins and latched the pedal for the coach's brake as Ming—in disguise—leapt toward the brass runner.

"Bolt the"—the driver then took a fist to his face—"doors!"

For a count of two heartbeats, and as Charles stomped at him, the Taotáva attacker lost his false countenance, which did more for his advantage than any blow. He dared not reduce his chance at success. So, he used the team of horses as a weapon and flung Charles headlong toward the eight hoofs he directed even as the brake activated. Better that he preserve his strength for the *true* intended, and not a soul who meant so little.

At least one bone broke, judging by the sharp crackle and ensuing howl. The sudden stop provoked the horses but withdrew no emotion from the false-faced Ming. He focused his might and, with a vile thrust, pried open the door to the passenger compartment. When a drawn curtain separated him from his prey, he reached into the cuffed sleeves of his jacket and removed two pieces taken from the branch of a buttonwood tree, filleted down to rods, and then sharpened to tapered points long enough to pierce through a body.

Afore he ripped open the curtain, a crystal decanter filled with hemp oil burst against his chest, shoulder, and throat. A hiss of uneven light chased behind and then a ripple of blue flame spread over him like a cloak. Ming writhed in pain, but as his hand slapped at the fire, another surprise stole the breath. His arm shrank in length and girth to reduce the amount of damageable tissue. The rest of his torso could not do the same, so he flung his full weight unto a bank of powdery snow that heat reduced to scalding steam.

Charles, who lay tucked beneath the axle of the coach's front wheels, squirmed away as he observed the change. The horses drummed with their hooves, but then an eerie calm settled across the valley. In this, as well as his suffered wounds, Ming took fright. He scampered away, sobbing at the blistered flesh and the matted wardrobe that hindered his left flank.

His intended victim—a descendent of Jacobians and Erorii, born a Shelbian, who explored the Carpenterian mountains and resided as an Archibaldian—emerged from the coach shaken, but not frantic, then stomped the littered open flame with the wooden heel of a boot whilst her brave driver chased away the already-fled attacker and held his crooked arm. When that heel proved too slender, his passenger stripped off her coat and smothered tendrils of flame. By the time Charles returned to his benefactor's side, he found her in a motionless stance and focused on the horizon of Sevier. She batted long, elegant lashes across pools of copper-hued irises that captured every light yet remained more brilliant than each source.

Within sight of Mumus Tower, Countess Sondrea Ebbe Conliffe backed away from the monolith with a lilt of avarice for all that the site represented. In that moment, the eldest of the Jacoby Territory's Fabray bloodline realized the monstrosity that spilled out even unto the tranquil valleys of the Archibald Territory. She felt rather like a soul who gained her sight after moons wasted on oblivious denial. Now she backed away further, with purpose, till she felt the nearness of the carriage again.

"'And straightway the deceiver forgetteth what manner of soul he was.'"

Her driver removed the knit cap from his crown and bowed his head in recognition of the parable she recalled.

"Charles, fetch Dory and Mim. We've a new destination to reach now."

SONDREA EBBE CONLIFFE

Sondrea represents the oldest Jacobian family to survive the Accession but is rooted in privilege that has come to her at tremendous cost. She has witnessed the possibilities of the Second Creation and the terrors of those creatures that the Guardians have yet to oppose. Her desires are to get back what the secondkind lost and to protect the soul she cares about the most—even at the expense of her character.

NEVER THE TIME

FIVE

THE 7TH EVE BENEATH THE MOON OF THE MOTHER'S SONG
THE 107TH WINTER SEASON OF THE ACCESSION
IN THE CARE OF THE HELPER, WHO KEEPS SOULS FROM FRUITLESS WANDERING.

ON THE HEM OF PARANTUA
THE CARPENTER TERRITORY.
SEVEN TICKS OF THE CLOCK DUE NORTH OF 111 BUXLEY CROSSING.

Three moonrises passed afore Tull and Asham neared Shannon's Inn to rejoin the outfit. The lights of Parantua offered more distraction and the setting nearer to the Loy River offered more amusement than their bivouac near the lodes. Even so, Asham had not relented with conversation long enough to gawk. Though still seeping from the imprints upon his flesh, he proved more long-winded in his attempt to coax Edmond's trinket from Tull than the soul he agitated ever imagined.

Tull was sore, too, from missing time with the Shannon family. In his present soreness, he would not relinquish Edmond's glass fox even to save Asham's soul from Ki'eoppa—the Pit. Though wearied by the Creightonian's nattering and the time spent atop Blizzard as they crossed the Carpenter Territory, the pace of his heart testified to his eagerness to be rid of his fellow traveler and in the company of souls he cherished.

No other place in the territories offered a better chance at mending or wearying his body with too much laughter than Shannon's Inn. Keeper Victor Simon Shannon, his bride Francine Laurette Mokuk, and she who was the first soul he rescued, deepened his purpose and counted him as family. Four moons—two spent south of the

Loy—passed since the Jacobian's last visit. Now he needed only to reach the pine plank door of the inn without another soul's attempt to delay him.

Asham's overlapping wounds and irritations drew the eyes of most travelers away from Tull. Though Olley would have kept distance from their unreliable fellow, Tull benefited from the distraction. A notorious gesticulator, the swing of Asham's wounded hands and the uncertainty of ailments kept back most souls and cleared their path. Those who failed soon fled from the sound of Asham's voice.

A backward glance proved that eight souls found the pair interesting enough to follow. This was a downside of their purpose. The Second Creation treated Guardians as celebrities, as legends, and as idols. All three descriptors troubled the Jacobian for he observed the elitism and the addiction to renown that rotted those souls who stayed too long in the outfit.

"If he lacked that wall-eyed stare, I tell you, he might at long last get a good peek unto one of the many mirrors he seeks and learn that he is no better."

Asham and Olley towed Cam's elitism; along with hints of Ganix's pompousness, Hector's coarseness, Mick's arrogance, and Perry's selfishness. The second Guardian from the Jacoby Territory left the outfit over such needs. What he left behind, others consumed.

"No, no—that's true—his wall-eyedness doesn't forgive his rodent-like overbite! Only an Archibaldian would favor vermin in look with none of their skill."

Between them—Asham, Olley, Cam, Ganix, Hector, Mick, and Perry—they claimed twenty plots, kept spoils of uncountable worth, and bedded a declared tally of souls that numbered near the population of the present setting. Cameron Lou Fenner kept in contact with two of his eight offspring. Picadura claimed upward of eleven but denied a twelfth, and Perry failed to keep a place amid the four sons he scattered around the territories. Ganix and Olley claimed no children, and Asham never stayed in touch with any soul he bedded long enough to learn of his progeny.

"But, forgetting his sight glass and George's sense of direction, what I'm asking is, if you had a map, would that information not prove worthy of a trade?"

"No."

For the first time since Olley bound him, Asham proved silent; but that soon passed. "Even now? After all we've gone through!"

The Guardian who refused to repeat his own words tugged the reins and turned Blizzard right at 111 Buxley Crossing onto Ketcham Leap. As for him, he kept but one plot in the territory of his birth. He loved—as deep as the marrow in his bones—one soul who exceeded his affections. Lest he risk her purpose and soul, he never intended on an heir. At least, not as long as he bore the purpose that made him travel alongside long- and foul-winded souls.

"I tell you, that surprises me, Nelson! All this time, I've counted you as kindred—nay, a brother. You are as near as a brother to me."

Tull nudged Blizzard sideways as he sighed, then removed Edmond's trinket from the lowest pocket of his suspenders and pressed the dull edges between his thumb and index finger. Asham batted his lashes, but still looked up to the Jacobian who sat one-half of a head taller than he. Tull then set the trinket in the outer pocket of his coat and closed the flap. With no other word, he awaited the reaction of the soul he unbound.

"You know, this is why we never groan over your silence."

Tull and his mount trotted ahead without argument.

"Do you not?"

Tull's grin reached an ornery breadth. He then basked as Asham's perturbed silence increased and the crest and tile of their destination came into focus. The sandstone face of the three-storey inn adorned with amethyst shutters and awnings that matched the eyes of the Keeper's daughter proved a welcome sight. Eleven strides on an eager horse let him determine a course through the gathering of onlookers that clustered at the half-moon windows of the inn.

Asham reached another standstill, as not one onlooker turned from the windows for him. This produced an opportunity for the simpler of the pair. Tull goosed him with his weapons satchel then slipped from Blizzard's saddle and nudged through the gathering with a polite, though unrelenting, step. One of the inn's workers noticed him, even waved, but an outburst from the gatherers interrupted a welcome.

"That's not them!" A stocky boy gasped as he shoved back from the inn window and elbowed the ribcage of a slimmer soul beside him. "Guardians stand twelve heads high I tell you."

The soul with poked ribs followed his prodder's hand and saw that he failed to reach Tull's height.

"Shoulders out to here." Though he exaggerated, the boy failed again.

"Uh-huh," the poked-rib boy agreed in jest.

Tull cocked his jaw, offered a wink, and then swatted away the blowhard with the pine plank door. "Much time has passed, Farrier Buford."

"As you say"—the farrier averted his eyes toward the gatherers and withheld Tull's formal title—"*traveler*. Might I shelter your horses in our stable?"

Tull agreed with a nod, a copper alms, and Blizzard's reins. "Don't let this one coax you out of any apples. He fed well in Wulfric."

"As you say."

Tull patted the man's shoulder in gratitude and received a swat from the pine plank door as the mouthy runt pushed back. Asham laughed, in recognition of his own kind, but proved disloyal enough not to lend a helping hand or give alms for the farrier's help. For this, the farrier let loose of the door. When the plank batted Asham into the inn, his fellow traveler sidestepped and let him stumble in.

67 Ketcham Leap

Shannon's Inn.

Where Guardians mend.

Souls of all ages and uncounted shapes clustered along the windows that looked in on Shannon's Inn to see what made the pair of travelers worthier than them. So enthralled were they with those Guardians inside the establishment that they missed the arrival of the two souls who completed the lot. Only he who took an ornery poke in the ribs smiled as he kept the watch over Tull. Even when the soul who poked him tried to nudge him away, he mimicked the Guardian's sturdy stance and let his agitator stumble.

The Guardian did not see, for he glanced upon the mantel of the hearth that Vic made during his daughter's first winter and brought with them in the move from Kanarek and saw the framed photograph of the Shannons with the entirety of the outfit. He then verified that the chandelier above head still dangled on three of the five leather braids that Vic did not cut the morn Harlan taught the Keeper how to throw a knife. An octagonal-shaped glass piece on that same chandelier still bore the crack from the impact of a cork that burst from a bottle that Francine opened in celebration of learning that same daughter received permission to study medicine with a bright and generous benefactor. He felt reassured that every corner offered him a tale and a sense of belonging and sighed.

TULL & EBBE

Shannon's Inn drew little more than devoted drinkers in the winter, apart from the local glassmakers and woodworkers who dispensed their alms for any drink served from burnished copper mugs. Another of the inn's hired hands, Mabel Eleanor Parker, whose poor balance worked against her over-proportioned frame, won over the lot with a smile as clumsy as her feet. She proved easy enough on the eye that even patrons who failed to woo her kept from passing out in the darkened corners of other establishments for a chance to make her their own. Still, the keeper who kept a keen eye on all kept her worker from becoming the next mark for certain Guardians.

Francine Laurette Mokuk, keeper of the inn and bride of Victor Simon Shannon, set complementary treats on a table for locals who corralled away from the center of the room where sat Ganix. She then looked to her husband, who sat in a booth furthest from the sour-scented Guardian. Many souls told how she wed beneath her; though, she never spoke of regret. She, like Mabel, did not greet their newest arrivals.

Her husband, a burly soul with an ornery sense of humor and a twisted tongue, possessed a loving heart far greater than any poet. This eve, though, he set his jaw and rested bloodied knuckles in a bowl of ice. He kept his eyes down and clutched at his mop of curls with another still-agitated fist. Tull recognized that ache and buried any form of heckling that he might have counted to garner their attention.

As he scanned the inn, he locked eyes with isolated Ganix, who sprawled in his seat till the rim of the back sat prouder than the oft arrogant and beady-eyed lump. His furious gaze burned like the embers that warmed the inn. Afore Tull focused on him, Asham cut between and approached the warm hearth. His motion reignited Tull's search, but he did not see the face of the keepers' daughter.

Though Olley waved him toward an empty seat at the table he shared with George, their headship matched Tull's posture. Between the trio and Vic, with a mindful eye on both sides of the inn, Edmond stood in boots so polished that they squeaked when he curled his toes. He dressed in a pristine manner, all the way up to the fashionable wig atop his head. All observed the neatness and immaculate care he maintained, so Tull returned the trinket with equal regard.

Unlike the oily sneer that spoke of Ganix's corruption, Edmond bore a delighted smirk that never frayed a single hair upon his false mustache. "I suspected. Did you see trouble on your way in?"

"Not even when I tried."

Edmond's gaze lingered an extra tick afore he nodded and set the glass wolf in a covered pocket on his vest—which matched his boots down to the thread color. He then closed his eyes and turned his head in the direction of Tull's travel companion. "Gera! You're to handle inventorying and cleanup alone till we're no longer beneath this moon."

"As you say, my headship."

Tull nodded in appreciation of Edmond's rule and received a pat on his back as he approached the chair that Olley pushed from beneath the table. This victory marked one amid few that the Archibaldian did not use to jab at Asham's character. In point of fact, he kept as placid as George kept timid.

In mockery's stead, the Guardian born of privilege and rugged confidence kept Ganix still. His chest measured so wide that his arms draped over the rests of the chair. What barbs he kept, he drowned with a swig from his burnished mug, but a gleam in his eye flickered when he looked to his oily peer. About the time when Tull wanted an explanation, a noise rang out.

Clumsy Mabel spilled another tray and, from the condition of her stained apron, not her first of that shift. Edmond's squeaky boot stopped a drained mug from rolling too far from her reach and shunned another soul's hope of watching her bend over when he stooped in retrieval. A pair of alms from her tray rolled contrary, around an overturned chair and beneath the drawn curtain of a room between the inn and the kitchen where workers caught their breath. Of these coins, no soul offered rescue.

Tull watched not out of attraction but because the soul he had not yet found hid from patrons in that same room more oft than she spoke to them. He half-expected the willowy array of limbs to swat back the curtains as if betrayed by the intruding alms. As the clumsy soul brushed back the veil, a stack of shelves painted to match the golden-crème walls and brimming with unused mugs and plates greeted his expectant gaze.

"I thank you, Francine."

Tull glanced around Ganix's head and spotted the crossed legs of the bear-like creature that held the voice he recognized. Harlan said no more, but let those who watched him see that he placed three silver alms upon a tray where Guardians drank for free. Tull identified Harlan's steely gaze well enough to understand why their host offered no rebuttal. The soul descended from three races looked to her husband, born of one. Even Edmond, who claimed a chair at Ganix's table, looked toward Francine's beloved and left the Jacobian unsettled and protective.

Of secrets kept—from Guardians and friends—none proved more veiled than one Tull shared with Keeper Victor Simon Shannon. When first they met, Tull *failed* to save the keeper's lone daughter. Seven spans since, and he still felt the grit beneath his nails from his efforts to dig her from her tomb afore she suffocated. No other instigator, minus the scent of baker's cocoa and endless pools, troubled him more.

In his time, he never observed a greater love between souls than what he observed between the Shannons in those eves afore she went missing. For that reason alone, he risked his permanent end. He convinced a grief-crippled father that a warring Minister called Enke'loi kept him from his end and then handed him Olley's saber. In a room without windows, far from Vic's bride's eye, he promised he would return–in success—if Vic ended him.

"Nelson!" Francine called out to him in a manner that brought relief. She carried an elegance too frail for her fierce build and a smile that hid the shame of whatever kept her husband agitated.

"Francine."

"*Oooo*, don't 'Francine' me." She laughed at her decent impersonation of him and opened her arms till he accepted her hug and proved that all was not proper when she spoke afore Vic. "How we've missed you!"

He oft wondered if, in that other land, the keeper lived and if he suffered punishment *there* for the success he enjoyed *here*. The smile on Vic's bride's face eased such wonders because her daughter lived again by Yah's grace and not Tull's deeds. Francine passed her direct stare onto her daughter but did not possess the same sparkling, amethyst-hued irises. Her warmth flowed through her touch, not her glance, as proven in the way she braced his shoulders and looked him over afore she hugged him a second time.

There she whispered her lone plea. "Would you see to Whispers?"

"I will."

She thanked him with a grin and looked with love upon her husband. Seldom did Tull enter the room when Vic failed to call out to him; either to greet him as family or heckle him with the tales of his feats. The Jacobian oft believed—*suspected*—that the amusing soul towed a faint memory of that previous land too. Given how he stared at Olley's scabbard, Vic offered no dissuasion toward Tull's suspicion.

TULL & EBBE

The keeper, who knotted with shame over a burdensome stammer, turned as silent as a plank once humiliated. Tull learned, too, that little needled that humiliation worse than his temper. The agitations of duties, the pressures of a provider, and the cruelty of unappreciative and berating souls brought out that side of Vic. Another moonrise might visit afore he spoke above a hush again.

Some might have observed how Francine never told the Jacobian where to find her daughter and how that Guardian never sought a direction. The soul who sought his end—fifteen lands ago—for the keeper's daughter learned well her habits and her secrets. In point of fact, he kept the family, their ways, and secrets nearer to him than those of his own kin. After so many lands, such memories of those he mourned never increased.

He exited the inn and the surrounding lot stepped back in a fluid ripple. In the same manner, they rolled back toward the Guardian's presence as if a tide called back to shore. Some, at least two per gathering, wanted to measure their toughness against that of a soul purposed to stare down terrible creatures. Others, still, found satisfaction from simple nearness.

Afore any spoke out or reached for him, he leapt upon an upright ash barrel and then again toward the stone basket where Francine kept potted flowers along a decorative window. A wilted petal fell, and he drove upward with the side of his boot tread against the face of the inn. His fingers took hold of a slab sill along the third-storey windows and he offered thanks that what supported a feathery soul provided him a place to pause without falling too.

While he climbed the inn's face like a ladder and delighted those who remained beneath—and a few who watched from on high—he recalled a tell he observed inside the inn during his brief visit. Amid Vic's shame and George's timid stillness, Olley's hands gripped the wooden spindles on the chair that he claimed. He heard the creak of wood as much as the grit of his boot soles against the stone ledge; proof that the Archibaldian restrained an urge to fight.

The brisk air outside the inn felt warmer than the mood inside, and Tull breathed in the aroma of anthracite kettles that lined the Carpenter Territory's roadways. A heckle from beneath vanished as the breeze redirected and burning coal surrendered to a scent of *fruit*. Peach blossoms. That fragrant air lured him away from every wronghearted distraction.

TULL & EBBE

In recognition of the fragrance, the easiest of smiles appeared on the Jacobian's face. Though she oft complained about her hair, she who rested above lavished her soil-black curls with blossom-infused shampoo. Tull admired her hair for the random strands of blonde that nestled amid the dominant black curls, courtesy of her paternal grandmother, but the scent was all hers. This scent proved her delicate way, letting pass the many walls she scaled in untold frustration.

A braided rope with a silken feel offered him a way above the third storey and onto the flat, recessed roof. Though his calves burned like the kettles and his heart outpaced the wind, he counted how he might surprise the first soul he pulled from harm. All ideas paled when he took the floppy toe of a boot sole against his brow and relied on the strength of the rope to keep him from falling to rejoin the crowd. Such a greeting characterized his pen pal well.

SIX

Through his unclouded eye, he found Novitiate Jules Baker Shannon sprawled on her tummy across the rooftop skylight in near-unflawed stillness; minus the anxious swing of her foot and worn, oversized boot. She looked to him like a ribbon, and he counted the ways she might twirl if he dangled her by the toe. In taunting's stead, he brushed her foot aside at the ankle afore her next thrash of his noggin and drew no response. Well-practiced was her inheritance of her father's silence in embarrassment—enough that she fled from her home to avoid every visitor.

"Worry not, Whispers! Your Guardian remains unmarred." He tugged his frame up and over the raised hem of the wall. When she withheld more than her nickname hinted, he proved unfettered. "I thank you for your assistance, though, J. J."

Beneath the past four moons, since last he sat with her, her limbs grew till she rested at a length greater than the inn's skylight frame but remained slight enough that she added no pressure on the glass that held her. Her foot regained the pace he had stopped with his brow and soothed a pair of sparrows who nested within the shared glow of false light. He looked to her with a smile, even plunged lower to catch her eye, but to no avail. Her cheek rested on her bent forearm, her attention fixed toward the corner of the receiving room where Tull last saw Vic seated.

As Francine told the tale, no soul in the territories ever stole a pebble of Jules's interest or awe from the heap she set upon her father. Her first words, her first steps, and her first plan each morn, revolved around him. Then Tull entered their lives. Francine helped Vic through the hurt—the same hurt she towed near one hundred sixty moons—and let their daughter's fondness for another take root. Once Vic accepted his daughter's interest, he too kept a tether on he who traveled from the furthest side of the territories and earned his right to rest alongside the opposite ledge of the skylight frame—though not alongside the keeper's daughter.

Tull stretched his back and admired the sky-fires above as much as Jules's devotion kept her focused downward. With the wind's song above them, he listened to how the sway of her leg added a tempo. She never insisted that Tull leave her alone.

TULL & EBBE

In the possibility's stead, and despite what commotion delivered her there, he felt peace-filled, and able to let the firstkind mind the watch.

No other worry rested on him. As he listened for her whisper, contentedness soothed him for, upon the glass, Jules's breast cast the rhythm of her heart. Since his third reset of time—where Enke'loi kept him from his end and frightened him from recklessness—he recognized and adored that pace even beneath the harmonic breezes and percussive swinging feet. Francine knew her daughter's heart well enough, too, to send after her the second soul in the territories whom she never resisted.

The slip of four cold fingertips across the forearm of he who was in his eighteenth reset of time and the single drum that Jules's palm made as she rested her hand upon *his* side of the skylight preceded the scent of peach blossoms that indicated a change in her nearness and a chance to remind him of past promises. "You said you would tell me why you call me J. J. this time."

Her huff skated across the glass and produced a film of fog. His nose twitched as he detected a note of cocoa on her breath. He preferred the stench of the mealy persimmon dross that her benefactor—and their advocate scion—Otto Meynell Chessy, bottled as wine to the scent of cocoa. As though she expected a rebuke, her palm crept against his arm and her fingers gripped tighter. Though she imposed no pain, she added her thumb for security.

A second time she leaned in. "Well, long spine?"

"This doesn't seem the proper eve for secret-telling."

When first they met, afore he plucked her from harm, he learned of the nickname that Francine Laurette Mokuk pinned upon her stammering child. To avoid attention—and teasing—the amethyst-eyed soul would whisper her every idea, belief, worry, and wonder into the ears of her mother and father. Her stammer improved some, though her parents heaped alms upon therapists who failed in their claims, and she outgrew her fear-filled expectations of teasing for the lingering fear of traumas that invited a Guardian's attentiveness. Still, around most souls, she proved strenuous in her silence.

The soul that she added to her safe list stretched his legs afore him and tucked his other forearm beneath his head with the sort of smugness that mingled well with a kept secret. With the hand of the arm she held, he took hold of a baggy loop near the waist of her trousers. "If Vic looks up and sees, I thank you in advance for any harm your account of our innocence spares me."

TULL & EBBE

She entangled his legs with one of hers and still managed to reach his ear. "Best to leave this land braver than you arrived."

Tull snarled in response to the breathy recital of his least favorite in Vic's endless supply of proverbs and challenges. He intended to share his disdain, which Jules remembered like his promise, and turned his head to face her. "Almighty!"

In the mingled light of the sky-fires and the skylights, he saw the greatest change in her appearance for the first time. Gone were her rich-black curls. Now, she bore waves a shade of purple that paled in comparison to her amethyst-hued irises.

"You held your breath so long in protest that your head unfurled and turned *purple*!"

"Not purple." She could not enunciate any better through clenched teeth. "*Pearl.*"

"As you say." He mimicked her enunciation and scratched at his throat whilst he stared. "Had they seen a pearl afore?"

She closed her eyes to his teasing.

Whilst he drew back from her, he kept her near with his hold on her empty belt loop and snuck his most recent writing into her pocket as the glow from the inn lit her features. "I approve of any color that flatters your eyes."

She poked his side but stayed as near as he kept her and opened her eyes. "You had best keep to foretelling storms, partner."

"Am I not?"

She shivered at the deep sound of his mimicking whisper but bit into her lip rather than reward him with a smirk of agreement. When blush spread across her creamy, cocoa-hued cheeks, she propped onto her elbow, braided her fingers, and jabbed him with combined fists. He provoked her to small talk afore she finished sulking. In surrender, she turned onto her back and rested beside him.

"The sky-fires have more pinks and greens as of late." He looked to see if she confirmed his observation and gauged the film of tears that washed her tremendous irises. "The lull will break. Then, all we'll see is snow. Not a speck of ash."

On the morn he rescued her, the glebe felt to him like he dipped his hands into the actual sky-fire. Abrasive rock and coarse sand cut into his knuckles and fingers, but he dug till he pulled her from a makeshift tomb that the foe the outfit sought prepared for her. Beneath eighty-six moons since, they rested in this way and spoke from moonrise to moonset. This late eve, she offered not a single upward glance to the sky-fires but, in gazing's stead, cast her awe upon him.

TULL & EBBE

"Ganix is disgusting." Her reaffirmed grip at his forearm exclaimed for her. "He—he's lower than a snoop."

He flicked his brow, aware of the value she put on privacy.

"He ought to have his soles cut and his tongue scalded as the judges would do to a thief."

Tull straightened his neck as Jules bent his ear.

"I—I—I find no wonder that he remains without another soul to invite near. He has the worst personality of any soul—even for a Shelbian."

"Imagine how you might behave . . . had you no kindnesses, no encouragement, no friendships, and no love."

"You argue *for* him?"

"I say his singleness forged his personality whilst you say his personality forged his singleness." He bumped her when he shrugged. "You would see him beaten like a crude meddler, but who would forgive whom?"

"He is crude."

"He is Shelbian."

"And your fellows sat there in silence."

"We take our rebukes—and our grievances—away from those we—"

She interrupted him with an angered breath and sat upright. Her favored Guardian watched as she maneuvered across the hem and decided how best to turn her toward wonders far more terrific than crude Barton Blinken Ganix. As she brooded, she crossed her arms and dug her nails into her sides beneath his watch. He let her stomp but relocated to the wall's ledge to provide her with a physical barrier from further pacing or trampling the watchful sparrows.

"Tell me anyway."

Her exhalation proved her inner debate and lowered her posture till she sat next to him with her back toward the fall. She hid behind a veil of pearl tresses and leaned toward him rather than hunt for his ear. "He asked if the color of my hair changed the tinge of my—"

Though she kept from repeating the Shelbian's true crudeness, Tull's abdomen tensed and his shoulders rose like a frayed shingle.

"He said I—I—I am worth an eve's alms for my eyes and my tight—" She dug into his forearm with the rage that she ought to have cast out at the top of her lungs. She wrangled one lanky limb over the ledge and straddled the wall that she might face him. "Is that all I—I—I am?"

When she started to tell her next complaint, he sighed like a gale and paced his words in a way that agitated her inability to shed her stammer. "This isn't why I crossed the territory with Asham's continual absurdities ringing in my ears."

His remark agitated, so she boasted on her first hero. "My dad defended me."

"Though you've shed your title of blamelessness."

"Ganix is bigger than—"

"Have I not taught you to stave off worse threats?"

Her solemnness provided answer at his hint of criticism.

"Ganix reminded all that he's a—"

"Guardians shouldn't get to bully us!" At last, her voice rose and moved the sparrows.

"*Partaker.*" In turn, he hushed. "We have sheltered you from Partakers."

"I—I—I am not naïve."

"Are you not? Be grateful that Partaker—crude and vile Ganix—is also a Guardian. He knows the laws and boundaries."

"My dad shouldn't have to serve souls who bully him in his—"

"Behold! Every soul in these territories who hears!
Behold! Your judges announce a new birth!"

Jules pursed her lips and turned from the Challis Signal House that broadcast through the lower territory and sat west of their location.

"This same eve, the seventh beneath the Moon of the Mother's Song, Bonnie Wallace Holroyd gave to her second husband, Zink Longfeather Holroyd, a son; named Zink Wallace Holroyd. He is beneath expectations, but peace-filled and blameless. Present at the birth were—"

"What does that mean? *Beneath expectations.*"

Tull did not hear who attended the birth. "Zink Wallace Holroyd is a runt."

"They are all runts."

TULL & EBBE

"STAND AND HONOR THIS NEW SOUL!"

Even from a rooftop, the pair obeyed. As two voices joined the uncounted souls who filled the roadway, all recited a verse spoken over every new soul born to the Second Creation.

"Our joy we share with you, blameless soul, and pledge never to turn from you in your need. May your struggles be ours. May our blessings be yours. We celebrate you on this, the eve of your birth, and three eves in full, Zink Wallace Holroyd."

"WE BID YOU A FRUITFUL AGE, CHILD."

In the tenderness of celebration, Jules reached sideways and held to Tull's wrist. When he looked on her, whose amethyst irises reflected the sky-fires, he found a glimmer of the pureness that once brimmed in her afore her rescue. In the spans since, her gaze provoked a soul to dizziness. Rather than letting her see him sway, he stood prouder and let her lean a shoulder against him as she observed those beneath who celebrated one more addition to their number.

"Those Partakers truly enjoy their *knowing*!"

"Truly."

"Not so sure that they un—und—that they *get* the effect of the act, though." Then the left side of her face stretched with an ornery sneer that hid the pureness of her eyes. "Otto says that's why more Shelbian novitiates are learning to be nursemaids than nurses."

"Tell me how Otto's crudeness differs from Ganix's."

Jules grumbled, and lunged as if to leap from the roof. Afore she departed from Tull's reach, he clasped her hand and spun her at the heels. Her limbs entangled, a drawback of those floppy soles, and those souls beneath heard her squeal of surprise as her hand slipped from the Guardian's. Whilst her end seemed certain, not a single strand of blanched hair fell afore he cinched at her belt and kept her from tumbling.

Her smugness took on the form of a grin that stretched beyond the breadth of Tull's hand. Whispers then let out a laugh from her belly that proved another of her father's proudest inherited traits. So loud was her sound that a mimicking chorus arose because her favored Guardian kept watch over her still. All laughed but him.

TULL & EBBE

Jules's expression faded when he whose orneriness was better-known to her dusted his hands and folded his arms across his chest. Her eyes screamed his name as the realization of his absent grip took hold, but her jaw remained too slack for rebuke. The soul who recorded all seven—if not *eight*—of Tull's expressions tried to reach for him but her splayed fingers missed every thread. Her failure, to be clear, was aided by his decision to kneel upon both knees amid her predicament.

Afore gravity tugged, she blurted in harshest disbelief, "Nelson!"

As her feet mimicked the pendulum of a clock, she chirped like a bird in the attic and thrashed her arms both as the clock turns and in the opposite arc. All the while, Tull remained still in a way that perturbed many souls. He never reached, never doubted, and never ceased the prayer that moved his lips but never touched her ears. With his whole heart, he trusted in those who kept her safer than a father's love or a Guardian's purpose.

"Nelson?" The tiniest voice crept from the keeper's still daughter.

His prayer ceased and his voice brimmed with gentle certainty. "Look upward."

Above Jules, an unblemished face of burnished bronze and eyes of pure light greeted her with a smile that bore a measure of Tull's playfulness. Smaller than Jules in stature, a Squire held her a head's height above the ledge. This fact offered peace. Yet, the stammerer's smile faltered as she observed her reflection upon the countenance of the firstkind creature who, she imagined, observed her previous smugness.

"Have I not told you that they listen evermore?" He arose and leaned onto the hem. "They enjoy big laughs and loud songs from small bodies."

He stared at various points as he visualized a path, then noted a prominent obstruction between his vantage point and the businesses across the avenue. With a sure hand, he reached out and plucked at one of her boots.

"I don't believe they mind big feet, either."

As though she had never noticed the size of her feet afore, Jules shook free from his pinch and tried to tuck away from further judgment. She then noticed the ribbon of fire that formed around her. Squires and Ministers did not have legs or feet; rather, their bodies were composed of ever-burning brass that took on the form, length, and breadth that they required from moment to moment. She tested the flame with a curious hand and felt tickled but not burned. As she giggled, the Squire mimicked her to the very note and invited her scowl.

TULL & EBBE

"Is she going to hold me till the morn?"

"A male Squire keeps you. You can tell by—"

"I—I—I don't—don't wish to hear!" She clenched her eyes and then peeked as both creatures laughed at her.

"Then let us leave talk of *knowing* and *nursing* to other tongues, gentle soul."

When she caught Tull rolling up his sleeves, she noticed in her peripherals that the forearms of the Squire took on similar effect. "*Nelson!*"

He waggled his index finger and required an additional moment's pause as he fastened the folded cuffs above his elbows. Then, with no word of intention, he leapt sideways off the hem and to the north, further from the pine plank door and the inn's receiving room. His leap reflected across the Squire and from the cooing and gasping beneath, he played to the crowd well. Both creatures moved faster than Jules's divided attention followed, and she twisted with enough delay that she missed the height of Tull's ascent but not the landing.

The Guardian renowned for his bow leapt further than intended and without the burden of solemnness he towed these uncounted moons. The calming presence of the Squire washed over him and upon those who watched beneath—and across she who stayed in the firstkind creature's hold. Even that brass face delighted over the antics and abilities of he who sought to amuse his kind. So rare was Tull's showiness that those who observed him seldom believed the truth in tales told of him. Now, the proof radiated like the Squire's train of fire.

Between Tull's landing atop the second-storey sill and the spiral-pivot around the copper downspout, he gained momentum through bursts of contact till he vanished unto the darkness. Jules gasped with a hint of fear, a burden of regard for her rescuer's well-being, and stoked the Squire's sympathy. They drifted three-fifths her length lower and the same fire that consumed fear lit Tull's perch. Illumination caught the Jacobian's warm smile as he rested on a wooden crossbeam that reinforced the load of a connecting walkway between Shannon's Inn and a storeroom that the family rented out for winter alms.

Jules did not need to call out to him, and he did not need to look toward her. With the sureness of a tether that kept two souls, one of Yah's gentlest creations carried the keeper's daughter on a guided path toward the Guardian. When he found her gaze within the brilliance of the Squire's light, as proof of his heart, he reached for her hand whilst her feet touched the beam that supported him.

TULL & EBBE

Tull steadied her as she sat next to him and kept her balanced when the sound of the Squire's flame made her duck in uncertainty. He gave her little time for stillness, though. She returned the favor of balance when he swung his right leg over her head, straddled the crossbeam, and faced her. His grin of appreciation made her arms tremble, but her knuckles turned pale as she gripped the pulp of the beam—and his wrist.

"I—I—I can't believe—why are—are you nodding?"

"You can believe." He admired her from the peak of her hair down to the wrinkle in her chin that appeared when she snarled. "You needed wonder. Now, I wonder, do you need *more*?"

"No!" She held his forearm with both hands and the beam with her thighs. "No."

He laughed and let her keep her hold. "Now you see."

When he leaned back and observed the sky-fire from their newfound height, she took hold of the fabric of his shirt and wadded a fist since his arms proved stronger than hers. "I—I—I fear I—I—I may heave."

He soothed her when he patted behind her knee and restored his balance as he lifted her chin. "Have I to ask you to look up again?"

When she followed his gaze, she saw—as he saw. The Squire who flung her rejoined a flock of eleven who watched over the secondkind; much like those souls who watched through the panes of the inn for a glimpse of their Guardians. These creatures of brass and fire and diminutive build delighted over them as though they were the treasures. In their sight, both souls felt adored.

This was the intention of the Creator. Neither the First nor the Second Creation were designed for struggle or lonesomeness. They sought such, refused to turn from temptation, and bore the shame of their choice. Those rare moments when joy flourished appeared like the brightest bloom of color that showered in the sky-fires.

"Look! See how they boast over the keeper's daughter!"

Jules heard the chatter from beneath and looked toward the Guardian who, by her measure, knew better than she about the truth. The radiance of his smile stoked her curiosity enough that she took more time than cordial to observe him. When the happenings around them appeared in her peripheral as twinkling light, she found the Squires departed. The breeze never reacted, and they disturbed nothing crafted by the secondkind.

TULL & EBBE

"When next a soul offends you, remember this eve. Remember Yah's First Creation delighted over you not because of me, but because *He* delights over you too."

His warming timbre made Jules look on him in a manner that dimmed the sky-fires and hinted at hopes kept unspoken. When he focused on her changing pupils, she bit at her lip and nodded in agreement.

"I thank you. And, I tell you, never again will Ganix speak to you without regard."

"You can't give me your—"

"My word is yours." He draped a pearl-hued ribbon of hair behind her ear lest she find an excuse to fidget and overlooked her blushed cheeks.

She peered down the length of her shoulder and chewed at the corner of her mouth. "Tell me now how you plan to get me down from here."

"Same way we reached the roof."

"I—I—I went out the third-storey window."

"You did?" He arced sideways atop the post and scratched at his jaw as his lips puckered toward the other side.

Jules recognized facial expression number four. "You don't have a way down."

"I have a way down. I am less certain that *you* have a way down."

The abruptness by which she inhaled mirrored his pace as he swept his leg over her again. Her stammer offered him the advantage, and he swept his left hand out from beneath her as he hopped from the beam. She offered a chirp and he traced her fingers to the second knuckle, then slipped his hand from beneath to overhand. When he dropped, she uncrossed her ankles and hollered.

As the heavier counterweight, he plucked her from her perch and slung her over his shoulder. The fall of a measure twice her height took as much time as she needed to clench her eyes shut. By the time she reopened them, she stood upon the balls of her feet. She held her breath, her foothold, and any complaint as she remained as near to her Guardian as he set her.

SEVEN

"Stand away."

At the sound of another's voice, Tull's instinct was to shield Jules. Then, he who stepped past the pair with the politeness of a Shelbian produced an uneasy twitch in the Guardian's sense of rightness—expression number six. The Jacobian kept Jules between him and the front of the implement and tool supply store, but never took his eye off the hatted soul. From the stitched brim to the smooth sole of his shoes, the passerby did not mingle with the locals in the slightest way.

"Perturbed but curious."

His brow furrowed as he felt a tug against his suspenders. The right hip pocket twisted, and he snagged Jules's wrist afore she found any sharp edges. "What?"

"That's the face you make when you're perturbed but curious. Do you not like tall hats?"

"As you say, dove."

She teetered to find his ear and lay against him lest he walk away. "There's no such thing as a *purple* dove. Or a clever *Jacobian*."

The return of humor invited a crooked smirk, which she let him see afore she nudged him to receive his attention. So few souls ever experienced her wit or admired her for the steady flow of cleverness she exhibited. He might have complimented her more oft, but the instinct or the regard of how his attentiveness mattered seldom registered with him in the moment.

"Do you see unusual birds oft?"

"I travel with a falcon who believes he's a peacock."

"What?"

"The Son of the Falcon," Tull spoke the name his ever-watchful Warring Minister used for Olley Hendrie Falk. "Archibaldians peacock worse than Shelbians."

A memory excited her and confused her tongue with laughter. "Remember w—w—when you said Asham would lick his own rear if he h—h—had to go two eves with*oooout* attention?"

"I remember citing Harlan's observation of him to you." He sensed the inward scolding Jules inflicted for her tangled tongue, but could not shake the passerby's presence and took a step in the same direction. One backward step allowed him to pinch her pinky between his index and middle fingers afore he led her along the same path.

"See another peacock?"

She withheld her grin, but squeezed his longest fingers and entrusted him to guide her. With each step, she noticed how those souls who hovered near the entryway of the inn and those across the avenue rolled away like the fog from heat. The more she watched, the more the realization amused her. A soul who moved with the current counted her amusement as an insult and hurled a snowball that struck the front of the inn but missed her in full.

Tull then pulled Jules ahead with a sweep of his arm, as if to serve as her shield. His action set them adrift across a slender patch of thick ice that accumulated along a trapped space between a string of plate glass windows and anthracite kettles. her laughter rose to the same heights they slid, and she let pass the hurt and discomfiture that aggressive souls sought to make her tow. As their makeshift skate reached an end, Tull swept her onto steadying terrane and held open the inn's pine plank door with his heel.

Jules's laughter drew an easy accompaniment from her companion and carried into the inn as they entered. Francine recognized the familiar sound and cast an approving glance their way. Tull withheld a response to her for he found the hatted soul, who spoke to Edmond, then lost any air of joy when he saw Barton Blinken Ganix, who no longer bled from the nose but kept his soiled hankie on the table so others might see *his* offense. If he who spoke to Edmond shared that offense, Ganix would heap trouble upon the Shannons.

"Your concern for the Larsonites is of no urgency to the bench. Let those butchers enjoy the independence they've sought since they cleaved themselves from the Creighton Territory as they cleave their sons!"

Only a Shelbian would esteem the Creighton Territory over the Larson Territory when he spoke with a Larsonite. The barb made Asham the Creightonian stir and fidget; proof that even he feared how Edmond the Larsonite might react.

"Is my directive to you unclear, Guardian Elragadó?"

TULL & EBBE

"No doubt our honorable judges will remember their choice when the count of taken souls rises by the next moon."

Tull heard enough of the newcomer's words that he let go of Jules's hand and stepped nearer to his headship's right hand. "Who's the Shelbian?"

"Judge Conliffe's current herald."

Though the Guardian from the Carpenter Territory reduced the visitor to a lower title, they stood amid the Advocate Scion and future judge of the Shelby Territory. Till he claimed the bench, Gary Lee Madár fulfilled the duties that his successor heaped upon him. Whether that involved standing afore Guardians or washing linens, Tull imagined the scion never let rest his contemptuous snarl.

"See to your appetite." Harlan looked over his fellow's shoulder and saw how Jules lingered. "I suspect we're about to journey without slumber."

Jules stared at her mother, as if betrayed by judges whom she still believed caring and greathearted. Francine shrugged from helplessness and then whispered to her husband. The buzz of voices multiplied, for all with sense followed the troubles in the Larson Territory. Beneath the past two moons, nine souls vanished, and none learned the cause or their whereabouts. The Guardians could not enter without an edict, but believed—afore now—that a consensus amid their judges neared.

Now, the scion for the judge from the Shelby Territory relished the decision to rescind any offer of help. No formal decree carried through the territories. More, the newcomer seemed to enjoy telling the Guardian *from* the Larson Territory, as if a personal slight. Not Edmond, but Vic reacted the loudest when he struck the table with a flattened palm.

Madár watched as the keeper hid his expression behind fidgeting hands but dismissed him to deliver the final portion of his message. "No Guardian is to set foot in the Larson Territory. You and your outfit of seven are to appear aboard the steam tram car listed on this card."

By the law, those in the territories who held no authority could not know the whereabouts of their lawmakers. Edmond accepted the card but made the holder sweat as the uninformed knew the value of the information he possessed. Against their purpose, every bright Guardian relaxed their postures and dulled their stares. Madár's worry formed on his brow as a lone bead of sweat fell and a gasp arose when the headship withheld the card with an obvious smirk.

"Guardian, I would advise that you not let your judges *wait*."

"Nothing instructs finer than a strong example, scion!"

Harlan held open the door of the inn and stomped the heel of his boot against the lacquered floorboards. Jules lost the chance to let the scion see her disapproval of him because Tull and the other Guardians took threatening stances that encouraged Madár's swift exit. By their posture, each stood ready to remove him from the inn and the Shelbian proved wise when he proved wise to Harlan's advice. Even so, the outfit headship kept his head down whilst he wrote in his journal and refused a show of courtesy or alms toward Madár.

> 1,987. Zink Wallace Holroyd, b. 12.07.107; mother Bonnie Wallace Holroyd and father Zink Longfeather Holroyd. Shelby Territory.

Since the Last War, and an era afore, those souls north of the Loy proved dismissive of those born to the south. As Guardian from the slighted Larson Territory, Edmond suffered the disregard more than most. Judge Dale Marius Conliffe, of the nearest territory to their present location, seldom relinquished his contempt for the *lower* territories—a true Shelbian. Amid the Guardians, none would side with Ganix over Edmond—nor would Edmond ask as much of them.

"Tull's abettor is imaginative. She might learn what went on in the talks with the Larsonites—"

"So might Nita." Asham received sharp looks from both Olley—who proved how he despised Shelbian women on the same morn he lumped raillery upon the Creightonian—and Ganix—who despised his own scion.

"Sister Lois might request that we set our attention toward her supply travels along the southern hem"—Tull hinted, in suggestion of another way around Madár's command—"if we provide her the idea."

Edmond swatted air with his journal in rejection. "She remains cross with me."

"Truly!" Asham laughed above all others. "She favors Tull still."

About the time Tull avoided Francine's stare and protected his sides from Jules's elbow, Olley planted a fist beneath Asham's hind rib. This drew another thump of Harlan's heel against the floorboards and a stern look.

"My apologies, Harlan."

"Apologies, Harlan." Asham rubbed his back and sought his breath.

"Boys, after all this time? How will you ever lead? How will you expect those we keep safe to believe they are safe? We have our orders. As distasteful as we find them, they come from those we serve. Do you believe your plans so unflawed that only you can imagine ways that this soul who leads us has not counted?"

Olley, Asham, and Tull said no more against Harlan.

"Boy, I—I'll tell you what I—I m—miss!" Vic Shannon's gruffness matched Harlan's, but he brimmed with an enthusiastic laugh as he wiped his mouth and smoothed his bushy beard. "I—I miss m—me them little corn dodgers that they sell out front of Monkshood Station. I—I had m—me a bag of them, oh, couldn't've been but a few scant spans back, when my papa loaded us up for our first ride on the No. 8 steam tram. The secret was how they fried them in honey, see? Though, my momma swooned like a dove over how they rolled them twice in confectioner's sugar and, and, uh . . ."

"Nutmeg." Francine completed his tale, and her husband waggled his finger in agreement.

Edmond shared Tull's compassion for the keepers and said nothing about the way Francine protected her husband from words that proved too difficult for his stammer. "I imagine we see to our purpose, then I send Nelson back here with a sack in time to celebrate your seventh winter of gladness."

The Larsonite's glimmer met Vic's eased breath just as the keeper's wink produced a soft sigh from his daughter.

Harlan teased, "Let Francine duplicate the recipe afore you eat the lot."

"With the size of that boy's stomach?" Vic's laughter flowed at a cost to Tull. "No. You best send him back with *two* bags!"

The Guardian from the host territory heckled the Jacobian but set a mighty hand upon his shoulder afore he offered alms that covered that coveted second bag. "I s'pose we'll be having corn dodgers then."

"Hold on, now, you know we—"

"*Never s'pose*. I do remember, my fine host. I let the cold dull me."

This time, Tull spared Harlan. "When I return, I'll bring two sacks."

Harlan's heavy boots offered a slight drag along the right ball as he leaned toward Edmond and imitated how Jules spoke with Tull.

"Harlan keeps a treat that might hold you over till then."

Most of the five earliest arrivals grinned—not Ganix—but not Asham or Tull. Harlan was gifted with a beautiful speaking voice. Even so, he withheld announcing self and ideas out of respect for Edmond's authority. In this, he taught the Guardians humility and obedience better than his occasional scolding let on.

"Cinch your gear, boys."

Vic leapt to his feet, too, oft the worst at keeping secrets and surprises, and patted Tull on the back with a hint more might than expected. His laughter roared, but he draped a gentle arm across his daughter's shoulders. She leaned her cheek upon him and set her arm around his soft midsection while Olley and George trapped them a few paces between Harlan. Francine followed Asham, and then Edmond—because none of the Guardians settled in their rooms till the entire outfit arrived, nor needed to gather a single possession not already found within their reach.

Tull lingered just enough that Ganix realized they were the last two Guardians who remained. Like Harlan, Tull's speaking voice soothed many. With practice, he also managed to withhold words. The Guardians of neighboring territories exchanged cold glances; though Ganix wore his with greater ease. Tull bore too much heart and too much regard for others. Ganix knew this, but also understood that he—not Tull—suffered the disadvantage of reach and strength.

"Where is that Nelson at?" Vic's gruff voice trundled between rooms. "I—I i—i—im—magine he ran to see about them corn dodgers!"

Tull looked toward that sound-funneling doorway and found Edmond. He found no chastisement and no encouragement. All towed the weight of the offense against Jules and Victor. Ganix kept still, but sensed that same presence behind him and followed Tull with his beady eyes as he, too, stepped away from the Shelbian.

"Don't forget a side of some of that apple butter!"

As Tull claimed afore, the Guardians took their punishments and grievances away from the sight and hearing of those they kept safe. Like the Scriptures taught, retribution against Ganix was not his reward. His heart toward the offended remained well-announced, however. Those who whispered upon his departure watched Ganix, who sipped from his burnished mug; but, beneath the table, his hand returned a hiltless blade to the sheath on his hip.

He who offended all he passed—and oft neglected his purpose—paid the onlookers no mind. Ganix fed off plates that others paid for and stifled his thirst with drink that the keepers gave to the outfit at no charge. Though the Shannons refused to charge the outfit for their stay, the Guardians oft repaid them in other ways. Only Ganix took more than he earned and more than his share—a true Partaker.

TULL & EBBE

Every sin that led to the soul's end proved a part of Ganix's purpose. He grew fatter in winter than other souls; a glutton. He proved lustful in the way he spoke toward Jules and prideful the moment he let her return to the inn and did not apologize to her. His indifference toward others—even the way he sat whilst the outfit saw to their hosts—spoke to his slothfulness. And, as he stole the alms that Harlan intended for Mabel Eleanor Parker in gratitude, he proved his greed—all without leaving his seat.

What ought to have counted as the *eighth* great offense, and as common to Ganix as breathing and whining, was his flatulence. The man produced a rancorous fog that wafted like the mist off the nearest millpond on a brisk morn. No Guardian crowded him or claimed a foothold behind him. With a thunderous racket, he announced a replenishing fog and fanned the proof toward a table of patrons who sat too close for his liking.

EIGHT

Now, in that back room, where a half-moon-shaped walkway led to the inn's stable, the Shannon family mingled amid the six Guardians and stalled horses that they divided in pairs. George and Asham, then Jules, Olley and Edmond, then Francine, and then Harlan and Tull, who found his place near Victor at last, skirted Harlan's surprise on the belly of the stone floor. Though Jules showed passing interest in Asham's wounds, and Olley a lingering interest in Jules's backside, she brushed Blizzard's mane as though her own but without ignoring the reveal. Victor offered his bride a wink and she grinned as Edmond spoke in her ear at a pitch that sounded like a distant hum.

"We found this beast," Harlan shared as he approached a shrouded heap, "grazing near the pecan groves south of Wulfric."

"Traveled up near the mountain-lands, did you?"

"Truly, and with utmost regard for our trespass."

The combination of Harlan and Victor's laughter warmed every soul and distracted a pearl-haired dove from the horse that ate an apple from her palm—as if to mock his owner. This was the magick that Vic's joyousness held over his bride and their fruit: that his mere rejoicing enticed their attention above any other distraction. Three of the young Guardians found solace in that bond and looked upon Vic with reverence. Their regard invited a calmness that loomed as Harlan stooped toward the still-disguised, pecan-eating beast and George helped with the reveal that made the horses snort and whinny.

"Almighty! A Wilkołak, I see!"

Asham denounced the creature's legend with an aloof snort of his own and to the surprise of none of the other souls that stood with him. A creature that tormented the Shelby and Creighton territories afore the Last War and up till the Era of the Reformers now was as rare as the talker's chance of spouting profound words.

He then nudged the sole of the beast with his boot. "Stout!"

"As you say, Asham."

TULL & EBBE

The romanticism of poets and the imaginations of artists paled at the sight of a true Wilkołak. A beast that was neither flesh like the secondkind nor a shape-changer found in Shelbian lore measured, at rest, two-thirds the size of the horse who flirted with Jules. Had the spine straightened, he would have stood higher than three-fourths of the Guardians. His coat of brown and white mingled hairs drew George's hand, and did not provoke his strong sense of superstition, for he loved all creatures of the field.

"He keeps no pulse still."

"That's a relief!"

"On this we agree."

The beast donned jagged teeth and claws as sharp as any blade in the Westonian's collection. They were hunters who tracked whatever soul they desired till they overpowered them. Even so, George petted his shoulder as though a common dog. In their time, the creatures roamed in packs and nested along the forests. To find one apart from the pack went against the tales each soul learned.

"I—I heard they kept nests in the forest, where they blended in with the brush."

"That was afore Zeck and Buster drove them past the lodes to the north."

"You believe there's more of them up there?"

"Worry not"—Harlan patted Vic's back—"we noticed signs of no others."

"Nor any report since afore this lot were called scions."

"By our count of the teeth, this is an ancient of their line. He survived the Last War and the Accession, but not an encounter with the Fallen First."

"The Fallen First ended him?"

"Left him wounded and then abandoned." He glanced toward their host's daughter's nearness and then their hostess. "When I said he fed in the pecan groves, I omitted that he devoured his own hand from the briars."

"Then you showed him mercy."

"Not to us! All but Ganix worked to tow him from the field, and your farrier lent a hand when we arrived."

Edmond's claim made Francine look around the stable for their wayward hand.

"Nelson and I might have helped," Asham nagged, "had Olley a better character."

"Or, had you a better mind toward your purpose," Olley challenged with a half-step toward his nuisance.

"He is a beast." Tull soothed rivals and redirected attention onto Harlan's trophy.

TULL & EBBE

"He smells like Hector!" Asham choked, and covered mouth and nose.

The most well-spoken amid the Guardians proved with a riotous laugh why he towed the nickname "Howlin'" Harlan. The echo stung every ear and invited a delight-filled smile that spread his beard and let his teeth see the light once more. He fought mean and dirty in the service of the Carpenter Territory and the secondkind for one-half of his fifty-four spans. Still, he delighted in a clever remark when the occasion called; and Hector Geirolf Picadura did bear a peculiar odor.

Jules wasted no time on laughter nor apology to Asham, whom she nudged aside to test her nose against the scent. She twitched her nose and traced a line where the musculature of the hip changed due to favoring and felt the aggressive wear pattern on the heel that came from constant, but recent, stumbling and abrasions across toes with broken claws. The creature's hind leg also revealed a rare marking that singed a thick coat and blackened the tissue beneath. While her desire to speak proved obvious to each soul, she shook her head and swallowed as she pursed her lips.

"What do you see, Whispers? And, speak up!" Vic pushed his daughter to overcome her impediment as he had given up on his own progress long afore.

"A handprint. Two fingers and a thumb." She tried to reproduce the pattern by splaying her own hand but could not mimic the shape. "He had trouble walking and picking up this foot. That must have felt cruel. I—I—I i—im—imagine that he roamed as he wanted afore."

The elder Guardians admired her wit as much as her heart toward all creatures whilst George knelt adjacent to her and measured the breadth of the befallen hand that tangled with the beast.

"See this, Jules." Harlan invited her attention as he reached for the left eyelid and exposed a murky-yellow iris. "His attacker blinded him with mire."

Every Guardian—even Ganix—could testify to the sting of mire. While the secondkind learned how to flush the toxic balm of the Fallen First, a creature that could not reason as they reasoned bore little hope of salvaging an eye once doused.

"And, see too"—he dragged his fingertip across the blistered edge of the left hand of scalded black claws—"how he fought back. As you say, he lost his ability to roam and administer protection but kept his instinct to war."

"Now he sits ready for the next bonfire—or the supper plate!"

Jules scowled at Asham's disregard. "I—I—I wouldn't eat him."

TULL & EBBE

"*Oooo*, you wouldn't, you say?" Vic tickled her anger-red ear with his coarse finger. "Not even with your momma's sweet potato gravy on top?"

Jules covered her mouth, but her consideration seeped over her digits.

Edmond stepped out and crouched nearer to Harlan than Jules or the beast. "I'd like to see prim Madár's face if he sees you hauling this brute up to the station."

"You working against the judge's orders, my benefactor?"

Tull dragged Asham backward afore Olley swung and caused the Archibaldian to circle wide as he shook off the impulse.

"Harlan would get arrested for traveling out of the territory without the proper vouchers."

"He'll be riding with those souls who issue the vouchers."

Olley's stubble teased Tull's ear. "Oft proves simpler to let me hit him."

Asham squeezed Tull's shoulder. "Most oft, his jolts amuse me."

Tull elbowed both pests away and yielded to Harlan again.

"A soul imagines you might charge four"—Harlan looked toward Edmond, who splayed a full hand—"nay, *five* copper alms per every head with eyes that wish to marvel over this creature."

"Oooo, maybe even six, if the mood sets in and the arranger makes him look daunting."

"I've spoken to those who helped me tow him over the foothills. George, Olley, and Edmond agree. We give this beast to you, Victor, and you, Francine, as we've noticed the harshness of"—he measured his words and dared not mention the financial strain they towed—"winter. In keeping with our own customs, Nelson and Asham, what say you?"

"This winter has proven unkind." Asham felt Olley's arm around his throat.

"He meant our parting gift."

The Creightonian nodded in breathless agreement.

"Nelson?"

"I share Edmond's view and recognize my bias against heralds." He then decided in his heart without the Helper's guidance and stomped his heels against the stone floor. "My boots still hold, my coat's warm, and I have the alms to see the thaw."

"Then all is well!" Harlan declared a victory as the two late arrivals agreed with him. "Victor. I trust you still have that agreement with the arranger who crafted my coat?"

TULL & EBBE

Choked with emotion and the much-needed kindness, the keeper proved who Jules took after when he nodded and swallowed his words.

Francine reached and took Harlan's hand in hers. "We thank you, Harlan. We thank you all."

"A Guardian seldom gets to enjoy looking after his own territory."

Though Vic and his bride would never speak of their struggle, the winter and the competition battered them atop the alms they spent on Jules. The price on the head of the Wilkołak towed uncounted value—for few souls observed an authentic Wilkołak that fell by the hand of a Guardian, with Harlan's reputable word, and not a clever charlatan who roamed the settlements in search of simpletons. That the Guardians would donate what belonged to them spoke of a side that the judges, or other naysayers, seldom recognized.

"There are better uses of alms than the amusement of drunkards," Ganix condemned from the doorway. Worse than his disapproval was the foggy stench that crept into the room and covered the beast's scent.

Whether the stench or the gesture of the others produced a tear in Vic's eye, he found cause to turn from the lot and push open the entry door that led to a less-populated path to the rail station. Tull captured Jules's eye with a wink as she wrapped her pearl-hued hair around her nose and mouth like a scarf and breathed the fragrance she preferred. Even mild George, who offended none, used the beast's covering like a canopy and sent Ganix's foul odor back toward him as he shielded the defenseless creature. Jules laughed and Vic wrapped an arm around her at the same time that Edmond smoothed the brim of his hat and smirked at her welcome sound after the way the eve started.

"Edmond, I simply must speak to you."

"There'll be time for talk as we travel."

The color flared in Ganix's eyes, as though offended by the dismissal.

"Claim your mounts, boys."

With that command, every Guardian snapped with obedience and marked the end of their time of mending—three moonrises indoors, except for Tull and Asham—amid the Shannon family. Ganix departed first and without farewell but kept Jules from further insult, and Vic from added cause to swing on him a second time. Each stomach missed the comfort of a fine meal, but none complained. The family gathered at the doorway and the Guardians formed a line of departure.

"Soon, I'll see you," Olley promised Francine.

"Be well." She patted his broad shoulder and moved him along.

"I thank you for your kindness," George addressed Vic, but both offered a hearty handshake that canceled out the other's measure.

"Remember to tell how I used my *right* hand to strike down the beast." Harlan leaned in. "My *bare* right hand."

"I—I will do that just for you, H—Harlan."

The laughter between two amicable storytellers drowned out the words that Edmond and Francine shared. Still, Vic noticed Asham and broomed him along afore he hugged Jules too well.

"Hug on a warm flask."

Jules proved contrary and did not reach for Tull lest she bear the teasing of her ornery father. She mimicked the way Vic dealt with Asham because none better than Tull would understand her heart. Even so, as she swept her arm along his back, she let her fingers brush him with the same tenderness that she showed the Wilkołak. Her eyes gleamed and made him woozy, but Vic saw that too.

"We'll have to set out some lemons and mint now that the Shelbians are leaving."

Tull hugged the soul who, in another land, meant as much to him as a father might. "When next I come through, I'll see that I stay longer."

"See that you take care this time. We'll be here a long while after."

"As you say."

"And stop all that growing! Makes m—me feel like I—I'm shriveling."

Francine's ageless features contorted as she snickered at her husband and fanned him away like Ganix's fog. She then swatted Tull's arm. "I gave you your hug this eve."

"I—I predict a shortage of flasks across the territories!"

As proof of her own humor, and her regard, she gave her daughter's favored Guardian another hug, with a kiss to his neck. She held longer than the others received but never spoke aloud of her gratitude for his seeing to Jules.

"Say! W—Why don't you hug me that way no more?"

Spirits changed for the better during the all-too-brief visit. Afore Tull spoke of his regard, Harlan patted his shoulder with a mighty reach and the Jacobian led Blizzard away in silence.

TULL & EBBE

"Soon we'll see you, Francine."

"Look after these brave souls, Harlan."

"As you say." He exited with a smile, then circled his mount and spoke in a hushed tone for Tull's ear and no other. "Jules fares well?"

"Would you?"

"She spoke of Ganix's insult?"

"But not why none of her Guardians defended her."

"This eve, she observed her father stand up amid a room that brimmed with Guardians and other louts to defend her. As moons are born, I tell you, she will come to regard him with the affection we've heard she heaped upon him in her blamelessness. They will stay hemmed close evermore. What happens to Ganix—or what does not happen—is Edmond's decision and no other's. I believe you hear me."

"I hear every word."

"And those between?"

"As you say."

Harlan smirked at the dour Jacobian. "I'll lead them out, Edmond."

They joined with the rest of the outfit but caught Edmond rolling up his sleeves.

Asham chimed in, oft useful at changing a subject. "Are we to bring our scion and abettor, my benefactor?"

"Gera, did you hear me say to any of you, 'Gather your scion and abettor' while we were indoors?"

"No, benefactor."

"Did you hear me give the order while we've stood out of doors?"

"No, benefactor."

"Was there a decree from the judges that gave away my authority to some herald whose tall hat and proper boots cost more than your instruction?"

"No, benefactor." He batted long lashes and stared as blameless as a doe. "I'll see if Harlan wants my hand in keeping the watch."

"No." Edmond drew an irritated breath. "Bring up the rear with me."

Asham turned squeamish. "Ganix brings up the rear evermore."

Tull and Olley shared an amused glance for his plight but dared not let their awareness—or expressions—register.

"As you say, benefactor."

"Tull, you be sure the rest keep an extra step ahead of us."

TULL & EBBE

The Jacobian offered a succinct nod of obedience as his eyes sparkled with realization. As he told Jules, the Guardians received their strictest punishments away from the eyes of those they kept safe. Seldom with the swiftness of this eve's example. There, on an isolated walkway along an ice-filled gulley, Ganix and Asham received a harsh beating from the outfit's headship for their waning integrity.

Now in his seventh winter as a Guardian, plus three spent as a scion, and he had never faced a beating from Edmond, or Mick, or Cam—only Nance. Still, he lived near others who needed discipline so oft that he learned the sounds of punishment. Asham proved as slow to accept his purpose as Tull proved toward understanding the hearts of those souls around him. He bore no pity and kept the outfit in an advancing line.

As for Ganix, long afore he insulted Jules, his hebetude contributed to the slump of morale. Now the sound of his pained shrieks from beneath a drastic heel made Harlan lead the others onward with a hastened gait. Neither Tull, nor Olley, nor George, nor Harlan looked back. No words arose between them, but all observed the shortness of Edmond's temper wither beneath each passing moon.

Tull learned, in his ten spans with the outfit, that Edmond Anson Elragadó never lived as a soul who sought authority. After the pageantry that he lived beneath whilst Cameron Lou Fenner enjoyed a farewell that lasted two spans, a low-key existence suited the outfit's present headship. When Mick Curtis Whigham rose as Cam's replacement, however bristled and arrogant some gauged him, Edmond believed the burden eluded him.

Tull learned, too, how Ganix craved Edmond's title. His deviance against custom and refusal to submit to the judges cost him. So, he connived, undermined, and humiliated Edmond, and refused retirement to spite them all—even his scion. He terrorized and offended as many souls as possible to make the judges regret their rule against his advancement. This mockery—like Asham's title by lottery—offended the eunuch whom judges entrusted with souls to be turned into upright Guardians, lest he took them from the land.

A Tailored Heel

An Interim

Still the 7th Eve beneath the Moon of the Mother's Song
The 107th Winter Season of the Accession
In the Care of the Helper, who keeps souls from fruitless wandering.

786 Halloway Courts
Grand Hall Station.
Within sight of Challis Signal House.

Edmond's discipline of Asham and Ganix—whilst cruel—satisfied him most when he saw the cold glimmer of disapproval in the eye of Advocate Scion Gary Lee Madár. The two souls who would have spoken up about the delay that Harlan's gift of a Wilkołak caused could not yet use their jaws. So, the outfit headship let their welts draw the full extent of Madár's judgment for holding the departure of the steam tram. As an added slight, he let the steadiness of his smirk bruise the scion's notion of authority and counted as the last soul to board.

Of the seven judges who ruled the territories, a standard routine followed. From a well-defended steam tram, six judges traveled and heard a variety of grievances from the secondkind. The seventh judge, whose identity changed with every moonrise, rested. Of the six who filled the bench, two sets of three presided. This, too, changed from session to session. Three sat at the front of the eight-car steam tram and three at the back—separated so no foe could rail against the court at once.

That the judges expected such rebellion spoke to their wisdom over the way they ruled. They further demonstrated their wit when they assigned the Guardians to abide in the same steam tram car that carried souls they defended, regulated, and even wronged. They too would find their numbers divided soon. Because of their authority, all seven Guardians could neither surround nor outnumber the judges in an enclosed setting—by law of the judges.

Tull made the best use of his time and sought slumber beneath the cradle-like sway of the steam tram. Olley sat across from him and propped the heel of his boot along his friend's thigh lest he spill from the tramcar bench. While loyal toward a friend, the Archibaldian also sought a chance to rile any soul who offended him in character, habit, or fashion. He faced the front and withdrew a crisp, brilliant-green apple that he carved with a blade that reflected both fruit and wielder.

George, who mistrusted this form of travel, blinked less than Olley and dared not let down his guard like Tull. Till he reunited with his horse and smelled the terrane, he would remain uptight. For this, Olley cast a glimmer of light from his blade into George's eyes. The east-facing Westonian accepted the offering of half an apple and broke that half with Asham. The fresh-whipped Creightonian accepted in silence but groaned at the first bite.

Olley proved his steady hand to their audience when he set half of his portion of the apple upon the arm that folded across Tull's chest. The Jacobian kept unstirred and the fragrant apple wedge mimicked the sway of travel with a more humorous wobble that made little faces giggle and whisper. Some passengers who had no grievance against nor fear toward them whispered and snickered too. A few more watched in wait for Tull's reprisal.

From behind Olley, Harlan made the wait easier when he tossed gleaming fruit to blameless travelers till each member of the outfit had one less treat in their allotments. He then sacrificed one more of his own. None offered greater alms than their looks of gratitude, and Harlan accepted each with a belly laugh. The joy faded as the advocate scion with unkind eyes and a set jaw returned through the eastern access. In response, most hid Harlan's gifts from Madár's sight.

The advocate scion then cast a scornful look upon the four Guardians made to wait apart from their judges. After his eyes counted them twice, he latched the divider that kept back any inferior creature who gleaned a look unto the traveling chamber of supreme souls. He shared that same sour expression with the elder trio whom he fetched. On the rest of the passengers, he would not look.

Harlan took a special interest in such effortless smugness and tugged at the frayed lapels of his bear hide coat. Madár's show of partiality hinted at the sort of judge he would become in his time. Given the short span of Shelbian advocates, a time they traveled toward as fast as they traveled now. Letting pass the future, the Carpenterian wasted none of his time pretending to hold undue regard for him.

As Madár turned his back on the passengers and corralled the three elder Guardians, a clean-sliced apple wedge struck his shoulder. A hush of breath and voices followed. The scion looked as tart as the fruit that claimed his attention as he faced those subordinate to him. He could not name who struck him, nor did he notice how Tull nestled toward the chill of the tram's outer glass shell. With a stare of equal temperature, he made a blameless soul who expressed bravery by touching the Jacobian's shoulder duck behind her adjoining bench in fright.

"Scion"—Edmond expressed with legitimate authority and spoke Madár's own words back to him—"'I would advise that you not let our judges wait.'"

Madár obeyed with a scowl, and Harlan offered the lot behind them a wink afore Olley led a chorus of laughter. Even George laughed aloud. Though Edmond offered a solemn response in exit and did not diminish Madár's stature, Harlan retrieved the apple wedge, which he then flung hard enough, and with enough accuracy, to dishevel Olley's immaculate hair. Not a soul for wastefulness—despite the privilege of his upbringing—the Archibaldian elicited a groan as he found the wedge, brushed the flesh clean, and tried his hand against Tull's stillness a second time.

None of the elders corrected him, for they fussed over their appearance—in attire and presence—afore the judges. Edmond offered a clean linen kerchief to the Shelbian he punished and spotted the fright in Ganix's eyes toward him. For this, and a regret he towed on the hip of his temper, he let *his* elder in spans lead the way and had never felt so grateful that bloatedness and irritation did not come over the Shelbian. As if they shared a similar gladness, Harlan reached and patted Edmond's shoulder.

"The lights will remain low till you're all settled afore the judges, lest you offend them in your improperness. You're each to remain silent in their presence till such a time as they speak to you by your"—Madár's familiar instruction stalled as Ganix entered amid his dialog—"purpose and name—or you receive dismissal from this appearance."

Edmond tested the rules of the chamber when he entered and did not remove the hat from his crown. Better he let the authority of the territory believe him uncouth than let them judge him for an unkempt wig. The brim almost scraped the bullish brow line that kept Madár's spectacles in place and the scion pressed backward against the entryway rather than touch the eunuch or retreat in full. His stern jaw faltered, too, when a sharp breath from Harlan teased the back of Edmond's neck.

"Afore I step in, I wanted to urge caution, Scion. You risk losing a button from your jacket"—he raised a coarse mitt to pat the shoulder of the uptight soul—"lest you relax your posture."

The bear-like Carpenterian heaped no other barbs and entered with a wobbling half-step that spoke to the condition of his hinges and not the sway of travel. He and Edmond lacked the time needed to accept and receive last words afore the lights on the court arose first on the bench and then the lower-seated Guardians. The headship held his hopes out for an appearance afore Judges Bliss—a faithful supporter of the outfit—or Katch; the latter from his own Larson Territory, who might compromise in Edmond's favor. In their stead, he faced a disinterested collection of long-standing and embittered rivals—of the Guardians and each other. He noted that Harlan's knee bounced out of time with the sway, and suspected his old friend towed the same sense of an ill outcome as he.

"The court recognizes the long-serving Guardians from the territories of Larson, Carpenter, and Shelby."

Scion Madár balanced a tone of menace toward the Guardians and adoration toward the judges. "Where are your alms, Guardian?"

Summonsed to appear afore the court and taxed for his obedience. Edmond counted this a heel to the neck. Harlan drew attention when he sank a hand into a trench-deep pocket and withdrew a stained sachet that once held the first alms he received as Guardian. He jostled the contents to determine their worth and, without a formal count, tossed the sum to he who salivated over the judges' authority.

Edmond swore the chamber tilted when the scion tried to dodge Harlan's alms pouch. Ganix snorted and stared at Madár with the slowest, coldest gaze the Guardian remembered seeing from a Shelbian. Not that he enjoyed siding with Ganix, but he appreciated how his elder railed against notions of another's authority. To add further slight, Harlan shooed Madár when he attempted to return the emptied sachet.

As for the judge whom Madár served, when last Edmond stood afore him, Dale Marius Conliffe tasked the outfit with the burden of seizing the assets of a soul who denied his daughter a novitiate's position. Though far from increasing the wellness of the territories, the outfit let Conliffe boast his increase of power over his daughter's offender and them. From the way he looked down his bullish nose with flittering eyes, Conliffe resented that Edmond learned of his shame for his daughter's failure but towed no remorse over the stench of his own corruption. Still, both kept an awareness of deeds far worse than that lone judgment.

"Honored Souls"—Edmond swallowed the acidic bile that rose over the lie—"I thank you for this order to appear afore your esteemed bench."

Soft in loudness but not in sharpness, he who showed no love to another soul let his impatience gleam in his cold eyes. "Be seated."

Edmond nodded in response to Lael but looked unto the empty space beside Samuel Herbert Gwynne, sage advocate from Harlan's territory. His incompleteness aside, Edmond preferred the proof of travel's sway on Gwynne's daughter to the sound of Madár's back teeth clacking as he stood ever eager to grovel. Mia Elaine Gwynne oft wore the scent of vetiver that wafted through the chamber's dry heat. From this, the headship took a reminder of sowing seasons in his blamelessness when his mother took him to visit his father near the lemongrass fields of the Weston Territory.

A snap of the latch of a silver pocket watch caught Edmond's eye and scared away his sense of the nostalgic. The judges never learned, or never cared, that those reckless play-acts needled the elder Guardian and eunuch. Chester Nicklaus Lael—called *Chick* by friends no soul had ever met—was the coldest of the judges and the last soul expected to sit in a confined space with Conliffe. The Shelby Territory and Lael's Creighton Territory towed notorious grievances against the other—worse than a Larsonite toward a Creightonian.

Lael's scion, his son Nicklaus Joseph, stood over his father's shoulder, but kept his eye on Edmond. Both were uncaring cowards. He who passed over his eldest daughter to make his male fruit his eventual replacement dragged out his words on an agitated breath. "Let us set this matter behind us."

Edmond gripped his knees in anticipation whilst Harlan wiped his hand through his beard and tugged the follicles in place of wringing pampered and narrow throats. Each Guardian—save Ganix and Asham—kept a cautious eye and trained ear pointed toward the burgeoning troubles in Edmond's home territory. Now they waited to learn what matter the judges deemed of greater consequence than the increase in missing blameless souls amid a lot who struggled to produce heirs.

Tull & Ebbe

"Two moonrises ago, whilst traveling the Coburg Road unto Sevier, the bride of Advocate Cyril Adair Mumus suffered an attack at the hands of a trespassing soul. A fire erupted within the coach and the offender fled. Neither the judge's bride nor her driver agreed on an identification or any manner of his character. In her state of undoing, she has . . . relocated . . . to her father's plot in the Shelby Territory without the counsel of this court."

Edmond glanced toward the welts on Ganix's hands but set his mind on their predecessor. Count Theodore Reaume Conliffe hid in the Shelby Territory since Beau Itzal Zeck struck and flung the magick-wielder through the mighty windows of Ebbe Demesne. Droves believed that Zeck broke Conliffe's neck with that punch. He then considered the Jacobian who seldom spoke of the count's condition in their travels together.

Judge Gwynne spun his fingers in a wheel-like motion. "We decide you must lead our Guardians unto the Shelby Territory—up to Ebbe Demesne—and ensure that the countess does not leave there."

"Lest she return to her esteemed husband with harm in her shadow."

Edmond stared at the remaining, silent judge on the bench and winced with pale-eyed disbelief. He held his tongue with such a willful bridle that his head trembled. The judges allowed no defense of blameless souls nor the hunt of a predatory soul. The half-sister—born of a better mother—of silent Judge Dale Marius Conliffe was the excuse. These honored souls worried about their heaps of favors and—yet once more—drew the Guardians away from mending to keep safe a favored soul.

"You're to make camp on Ebbe Demesne and keep your presence discernible but not visible." Judge Gwynne kept his eye on Edmond as though ready to dive from a perch and pluck his next meal. "If a soul comes for her or she attempts to leave the territory, we require you to be ready to prohibit them."

"Elsewise, leave as small a mark as imaginable and then reduce that."

Edmond turned his whole head toward the outspoken judge who sat at the opposite end of bench from Conliffe.

Lael pointed a stern finger at the headship. "You're to use this as a time to prove your mettle and your ability to abide by our orders. You further remind those souls not in this chamber of our fine and unflawed expectation of them; for I say they have grown insolent and playful."

TULL & EBBE

Now the headship of the insolent and the playful pressed downward at his seat till the lacquered planks creaked.

Lael removed a pair of half-lensed spectacles and huffed as though Yah blessed no other with a mind like his. "We must keep this era of irresponsible souls reliant on our wisdom."

Harlan folded his leg and rested chin in hand, as if enthralled, but the bewildered sparkle in his walnut-brown eyes spoke to malicious thoughts.

"We must set them afore the water we want them to drink."

Harlan withheld his objection, but had he a lesser appreciation for the inventiveness and purposefulness of other souls, the chair beneath him would have turned to matchsticks. He was a Carpenterian to the depths of his heart and railed against the manipulation of authority found in their judges. This is why the judges dared not risk his advancement to headship; for they would then have to recognize his presence. Still, he respected the rules of order as best—nay, better—than he ought and drew Edmond's curious stare.

"Have *you* found error in *my* judgment, Guardian Elragadó?"

"Who am I to gaze so recklessly unto your understanding?"

Lael's stillness held long enough that even the sway of travel fell shy of moving him. "As my understanding exceeds your own—by your own admission—I tell you that your gaze is better spent on your successful passage through the droves of Shelbians who despise you and the Behemót Woods . . . this time."

"I thank you, Honorable Soul, for your regard. This is our purpose"—the headship sniffed at the stench of their rule—"in full?"

"In portion."

Gwynne showed caution with a straightening of his posture.

"I can imagine"—Judge Lael's droll voice grated the ear as he leaned toward those who guarded him too—"no conditions where that Jacobian you lead should be allowed to enter the Behemót Woods. Lest you wish to see him tempted by her whom you corral."

Edmond cocked his head as if to size up whether the smarmy advocate would better pass through the flue head-first or sideways.

"Are these directives unclear to you?"

"In no way, Judge."

Tull & Ebbe

His thick eyebrow pressed the wrinkles nearer toward his hairline. "You are dismissed from our presence."

A smirk never looked as vulgar as Edmond smirked. Even so, he proceeded back to the other insolent souls and let his smirk spread to a full smile as he counted his former headship's last words to the court afore his farewell. Mick Curtis Whigham told Judges Bliss, Lael, and Elwell that a tailored heel set against the secondkind's neck was still an oppressive heel; oppressive with a steep sense of value. That Mick had sacrificed a leg to his purpose enhanced the sting of his barb. These judges were thieves of more precious commodities than alms or purpose; they were vultures.

Harlan, who followed in step but not in manner, patted Scion Madár's shoulder harder than deemed cordial and, without a call for alms, wiped the pads of his fingers against the unblemished fabric of Madár's bespoke overcoat. In this, he tucked his disdain for the judges beneath an aloof—almost incessant—need for tactile edification.

"I tell you"—a few paces, and Harlan's hand came down on Edmond's shoulder next—"had we an audience afore Ernie and Samuel *together*, our judges would set us across the Loy, where we might be of use. Even Marvin would have riled this court."

Edmond slowed and let his shoulder prod Harlan. "You mind your observations well enough to lead if you aren't cautious."

"I beg you to hush"—the bear-like soul leaned nearer to mutter—"lest the judges order my end to avoid your claim."

Edmond's same vulgar smirk looked as playful as Lael accused their underlings of being and both he and Harlan laughed at the legacies and impressions they forged in their younger counterparts. "Better they put such an order on my head."

The engine hissed as the steam tram slowed and produced an unsettling, to-and-fro sway that mingled with the heat from the judges' chamber and the tart fog that Ganix expelled afore he brought up the rear. Both Edmond and Harlan saw an unflawed recipient and stood aside as Ganix's stench affixed to Asham and turned him sideways.

Afore they saw if Asham retched, the young foursome's most boastful member arose, too smug to let true offense rankle his expression. "Have we a new directive?"

Edmond proved as rooted as the bench, further proving his disinterest in Olley's determination to lead, and turned his head toward the senior-most of the foursome as he let his right-hand dole out their orders.

"We're to report to a plot in the Shelby Territory."

TULL & EBBE

Tull did not budge from slumber and made Edmond and the gatherers at his back more curious.

"Upon what soul?"

Edmond dismissed Olley's curiosity for his own again, as he proved eager to see Tull's response when Harlan poked the sleeping Jacobian's thigh with the hilt of a carving blade that possessed more girth than Madár's neck. "A soul we needn't name."

"Can we not let George choose the pack horses this time?" Tull proved lighter in slumber than his expressions hinted. "The last team moved slower than his herd."

"They were marvelous creatures!" George objected, not in anger, but with a proud, song-like tone.

"I *ran* faster than mine," the Archibaldian chimed in.

"And I mine!" Harlan's claim drew laughter from all around, for he lacked the build of a runner.

A custom amid the Guardians dealt with their purchase of pack horses. Though they traveled with their own mounts, they oft purchased additional horses from local stock. When they completed their labor, the headship gave away their recent purchases as a show of rebuilding the settlements that needed kindness. This custom, instilled in them by Edmond, drew this era of Guardians further from the previous era of self-seeking and hoarding members that the elder trio once traveled alongside.

"I . . ." Harlan kept from spoiling his friend's mood.

"Tell me anyway, you old bear."

Harlan folded his arms across his broad chest and ran bejeweled fingers through his lush beard. "I believe this won't end well."

"We have our directive, and we've trained them well."

Harlan gave the slightest tilt of his head in doubt. "As you say."

"Guardians! Look upon the faces of these souls who look to us to find a way through the darkness. They look to us for we are purposed by our Creator to keep back the Fallen First and to trust in the wisdom of our judges. We will not fail in our purpose for Yah sees our obedience. Cinch your gear"—he looked toward the two battered Guardians—"whilst our host Guardian chooses the pack horses and Gera chooses the wagon."

"Ask, too, which farms would benefit most from a sturdy team."

"As you say, Edmond . . . Harlan." The beady-eyed Shelbian offered Asham less than a half-glance afore he exited through the opposite end of the passenger car.

TULL & EBBE

Though the whipped pair moved away from the lot without protest, their headship's eyes did not stay on them. Edmond saw how the passengers watched his three remaining subordinates. He saw how Tull and George observed in silence as the eve broke and brought color back to the Shelby Territory's oldest settlement and the way that Olley guarded their back as they, in turn, guarded his. He then sensed the Carpenterian who lingered in defense of him.

"Many spans have passed since a crowd looked upon us that way."

"Not so many spans."

"As you say."

The pair observed the trio without further comment. As his character required, Olley found cause to speak to the most alluring soul in their passenger car. Not to be dismissed, George withdrew further from the crowd with each trip, for he found accolades and attention contrary to the humbleness he lived beneath. Tull, who managed to stroll the hem of both mindsets, pretended to drop nothing—that his retrieval of nothing might distract the eye and offer him the chance to add a pair of silver alms into the coat pocket of a slight soul whom all the outfit's members might call weary.

The Larsonite cast another glance at loitering Madár and felt the chill that emanated from the gathering shadows as the steam tram reached a full halt. He adjusted the lay of the hat upon his head, covered his chin and throat with a fine scarf that matched his irises, and then put on his gloves—all without glancing away from Conliffe's future successor. Edmond protected the Jacobian and distracted the Shelbian with words once familiar but now seldom heard. "May the warmth of Yah's mercy travel with you all!"

As Harlan patted his shoulder in approval, those travelers at his back supplied the next verse of a tune of devotion. "May the light of Yah's lamp guide your way!"

THEODORE REAUME CONLIFFE

The first Guardian of the Erori Territory and Count of Ebbe Demesne in the Shelby Territory. Sondrea Ebbe Conliffe's father was seldom good, let alone heroic, but his purpose in this tale goes beyond providing a heroine. This character's introduction came in 114, *Tull the Guardian*. Though not addressed by name therein, he is referred to as "Papa" by Katerena Yvette Mumus, who hunted fellow Guardians and creatures with him.

PURPOSE & PRIVILEGE

NINE

THE 7TH MORN BENEATH THE MOON OF THE MOTHER'S SONG
THE 107TH WINTER SEASON OF THE ACCESSION
IN THE CARE OF THE HELPER, WHO KEEPS SOULS FROM FRUITLESS WANDERING.

1212 CONLIFFE'S LANDING
MONKSHOOD STATION.
AT THE NORTHERN BANKS OF THE LOY RIVER.

The outer door on the steam tram rolled upward on the same copper rings that provided relay frequencies between signal houses and the chief inspectors of each hosting territory; lest harm befall the judges beneath their noses. That action, though well-oiled, let the murky lights that drifted on the haze of fog and incense smoke draw the eye away from the lower portion of the door, which stretched outward on rods that formed a footbridge for exiting travelers. Afore the scents of incense and those that the incense masked reached Tull's nostrils, he identified a sound that meant the outfit's arrival in the Shelby Territory. With that sound of gurgling and churning came the vibrant curses of the conductor's hand, whose purpose meant that he leapt first and secured the footbridge for those who departed in Conliffe's Landing.

He who swore and sank his entire left leg from heel to groin then looked upward to the awaiting Guardians. The slosh that collected along the banks of the Loy River turned the leg-swallowing, trouser-ruining mud rancid. Stagnant water gathered where tentacles, malformed hands or feet, and scorched wings of the Fallen First arose and mingled with the mire they dispelled from their husks. This was a shelter territory for the Fallen First; a place given over to those who fled from the Triune.

TULL & EBBE

Those who defended the judges kept an eye out for travelers who sought to overtake the railway and nudged the outfit nearer to the exit. In suspect's stead, they found no other soul who meant to travel, just as none other than the Guardians meant to exit. Most who journeyed out of the Loy crawled on their bellies and left behind grooves where water pooled. This drew insects and reptiles, kept alive by torches that burned along the waterway and landing. These pests infested all that gathered too long, a point reinforced by the jittery hiss of the steam tram's bowel cannisters and the muddied conductor's hand's desire to move to another locale.

Conliffe's Landing once rivaled Bel Geddes—a remnant of the Gierig Territory—and Sevier of the Archibald Territory. The Second Creation gravitated near those settlements and left this darkened municipality to a multitude of boasted sins. The spectacle of the copper dome atop Szélhámos Shrine, etched with the likenesses of Ministers, Squires, and birds, appeared dull and dark, though the morn was upon them. Further along the landing, Van Enger Opera House stood as dim as the thistle-hued clouds that withheld the light of the sky-fires.

From the rail station, an avenue of shops, inns, Kovács Motion Theatre, and other businesses once swelled with patrons who stayed out all eve and unto the morn. Now, every glass bore the hushed darkness from within. Since the onset of winter, and a portion of the moon afore, murmurs circulated of sickness from deeds that kept most Shelbians hidden from the light of judgment and the burden of compassion or reputations. Few believed; except for Reformers. They accused Partakers of having gone too far, as was oft their way.

Seeing now the proof, Tull shook his head. "This is worse than they told."

Tull's remark fell short of how Olley cursed. "We have greeters."

The local model of authority stood in wait like an overripened garden ready to spill out upon the slosh-ruined terrane if prodded. Chief Inspector Rusty Waltman Guild made deputies of his sons—Will Waltman, an eggplant-shaped soul, and Rusty Wade, who mirrored the pumpkin-like, squatty build of their mother. Like many Shelbians, the Fantastic Guild Trio detested the outfit. These were not well-educated, well-dressed souls like Scion Madár but, like him, they could get away with *more* abuse of the outfit than a common soul.

"Where there's a Will"—Olley looked from the eldest Guild brother to the youngest—"there's a Wade."

TULL & EBBE

"Cinch the gear, Falk!" Edmond called from behind them, and made Tull reduce his smirk.

"How this dove smells worse each time we return to her!" Harlan then hurled out a trunk that landed near enough to the trio of law-keepers that filth and river slosh freckled their trousers.

Chief Inspector Guild's face reddened but a worn sneer crept over the left side of his face. His eyes, blue as the bird, then pecked at each member of the outfit till he found the Shelbian amid them. By custom, the host Guardian presented the outfit to the host inspector. In tradition's stead, Ganix gave a fleeting glance to the inspector and then hocked bloody saliva toward him without descending from his perch. Whilst Guild's two deputies sought to add to Ganix's wounds, their father held them back with his forearms and a laugh.

"We must work on your welcome, Barton," Harlan offered a hushed reminder toward the spitter.

"You're to turn over your weapons till such a time when you leave the Shelby Territory!"

No such law existed.

"You're not to leave by way of the Jacoby"—Chief Guild jabbed his thumb westward, then changed direction and jabbed again—"nor the Carpenter Territory."

No chief—however rooted in his purpose—had such authority as to tell the comings and goings of the Guardians. Let alone Tull the Jacobian or Harlan the Carpenterian.

"As you've entered, so must you leave."

The six Guardians not born of the Shelby Territory sneered in contradiction. How and when they traveled fell on Edmond's shoulders and the judges' decision. When none trembled, Guild hoisted a proud gut and revealed a shock baton at his hip. His inhalations sounded like the last breath of a kettle afore steam burst from the orifices and prompted each soul in earshot to listen for his next barb.

"Your weapons. Now!"

"Sabers too, Falk."

Chief Inspector Guild's eyes and shoulders showed his change in mood. His firstborn son and second-best deputy *had* to speak. This undermined his authority and agitated the Guardians whose age neared the same as Will's. He saw the anger in his father's glance and the Guardians watched the knot in his throat sink with his brash posture.

"Worry not, Guardians." Harlan leapt from the footbridge, stepped on fractured stones as he unbuckled a belt that weighed half as much as the chief's firstborn, and draped his possession over the deputy's soft shoulder. "We can do more harm to this territory and her troubles with our wits than with our weapons, can we not?"

Tull joined Harlan and angled his bronze bow in a manner that threatened how well Rusty Wade's hat sat atop his apple-shaped head. George followed the Jacobian, laying out spears and knives blade by blade without looking away from the law-keepers. This made Guild's second-born nervy, and he marred Tull's bow with oily fingerprints. The best athlete—and deputy—in the territory fumbled a clutch afore uncounted onlookers so even the muddied conductor's hand laughed at his expense.

"Might ought to tell him which way to point the arrows, too." Olley set a barb upon the deputies and removed his tethered barrage of sheathed knives and hatchets as onlookers laughed with him.

The Guardians tossed the gear atop a parading carriage—a two-wheeled cart with little more than a flatbed due to the softness of the glebe and an inability to maneuver a heavier cart through the mud. The deputies meant to humiliate the Guardians by boasting how they disarmed the territories' protectors. This was no more than a show for them. Then again, only fools expected less when leading into an election season.

"The saber too." Chief Guild's unforgiving stare settled on the soul who slighted his favorite son.

Edmond recognized Guild's play and disciplined his own showy underling. "Hand over your saber, Falk."

Olley's posture turned rigid; much to Will Waltman Guild's admiration. Both sides adhered to a common and right-hearted rule. Those with authority spoke. Their subordinates kept silent. Harlan, who mothered and corralled, held dual—unofficial—authority. The Guardian from the Archibald Territory did not.

Though bristled, Olley showed obedience through fear; though fear *without* silence. "Be grateful to your purpose, Shelbian. That is all that keeps you upright."

In response, the conductor's hand, who lived beneath the same rule, chose this moment to creep back onto the tramcar between Ganix and Asham as even the Guild Trio fell silent. Asham batted away the muddied hand and showed higher regard for his boots than Olley's offense till the boots on Edmond's feet creaked and stilled him.

TULL & EBBE

Then the chief batted his eyes and shooed away the Guardians' theatrics without an appreciation for talent. "You can reclaim *all* your gear on your way out of the Shelby Territory."

"The axe." The firstborn of Guild's fruit proved slowest of all to learn and hardest of all to teach.

"That axe is for chopping wood." Edmond swiped his vigor. "He keeps his axe."

The firstborn deputy's eyes wavered like a flame to wind as Edmond challenged and his expression changed from arrogance to uncertainty as his father pivoted away, then removed the hat from his snow-white crown. His son did the same and jabbed the rumpled cover in the direction of Tull. "He's never broken kindling with that blade!"

"Guardian Tull." Snowflakes fell with less grace than those syllables from Edmond's lips. "What say you?"

"My axe"—Tull proved a rigid hold—"but *he* does the lopping."

The Jacobian plucked his possession from the deputy inspector's soft grip, spun the axe till the blade rested at his side, and pointed the handle at Olley. Jilted, obedient Olley. The proudest soul in the outfit. The *angriest* soul in the outfit.

The Archibaldian swelled with delight and accepted his truest friend's offering. With a breath that pulled their nemeses inward, he raised the gleaming axe above his head, then pivoted and swung downward with all his strength. Tull's blade—backed by Olley's might—splintered the tongue of the parading carriage and lopped the wagon from the deputy's rig. The shift in balance scattered the confiscated gear.

"Falk!"

"Step back!" Rusty Waltman Guild seethed and swatted his eldest with his hat. He looked toward Olley and then Edmond, but not Tull. "*Get!*"

Edmond tipped his hat, which did not cover his smirk.

Olley returned Tull's axe. "On behalf of all Archibaldians, I thank you. I'm half-inspired to ask that Ganix rent out the farrier's dullest ass on the Guild boys' behalf."

"Attempt, and Edmond will have yours down in the slosh with that secondhand saber of yours to your chin."

"Secondhand?"

Tull inspected the overarching rigidity of the offended Archibaldian's posture, then watched him run a gloved hand through a wave of his not-unkempt hair.

TULL & EBBE

"I tell you, the age of this saber exceeds the stones this territory is built upon. This blade's provenance reaches higher than the tarnished cap of their shrines. Rest—"

"Will *you* rest"—Tull waved a hand—"afore your spine cracks?"

Even George chuckled with Tull at the expense of Olley's lineage. Afore they rode out, the soft-spoken soul leaned nearer toward the Jacobian. "My friend, Olley told me that saber belonged to a great ancestor who led the old fathers unto battle."

"All Archibaldians claim greatness, George, even their boors." A gentler smile lit Tull's face and he turned from those who watched their every move and sidestepped the Westonian's horse, Salmah. "Remember his is most, as of late, the fruit of thesps. He must have some outlet for their creative sway on him."

George nodded, though he did not understand. Those from the Weston Territory seldom took the time for amusement or storytelling. The son of thesps Betty Kay Olley and Silas Hendrie Falk Junior worked hard to bear his purpose as Guardian Olley Hendrie Falk. From time to time, though, the privilege of his upbringing seeped. Like most Archibaldians, Olley loathed being told to whom he must prove obedient.

Tull climbed onto Blizzard but offered the thesp's son some direction. "The nearest route to Desard Bridge is twelve—"

"The mood has turned in me, Nelson." Olley rode through, as pompous and rigid as ever upon Firefly, who mirrored his imperiousness.

This behavior George understood and laughed over.

"Stand away!"

Tull followed the cola bean-hued steed's trot but gave a patient glance to downtrodden Asham and soured Ganix. Though he felt a nudge from within to ride alongside them, he cast a dismissive breath and nudged his mount to hurry afore Olley created greater distance than even strong-legged Blizzard could endure. With a cluck of his cheek, they trotted after George, who followed Olley, who followed Edmond and then Harlan, across cobblestone roadways across the trampled paths northward.

TEN

Silas Hendrie Falk, Jr. never bore his son's bounty of fanfare. The theatrical lot reenacted the exploits of the Guardians and sought their approval in this land—never the other way around. Father and son were stubborn and withheld praise for the other. So irritated was the thesp's son by the outfit's welcome that he ignored even the fanfare of young doxies who gathered as the names of the Guardians lured them out of doors. Though plenty of Partakers turned out to jeer, Tull counted fourteen head who applauded them.

"Not this time; my sympathies." He spoke to a crowd of blameless souls and women who offered pieces of their lives—or bodies—for a moment of attention from those whom the Guild Trio offended. Even they stood as potential victims for the law-keepers and Partakers who sought an opportunity for violence. "Return to your homes, for the morn is bitter!"

The winds off the Loy proved their bite through the many cold hands that swept at the Guardian's leg as he rode past. By the law, the outfit could not offer alms unto Shelbians because their judge—vile even to Partakers—wanted all souls reliant on *his* mercies. As a Jacobian, Tull heard and observed under protest the accounts of terror that Judge Dale Marius Conliffe exacted upon the tormented and threadbare.

The son of Guardian and Count Theodore Reaume Conliffe and Shelbian Vivian Lizzie Dale, a failed thesp but an easy consort, was the breathing semblance of all that was wrong with Conliffe's Landing and the territory. Their advocate saw their need and kept them broken, lest a soul challenge his authority. This was the opposite of what their elders meant when they appointed judges to keep them. Tull reasoned that Conliffe found great success in stealing from those who lived beneath the distractions of depravity and infestation.

"Truly! The best reason why we forfeited our weapons." As he sought a peace-filled breath, he reached down and shook the hand of a blameless soul and, with tear-filled eyes, forced a copper alms into his frail hold despite a cruel law. "Blessings and mercy on you, young soul."

TULL & EBBE

"Blessings and mercy on you"—his soft voice rose with uncontained delight as he hid the offering—"Guardian Falk!"

The heckling crowd mirrored the feeling that Tull contained and dampened even the billow of hot air from the departing steam tram. Seven spans as Guardian, and still souls mistook the grandson of the Jacoby Territory's first female judge for the son of the Archibald Territory's oddest thesp. This made him squirm in his saddle and set Blizzard on a trot that led them away from the gatherers. He rubbed at his jaw, not too unshaven, and counted that a beard might set him apart.

Once he chuckled over the slight, he gauged the angle of horses and rigs along the roadway. In a none too subtle manner, those on both sides of the Guardian's path turned toward the north too. He saw how those on his left whispered and, in his peripheral field, observed how George counted those on their other side. Even the lopsided clack of hooves beneath Ganix struck with an increase of swiftness.

The doxies who clustered at the roadway crossings covered their bite mark and bruise-adorned shapes; though, not due to the cold. These shivered in fear and clamored toward the sturdiest beams; not beneath the awnings that sheltered them, but in the open. A staggering doxy passed out as two souls turned toward the shadows afore their faces vanished in a pungent fog afore Ganix. Then, the stench of salt and ammonia stung the Jacobian's keen nostrils and took his breath, till he covered nose and mouth with the red balaclava around his neck.

"Salt bomb!"

One who turned from him then recoiled. "See your end, Guardian!"

No end greeted Tull, for Harlan proved as aware as the Jacobian and twice as strong. The seasoned Carpenterian overturned a plank wagon and made the threat-hurler cower backward. As the wooden hauler fell, a pressurized mixture of salt and ammonia burst. The rain blistered the wagon and the soul who meant the outfit harm. Two accomplices—judging from their matching black coats and acid-stung hands—fell into convulsions alongside the first.

"May Yah refuse your soul!"

Harlan looked upon the soul he crushed with the wagon. "I tell you He is more certain to refuse yours."

The sound that Harlan's heel made as he crushed the bomb-wielder's throat turned the most defiant soul pale. Those nearby backed away in retaliation's stead. Few Guardians deprived a soul of their repentance without heavy consideration of the burden, and this expectation of time to repent afore their end proved the cowardice of most Partakers. Such arrogance provoked a crazed discoloration in Harlan's irises that matched the fog's wayward flow.

"I warned of the harm we might do with our hands alone."

Tull watched others step further back but remained calm.

"They believed us frail."

"They now turn from such error."

"I believe so! You keep unharmed, do you not?"

"Unharmed and unsettled."

Harlan's laughter, however boisterous, deepened the intensity of his incited stare as the warmth returned to him. "As am I! Cuss!"

As the brute called for his horse, Tull doubted that Harlan could fall. He took more blows and shed more blood than any Guardian, yet never took a knee afore any other in the outfit.

"Let us join Edmond."

"As you say."

Harlan snorted like a stallion then patted the Jacobian's booted calf. "Lead!"

Tull coaxed Blizzard, who whinnied an apology toward Harlan's bowed stallion, Cuss. That same weary creature proved sly enough to make his rider work for remount without Tull's help. The Jacobian kept his gaze set on the brim of Edmond's white hat, for the rest of the outfit handled the reactions of the crowd and the determination of their next move. That spent bomb dispersed the fog and let them follow an unhindered path till such a time that George reclaimed the squeamish foal who towed supplies for them.

Ammonia bothered the eye, but none of the Guardians took offense at the Partakers' attack because such attempts set the stage for their every entry unto the territory. Less might offend them. As a whole, the Shelbians were not revered for their hospitality or friendship. They were a peculiar lot who, in revenge's stead, celebrated the failure of their own lot and worsened their suffering with glee. Even Ganix laughed as their would-be attacker's skull caved beneath the heels of those who mimicked Harlan's rebuttal.

"Stop your skedaddling!"

Tull understood that Harlan chastised Cuss and blocked the ornery mount on his fellow northerner's behalf.

"I thank you, lad." With that, Harlan took hold of the reins.

The side's trio—Tull, Ganix, and Harlan—bore ways that were their own and yet appreciated one another well enough to take no lasting offense. The trio from the southern territories, and perchance Asham, had Tull looked toward him, watched in condemnation of the Partakers bloodlust.

"I allow for much, but I will never forgive the stench!"

"I weep for them." He breathed through his mouth. "The place turns a soul in ways they do not see."

"I tell you," Harlan marveled, "from this angle, you do take on a thesp's pleasant mien. If only you had chosen the purpose of a Reformer!"

Pleasantness surrendered to sneering as the Jacobian stooped to his right and goosed Harlan's horse. A whinny of disapproval led to a hard gallop that prompted a tremendous bark from the Carpenterian. Then, that pleasant mien returned.

"Abate, I tell you!" Harlan shouted above burdened hooves. "Abate!"

Eager to learn of their purpose there, and certain not to leave Harlan to wander, Tull leaned into the angle of Blizzard's neck and raced ahead. George let him pass, but Olley would challenge him. Soon, the pair neared their headship as George held back for Harlan's benefit. Edmond sensed the pair, shifted both reins to his right hand, and pressed down on his hat. About the time that Tull reached his peripheral on the side by which he held his reins and Olley on the other, he hooted and lunged till his stallion led the way out of Conliffe's Landing.

Behind them, a swarm of locals mounted horseback and bench seat and pursued. Like the pressurized bomb, this too proved part of their usual welcome. The pursuit of uncertain intent oft provoked the sort of misstep their detractors longed to feast upon. The Fantastic Guild Trio knew this to be true; still, they took away the outfit's weapons. The harshness of the Shelbians turned them into judges—every soul—as if they set themselves above and apart from other territories.

Though a spirit of unaffectedness bloomed within the outfit, the past still haunted. Letting pass how the terrane opened to fields of untrampled snow, Tull saw how Olley ducked behind the neck of his horse and directed a fearful eye both ahead and behind. His horse's arrow-precise path blurred, then he surrendered the lead to the Jacobian. Further back, their own headship put up a heavy-hearted but flimsy challenge. In no other territory could fifty to sixty souls chase with such easy gain.

Their headship then smiled. "Go tell the Guilds I have reconsidered!"

TULL & EBBE

Tull matched his smile and spoke in a low voice unto his horse's ear, "Vo Yah ohi'ea avat polq i'ea suo i'eaa sydäntä i'eäste äväm'me, Blizzard."

With a right-handed cinch of the reins and a shift of weight in the opposing direction, the Guardian turned his horse till the beast stood on his hind legs. Once down, he reversed his course for the sake of his fellows' peace. To confound the nuisance and protect them from what the outfit sought, each racer then circled around and darted headlong through the pack of locals without slowing Tull's lead.

As their course set them back upon the roadways of Conliffe's Landing, the two fastest raced harder toward the Loy till they found what passed for foils so soon in their visit. Deputy Inspectors Guild and Guild put up no fight, but fell apart and sideways as the Guardians reclaimed the wagon that held their confiscated weapons after Tull sank the blade of his axe into the pulp of the wagon's oak bed and hooked an iron tip beneath the plank frame. Olley lent a hand to the haul and a boot to Will Waltman's shoulder that cast him back unto the river mud.

Tull ducked a hurled stone and forced Olley to bow. "Best to hurry!"

Olley considered a barb, then ducked a fire-capped bottle. "As you say!"

"Now!"

Each gave an opposing tug to the axe handle and broke the oak plank. As the tongue dug into the glebe, those who still chased them trampled the hauler and lost the pair. Broken boards took flight and knocked riders from their saddles. Another timber wedged between the front tire and wheel well of an oncoming rig. Both Guardians cleared the rear fender in time, but the rig twisted sideways and blocked those who managed to avoid the wreckage.

As they wove through the swarm a second time, this time swatting at those who meant to upend them, they proved who held authority—even as visitors. At the pace they traveled, through scents of shops and industry, to the voices of surprised and bemused locals, the cobblestone roadways soon delivered them to snowy hillsides and awaiting fellows. Eager to disperse their reacquired gear, Tull and Olley almost rushed over the slow-moving mount beneath bear-like Harlan. In the process, they chased away a caravan that sought to overcome him.

Rather than strain their backs trying to offer his gear to him, the Jacobian and the Archibaldian patted the nearest Carpenterian on the shoulders as they cast snow upon him in passing. He swore against them in his father's tongue—from a language spoken afore the Accession—and grunted as he sought to thrust both him and his horse faster in claim of his gear. His horse seemed to understand his tongue and proved contrary. So, the younger, faster, and *lighter* Guardians tried their best to corral him with taunts that he would, no doubt, settle with them once they made camp.

Edmond, on the other hand, let Tull come alongside with little fuss and a softer hand atop his hat. "Mind the snow you churn, Jacobian."

Tull's grin showed beneath his balaclava.

"You took a chance that all might work as you imagined." The headship proved patient amid the silence. "Did you not?"

"I imagined only that we are traveling further north than even you care to take us without proper weapons."

As a test of his subordinate's wit, Edmond gauged the distance between them and what remained of their pursuers. With a whistle and a thrust of his ankles against the belly of his mount, he pushed harder and kept up the pace where they could either ride or make confession. Tull appreciated that and adjusted his balaclava to protect his chest from the cold. He gave Blizzard a pat on the neck and then sought to match the Larsonite.

Edmond led outfit and pursuers on a gradual curve behind the plots and villages that settled along Villám Fork. They traveled further still and far from Zatopić Lock & Dam, which employed mighty backs purposed with the lifting of bridges to protect the secondkind from creatures that overfilled the waterway. When they crossed the ice fissures near Lenyelt Aquifer, marked by the hollow, pained echo as the hooves broke the crusted surface, most of their pursuers scattered. The remainder vanished in a former riverbed where all turned white with fog.

An instinct to scatter disturbed the horses, and every Guardian struggled to hold their course as they pushed further north. Many battles were fought on the same terrane during the Last War. Some, like George, believed the spirits of those who saw their end afore the Accession still roamed. Given the violent, taunting spirit of the wind, Tull caught a suspicious glance from Blizzard that hinted he might agree with the Westonian.

"Äi'elä ha i'eolae." Tull heard uncounted tales of horses trotting with such might that the snow seeped with the blood of their ancestors. Still, he no longer believed fright-filled tales. "Naen . . ."

TULL & EBBE

Where the light stung his eyes, he found Harlan in wait atop wheezing Cuss and overlooking the old riverbed. The fog swirled with the breeze, and Edmond's unwavering eyes fixed on him. Bear-like Harlan offered a mother's grin of sorrow, which deepened the chill. All proved calm, and Tull stared unto the fog for wisdom.

"We have arrived." Harlan spoke for their headship and the learning of the pair who retrieved their gear. "Mark a post till the others meet us. Olley to the east, Nelson to the west. Then gather your tethers."

The calm Jacobian's heart raced till Harlan's orders went unheard by him, for his heart told him more about their whereabouts than an elder could.

"Nelson."

When Harlan nudged him with a packed snowball, Tull blinked and then gave Edmond a passing glance afore he obeyed his headship's right hand's order that failed to draw his audible confirmation. With breath held and eye wide, Tull rode out of the spent riverbed and stared due north.

"I've not seen him make that face for a spell."

"He has so few to make. Our Creator created this place too. He will overcome."

"And you?"

Edmond proved why he led longer than any other Guardian when a smile formed upon his face and revealed both the gap between his teeth and the joy he had lost in his time. He looked upon the soul whose friendship paralleled that shared by Tull and Olley, and a forgotten chuckle rose above the knot in his throat. "All I heard in the fog was the creaking of those tired joints. You're turning into a kettle."

"That I am!" Harlan's boisterous laugh disproved even a whiff of offense as he checked the positions of his fellows. "I cannot remember a time when I moved with their determination."

"You forget we were there with them."

"As you say." Harlan offered a heavy, if not wobbling, nod, then showed regard neither for ears nor emotions. "The judges test us."

"Evermore."

Harlan lowered his voice. "And our withdrawn Jacobian remembers this place."

"They knew of his past when they approved him."

"And we've taught them of our habits of forgetting their orders."

"As you say." Edmond considered their judges' stern demand. "If I obey and keep Tull at the hem, he will be crushed if we fail at this."

"Disobey, and any failure will heap madness upon him."

"Whilst the judges gain authority."

"And turn hearts against us."

"As long as we're in agreement then."

"I believe I have three"—Harlan groaned and reached into his pocket—"yes, *three* copper alms that stand for Nelson's ability to lead us blindfolded."

"Here?"

"I'd make nary such a claim if we sat in the unflawed fields near Heathland Hill."

"I cannot afford such a sizeable loss." Edmond chuckled a second time and offered Tull a nervous glance in the face of an open compliment. "Where are those lags?"

Harlan held the alms between his fingers, raised his hands to either side of his mouth, and screamed encouragement for the ears of Ganix, Asham, and George. "Souls from the lowlands haven't the cullions for a proper ride through the fog!"

His headship nudged Gallant out of the riverbed.

"No offense, Edmond." Though the eunuch joined him in laughter as he withheld apology from Olley—the fourth soul from the lowlands—Harlan let the Archibaldian stew as he faced an entanglement of limbs that blackened his irises. "O, Yah! I pray this accursed weald has forgotten us."

ELEVEN

<u>THE BEHEMÓT WOODS</u>

A FOREST OF 4,015 TREES.

HIDING PLACE TO UNCOUNTED CREATURES.

The Behemót Woods bore a memory like no other created portion across the Seven Territories. Since the Era of the Reformers—whose era preceded Tull's by two—legends arose of the thirst that the trees kept for the souls of the secondkind. Their imaginations, rich with the fear of sounding foolish, and their tongues, weakened by the weight of conviction, failed to tell the truth about the terrors that awaited. For this reason, Tull bound the tethers amid his fellows and their horses with cruel reassurance.

Since the Accession, one-five-hundredth of all the souls lost to the secondkind met their end in the Behemót Woods. What sounded as though a pittance equaled one thousand four hundred forty souls in one hundred seven spans. Believers blamed Partakers, who blamed Reformers, who blamed the Fallen First. Still, souls fell with no regard for their beliefs or stature.

"When next you see us, fellows, the trees will stand at your back."

Edmond's boots creaked in the stirrups of Gallant's saddle as he leaned down and let Harlan secure a blindfold that upset his wig. Tull checked the faces of the others, all wrapped in blinders, and then the knots that tethered their ankles from beneath the bellies of their mounts. Then Harlan tested those tethers that looped from the horses' necks. However unpleasant, these woods demanded such precaution.

"Fine knots"—Harlan squeezed Tull's shoulder—"and better than other Jacobians in this outfit ever achieved."

Harlan boasted for he taught Tull more about knots than he who called him scion.

"When Yah cast out the sins of our kind, He cast them unto these woods!"

TULL & EBBE

Even a Jacobian appreciated Harlan's love of the dramatic but soothed the others when he held his tongue and encouraged no further performance.

In his stead, Asham filled the calmness with jarring laughter. "You ought to have rode straight for Bel Geddes and not settled with this lot, Harlan!"

As the wiser and their horses stirred, Tull ducked the tether that separated him from Blizzard and climbed onto the saddle as if to coax Harlan to let Asham's stupidity pass.

"When the eyes of the prophet son of Amoz were opened"—Harlan spoke against insults, coaxing, and what nested in the entangled forest—"afore he accepted his purpose and traveled unto the southern kingdom, he saw the same creatures who now fill these woods in their pure and resplendent glory."

Still the Creightonian proved slow to hush. "Their what?"

"What we keep you from seeing are the forms of what remain of those who stripped off their burnished hides and tore away their magnificent wings. They are evermore the semblance of their souls in the moment of their betrayal. Believe my friend and I will keep you from them." Because he had traveled a long time with Tull and shared uncounted moments when they learned the other's histories, he faced the Jacobian and no other. "Will we not?"

"As you say!"

Some counted Harlan with the loons, and for good reason. Tull believed his mentor and fellow northerner carried with him a spirit of aberration that invited lunacy and darkness. Not the maniacal sort; rather, the sort that made other souls fear the loss of the light. Tull respected him as much as he feared for him but never lost an ear for what others spoke against him.

"Ride by your ear and not your eye."

Harlan smiled like a well-fueled flame. "There'll be no turning back."

"No turning back."

"There'll be no ceasing of prayer."

"No ceasing."

"And, there'll be no hand offered to the fallen."

Tull agitated with his slow response. "As you say."

"If you feel the alms dropping from your pockets, lads, we've rode too fast and twisted about!"

TULL & EBBE

Tull side-eyed the others when the whispers of prayers hastened. He kept a light-hearted expression upon his face even as he wrapped the final tether around his gloved hand and the saddle horn. The sound of Olley and Asham fumbling their recitals of prayers that stood afore the Era of Despair amused him more than the smile that parted the thick beard of the bear-like soul who would lead them through the same woods that intimidated Tull in his blamelessness.

"We ride!"

The blinded outfit set their trust upon Harlan and Tull, who led them through a forest that offered no true passage nor a straight path. The terrane conspired to reroute the swift team and currents in the fog rippled to upend them like the creatures who sought to pluck blameless souls from the light. Each Guardian rode close to the neck and held to the tether of another Guardian. If a soul fell, the other would fight by his side and let the lot ride on. This was Edmond's strategy, and a tactic that had kept them without a fatality since the judges granted him headship.

In the Accession, the Behemót Woods turned over and twisted thousands of well-rooted trees upon the caps of unmoved trees of equal sturdiness. Some grew upward whilst others grew downward. The roots of those overturned trees draped in such a way that they grew into one another and narrowed the passageway travelers carved between the teeth of a forested mouth that blotted the sky-fires and created a rare internal environment. Till Harlan and Tull found a way through, the braided foliage that grew so thick that the sounds of their passage no longer traveled with them threatened to erase the entire outfit from the territories.

There, in the ninety-eighth sowing season, the former Guardian Mick Curtis Whigham and Harlan forced Gaweł Jolyf Moreau and his Berserkers to flee after they ambushed and then dragged unto the Behemót Woods the bulk of their fellows. They overpowered Guardians, made them suffer uncounted forms of abuse, and took the second era members—like Edmond and Ganix—nearer to their end than any other foe. Because of the woundedness they bore there, those who remained in their purpose shielded their faces lest the spirits of fear and devastation remember them.

Though they moved as a unified lot, a competitive nature remained as they challenged an untamed foe and trespassed on the fissures of a former land that possessed an unmeasured depth. Olley's Firefly moved fastest, though Edmond's Gallant proved poised for a challenge. A visible smirk spread along the Archibaldian's shroud till a tug at the reins stole his posture and demanded he surrender his arrogance as his horse's hind end slipped. Nearby, where warm air rose, the snow melted away and created tendrils of ice that bolstered stones broken in the overturning by the firstkind's arrival and trees dented with triple blunt wounds in clusters of six triplicate sets—the imprint of the Kuusa Si'epä.

The shadows chased the heat and sought to devour what the trees could not digest like the thick mud that coated the hooves of every beast. As bleakness ascended powerful legs; Harlan pressed Cuss onward with devotedness to see the other side. How he learned his way, he never told. They traveled opposite the routes that Tull learned at such a speed that the Jacobian could not take his eye off Harlan lest he veer astray with one-half of their fellows. When they avoided a knot shared between three red elders, Tull cinched the tether that held George's Salmah and caught a peripheral glimpse of scurrying limbs.

Indecisive Perry Wallace Rudat dragged out the selection of his scion longer than any Guardian. Cam tired of his amicable ways and sent Sebastian Wredden Shaw unto the lowlands with Ember Willows Martel and Herb Atkins Benest. He sent Tull into the foothills with Mick and Harlan. His decision led to the egress of six Guardians and four scions in the two seasons that followed—and then evoked his surrender.

Mick, Harlan, and Scion Tull completed their tests and traveled unto the woods where they found the lot in battered, traumatized states. Moreau and his Berserkers fled toward the lodes of the Ice Clans and—as of the counted morn—never resurfaced. Most believed that Mick and Harlan hurled them from the bluffs unto the Forbidden Sea. Cam—like Olley—never spoke of what happened in the woods; ever true to their Archibaldian pride. After that, he let Perry keep both scions.

The mention of Gawet Jolyf Moreau's name inflicted painful reminders of all that was suffered there. To send the Guardians back unto the Behemót Woods proved the contempt that certain judges kept toward them. Snivelers—like Conliffe, Elwell, and Lael—composed rumors that the lot never recovered; that Moreau bested the bravest souls in the territories and set them down a path of listless uncertainty. As such, they—and not the Berserkers—stole the reverence due Olley, George, Kim Debney Byrne, Rhys Lux Garver, Colborn Ziba Shelley, Ganix, Edmond, and Cam—the survivors.

"Break right! Then bear down till the north wind slows you!"

Tull did not confuse their blinded fellows with added direction. Harlan held authority over him and, by his own silence, sway over the outfit. One voice would lead them from harm, two would divide them. If the Jacobian spoke, he would confuse the ear and break the peace instilled in them through Harlan. He trusted Harlan and broke toward the north—his right.

He never once looked behind him or let Blizzard lead him in the opposite direction. Though he intended to offer a better prayer, he asked only that he please Yah without utterance of, "Please, Yah," or any mealy words that precede a selfish request. Humbleness proved necessary to all forms of obedience. He did, however, add in a note of thanks that none fell from their saddles, for this would have made him dishonor Harlan's third directive.

Like his mentor, he leaned to the right side and far from center as the glebe shifted and their horses struggled to trot upright. The stringy coat of shadow surrendered to the wintry brittleness of shriveled leaves and starved vines. There, the light drew them toward textures and colors—toward an unproven route that they tread with the trusted hooves beneath them. A breeze carried light and level terrane toward them, and a sigh went out like praises.

"Settle now!"

Harlan called to Cuss, but Tull noted that Blizzard obeyed too. As the entire team heeded the command, all seven Guardians emerged from the Behemót Woods unscathed. Their color and swell returned as each soul stripped the coverings from their eyes and broke loose the tethers that hemmed them together. None peered back, and each savored the bite of the wind that greeted them.

"I now remember," spoke the Carpenter Territory's first Guardian, "that our judges ordered us to keep our clear-sighted Jacobian on the other side of these woods."

"You offer to lead him back, do you?" Edmond cleared his throat and Gallant fidgeted, keen to the uneasiness of what sounded like a stranger's voice in her ear.

"We remain devoted to the efficiency of our task if we remain here."

Edmond soothed Gallant and offered Harlan a delayed nod.

"Gera! Retrieve and wrap the tethers and blinders."

"As you say!" Bruised, yet still handsome, the outfit's current Creightonian obeyed Harlan but not without remark. "Truly! This time paled to those dread-filled whispers you lot have heaped upon these woods!"

"Keep making racket."

Asham looked toward Ganix, who slung his portion of tethers at the soul he oft treated as the lowest in creation.

TULL & EBBE

"See if the woods are done with you."

Now, a seldom-revealed fact about offensive Barton Blinken Ganix was that he trained his voice with operatic skill. That was his escape and his joy. He could carry a tune in a way that reduced Asham to an absolute and profound hush. Against the emptiness that lay afore the woods, he let his voice echo a tune about soldiers who died in a war that none of them observed or comprehended.

The lyrics told a tale of courage and the nobility of sacrifice above exultation. In those moments, none of them minded Ganix's presence. The richness of his voice coaxed the hearts of every creature till even the trees seemed to bend toward him. Edmond and Harlan allowed their elder to lead and, for that tune, every Guardian remained behind him.

Then, as Olley loosed his tether and flung the cord at Asham, Ganix's unsettling character reemerged. "Let us set camp, Edmond. Truly! I must see to my bowels."

Olley huffed as Edmond hung his head and billowed against the bill of his hat. "Get up there with him, Gera!"

"I'll not stay pinched for you!" Ganix called back with a lyrical value that made the skin chill.

Once Asham flung the tethers back at Olley and rode off to match Ganix, Harlan offered Edmond a direct glance. "Our passage found us with ease."

"Much?"

"Look to the Jacobian."

Tull, who removed the blinders from his horse, felt three of the four souls look upon him. He wet his lip and kept Blizzard turned away from the woods. "I believe she shed her warmth on us. When comes our time to go, we'll see how bitter she gets."

"We ought to set her every limb ablaze." Olley then spat to prove his disdain.

None approved of the Archibaldian disregard for nature. Their territory boasted glass structures and technological trinkets of endless design. All the while, their trees withered and their terrane suffocated beneath roadways and foundations. While Harlan led Edmond and George away without remark, Tull remained still. He stared at the place so long, in point of fact, that he developed an immunity to the sound of his own name.

Olley shook him with a nudge of his boot to Tull's shoulder. "Is there a matter?"

"I cannot say."

"You can say what you like. I allow as much!"

TULL & EBBE

Tull proved calm.

"Why would our judges order you to keep outside the woods?"

"That almond tree—with the trunk shaped as crooked as Cuss's back—bears the marks of a hatchet."

Olley strained his eyes, as if to see through the same tree.

"An uncountable lot on an oval face where the bark has been plucked clean."

"George!" Olley withheld till he looked back. "Does the almond tree afore you—"

"To his left."

"That is, to your left"—he looked at the identifier of trees, who shrugged and nodded for him to continue—"bear a distinct pattern, by chance?"

George furrowed his brow and Olley whipped his hand in the air in a circular manner to emulate rounding the tree for a look-see. The good-natured but not inexhaustible Westonian rounded about and leaned to the left side of his saddle. "Much of the bark has been removed."

"Is that all?"

"I count . . ."

"Almighty!" Olley hanged his head. "I believe he means to count every stroke."

"An uncountable number, George?"

Olley squeezed the bridge of his nose and missed seeing George's nod. "Say this is an elaborate plot to dupe me."

In a lie's stead, Tull again kept still in the place where the first Guardian of his territory and Zeck's fiery-haired granddaughter defended him with little more than a brilliant horse and faith in Yah's compassion.

"You've visited this place afore." The Archibaldian cursed beneath his breath and wrung his mop of chocolate-brown hair till a wavy lock fell from position and scraped beneath his lower lip. Then, he repeated his curse.

"Say the memory stems from a good experience."

"When, Nelson? When has a memory of yours stemmed from a good—"

"Why the delay?" Edmond called out. He then waved his arm in a wide, crescent-shaped arc. "We'll set camp over the next hill!"

Olley slapped Blizzard's hind end, then negotiated his own mount into a soft trot. "Tell me. I won't look at the tree, but tell me what awaits us over the next hill."

"An ornamental faucet tapped into a spring. A millpond and house to the northwest. A stable house nearer to us from there. An orchard behind them."

TULL & EBBE

"An orchard?"

"Falk! Refill the water satchels as you pass this faucet!"

Again, Olley cursed.

"You wouldn't hide from me a flaw so great as being a Shelbian, would you?"

"You must let go of your hatred."

Olley stared as though uncertain.

"I tell you; I am no Shelbian." Tull's voice stopped cold as Blizzard sidestepped and whinnied. "Almighty! There are not enough moons in my time to forget such a sight as that."

"What?" Olley swore a third time and turned sharp enough that his horse ambled around Tull in a broad arc.

Ganix crossed afore them, stripped of trousers and all that covered him from the hips down to his knobby knees. With a roll in hand, he stomped toward a cluster of trees without covering his endowments.

Olley's laugh escaped on thin air and he rested his elbow against Tull's shoulder. "I tell you; I dare to risk blasphemy just to see the face of the poor Squire who swoops down and finds Ganix taking the bark off those poor elderberry trees."

Tull chuckled like a blameless soul. "They're walnut trees."

"They'll never be the same." He prodded his friend. "The dullard is about to—"

Asham snapped at the neck and hips as he spared his mind from the full spectacle of Ganix's clefted trunk. Tull covered his face at the sight and hid behind the neck of his horse to spare the Creightonian further ridicule. Olley, who seldom employed reservation, took the hankie from his pocket and motioned as if polishing the filthy sight from his eyes. The distraction eased the oddness of Tull's memory, but the Archibaldian at his side soon discovered better sights.

"Look, Nelson."

Tull bristled when Olley turned his jaw.

"George has made new friends. This must be a record!"

Three tender goats chewed from the wild grass of the fields and kept a curious gaze upon the two ornery Guardians, till the sounds from Ganix startled the furthest animal from her next bite.

"Not here two ticks and he's become a shepherd."

"Those are goats." Tull stepped from Olley's reach and stowed his tethers. "These surroundings must seem strange, so far from Sevier glass and Bel Geddes crystal, but how could you not have watched *The Kenite's Bride*? Next to *Betty's Bouquet*, that was your mom's finest performance."

Olley grumbled as Tull gathered Blizzard's reins in his right hand and took hold of the saddle horn with the left.

"I shiver each time she offers me a drink." He ran his left foot through a stirrup of Blizzard's saddle, whilst Olley's nostrils rose in offense. "You ought to see her in more roles than *The Forbidden Sea Monk*. They aren't all filled with such fright."

A metallic jingle preceded a slight thud, but the sounds proved loud enough that the Jacobian inspected beneath. When he found a hook-shaped disruption in the snow and heard what sounded like a cable and spool, he sought proof. Clumps of snow leapt from the surface and then a coiled line broke free. The same line ran taut, and he followed with his eyes where he found a figure cloaked in shadows.

"Ci'sóla!"

TWELVE

Tull plunged his right hand at the cable and took hold of a hand-bent hook with a blunt end dipped in paraffin. Where the hook and line met, a loose copper sleeve rolled and provided the jingling sound. He gave a tug and the soul who controlled the spool tugged back. What ought to have been a fair draw devolved unto a test of wills.

Afore words reached his lips, Olley rose in his saddle with the snap of iron and the groan that accompanied Tull's sudden bow. What seemed at first like a slip soon proved elsewise as a sharp jerk at the cable pulled the opposite foot out from beneath the Jacobian. A line of light rustled the branches and corrected every misconception. Tull shouted and clawed at the frozen terrane and spooked his horse.

Blizzard's back hoof almost trampled his rider's hand but the cable that rustled branches and dragged the Guardian also removed him from that harm. As slack left the cable with a series of heaves, the Behemót Woods consumed him. Brush and leaves erupted from beneath a snowy hem and took away his chance at umbrage. His whole body took to the air and the iron teeth around his ankle tore through the fabric of his trousers.

In need of help, Tull observed that Olley proved helpless, too. Bullied by his experiences in that twisted forest, neither he nor his steed reacted in pursuit. He did nothing at all. Fear crippled him, deprived him of swagger and tongue, and turned him small beneath the weight of failure. When faced with his fears, he wilted.

As for Tull, his ascent ended when he bottomed out against the trunk of a honey locust tree that grew downward from an overturned crest of lush terrane. Though capped with ice and snow on the topside, beneath proved as fertile and warm as an eve beneath the Moon of the Sower's Hand. That moon, when the mist burned off and the seed flourished, went unseen from his present location, so the terrane had no way of sharing in the beauty. Even so, he proved gentle rather than swatting away at foliage or scarring the bark.

Two semicircular bands of iron, torch-cut into a serrated bridge and fitted with a coiled locking mechanism, held him. The tension of the spring proved taut enough to

TULL & EBBE

twist the Guardian's foot but not to rip the flesh of his boot. With his elbow as a lever, he pressed against the tree and shifted his weight to pry at the trap with the heel of his freed leg. The cable that kept them both, however, coiled tighter, and the spring hammered the inner band of teeth against his leg for a renewed hold.

He tightened the muscles of his core as the teeth bit deeper, lifted his full weight with his ensnared leg, then craned his head till he swayed like a pendulum. His eyes throbbed now. Still, since blamelessness, he loved the intricacies of trees and the paths that their branches chose to travel. As a creature of peculiar travels, too, he felt obliged to treat all but the fig tree well and put to use the condition of his body over any weapon.

With a stomach-straining reliance on every abdominal muscle, he performed an imbalanced and inverted sit-up that let him hook his left arm around his left thigh. He had strung enough bows to learn about resistance, and let loose his hold to turn his form into a counterweight for the device. He lifted his full weight till his unhindered leg bent around a branch of the downward-growing tree. Another hoist of his frame tricked the coil and let him pull two lengths of cable as long as his arm to create slack in the line.

He repeated the feat and claimed another arm's length as the cable unreeled. The exertion mingled with suspension and, more than once, taunted him with a loss of light. Because the ever watchful and fiery Minister loved him, she blew the slightest of breaths and restored his acuity. In unwasted alertness, he kept a gloved hand on the cable and lowered his body till he reached the highest limb of the adjoining tree.

What scent Tull smelled as he inhaled in relief was likened to that of smoldering wood; not an unpleasant stench, but a lure that let creatures prey upon travelers. The Kuusa Si'epä produced the scent by touch. Because they were not intended for the secondkind's realm, they cast off a frequency that proved contrary to all that Yah created there. The frequency mimicked heat and made scorch marks upon trees without the presence of flame.

This was not their sole oddity. None showed the signs of being born, for they were each created by Yah's direct intention. Many went without the full use of eyes, tongues, or other sensory organs. All went without noses or ears. Most were as smooth as Edmond's scalp and counted as the sole kind of creatures who lacked an odour.

TULL & EBBE

Since their flesh blended amid wood and stone, Tull relied on this smoldering odour to indicate their nearness. The Kuusa Si'epä prowled in silence but the trees still reacted, and he counted six distinct groanings from the wooden paths that led to his location. From his left side, four approached. Two others crept from beneath. They were fierce and chaotic, yet a sight unto themselves to behold, for the brutality of their betrayal against Yah was heart-wrenching.

Afore they fell, they who stood in the throne room of the Creator saw—in absolute focus—His immaculate glory. When turned to wrath, Yah's awesomeness extinguished evermore those eyes which once burned as pure flame. The face that all created species would bow afore at time's end, and the last these creatures ever saw, haunted the Fallen First with every tick of the clock's hand; or so Tull prayed. If they were not haunted, then of what gain was remorse?

When the Behemót Woods's dwellers fell, they tore away their fiery wings by cleaving their limbs at the bulbous joints that let their adornments serve as a shield for what the created eye was not able to look upon without suffering blindness. Those joints oft tore open but retained muscle function well enough to serve as hand-like instruments; of which they had six that served as both hand and foot.

Their former arms and legs were lost when they cast off their burnished, flame-fed armor. A serpent-like tail extended from their haunches and coiled, as if to steady them whilst reaching as their heads extended from their shoulders as if seeking and never finding stimuli. What looked like fingernails at the ends of their ragged fingers were the remnants of ducts that kept the wings silken in texture and strong as a shield. Tull found them as far from silken and glorious as Ganix's clefted trunk.

One after another swung from limb to limb with their self-created hands. They gnashed their teeth so hard that even now their jaws trembled within seared mouths. The sound that emanated served them—as an echo served a bat—and let them find he whose heart beat fast from an upended setting. All six landed on the bottoms of limbs that now served as the tops and let the sounds of chattering bones unnerve the once blameless soul who returned to their woods.

"'Yah, our perfect Creator, makes war in my name'"—even after sixteen spans, he relied on the verse and then spoke the half that counseled him when he felt alone—"'so I must keep still.'"

TULL & EBBE

The lowest took hold of the tether with three limbs and leaned till the snow beneath no longer made Tull wince. Another set a high hand upon the sole of his boot and brushed a malformed cheek along the Guardian's leg.

"Mi'enu poede tänä truvasoa Yah vahvuudessa i'ea aermuessa."

An oblong hand swatted and drummed against his taut stomach.

He looked unto the pits of the extinguished sockets on the cable-gripping creature's face. "Can you say the same?"

From within, but without lending his voice, he screamed the name of their mutual Creator. Stillness then ran through the woods like the mightiest of currents. In reaction, every creeping thing—even the six six-limbed creatures—scattered till the limbs of trees and the trapped Guardian were all that drifted. Tull offered a solemn prayer of gratitude and breathed an untroubled breath.

Beneath him, on the unmarred glebe upon which the secondkind built, ice crystals compressed as heavy soles crushed new fallen snow at a frightened pace. A faint sound of windedness—a result of held breath and an excited heart—filled the silence between steps. A squatty brute roamed with an uncertain side-waddle that upset branches and scuffed the ice from roots. Not even Harlan, at his drunken worst, or Ganix, with his usual disregard, ambled with such a lousy step. With a brunt hand, the brute clenched at a rugged branch that served as little more than reassurance against the plucking hands of a creature that frightened even a low wit.

Tull curved his full body to confirm suspicion, but that soul withheld from him and plucked at the cable with his opposite hand to rouse him. With that, Tull roused right back. "I am Nelson James Tull; fourth Guardian from the Jacoby Territory, sent here by order of the judge of this territory. Truly his name is known to you."

A grimy side-waddler stepped nearer, beneath jagged limbs and through pools of ash and mire that stained the snow. The Infested ambled with the same sideways step, but seldom without a tow of voices in a single throat. Tull heard only the muffled wheeze of a soul who wanted to sound more imposing. The stench of nervous sweat further reduced that chance.

"I am no longer blameless. These woods and her dwellers no longer frighten me."

He discovered a patch of skin, like the scalp of a soul who shaved their head, and then identified the underlying body adorned in a pelt. The bite of iron teeth against his ankle proved their first purpose.

"Nor do the tales of a wit smaller than their teller's stature upset me."

TULL & EBBE

A stripped piece of bark crumbled in his foe's hand. Though strong, he lacked the mind to hunt. The pelt, the trap and cable, and even the use of the twisted woods were all passed along from another, surer soul.

"Zeck would swat you like a rabid stray if he saw you now"—the pet name of his captor felt vile on his lips—"*Mim.*"

Moses Ian Merill stepped into sight, though still hidden from Olley, and looked up till he found his catch. His bleak eyes appeared as cold as the wintry sea though his skin proved as rumpled as the stained shirt beneath the pelt that Tull's eldest predecessor—and Mim's former benefactor—gifted him. Though he looked all around for signs of the creatures, he offered a smile that boasted his victory over a soul he had tormented in blamelessness as though he obtained the last laugh in a long-played game. Still, he withheld his words.

"I've not missed you once."

The reeve by trade expressed a vicious smile for Tull to see. He then turned his back on the Guardian. Now, by the law of the judges, a soul ought, at the very least, to offer their hand of assistance when confronted by an agent of the judges. Then, he remembered Mim's poor manners and heard him walk further from the direction of the camp and the paths which the fallen creatures chose.

He did not call out for Mim, for Olley, or any other soul's help. This trait of his disturbed she who watched over him. She of a burnished brass body and fiery train did not reach in to free him from his trial this time. If genuine harm arose, she would pummel them unto the dust that formed the Second Creation. Till then, she observed the Jacobian through a veil that his eye did not identify.

That eye, however dimmed toward the supernal, sought the weapons that adorned Blizzard's hind section. Apart from a nail knife, the pencil in his boot, and two tongues' worth of ill-tempered words, his arsenal ran low and without a device fine enough to undo the cotter pin that held the hinge of the trap in place. This did not keep him from a two-handed search for an uncounted inventory, however.

Tull remained still, except that he cross-reached and reacted to a sharp edge in his trousers' right hip pocket that poked beneath the nail bed of his left-hand ring finger. With some adjustment and a crane of his hips, he tugged what seemed as thin as paper yet bore the fibrous texture of fabric. He minded the clench of iron teeth and the wooden cradle that dug at his shoulders and crown as he unfolded a slip of cotton paper folded once into an oblong shape that displayed two statements side by side versus stacked top to bottom; a writing style accredited to a single soul in all his travels across eighteen lands.

"In all fairness, she distracted you with that purple hair."

"IMAGINE, IMAGINE! A HARD-TO-IMPRESS GUARDIAN MADE TO WONDER, 'HOW DID SHE SNEAK THIS INTO MY POCKET?' IF A HARMLESS NOVITIATE CAN SLIP HER HAND IN YOUR POCKET UNNOTICED, YOU OUGHT TO CONSIDER WHAT A CREEPY CREATURE IN THE SHADOWS MIGHT DO, PARTNER."

"Some find her smugness adorable." He smirked, then brushed aside a frond in search of creeps other than Mim afore he read the right side of the note:

"LEST I FORGET, I DON'T BELIEVE A GUARDIAN SHOULD SERVE THE TERRITORIES TILL HE ACHES. I DON'T BELIEVE YAH MAKES TROUBLE OR ISOLATION A SOUL'S PURPOSE. BETTER THAT YOU FIND A BRIDE AND BUILD A HOUSE SOMEPLACE PLEASANT. YOU COULD LEARN TO BE JOY-FILLED IF WELL-LOVED, COULD YOU NOT? SOON, YOU'LL SEE ME."

Tull gained little time to reread Jules's note, let alone consider her words, for the sound of drumming and crackling drew his ear and turned his head. A slow-moving seventh member of the Kuusa Si'epä plodded along a downward-growing tree toward him. The breeze caught a fragrance in the paper that reminded him of that soul he found hiding upon a rooftop and drew the creature nearer. This scent, though subtle, arose like candlelight in the darkness.

The limb-over-limb-over-limb travel took a sharp misstep when a clump of moss-rotted bark broke loose beneath the creature's hold. A sideways plunge led with a kick to Tull's crown as the Kuusa Si'epä fell. The creature's wet, slick texture brushed the Guardian's arm afore the Jacobian lost consciousness and let the perfumed note slip from his jarred hand. Both Jules's message and the clumsy straggler fell unto the shadows of two trees—neither of which struck the terrane afore they vanished.

An intense light offered no warmth, but cast further harm away from Tull when he needed a defender. From that light, a burnished-bronze hand reached through the veil of a territory's unbelief toward the Jacobian's ankle. Beneath the touch of a pristine fingertip, the hinge of the trap fell as disassembled bits. That same hand took hold of the Guardian's leg, then another supported his neck, kept him from injury, and carried him unto the glebe outside of Behemót Woods.

When Tull sprang upright with energy, he found no other soul around him. The glebe beneath, void of snow and lush with flowers, kept his body warm for the time he needed to recover. He suffered now no dizziness, no throbbing, and no flawed vision. Time's loss aside, he suffered no confusion regarding *how* he landed there either.

As the weapons at the end of the Era of Despair were destroyed, he discovered the iron of Mim's trap reduced to a solidified puddle in the snow beside his resting place. When he pulled his hand free from his pocket, he learned his pocketed nail knife underwent the same change. No weapon withstood purity lest those creatures who held the Light allowed. He paid the loss no mind and set his full attention toward the cover of clouds above the plot.

"I thank You."

Deeper than those spoken words, a feeling of unworthiness pooled in his heart and humbled both his posture and his want for retaliation against Mim. The proof that he remained heard by his Creator took away every hurt, every bitterness, and every doubt. In their place, a cleansing breath rejuvenated him and let him continue onward with his purpose toward the secondkind and the slow reveal of a place that once served as home to him.

What he had learned of Ebbe Demesne in his time now pecked at the absence of worry that filled him. Wife and mother, firstborn son, second-born son, and then father and husband all met their end on the lush plot. Two fell by the same hand. He could no longer remember the culprit—except that their tree withered, and no other bore their name again.

After the Accession, she who remembered that second-born son of the withered tree returned from the forested shores of the northwestern hem with a husband. He—Howard Alexander Fabray—was much younger and less reasonable. Fabray purchased the ancestral home and the legacy of the curse with the alms of his bride, Elsa Betty Ebbe. She, who survived the Accession, did not outlive her young husband. She kept the curse from their daughter, whom she sent back to the forests and schools

TULL & EBBE

of the Jacoby Territory, and as her end neared, sought out a judge who recorded unto the annals every observation the keen elder made.

Elsa's brother, Saul Martin Ebbe, served as witness, but idolized his sister's husband. He spent much time at the plot, which bore by then the name Ebbe Demesne. The two became like brothers whilst Lea Christine Fabray stayed away till she unraveled ways to turn Creation's rhythm into an energy source that made kettle lanterns burn with light and outshone Randolph Hereford Wylie's identifier beacon design. Still, the curse lingered and divided the hearts upon Ebbe Demesne like the twisted forest outside her walls till a single soul proved weak.

The curse—a gathering of spirits—promised greatness to Saul Martin Ebbe. Greatness towed but a single demand. He had to end his sister's husband's time and set free the gathering. Till such a time, the bleakness that settled on the place chipped away at the *trappings* of peace, gratitude, and richness. Fabray retreated deeper unto tragedy whilst his bride's brother studied every book from afore the Accession in search of a way to attain the utmost power.

"I still do not believe in curses"—Judge Juanita Gene James's lone descendant looked from the clouded sky-fires toward the shattered and cobweb-filled atrium atop Ebbe Demesne—"yet here I stand again."

He saw once, then never again, a fantastic telescope that sat within that atrium above the manor's third storey. The same might of the Accession that forged Behemót Woods also twisted the gazer's dream and shattered both lenses and every pane of glass that encased the room. The library that formed the recessed study at the foot of the observation terrace rotted and deprived the secondkind of volumes of history, advancement, and other wondrous imagination. Tull felt no bitterness on the matter.

"All that was will be made new." He ran his hands into the pockets of his trousers and sighed. "Believe me this."

He turned from the atrium that Mim once described to him as haunted toward the cause for vibration in the terrane. An easy grin fell over him. Blizzard slowed as though uncertain and the Jacobian looked upon the sorrow-filled expression that benefitted no soul—least of all a true Archibaldian. In Olley's left hand, he held the reins of the gray stallion with the spotted white belly.

"In that atrium sits a telescope that would make my friend beam with approval."

"Not this peak, Nelson."

TULL & EBBE

"Yah destroyed the lenses"—he accepted Blizzard's reins even as Firefly whinnied at him—"lest we see unto His throne room."

"As you say." Olley then paused. "Not you, horse."

"Not I! I repeat only the tale that was told to me. No longer do we sit low amid the southern hem. We are in the north! Here we stay within His reach and feel the breath from His nostrils."

"That sounds unsavory." He who failed a friend hid his shame-pooled eyes from the truest soul of the era. "I set your place at camp."

The Jacobian offered a gracious nod and mounted Blizzard's saddle.

"When next we mend in a town with purposeful roadways, I'll see that a new tent finds you." He cleared his throat and bared his teeth as a tear fell down his face for his failing bravery. "You sorted the matter, did you not?"

"An unsettled grudge."

Olley sniffled and mopped his face.

"These woods will not be our end."

The Archibaldian's brow told of his greatest fear.

"As I say."

His smile held till Olley cocked his jaw and sneered over the display of belief. Whilst he lacked his own, he could lean on his friend. This much remained proven, and Tull held no grudge against his inaction. With a pat to the back and a hearty laugh, the Jacobian maneuvered with Blizzard and followed an easy path toward the outfit's camp with the Archibaldian at his right side and the cursed manor on his left.

Once Having Six Wings

An Interim

The 3rd Morn beneath the Moon of the Frail Dove

The 93rd Winter of the Accession

In the Care of the Helper, who keeps souls from fruitless wandering.

In the current of shadows

Between two times.

Beneath uncounted lands.

To those who lacked understanding of the firstkind's hand upon Tull, the shadows went unnoticed. To those whose belief wandered, what was once unnoticed turned into a prowler. In point of fact, the shadows were a part of creation, and all that was created was intended for a purpose. In this land, and the others where Tull once lived, the shadows smoothed new paths and took away obstructions.

Each time Enke'loi the Warring Minister set her hand upon Tull and kept the Guardian from his end, effects changed. What was once fashioned and necessary changed. Those tools that required furtherance of the secondkind's paths changed with them. Every misplaced object, every disappeared trinket, and every possession lost evermore fell unto the shadows. In this was their purpose: that the shadows take from the secondkind's reach what no longer furthered their paths as Yah intended.

Those who fell first could not deny such belief. This included that creature who took from the Jacobian the much-lamented love note from a soul whose tongue so oft betrayed her. That slip of paper spun end over end through the shadows and unto those lands where Tull lived no more. The current was not written over the former in full; rather, each shared the same light. In turn, the shadows between every land flowed like the Forbidden Sea.

What once served in the supernal throne room that the Jacobian imagined at the other end of the atrium telescope now fumbled for his scraps. The Kuusa Si'epä lost much. Those who declared Yah holy lived now in filth; afraid of the Light and tormented in the dark. To them, the shadow was a blanket—a covering—that neither warmed nor hid. Still, the hope remained. Better to drown whilst seeking, after all.

Without eyes to read or voice to recite, the message upon Jules's note served no purpose. Her scented paper and the sound of rustling piqued what senses remained in the creature. If the shadows coveted the note, then a chance of barter remained. A moment without the anguish of a grave error justified drowning in shadow's flow.

Had the creature not eyes doused like spent candles, the oddities of such a place might have replaced the desire for the trinket that prompted the chase. As such, fear increased with the stream of every disembodied sound; like the noise on the other side of a wall that might never be identified. Bodies of other travelers swam through the shadows; aware of the creature, but given over to their own pursuits. Lands flowed by as a clefted nub still swatted for a grip at the tail of the lost love note.

Another hand took hold first and pulled the slip of paper unto the light. The Kuusa Si'epä reacted to the loss of scent, then scurried end over end as all six limbs worked to redirect a course. Time flowed like the current, and the shifted position appeared as a stone that jutted up from a stream. In this, the creature exposed the neck for the hand that matched that which held the love note. As a hungry creature who plunged a hand unto the water and drew out a fish, so caught and so plucked from the stream of shadow was the Kuusa Si'epä.

Saturation dwindled like the appearance of colors beneath a full eclipse; neither muted nor enlivened. The shadows fell from the creature's limbs and the severity of cold air stiffened every joint. Flakes of snow the size of silver alms fell from charcoal-hued clouds that hid much of the sky-fires. From amid a setting of snow-covered trees and frozen rock, a Somers Roundabout—a great attraction of the secondkind's past expositions—stood entombed in ice.

The circular arrangement of suspended benches and decorative trusses went missing at the end of the Era of the Falling Lands. Most souls believed the attraction fell unto the sea. What once stood on the shores of the Archibald Territory, however, now resided upon the mountainous barrier of the Carpenter Territory. Encased and preserved, this spoke to the harsh setting that soured the mood of another soul.

Vi'emane the Last, who gripped a lost note in his right hand and a fallen creature in the left, bore no sense of wonder in irises that matched the color of ancient ice. He stood greater than any member of the Second Creation, smallest amid his kin, but with the same visage. What portion of his face remained visible beneath a mane of wild hair and a thick beard wrinkled as aged eyes sought to focus on delicate letters. He cursed the mighty winds, batted lashes mingled with snow, and struggled with the text size.

"Kéap, kéap!"

At the sound of his tongue, the frigid Kuusa Si'epä went slack. Now the brilliance of the sky-fires shimmered beneath this soul's cold irises and plumes of color like molten bronze spread from the pupils outward. Teeth, not unlike those of a lion, pressed against a worn mouth as the member of the Seko'tae—an accursed race—spoke to the fallen creature who surrendered a supernal home on a Liar's crusade.

"Mundd i'el, motyl áttál, hí'er nöka?"

With the swiftness of a batted eyelash, this new foe slung the Kuusa Si'epä upon the exposed rock and pinned a tarnished, bronze foot across the creature's chest. He then gathered sediment into the palm of his idle hand, spat, and spread the mingled paste across the empty sockets of the trespasser. This proved the firmness of his belief in I'Esh, who performed the same feat long afore the Accession.

"Nēm szábád ni'ekem i'egy jágyátte."

As he tucked away Jules's note to Tull, the Seko'tae foe watched the flames reignite in the Kuusa Si'epä's eye sockets as a thirst for pure air made the creature squirm underfoot.

Certain Souls

THIRTEEN

The 7th Peak beneath the Moon of the Mother's Song
The 107th Winter Season of the Accession
In the Care of the Helper, who keeps souls from fruitless wandering.

Beacon 072.19.434 recognized at 191 Taurog Roadway . . .
Identifier confirmed—Sondrea Ebbe Conliffe.
Observe at all times beneath Edict No. 112009-11B.

Howard Alexander Fabray was neither as gentle as his façade hoped nor as scandalous as his reputation hinted. The loss of his bride made him love Elsa Betty Ebbe more. By then, he no longer knew their daughter, nor held hope for greater than his erasure from time's thoughts. His solitude drove him toward desperation till he no longer expressed the workings of his tortured mind; that another might save him.

For Lea Christine Fabray, her father took on the curse—that no other should fall. He gave all to his daughter except Ebbe Demesne. Then he raised his hand against his heart and brought about his own end. The line of spilt blood flowed once more.

Fabray's ill-hearted choice drew his brother-by-law and that soul's powerful friends unto Ebbe Demesne. With their backing, Saul Martin Ebbe sought to seize the manor afore his niece received her inheritance. They traveled with an intent to destroy Fabray's testament. What awaited them at his home proved worse than any coward might fear.

By the time Reformers surrendered to local panic and approached the plot, the Kuusa Si'epä swarmed Ebbe Demesne, unbothered by the flames of torches that Ebbe and his friends wielded against them. Creatures seared in Ki'eoppa suffered far worse than the fires made by Yah's favored secondkind. The six-limbed terrors tore apart the trespassers and their horses and flowed from the Behemót Woods upon Ebbe Demesne the way that salt spilt from a shaker.

Adorned in the fire of torches and the blood of elitists, the Fallen First turned against those whose arrogance cloaked their greed. Their veils withered and their fear showed. Those who set their trust in fire above faith bore no factual insight of darkness's grasp. They might have met Yah had another—a friend to Saul Martin Ebbe—not hidden amid the carnage.

Imbued by the lessons found in books and a title that amused him, Erorii Theodore Reaume Conliffe declared himself the sole authority over Ebbe Demesne, over those he saved, and over most of the Shelby Territory. He forced back the creatures and shook the untested belief of staunch souls; souls who limited even the measure of Yah's power. On that bitter eve, those who sought to destroy bowed at the feet of a magick-wielder.

Afore the next moon, Judge Kieran Randall Bray awarded Conliffe the plot and named him a Guardian but traded a curse on one house for another that fell upon the entirety of the Shelby Territory. The accursed lineage—now stricken—joined the spirits that fed Conliffe's magick and hardened his heart. He sought to turn every soul into a servant; a subject too afraid of what he might do to them if they grumbled against his ways. By Bray's end, that judge ruled only in the manner that pleased the count of Ebbe Demesne.

"Again, the Reformers come . . ."

Bray's fellow judge, who heard Reformer Angus Waggner Stanley's tale at the request of Lea Christine Fabray, regretted her involvement till the morn her end arrived; many spans after she taught Conliffe's fruit how to hold a babe. By her journals, she believed that the curse took hold of her home, too, and warned her son to stay prepared. Whether her son obeyed or attributed her request to fear, he never told. If he told, his son—that held and cherished babe—shared no awareness of the remark.

"Pray that I have prepared you against the monsters that dwell here"—the faint reflection of Conliffe's fruit overlaid a still image of the Jacoby Territory's current defender—"Guardian of mine."

Further from the coldest portion of Ebbe Demesne than the Behemót Woods stood a wing of thick glass panes reinforced by ornamental trellises of iron and copper trim. Spruce drapes and holly blanketed the outside. On the inside, beneath tapestries as thick as a blameless hand, a home set apart from magick still bore fearful observation of the count's nearness. Though slight and hushed, all trembled, and complete stillness never visited such a restless plot.

Maia Espe Zeck spent her last thirty-three spans in the cold of Ebbe Demesne. She watched the cursed house of her husband and delighted over the occasional visit of Yah's Third Creation—animals—who crossed the shadowy terrane unaware of the upset that settled there. Few visited twice. Since she departed two spans afore the current winter, even fewer souls discovered the neglected wing.

In the aftershock of an attack, she whose first steps occurred upon her mother's floors returned and took down every covering and relit every wick and pilot. Now, the countess moved with the subtlest of missteps; not caused by the attack or the imbalance of magick. She was not an unflawed creature. She had greater beauty than her mother and grander presence than her father, and some counted her as the secondkind's nearest-to-perfect soul, but she never made such a claim, for she knew whose genes helped shape her heart.

At the writing table of her departed mother, the first countess of Ebbe Demesne sat behind a fortress of resources that held no interest for her father. She consulted the journals of her grandfather, the diaries of her mother, a recreated private ledger that she kept hidden in her coach, and a collection of articles hemmed together in a scrapbook by a devoted reader of the late Philip Clapham Tarry. Add to that a journal of her own notes and a sketchbook of designs by an inventor friend, with a library of archived reels from uncounted minds, and she proved determined to find the motive behind the recent attack against her and her incorrupt driver.

Her grandfather's journals named her attacker Taotáva; that is, a soul with a malleable form. Her mother's diaries told her about the troubled wanderers and spirits who disturbed the unsettled lands between Ebbe Demesne and the Court of Learning, where she and her fellow overseers met. The investigative writings of Chronicler Tarry spoke of the first collection of Guardians' redacted discoveries and the attacks withheld from the secondkind of the Eras of the Reformers and the Falling Lands. Such learning oft reinforced why she was not a soul who sent others ahead or into the unknown in her stead.

As she had relived those brief moments of the attack uncounted times across the past three eves, she felt certain that the third-most intrusive of Holston Lucius

Buckler's machinations observed the attack too. She supported the wily inventor since she first encountered him in the ninety-second gathering season when he imagined a solution that kept the secondkind's food supply from spoiling from premature winter. He spoke to her as an equal and marveled that she—who was no inventor—grasped the principles of his works. Though she did not count him as a betrayer, she never pretended that he placed friendships above his purpose.

The recreated ledger stopped eight moons afore her attack, but she found two identical investments in Buckler's research for the sum of seventy-two hundred silver alms. Her coach and horses cost one-fifth that amount. Charles's salary cost another two-fifths. The ledger—a private account of Judge Cyril Adair Mumus—riled her. Even so, she held onto a tingle of suspicion that the Shelbian advocate—her half-brother—worked against her too. That he sat on the bench that decided the Guardians' purpose provided her with further cause to suspect him.

The pair never bonded. Her half-brother's own shadow kept from being seen too oft with him—or so her mother claimed. Their mothers were rivals, and neither drew the love of their shared father well enough to accommodate the other through the difficulties he presented them. She wanted fairness, and Dale Marius wanted authority. Even over her, he sought to rule.

She limited her time in the Shelby Territory because of father and half-brother. They relied on her to offer charity to the souls they riled. Her father's son excelled at creating offense in others. So well, and so oft, that she sold some of her mother's belongings to ease the burden he set upon others. He was not the sort who would invest alms when he could resort to intimidation.

As for the attacker, she leaned on her grandfather's simpler logic to make sense of creatures she did not understand. For who could understand a soul that seemed without soul, without proper form, and without good? Another trait she noticed lacking was her attacker's voice. Short of guttural moans and whimpers of pain, he never spoke. Neither she nor Charles learned their attacker's motive or benefactor.

She invited neither handwringing nor navel-gazing. He who attacked intended harm, and she kept no regret over her counterattack. There were enough creatures amid the secondkind who sought to upset and uproot them. Not even she kept the purest heart; elsewise, she would have refused her seat as an overseer.

As for the soul who educated her, he was neither well-read nor a student of learning. In no way did these traits diminish his stature in her eyes, though. He struggled with the secondkind's tongues but learned all the syllables of the firstkind—unlike the countess. She counted so few souls as true and fine, for so few lived up to her grandfather's example. He lived by his heart, and that strength intensified his writings in a way that made him seem still present in the past ten spans without him.

Met Js. James, McCook, and the new Shelbian. Three Shelbians since the sowers' season. This souls' no differ from last two. Suspect I am to meet next afore winter gets. James, McCook want maps of whats' beneath. Theys' so close to our feet theres' spots where the glebe rolls like a snake in me bed. I go to the woods while the moons' up and I wait to see but theys' hidden. How can I ever forget those sounds?

This corresponded with a passage found in her mother's diary that she read aloud to stoke the solemnness around her. "'We heard the cries from beneath the Woods again. They are hollow and weak, yet carry through the walls as an endless chorus that breaks my resolve. I believe that these are children who've no mother and no father to care for them in their sickness. Now, I fear, they have no claim except this twisted glebe to cover them as winter stays longer than afore. I fear what those cries will mean to the babe I carry. Theo reminds me, with indignity, how motherhood turns me foolish.'"

She counted the memory, remembered times when her father dismissed her mother's gentle-heartedness, and let the burden settle upon her heart afore she returned to her grandfather's journal to another earmarked passage.

I ought to have took his head. He is the root to this wickedness. He is the reason that theys' suffered. He swatted them and sent them beneath. I nay'ver ought to have let that majick taint us. I must see Her. I must ask Her to heap the white fire upon our rot. Theo must burn.

TULL & EBBE

She read the same passage four times and still did not glean more than her grandfather's woundedness and contempt for her father. Reformers claimed Yah had cut her off because of her father's magick. Believers claimed Yah would not hear her prayers for she had never descended low enough—common enough—to prove faithful to the Triune. These were not unproven arguments. Even so, at times she wanted to hear the Voice that calmed fears and silenced accusations in other souls.

So, she cycled through the heaps of wisdom her ancestors offered in search of a key to her grandfather's reasoning or the observations kept by father and daughter. The rest she would sift through the mind and heart of a beloved fellow Jacobian who spoke with the tongue of the Ministers and reasoned with the wit of Guardians. All she learned from her grandfather she recited back to him, after all. He seldom forgot a lesson from her lips.

To her delight, he now stood as near as he had since their paths last met at the gate of the church at 707 Little Oak Way on the previous Feast of Hivi'ern. There, he walked with her to lay a wreath of purple hyacinth and larkspur at the foot of her grandfather's copper statue and she kept near to her sweet Jacobian as they visited his father's wooden grave marker—absent of flowers till his bride returned—but in remembrance nonetheless. This tradition was theirs since the ninety-first winter. That tradition rooted Nelson James Tull to her, for she took no other.

"The outfit departed from here this morn afore the moonset. Seven members with no scions or abettors." Rusty Waltman Guild then exhaled with fondness, "A pair of fine stallions in the lot too."

She made no remark to the gruff voice that filled the parlor, but adjusted the lay of her grandfather's journal.

"I warned them they were not to leave except through me and by way of the steam tram."

"Oooo, Rusty. How shameful!"

"We confiscated their weapons with minimal fuss. They—They managed to reclaim them."

TULL & EBBE

No reaction to her words followed for the voice came from a recorded reel that she played upon her personal display plate—a thin slab of glass and copper that relayed data back and forth across the territories.

> "My deputies might have hunted them down for that slight, but some fools saw fit to discharge a salt bomb near the landing."

She doubted ever-boastful Rusty Waltman Guild carried a display plate of his own. Such devices proved the thinness of his boasting.

> "Three souls. The Carpenterian turned over a plank wagon on the soul who set off the bomb. He and the Jacobian rode off whilst the crowd turned on the wounded."

This made her lean nearer to the device as she twisted at the waist and rested breast upon folded arm.

> "Well, I should add that we see this amid the Partakers. They're worse than rabid dogs this deep unto the winter. No imagining how much worse they'll turn afore the thaw. I doubt they find their senses even then!"

The chief inspector kept an array of expressions that suggested some sort of deficiency or lacking acuity. None hinted at regard or compassion for another. He suffered a perpetual nod even as his eyes proved glazed and his jaw slack, but never inspired confidence in his wit. Without a doubt, he was the dullest form of amusement except that which accumulated at his expense.

> "The Jacobian and that—that loud-mouthed Archibaldian—"

The reel whined as he spewed his disdain for Olley Hendrie Falk.

TULL & EBBE

"Chased every soul that tried to chase them. I've never seen such a sight. Two riders versus fifty or sixty."

She believed *the Jacobian* would provoke sixty souls without worry and smiled.

"They out-rode every last soul."

Her laughter shocked the room and seemed to set all rattling objects upon a different course.

"I remain certain that they will obey you, Honored Soul. They suffer the aftershock of their headship's castration."

The judges attempted to castrate the Guardians by naming a Larsonite as their head and made Edmond Anson Elragadó's name a joke amid their chambers.

"No, no! I am certain that the Jacobian will not cross through. I looked him in the eyes. The reports of his softened heart hold true."

Though the intercepted relay told but one-half of the conversation, she who set an attacker on fire chuckled at the law-keeper's certainty surrounding the Jacobian and his heart. In all her seasons, she had never once heard a hint of apology nor an admission of doubt from her fellow overseer and current chief inspector of the Shelby Territory. With his dizzying compulsion toward wrongheartedness, a steady soul might imagine with a proper heart that Guild would be less prone to assumptions of complete misunderstanding. When all else failed, he propped his ego well upon his notion of certainty.

"Why has there been such fear of him evermore? Even in blamelessness, he could not find enough kindness from those whom he needed."

Her breast swelled with a short breath as she purred with disapproval. She dug the nails of her left hand into the pulp of the rich, white tabletop and the other against the glass face of her display plate. Though she tore at the first surface alone, the second pulsed with light through a ripple of color and pressure. Those same hands that held the babe on his first eve never stopped seeking an advantage for him.

TULL & EBBE

The countess drew nearer her private journal and thumbed to an earmarked section that she composed in a contrary manner—from right page to left page and upside down from the binder's setting—to misalign speculation from proof. She glanced at phrases and heavier-written words and felt anger's fire for all she learned. What she committed in ink fell beneath a header: "The Colonel."

"You fear him more than any other, do you not? He's proven you a coward and"—her laughter seeped with annoyance—"I can tell you he's not yet set his intentions against you in full. I have withheld so much from him for your sake."

She then read the last phrase written upon the next page: Lu'qem Atoaen Si'el.

"Perchance I ought to defend you less. Did you delight afore your seven seasons of slumber believing you might set fear upon my heart? Ought I undo your bindings as your foes pray I will? You deserve worse, *Colonel*."

Such a title stood out, for the secondkind had no military. Nor did they observe a chain of command beyond the titles of advocate, guardian, chief inspector, abettor, deputy inspector, and scion. Even a countess bore less authority. Still, given the opportunities her title afforded her, she had learned of a pre-Accession rank. With so many eras afore them, there was still much to learn and revel over.

FOURTEEN

As a chime shook the chief's still image, the countess prodded the neighboring display plate. That display split in two and showed the image of a woman with a radiant glow and stormy eyes who awaited a response. Those same prodding fingers tapped once, and then the chime stopped. The still image of the woman overtook Guild's share and then moved further when a smile spread across olive-hued cheeks.

"My heart leaps!"

Law-writer Celia Freyja Kind Hand drew every breath and word from the Light. "I gave thanks to Yah that you were kept from harm."

Those souls from the lost territory of Damaris spoke with great openness toward their belief and an innocence that kept them from considering that not all shared their devotedness. In that way, she reminded Sondrea of her grandfather's parents, Kistiñe Aroa Itzal and Norman Beau Zeck, who were ardent Reformers. For their memory, Celia earned a covert benefactor who foresaw a time when she and those with similar hearts might serve the secondkind.

"You remain unharmed, do you not?"

"All is as you say."

"Yet you sit in a dark room?"

Sondrea ran her thumb beneath the lip of the desktop and activated the overhead lights. She had mourned her mother and reminded once-familiar settings of her ways. She still had much to learn, but could not stay tucked away from the secondkind any longer. Now was the time to begin receiving guests, and few proved more pleasant than Celia.

This change in lighting softened the tones from the relay lens and drew the countess's eye not just toward her friend's smile, but unto a cleft in her chin and dimpled cheeks that seemed too cute for a soul who wanted nothing more than to write the laws and learn of their Creator. "Are we not blessed this beautiful peak? How we learn the greatness of our Creator even in troubling times!"

TULL & EBBE

Sondrea found her use of *we* interesting, as she knew of no troubles in the law-writer's path; minus an identical twin who oft confused eye and mind.

"Forgive me. I've returned from a walk in the snow!"

The countess laughed in a way that repulsed gloom and made her visitor of sorts blush with joy. She too loved the elements but abstained, for obvious causes. Now that another former resident returned to her first home, she counted a way to make time for both. "Your home in Wulfric suits you."

"The northern territories fare better than those . . . beneath."

She flicked her brow in agreement. "I learned to ride my grandfather's colt in a winter like this. He insisted I teach Ligurus to trot without upsetting what he measured as too much snow."

"And you learned?"

Her slight smile proved earnestness and delight.

"I never would have believed another outcome." Celia then hinted, "You adopted the same habit for your own footsteps."

There were few who teased a countess, and fewer who understood her sense of humor well enough to know the time for riling versus tenderness for mending.

"How is Katerena?"

"Gloria keeps watch over her now"—Sondrea then clarified—"from afar."

"As you say!"

The countess of Ebbe Demesne, who admired Guardians and entertained law-writers, brushed away a natural wave of the fiery tresses she inherited from Kistiñe Aroa Itzal. Whatever the true purpose, this characterized a desire to cast tenderer matters from her focus.

"Now that we are nearer to being neighbors, is there more I can do for you? The snow is deep, but not so much that I cannot find a path through should you need me."

"Do not dare! A swarm of Guardians surround me."

"Oh?"

She heard the same lilt of curiosity in the voice of most when she mentioned her tether with the Guardians. From this soul, the sound seemed odd and unexpected.

"I have never met them."

Sondrea grinned as no hint of invitation arose in her mind.

Celia then squirmed. "Zoe Willa Köcsma sought in our eve most recent the curate of Ronald Mikolajczak Kovács. He invited her unto that *church* for their feast."

Tull & Ebbe

"At what cost did this Shelbian's favor come?"

"No alms! She remembered her chit. We await proof, I ought to tell you, but I am told proof is nearer than imagined. She travels with the curate to a nest in the upper Larson Territory. I will seek kindness from Marvin afore the moonset."

No woman in the territories needed further warning to beware kindness from Marvin Elam Katch—*honorable* judge and fellow overseer. On the topic of nests, though, Sondrea believed the law-writer, and their agent, might benefit from suffering those who abhorred all that was upright. Ronald Mikolajczak Kovács and his *church* stood as a feasible benefactor for Sondrea's peculiar attacker. She suspected him of matters that had not yet turned the heads of the judges but considered, again, her Guardian.

"He tells me Rusty still rages!" Celia never slowed. "From what I gathered amid outbursts of laughter, the Archibaldian offended Rusty's eldest son's wit."

"A fruit gnat would offend that soul's wit."

"He is as dim as the eve"—she remained ever considerate—"but his title requires dignity be added even to his dim soul."

No soul in the territories bore a name more appropriate to their character than Law-writer Kind Hand, either.

"I am further told that the soul you favor made an awe-worthy shot with his fabled bow of bronze and spared Gustus's seed. His reputation echoes the deeds of your grandfather."

"The soul spared?"

"Cora mends well. Her mother riles those who keep the Church of the Fallen Star to protest but Gustus shows honor. We *do* see to the needs of the weary too."

The words felt less like a barb than a reminder of decent roots.

"The Reformers will hush Magdalena's rampage."

Charity. Purpose. Rescue. The overseers noticed and reshaped all.

"She paraded her daughters, as though our Guardians deprived them from harm."

"Let us leave that inciter to Burghardt."

Celia shrugged. "I am told that the incident has deepened Cora's slumber."

"She dreams?"

"By Burghardt's word." Her eye followed the flick of Sondrea's brow. The law-writer then turned pensive and sought the corners behind her afore she furthered their discussion. "You read the transcriptions?"

TULL & EBBE

"I thank you, yes." She was not ungrateful. "I destroyed them, as you requested."

"I kept no doubts. You've seen your brother's hand was not set against you."

She observed no such proof.

"Samuel—Judge Gwynne—stated afore me that Judge Lael served as their eminence. A true Creightonian."

Some of the dampness that seeped from behind Law-writer Kind Hand's ears during their first encounter had since dried. Sondrea remembered that some had been removed with force. Still, she retained her essence. This made the countess see a greater purpose for her fellow overseer than she first conceived. Till then, she found other ways to instruct and encourage.

"Have you received your new acquisition?"

"My relocation has delayed the arrival. I expect all by the next morn."

"Should you see my name on the pages of Lee's journals . . ."

"I will see that you receive those pages with utmost discretion."

"I pray that Noble Joe affords us such discretion." Her shallow breath replenished her glow. "Have you spoken with Cyril?"

"Not as of yet."

"As you say." Her glow dimmed. "I shall pry no further."

She never committed to meaningful conversation except face-to-face. Sondrea respected that portion of her character.

"Should matters change . . ."

"I thank you, truest Celia."

Law-writer Kind Hand vanished from the display plate and she who received her call leaned back in a chair that exceeded her need for a sitting place. Her friendship with the vibrant and belief-saturated Damari proved a delight. The departing mention of certain men—certain in all their ways, if not their morals—dizzied her mind, though, and she looked toward the windows of the parlor as if to find a certain soul lurking as she sifted all the matters in her time.

"You taught me to mind my time, as Grandfather taught you, Mama."

The countess of Ebbe Demesne tapped the display plate that kept Chief Guild's image in place. From an array of options that dissolved her fellow overseer, she chose a method that would relay her voice to her succorer wherever she might reside upon the plot.

"Dory, where is Mim?"

Tull & Ebbe

"I've not checked beneath the furniture nor the shrubs for a sign of him."

"I sent him to warm the horses at the top of the peak and have not heard his grumbling since."

"Shall I seek him?"

"I believe I can imagine what keeps him."

"Shall I send him to you if I *do* see him?"

"If you believe you can convince him to acknowledge you."

"I'll attempt no undue exertions. Wilfred has asked again when you will receive him. He is—"

"He is promised no invitation; least of all to my father's home." She searched the gaps beneath the doorways for signs of shadows that fled afore she recognized their shape. "Are you near?"

"I . . . am not. Need I be?"

When she rose, a noticeable limp hindered her gentle gait. Even after thirty-five spans, her elegance remained, and not due to the ease of her time. She observed darkness as oft as she chased darkness, but she retained joy and hope. Whilst not comparable to the abundance that Celia cast, she felt a weight lift from her neck and shoulders equal to the stress that certain souls applied.

Such stress arrived on the heels and faces of trusted souls, and she counted the many eyes that lurked around the plot afore she fastened every curtain in the parlor. This habit, her mother instilled in her. Shelbians were not a moral lot. Their decency drifted like the loose snow on the wind.

Within her, she heard her father's shrill laugh and a reminder that Shelbian habits were her habits too. She never denied as much. She also never sought counsel or aide from those with the local blood. Too many foul ends and unchangeable regrets plagued this territory. Unlike most, she found a temporary means to reduce their plague.

Once she fastened the last curtain, she pushed back a copper shield on a cylindrical tube that stood in the northeast corner of the parlor and freed beams of interrupted light. The morn and the peak escaped her as she spent much time with her work. Her limp, the Shelbian curse, and the grip of time were no match for her mind. Not even her succorer's impatience kept her from her intentions for her flaws or the fast-approaching eve.

"Countess?"

TULL & EBBE

"I am to remain undisturbed. When the moon rises above the persimmon tree that marks the deer trail, I want you to fetch the most handsome Jacobian you'll find. He'll answer to the name of Nelson James Tull and none other."

"As you say."

The countess laughed at the emptiness in her succorer's voice, for she found Dory's lacking interest in the Guardians strange, letting pass her many other peculiarities. In a lie's stead for her response, she ended her relay. "I thank you."

Lest her grandfather's reeve—who served her mother afore and now served her—lurked beneath the furniture, the countess resided in true seclusion behind locked doors and drawn curtains. Only then did she cloak every journal with deceptive covers and set them on shelves in a pattern that made sense to her. In her mind, however, she believed in a soul who might detect her pattern and follow her lead if she could not advance her many interests. For him, she lived beneath the burden of many eyes and towed more secrets than a soul ought.

The arrangement of journals wore masked covers that spelled out his mother's family name. Those she set in every eleventh and nineteenth position from the top shelves down and from her surer right side. Eleven marked the moon and nineteen the count of risings and settings beneath that moon—upon which they—she and Tull—were born. Since she developed a mind for such puzzles in him, that had stood as her manner of hiding her secrets in open settings meant for him to discover. With this peak counted, forty-four unsolved puzzles remained across the territories of the eighty-four she set for him.

"But"—her voice lacked breath—"I am preparing you."

She then focused preparations on the display plate affixed to the cylindrical mending chamber that belonged to her departed mother—of whom she shared the same stature but surpassed in shape—and prepared for the first of her three prescribed sessions beneath the Frail Dove. The regimen came preloaded by the courtesy of another overseer whom she cherished as a sister. That dear soul would monitor all the countess's vitals from another facility and kept an override should there be trouble.

"Truly! You'll forgive me this change." Because she felt displeased about the prospect of a new wrinkle on her brow, she added another five ticks to the pre-arranged restorative process. "O, to have the everlasting beauty of the Damari or the undisturbed slumber of the Westonians!"

TULL & EBBE

She then paused between the buckles she unfastened from her gown and remembered a detail about her attacker, whose fiery departure—and the dousing of that fire—agitated her limp.

"I cannot imagine you've ever required a swim within our fish tanks though I do wonder how you mend." She then resumed her work on the next buckle. "Believe I have my grandfather's interest in beasts I ought to avoid, but I would welcome the chance to learn more about you, and not just why you sought to end me. That answer does rise to the heap, though."

Her thick gown fell from her arms and she sought her reflection in the chamber's unspotted glass lining.

"Say, also, that I do this to see if you'll make another attempt at me."

With her dare spoken and the chamber prepared, the countess set foot inside and positioned her feet away from the faucets that injected the recuperative gels and breathable fluids. The glass sheath enclosed her, and she fastened a porcelain disc fitted with eight piercing needles against her svelte abdomen.

"Last"—she shook as their barbed ends found familiar perches in the underlying musculature—"breath."

Those secrets she kept—of overseers, journals, certain souls, and wrinkles—faded as she fell idle beneath the cradle of the apparatus that lifted her off her feet to cleanse her of all ailments. Her identifier beacon then relayed her status. As light and gel cascaded over her and cast the parlor in copper light, she kept open her light-matching irises and watched for her shape-changing attacker as she imagined a certain Jacobian doing the same. He, too, proved welcome in her time of mending.

FIFTEEN

The 8th Eve beneath the Moon of the Mother's Song
The 107th Winter Season of the Accession
In the Care of the Helper, who keeps souls from fruitless wandering.

In the darkest moment of the eve—just afore the moon rose above the trees—the outfit gathered at their camp and kept from the windows of Ebbe Demesne. Tull, who finished his patrol without incident and explained to Edmond his *accord* with Mim, settled last. As such, he dined last. Still, the headship proved he was not unkind, for he preserved the best of biscuits and an extra serving of sweet potatoes for he who understood their present locale the most.

With the iron trap destroyed by she who rescued him from the Behemót Woods, and nothing more than his account and the markings on his trouser leg and boot as evidence, Tull bore no interest in vengeance. Harlan, on the other hand, mingled fearlessness with an appreciation for the laws of the Triune and the judges and plotted to ensnare the meddling reeve with the devices the outfit kept at their disposal. The attack was little more than a sour greeting—a greeting Tull admitted he earned in some unremembered way. Still, Harlan proved protective of the brood and thirsty for an encounter of his own with Mim.

For as long as the Guardians were in the territory, the Shelbians would rile them, but Mim's taunts toward Tull dated back further than the Jacobian counted. Edmond and Harlan conferred that their own necks fared safer without an outsider's meddling and dismissed Tull from their plot. Clever though he might prove, sooner or later, Mim would stumble into a trap. Till then, Tull satisfied intrusive doubts and dodged barbs from those who considered their efforts better spent south of the Loy.

While Tull fed, Olley loaded an embarrassment of provisions into his satchel, that he might take the next patrol with Harlan to avenge his own shame, and sought counsel from the outfit's slowest eater. Tull's habits—one of chewing a bite umpteen times, the other of not speaking with food in his mouth—grated even his truest friend. The soul raised on formality and privilege forced patience into his arsenal. Even so, Tull seemed to enjoy his meal more than any glutton.

"As you say."

"Truly, Nelson, such time has passed that I no longer recall my last words to you."

Tull looked at his next bite, then to Olley. The pleading eyes won out over the alluring scent of vanilla, and the Jacobian relaxed his feeding hand. "A direct ascent toward the Loy proves wasteful. This time of season, a patch of ice will steal your step and cast you headlong unto the basin."

"Once the"—Olley seized Tull's hand and kept the next bite away—"moon clears the lower forests, we'll have a better view of the ice fields. Will we not?"

"Not with the light of a half-spent moon."

"Better you travel away from the Loy first and return there at the moonset."

Tull bent toward his next mouthful and nodded in agreement with George.

"The winds will come from the bluffs this eve. Even a common fool will smell Harlan's liniment afore you can see whether he lies in wait. Better we come from the side of the Loy and avoid detection was my point."

Tull crammed in a second mouthful as he shrugged off unnecessary clarification.

"Remember that we sit beneath the same moon that saw the churning tide that took Gierig from your territory's shoulder, Olley."

The hungry Guardian then nodded, as if George spoke what was on his mind.

"I thank you, George."

"Forgive me, my friend. I believe you addressed Nelson and do not wish to be counted as one who speaks in an unwelcome way."

"In this lot? You needn't fret."

Their first moonrise in the Shelby Territory proved the only spectacle other than an oddity of malicious icicles and a chorus of screams that bore no rational explanation. Blinding snow proved a deterrent and an agitator and kept the outfit away from fire as they sought every track's path afore the weather erased proof of travelers. Olley refilled Tull's cup and then George's. Asham knelt, jiggled his empty cup at his Archibaldian thorn, and made Tull protect his plate.

"Get a look . . ."

Olley reassured George. "See?"

TULL & EBBE

Edmond and even Ganix noticed from afar, or they noticed the way that Asham leapt to his feet, but the approach of another on soft and uneven steps did not provoke them or startle George. Olley applied a visual once-over, then refilled his tin mug as if disinterested. This tell informed Tull that his friend found their visitor gentle on his eyes, yet too haughty for his ego to get caught playing the admirer. He wondered how long afore a soul close to their host appeared; reeves and hands uncounted.

Even as Tull swallowed a bite of mingled starches, he used his fork to pry the strap off the knife in the sheath on his boot. Ganix moved in the distance and then vanished from sight whilst Edmond kept still. Olley prodded the nearest fire, but he held to the stick as flame crept toward his hand and supplied him with a torch. George needed no weapon, and Asham served as a decoy when he sprang onto the path so fast that he forced their visitor to cast a spiced breath that confused her visage.

"Is this your assailer?" Olley heckled with a soft breath.

A woman who hid mulled rose-colored hair—frosted at the tips, but dark near the roots—stood in the shaped light behind a kettle lantern. Her smooth face drew attention to a long, narrow nose and pointed lips that showed her disapproval. The lantern light bore no reflection in her eyes, but she still seemed bothered, and never slowed her step as the moment neared when she would either stop shy of the foursome or prod one from her way. A keen eye observed the swell of Olley's chest and the flex of his musculature as she angled onto a direct path toward him.

"Are you the Jacobian called Tull?"

Asham laughed loudest; which offended their visitor more than the soul she mistook for the very soul that sat at her immediate right. Olley let his friend enjoy another bite of supper and agitated the asker with a slow sip from his cup.

"Need you the time to remember?"

"I am . . . an Archibaldian."

Slim-shouldered and cinched at the waist, she went measured by the eye of him who she approached first, though her nostrils rose as Ganix crept nearer. Then the tip of her nose turned from the next flirtatious Guardian who drew a seat between Olley and George with a none too subtle brush of her draped sleeve. A plume of objectionable breath, like a wheat field in the gathering season, escaped her lips and flowed across Tull's crown; for she stood almost as high as he who perched on an overturned log. She dismissed intrusive Asham with an unimpressed flick of her brow. "You are not who I seek."

TULL & EBBE

His mouth all but vanished from his face. "Why would you say that?"

Her retort burst from her nostrils with an amused fierceness.

Afore she offended George, the soul she sought put aside his plate. "*I* am Tull."

Her nose and brow scrunched when she looked on him, but her pupils bore no response of pleasure for her success.

"Fourth Guardian from the Jacoby Territory"—he tossed the apple to George—"The sole grandson—"

"The sole grandson"—Asham intercepted the apple and interrupted long enough to earn another glance—"of Judge Juanita Jane James"—he then flung the apple—"the only fruit of Kara Doe Nelson and Patrick James Tull . . ."

"And"—Olley caught the errant throw—"the slowest eater in the northern territories." He then struck Asham with the fruit. "His grandmother was Judge Juanita *Gene* James, you dullard."

Tull flung his last bite at Olley and struck.

The latter brushed his vest clean. "Will you tell us who you are now?"

Their visitor held a sash to blindfold Tull and calmed Olley with her disregard. "You are to let me take you into the manor."

"Even blindfolded and spun"—he stood two heads taller than her height—"I could find my way to the inner parlor or the food bin without a guide."

"You make yourself a target for our enemies. You will not shame your host nor tell of the pathways to the place where I lead you."

Tull gauged her mettle by the breadth of her mouth, which held that same dissatisfied sneer over his debate. He trusted in Ministers and friends, then he shut his eyes and stooped to claim the apple that struck Asham. He tossed the fruit to George and turned toward her for she seemed to protect her forearm and wrist.

"My arms reach. You needn't boast your height or infer that I am incapable."

He made no comment about her arms but his grin riled a soul.

Her breath smelled of spiced leaves when she huffed, and her hands proved cold and strong as she tied the blindfold as if a noose. She removed and flung the knife from his boot sheath onto his plate, then seized his elbow and used her full weight to maneuver his first step. "I'll guide you. Play the buffoon or behave like your friend, and I'll deliver you in tatters."

Tull drank down his cup—somehow immune to the heat. In his soberest, calmest voice, he prodded her well. "Lead on."

TULL & EBBE

"Wait!" Olley called out, and another minted breath clouded Tull. He removed a dirty rag from a hind pocket but tucked a hiltless blade beneath the Jacobian's belt, at the small of his back, and away from her line of sight. He then patted his backside. "Behave now."

"I thank you."

Her eyes proved dull in Olley's presence and she shunned him the way she neglected George; an absolute refusal to look on him. "If your friend approaches me again, I will take his knees from him."

"His ankles prove weaker." When he sensed from her breath that she faced him, he shrugged. "You seem to favor your step, too."

"Tull? You seek Tull in my stead?"

"You offend your host Guardian."

"Do not delay me. The countess expects my prompt return with her guest."

Tull sighed.

"Need I remind you of my provenance? I alone deserve—"

"You alone?" Olley interrupted Ganix when he took Tull's turn to speak.

The high belt that cinched Tull's guide's waist squeaked with stiff newness, still unlearned to her shape, as the temperature constricted the material further than the laces. In this, he gave a reason for her agitated breaths and used the durations to determine how near or far another stood to them as his fellows bickered. Then, her belt creaked away from a huff out of Ganix that bore the stench of soured leeks and bitter walnuts and made her squeeze Tull's arm for leverage.

"You do not lead us, Ganix."

"I demand that I enter—"

"Not above your host's wishes."

Tull smirked at his guide's *salt* for she silenced Olley and Asham.

"Stand away from me.

"You do not want to rile me."

"Stand away from me, lest I open your belly for keeping me from my purpose."

"You do not *dare* rile—"

"You tow no invitation here, Shelbian."

Ganix roared and cast spittle from his lips with a stout breath. "I am Barton Blinken Ganix, first Guardian of this territory! You will show me the proper due."

"I am sent for this Jacobian—not a *Guardian*." She wiped his spittle on Tull's sleeve.

TULL & EBBE

A bent knuckle prodded Tull's chest. "I warn you, Tull, you show me my due. You refuse the invitation, and send me in your stead or I will ruin—"

Ganix's breath and voice halted with such swiftness that Tull wondered if the woman made good on her threat. He smelled an oiled blade and then the aged and nervous sweat that oft soured Ganix's outer garments.

"Who do you believe you are?"

"Why would I obey you this third time? Stand away from me. Truly! I will not say this again."

The sound of spitting preceded the tightened hold upon Tull's forearm that led him onward. Then Ganix's wheeze soured Tull's next breath.

She hissed so low that both Guardians took a collective step from her.

A brunt arm struck Tull's back and a shrill sound of retreat signaled the confrontation's end. "Edmond? Edmond! I have a grievance."

The headship groaned over Ganix's newest gripe. "As much I gathered."

Though jostled, Tull did not fall from being struck as his guide led him. Afore he boasted, tendrils of withered branches swatted his face.

"Speak one word of my measured height, Guardian or not, and I will—"

"Better I kiss a few branches then see the stain of my belly on the snow."

"As you say."

Another branch, then nothing; and then, another branch. Tull groaned, but she who led him delighted.

"I thank you."

"Your kiss means nothing to me."

"Not for the path." He measured and matched her step, but crouched toward her voice. "Few set Ganix in his place with enough certainty to turn an Archibaldian and a Creightonian silent."

"I'll mourn this eve and every moonrise that follows"—her pledge hid a barb—"for I'll know evermore that I stood for a soul who would not stand for his own gain."

His sudden breath spoke to the response on his lips, but a swift inhalation drew back the barb. Whether the blindfold, the setting, or good manners intervened, she never asked. She led him alongside but not within a corridor lined with drapes and windows that let the reflection of sky-fires dance across the tiles underfoot. The walkway appeared like a kaleidoscope, and she kept the Guardian from the sight. Such choices spoke to the temperament of her character.

TULL & EBBE

"We enter your host's home now. Mind your words, your hands, and—once I unbind you—your eyes. I've allowed you to slight me only because I am well-compensated by she who adores you."

Tull swelled beneath the compliment as good humor righted his posture. She tugged him indoors, upon a dense rug and then across cob-faced stone. Designed to massage bare feet, the stones pulled the snow from his boots and produced a grated sound that rose to a height and breadth not greater than Tull's extended arms.

"I tell you I've yet seen a reason for such regard."

"Better you worry over the way Ganix might respond when next he sees you."

Another snort. "An unwashed mutt is an unwashed mutt."

"Larsonite or Creightonian?"

"What?"

"Only a soul from those territories remains so near to an agitated spirit."

"I am on my best behavior, Jacobian."

"Your benefactor does not entrust Shelbians, nor do you bear the skin of those who dwell in the shadow of the mountains and foothills."

"You'll show me the same proper behavior."

"Are you the soul our judges have sent us to protect?"

No wisecrack. Not even a snort. Her next step landed harder, but her hold remained equal and unchanged. Still, no remark.

"You're from the ash fields, are you not?" His curiosity loosened her hold. "The blindfold distracted me, but your last step proved—"

"Proved what?"

"You have an unsure foot, si'sar."

"I am not of your concern."

"But, I am your Guardian. Have you a name?" He leaned as she led him around a bend. "I do make an effort to remember all, letting pass how seldom I see my territory."

"Have I not proven my disinterest by now?"

"Well and beyond." The toe of his boot echoed against stone. He then stepped up a single step unwarned and unguided. "As if disinterest masks your interest."

She offered no rebuttal nor challenged the curve of his upper lip that mimicked his bronze recurve bow. Though he detected the scent of oil again, the jangle of keys proved she held not a knife this time. Then, and because he had too slight a hold on his tongue's restraint, he nudged further.

"That's a trait you and the Archibaldian share."

She stopped in her tracks and let him pass far enough ahead that all her weight failed to stop him. So, she swatted at his head and let the keys graze his hair.

He turned away from her commotion. "You've my attention."

"I have nothing in common with any scarecrow."

"They would not let you dwell along the southern hem with that haughty mien."

"Stand still."

"When my legs were nearer to yours in length"—her sigh met his ear like cursing—"I required forty-four steps west once I stepped up and entered through the garden door, one uncounted upward step, twenty-seven more steps through the breezeway, one more step upward, and—as of your past nine paces, a turn northward. The howls from the atrium make the panes along this walkway chatter, do they not?"

The pitch of laughter startled her enough that she looked toward the atrium's crushed silhouette.

"Three hundred seventy-seven steps!"

She scowled at his wit and appeared ferocious in visage.

"The third-tallest structure in this territory and fifth-most frightening." He then stooped toward her ear, allowing the correct distance and height. "Even whilst blindfolded and distracting you, a scarecrow dares not lose the way. I never could've survived my time in Sanger Lode if I had. That was five thousand seven hundred thirty-three steps with a snarling and bloodied Creightonian who swore she would end me clutching my neck as you clutch those keys."

"Such prowess." She let him sense her nearness. "Yet a lopsided buffoon ensnared you with a trap that no animal would be ignorant enough to approach."

"And you brace when you move." His words fell away but he made her uneasy when he reached between her arm and waist, then turned the knob on the door she unlocked. "Am I to enter afore or behind you?"

She strained but crammed him through the doorway. Given the placement of her hands, between his broadened scapula, he reasoned that she shut the door with a sweep of her foot, and grinned. The winds and terrane along the bluffs of the Jacoby Territory required a well-aimed step. In the past thirteen moons, as many souls met their end because of a non-committed, indolent step.

When the destination greeted them with stifled warmth and dim light, the guide nudged Tull with a splayed hand onto a padded seat—no doubt counted a deep seat to those with legs as short as hers—and kept the sash around his eyes. He made no attempt to remove this as he remained aware of her nearness by fuming exhalations through her nostrils. Once he convinced her of his stillness, she returned to the doorway and shut out the lights and the eavesdroppers. The wind rattled the door, and then rolled down the corridor by the bristled boards within the dividing wall.

"In no way like the haunted houses along the forests near my home. No. Too hollow for a proper startle." He held his sneer. "Plenty of other adventures to be had, though. Plenty of startles too. The canneries unnerve some."

As he embellished his next breath, isolation settled. Far from his home on Appledash Road in the Jacoby Territory and the rooftops of inns in the Carpenter Territory, the Shelby Territory made both neighbors seem further away than they sat. He noted how his guide left the key in the door lock and believed she stoked the fire to her excessive liking—as she never sought to learn of his comfort. An ability to move on silent steps, even with snow melting from the soles, stood as a credit to her character given her misstep out of doors. Her lacking conversational skills and agitated breaths, on the other hand, shouted her physical whereabouts.

Sounds mapped a room he had not visited since his blamelessness. Still, he remembered what did not change. He remembered how the daughter of Beau Itzal Zeck managed the fire on another eve that cast him at odds with Mim and unto trouble. He remembered, too, how Maia Espe Zeck's daughter kept him near till he found slumber in a similar chair and near the sound of her heart.

He remembered that this wing held five oblong rooms. He sat in the first, the parlor, which was of equal size to the last room, which served as a dominant bedroom. The rooms between were smaller. The nearest and second-furthest shared the fireplace and kettles of the end rooms. The room in the center, which proved of an irregular size—smaller than the outer rooms, larger than the neighboring rooms—served as the dressing room of the countess of Ebbe Demesne.

The chime of glass made him reopen his eyes and the rising flames teased his eye from beneath the blindfold and mingled with the shimmer of marbled light that reminded him of the sallow beams cast from a mending chamber. Outside the chamber houses designed for mending, those who afforded personal chambers oft held titles like Advocate and Reformer. Most souls could not afford the maintenance regimen—even if they understood the workings of the chamber—or the medical staff required for the chamber's operation. Still, the light made an unmistakable influence on the room due to the recuperative gels within the glass-and-copper chamber.

Then, all ornery playfulness ceased as he felt a hand rummage through his pockets. What trinkets remained in his care, minus Olley's lent knife, were items that never fell from his reach till the hand turned the claim untrue. He blamed his guide for removing the journal and two cherished photographs he kept therein as well as a pre-Accession campaign medal. Anxiety surged at the sense of separation and his heartbeat rose above the sound of dripping water—as if a body arose from a calm pool—as his agitation surfaced.

"Believe that I will take the hand from your wrist, si'sar, should the slightest harm come to what you've taken from me."

SIXTEEN

His guide slapped his mouth with what felt like the journal afore she created a flicker of shadow between the two warring light sources at her back. "Now hear my threat: Try to peek, and I will gouge out your eyes with what trinkets I've let you keep."

The mint of incensed smoke, not perfumed but boiled, adorned her gloating scoff. He wriggled his nose, as if he found her pungent, and she surrendered her advantage when she stepped back toward the fire. No doubt she preferred the fire after time spent out of doors—not to retrieve him, but to sneak a cigarette ahead of her duties. She looked down her nose at the outfit well, wanted them to consider her their better, but the façade fell like those droplets that returned to the tub behind him when confronted by true prestige. Tull learned that about her from listening to the measured change in her breath.

"He returned to camp last and ate with such devotion that I dared not stand too close. His elder approved of his visit."

No response reached Tull's ear, and no sound of motion hinted where his host stood but the powdery-sweet scent of clematis terniflora replaced the stench of boiled leaves.

"His trousers are torn at the ankle and he carried these with him."

Then a laugh as faint as a flicker of light gave way to an affectionate purr that sounded like building thunder. "I oft imagine what became of the frightened children in this photograph. The fairer of us grew to be even more pleasing."

Tull's guide scoffed at her benefactor's flattery.

A certain touch smoothed the hair on Tull's head made unkempt with a swipe of keys. "I instructed Dory to approach the most handsome amid all the faces that she discovered out of doors. To whom did she go first?"

He drew a hesitant breath.

Now she stroked his ear lobe. "Tell me anyway."

"If I am to s'pose the name of my guide, then she went to Olley." He cocked his jaw, but Dory snorted in defeat of his honesty. "I prove accustomed to such slights."

TULL & EBBE

"O, you displease me, Dory Orlean Sevilla!" The sound of fanning photographic paper mimicked a nervous heart. "Never have I admired the Archibaldian. Or his chin. Or his bluster. Or his preening."

"You've not seen him in his waxed moustache."

Airy laughter preceded her words. "Long have I proven biased toward sparkling, pewter eyes."

That voice, rich with warmth and confidence, exceeded Dory's in every way. Warm, without a need for fire. She spoke with a dignified timbre—less arrogant than the local accent, and more refined than the trained habits of Archibaldians. Hers was as unflawed to Tull's ear as any sound in the secondkind's range.

"As you've traveled here, you must say. How did you avoid the Behemót Woods?"

"We traveled through the rut in her belly."

"Then you proved you have no fear."

"I proved I am no longer blameless."

"Truly!" A sound like unfurled fabric whispered beneath the crackling fire and then she let out another purr that jilted the briskness of two ends of fabric overlapping each other. "My cherished guest and I are not to be disturbed."

"Till?"

Sondrea's brow arched as she turned her full attention from the view onto her succorer. Her musculature and profile never changed, and she proved who asked and who answered between them.

"Yes, Countess. I'll remain keen till you beckon."

"You'll tell Mim that I am beyond displeased by his antics. As he likes to play out of doors so well, he's to stay the eve in the millpond house away from our provisions. Those are *my* orders."

"Yes, Countess."

For the first time, Dory's shoes squeaked as she departed, which made Tull admire his hostess even more. Then he heard the door latch and the lock set.

"Why do you grin?"

"The reason escapes me."

"I honored your birth beneath our former moon."

"As I honored yours."

"At my age, I needn't be locked away alone with sweet cake." The drum of fingers against a hollow torso told another tale.

TULL & EBBE

"I imagined you'd say as much, so I ate two cakes." The way she sighed made Tull sit prouder than the compliment over his eyes.

"You were the smallest creature I ever saw when first I saw you." Her sigh spoke of her heart. "Still you carry my grandfather's memento to you. I'll not ask if you've deciphered his last words to you nor pretend you've come seeking my help with the translation. How many words have you . . ."

"Five." Keep, brother, from, my father.

"One more than the last time."

He studied the tongue of the firstkind for ten spans but failed to translate the full nine-word challenge Sondrea's grandfather made to him in the final ticks of his time.

"Nelson . . ."

He smelled the nearness of her scent, then the chair creaked as she added her weight onto his. Warmth and dampness remained on flesh as soft as her sigh as she teased his cheek with her form. Then she pushed against him till the sound of her heart deepened and her nudeness was proven unto he who sat blindfolded. The marbled light from the chamber flickered as she rested her proverbial near his knees, faced toward him, and tucked her grandfather's gift of a worn campaign medal into the pocket of his undervest afore she rested her brow upon his.

"When you say to a soul, 'Soon, I'll see you,' oft does that soul expect you to uphold your word." Her lips grazed his as she spoke, and she shifted at her hips till her arms draped over the shoulders of Guardian and chair. "She does not expect to retrieve you after six moons in your absence."

His host shifted onto her left arm till she saw his features well enough to pinch his chin. The Triune gifted the Second Creation beyond measure when They created Countess Sondrea Ebbe Conliffe, but her ways toward Tull confused many. She doted over him with a superiority that crushed souls who could not compete against her; not that he oft let other souls so close for fear of losing her approval. Even so, he prayed for a calm heart and obedient resolve as she ran her hand along his chest and shoulder.

"I could have Mim ruined if the Kuusa Si'epä touched you."

"They did not harm me."

Her copper irises watched his mouth as she moved close enough that he could again feel the softness of her lips. "You are in no pain?"

TULL & EBBE

"The chair proves soft." He withheld too, confident that she understood that he, too, counted as a soul who could not compete against her. he corrected his posture to uncomfortable rigidity and let her feel enough of a bounce that she understood his strength as well as his restraint. "Shallow cushioned."

Sondrea laughed as though amused, then swung her proverbial back, till her fingertips squeezed his knees and she dropped to his feet. When he remained peace-filled, she turned toward the mending chamber tucked into an alcove and mounted atop a slide-out cart with a polished brass gear train. As she rose, she plucked from a polished lever her discarded robe and covered her form with an expression of disappointment.

"I heard your appeal against reclamation of Forgney Bridge at Holly Landing."

After she set the trio of buckles, she circled her guest.

"You made our territory proud."

No other soul in the territories cast a shadow upon her, though a mural of the first four Guardians tried. She smiled at their ever-watchful faces, and unknotted the blindfold her succorer put on their heir. "I heard whispers of your sighting there."

Tull reached for the falling sash and clutched afore his vision focused or his ears determined the direction she moved.

"I would have seen you at Dozier Station Signal House, had the judges granted you a longer stay near Gardner Pointe beneath that same moon. Your weak-chinned fellow had much to say to all who listened about his missing the unveiling of the new observatory lenses. Those of us who attended were all impressed by the sight of, well, no more than the previous lenses showed."

He turned his entire head toward the mural of Guardians that once mesmerized and intimidated him but offered less than a glance afore his pewter irises rested upon his well-formed and dizzying hostess.

"I resisted the sweet cakes there too."

He reserved for her a smile that made her flutter for her next breath.

"I believed I honored my grandmother when I named a soul from our Taft Bluffs as my succorer."

He snarled and a grin creased her face from the nostrils down and her copper irises sparkled as she looked upon his complete face. Sondrea purred as she rushed and straightened the lay of his balaclava with blatant pride. "How I have missed you! My dearest Guardian,"

TULL & EBBE

In flattery's stead, he spoke of Sondrea's most obvious, yet most unsurprising, trait. "I believe you have outstepped your hitch."

"As you say!" The brightness of her smile exceeded that found in a string of subdermal lights fitted into a porcelain sheath that held together the countess's left femur and remained visible through flexible webbing, flesh, and the absorbent fabric of her robe. "The moments we miss whilst you're proving you're no longer blameless."

For seven spans and uncounted missed moments, she withheld the cause of her injury from him. He learned six conflicting accounts of how the countess suffered a strike that made tissue and bone erupt beneath the force. All reminded him that he did not keep safe the soul who once kept him.

"At long, long last!"

His heart rushed and his core tightened as she fanned away the hem of her robe and bared her hip and leg to him from waist to toes. Not presented as an offering or to gather more interest than he devoted by now, rather, to let him see the lights ripple as she kneaded the overlying tissue with her fingertips. Like a droplet of rain into a puddle, the pressure of her touch drowned as the light turned still. She flexed onto the ball of the foot, accentuated the muscle, and let her knuckles hold back the robe as her other hand patted the smooth face of the room's mending chamber, which repaired an injury that ought to have cost her the limb.

"Oft have I wondered how my grandfather might have led us had he the benefits I've enjoyed." The fabric slipped from her knuckles and hid her adornments as talk of Beau Itzal Zeck softened her. "I tell you, our souls would have prospered in uncounted ways had he accepted such advancements."

Tull nodded in sympathetic agreement, yet his eye returned to Zeck's visage on the northern wall, even as he set the entrusted campaign medal into the proper pocket of his coat. The canvas stood four-fifths of his hostess's height and every bit as long as her if she stretched upon the floor with her arms extended over her head. Tull knew each subject.

"Since your blamelessness, you see those faces and forget your words." She teased him with a twist of her figure that went unnoticed.

"Oft do I search the shadows and hilltops for sight of him."

"As do I!" Her smile cast away shadows. "Such a habit steadies me."

He who now bore the burden of a Guardian, towed regret that his blamelessness kept him from learning Zeck's ways or better defending his hero's granddaughter.

TULL & EBBE

"You have regrets of your time with him." Graciousness and anger flared in her. "All might show your regard if Eidolon Pictures echoed the tale of their ancestors."

When Eidolon Pictures made their film about the four Guardians, they cast Danele Gertie Zuriñe, Tull's mother's favorite thesp, to portray Sondrea's mother. In the act that tore apart the countess's father and grandfather, Danele performed the lone, lengthy nude scene of her thirty-seven-film career and humiliated those who showed Tull kindness.

"Truly! I hope you, my Guardian, never learns."

Spans after the role catapulted her unto success, the thesp lamented that Controller Gary Adamson Clark sullied Maia's name, declared her role in bolstering the offense, and made an overt plea for forgiveness. Whilst Reformers touted her repentance, admirers turned on the near-flawless thesp and cast their affections upon Maia's daughter, who showed grace but withheld forgiveness from the soul who made other souls believe the worst about her mother for gain.

"This I tell you, that letting pass how Henry Eugene Forster dressed when he portrayed him, and those uncounted artists who depicted him, my grandfather towed no more than a passing appreciation for indigo fabrics."

He looked upon his hostess, who hovered near his shoulder with a sly grin upon her face. His reaction pleased her, and a smile brimmed till her eyes sparkled and her nose crinkled. She then squeezed Tull's shoulders and kissed the top of his head. The soul born of noble lines and magick-wielders charmed the Guardian as no other ever had across the lands—variant times—in which he dwelled.

"Mama told me that Papa had this painting moved here because he *feared* that my grandfather watched him through the canvas." She let the force of her voice tickle his ear. "I've oft wondered if the real reason had more to do with the fact that the artist painted him with a mad shimmer in his eye!"

This time Tull laughed, and she smacked his chest without rounding his chair.

"You must agree!" She dragged her nails as though she petted him. "You remembered this plot well?"

"I remembered the tree where Mim threw hatchets but had forgotten the sounds from the millpond. My ear is drawn to the creak and grind that provides current. Edmond enjoys the sound, though Ganix complains."

"I've never related well to Guardian Elragadó, apart from our both dressing well, and I've oft doubted that Guardian Ganix's heart grieved for another. As I've never *met* Guardian Vosburg, I imagined I ought to seek counsel from a soul whose sweetness toward me never wavered."

"Harlan's favorite topics are the interwoven threads within our laws, fruit wines, apiculture, and the hot wells protected by the Ice Clans on Greely Mountain. He dislikes speak of progress."

"I'll leave you to enjoy or avoid such talk. You'll leave me to deal with Mim."

He bristled with embarrassment and realized how she used the same tone on him that Dory suffered. "You needn't protect me."

"You will let me deal with my reeve in my way if you seek to learn the favor I ask of my Guardian."

The countess offered back the belongings that Dory swiped as if a treaty between them. He took back his keepsakes without protest and returned them to his coat pocket. So, the reunion defined them. While he fussed with keepsakes, she sat upon a tufted lounger and drew her bare feet off the floor, but savored the sight of him as she awaited his direct stare afore she delivered on her word.

"I ask you, Nelson, and no other, to learn if my husband has arranged for my end."

An Historic Cruel Memory

An Interim

The 21st Eve beneath the Moon of the Reaching Sea

The 92nd Sowing Season of the Accession

In the Mercy of Yah, who gives the rain, the seed, and the bloom.

In a scant gown that no daughter ought to wear in her father's sight, and no fruit-bearing woman ought to flaunt afore a blameless soul, Sondrea felt jarred from slumber as lightning pierced glass. Her heart pounded through every portion, doubled at her ears, and made her limbs tingle. Even in piqued agitation, grogginess of wit slowed comprehension of time and place. Peculiar colors bled from the shadows, and every sound reached pain-filled heights and muddled lows.

The magick-wielder's daughter suffered his manipulation afore. Now, her spirit proved resistant. As singed attire proved, she was no longer the tear-filled innocent who witnessed her father's pillage of her mother's wit. Neither was she the heartsick novitiate who begged him not to ruin her first love's mind for the sake of his own pride. And, nor was she the fool who still believed he sought amends for his mistreatment.

The putrid-green hues of light that flooded Ebbe Demesne washed over her with tendrils of lightning that burned her gown and stung her flesh like hornets. Beads of sweat crept like slow-moving spiders delivering the poisoning awareness of impending harm that produced a field of goose-pebbles across her body. This was not a sense of harm to self or mind. Rather, she believed that her soul would soon suffer irreparable and excruciating abuse far worse than his magick.

"Papa, I beg you—please—you must!"

"Hmmm?" He never looked up from his journal.

"Papa!"

A blot of ink spoiled the page and produced a flutter in his cheek as he bared his upper teeth. His pale eyes moved as if too heavy to lift and savored her as if she were not of his tree at all. "My! You bring to my mind the allure of your mother when first I set my eye upon her true self."

"Papa"—Sondrea's wearied voice towed a rattle of frustration over his infuriating lack of respect for her heart as much as his lust-filled responses—"I need you to listen to me."

"What was that verse she oft recited?"

Sondrea's shoulders fell, as the strap of her gown followed, and her defeated sigh teased her breast with warmth.

"Say that verse to me now and I will hear you!"

"'Yah, our perfect Creator, makes war in my name . . . so I must keep still.'"

The magick-wielder giggled that same frustrating, infantile cackle that defeated Maia Espe Zeck and soured his regard for daughter, bride, and Creator.

Every muscle turned rigid with disgust till she dug her nails into the palms of her hands to keep her mind sharp. "Papa!"

With an agitated twist of his hand, the once-praised Guardian tightened a bolt of violet-hued lightning around his firstborn daughter and sprang from his perch without breaking the tendrils of magick. He looked her over in a way that a predator admired their prey and circled unafraid while she could only follow with her eyes. Though not enough to injure, an overload of humiliation between them would endure till such a time when she calmed to his measure of approval.

TULL & EBBE

"As I look on you, I see now"—he traced a line with a sharp nail till he irritated the skin beneath the gown from the nearest side of her navel to the furthest in a procession as the clock turns—"now I see. You are not a fit rearer at all."

Sondrea's ears rang with the burrowing sound of his concocted trespass and vile barb.

"His soul is better without you."

"Papa . . . I beg you!" A tear fell as she resisted his magick, but his hold proved too great. "Do not speak such words."

"'Do not speak such words?' You are your mother."

Her musculature shook and the threads that created seams unraveled a stitch at a time as the tendrils of lightning coiled. She wanted to scream out, for she remembered how oft he humiliated her mother with the same trick; evermore in front of another who did not deserve to look upon her. Evermore on a whim to turn two souls to shame.

"Your purpose here is finished?"

Sondrea's eyes widened as she discovered her cruel father spoke to an unseen soul and she struggled against perceived shame. The light of the parlor distorted the shape of he who stood behind her, though her father's eyes reflected the soul's whereabouts.

"Mind your elder, poi'kai."

"We have him."

Sondrea heard but did not recognize the coarse voice.

"We now take guardianship."

"Marvelous!" The count of Ebbe Demesne proved alit with a playful smile and batted his eyes at Sondrea afore the color left his cold irises. He then loosened the bind of one arm, that she might cover her breast.

With a tormented heart and a clenched left fist, she sought to strike her father in modesty's stead. The chill on her skin mingled with sweat and the intensified colors of the parlor met the intention of violence like brushstrokes on a canvas. She would take her revenge over her father's betrayals. Except, a stern hand restrained her fist and jostled her away from his blindside.

"I tell you, si'sar, you are not favored by this."

None—in that time—defied Cameron Lou Fenner, first to take up Randolph Hereford Wylie's purpose in the name of the Archibald Territory and the new headship amid Guardians. He who isolated her fist and full arm without the amount of effort she imagined showed no regard for her shame. Air passed from his nostrils with the same ease that fueled her father's smile, and his jaw relaxed till the count's cackle extended the field of goose-pebbles from his daughter's skin then across Cam's forearm too.

"I needn't remind you of your—"

"This is my family's home, Guardian"—she saw his heavy, battle-worn eyelids open and credited the steadiness in her voice when he released her hand and let her correct her gown—"where my mother reared me beneath the blessings of a patient and wrathful Creator. Do not dare to speak to me of where I belong."

He who led the Guardians took a patient breath but not a customary or docile step back from her. "By the arrangement of your weddedness, you are to reside in the Archibald Territory in the home provided to you by your husband—my judge."

"A husband is a soul who loves and cherishes his bride. A husband—like a father—provides and nurtures and protects his beloved and sets her needs above his own. I haven't a husband. I am kept in a jar by a greedy collector."

"Letting pass your claim, he expects you back in the territory by morn. You, and not the orphan."

"You haven't the weapons to tear him from my arms."

"I needn't weapons." Cam held up a brass ring oft seen on a reeve's hip. "I had the key to your bed chamber."

"Papa!" Again and again the count tormented her.

Behind Cam, another passed through the doorway with the blameless soul that Sondrea cared for in tow. Though she looked pleasant, she had a reputation for vileness that ruined many plans.

TULL & EBBE

As proof of her well-earned reputation, whilst the blameless soul remained still, she who held him bit his soft cheek till he shook with pain. This made Sondrea lunge, against magick's harm to flesh and spirit, to keep him from further hurt.

"Nelson!"

The blindfolded soul's crying ceased, and he reached in the direction of her voice.

"If you harm him, I will murder you all!"

"An end we would deserve."

Sondrea fell silent—but not from Cam's regret—when a silhouette took shape in the open doorway. Beneath the eve's heat, but on a plot where he did not have an invitation, the darkened form of her husband stood far from her reach. A glint of light withered in Cyril Adair Mumus's empty eyes, but his posture provoked a chill deeper than her father's wicked magick.

"Your judge requires your loyalty"—Cam sought to correct her—"so you must let this blameless soul go."

Sondrea trembled at the sight of her husband taking Nelson.

The count chuckled and broke magick's hold as he clapped his hands. "I tell you; we will find you another pet."

His daughter fell hard to all fours and trembled as though her body temperature plummeted with her. She kneaded the muscles of her arms and mist escaped from her lips as she heaved. Her pupils shrank as her eyes turned slender in anger. She would forfeit all to strike them; even the Archibaldian who crouched beside her.

"I beg you, be still."

The countess struggled against the film of her sweat upon the slick floor, but her silent rage found the carnivorous smile that bared many teeth upon the face of she who gave Nelson to the judge. She who traded shame for rage swiped the borrowed set of keys from Cam's hold and jabbed an elbow against her father's jaw as she leapt upright. With those taken keys she bloodied the face of Nelson's biter. In response, Cam seized her ankle and swept her feet from beneath her. She landed hard, and none rose to defend her.

TULL & EBBE

His hush never sounded more defeated. "How can I protect him if you oppose your judges and your Guardians?"

The parlor's other woman took from a clasp on her thigh a brass nozzle fitted with a shielded hose that led to a fuel cannister on her back. She almost waited for Cam to step away afore she aimed at the countess. Sondrea still stretched a hand toward the blameless soul taken from her and did not give her foe the proper due. Afore she corrected that fault, an open flame burst from the nozzle in retaliation.

The afflicted soul buckled at every joint and hinge—writhing and exposed to the vileness that abounded—as broken in spirit as she had ever experienced. Boils covered her fingers and blisters spotted her smooth hand as the pain marred wit. Her beautiful voice, now rich with agony, let loose a shrill cry that terrified the soul she sought to protect. Then, she who burned her blocked sight of him and took hold of Sondrea's fiery-red tresses near the peak of her crown.

"Now you see"—her nemesis cinched tighter and pulled back till Sondrea's ribcage bent away from the floor and abandoned her ruined gown so she might stare upon who defied her—"I do have the weapons to tear him from your arms."

Titles & Tales

Seventeen

The 8th Eve beneath the Moon of the Mother's Song
The 107th Winter Season of the Accession
In the Care of the Helper, who keeps souls from fruitless wandering.

Her mother's mending chamber restored Sondrea's hand to full use and silkiness, but the unseeable wounds never mended. Even now, as she covered that hand with the other, her downturned mood darkened the brilliance of her eyes and made her face flutter with rage. She who wore the ring that marked her as the bride of Judge Cyril Adair Mumus fought at risk of her soul to keep he who became her husband's most devout foe from harm. Her pain made Tull despise the Archibaldian judge and her father the magick-wielder above all other souls in Yah's Creation.

Ebbe Demesne represented tremendous hurt for Sondrea and, from the way that Tull shifted, he had not mended in full either. Since that moment of her father's and husband's mutual betrayal, she sought ways to restore her failure and her loss of the Peace. Her shame and anger fueled her efforts to undo her traitors in the spans since. That she returned here—with all her options—spoke to her concern and, by her imagination's measure, invited clarification for her guest's continued trust in her wit.

"When first I learned of your return to this plot, I believed our judges sought to embarrass those who've outshone them in the eyes of our territories."

"I am nearer to having a Reformer's visions than understanding our judges' motives."

She rested her arms along the cushion at her back and let her foot point nearer to him than the fireplace. "What have your elders told you?"

TULL & EBBE

"Only that the judges ordered I not pass Behemót Woods or see you." He admired how her shoulders spread and her posture improved that he might see her more.

She winced as she counted that detail but grinned when she realized his brow furrowed for her confusion. "Do you know which judges sent you?"

"I saw the Shelbian who assists your father's son. I did not see signs of my own judge, nor Marvin. Nor did Harlan fuss over his hair or nails as he oft does when Judge Gwynne's daughter stands in chambers. Any other, I do not know."

"Gwynne *was* there. He sat on the bench with Lael and Dale Marius whilst his daughter keeps near Kingston for the winter . . . or till the persecution of her father by those same judges ends." She then volunteered, "I've not spoken with Papa's son in moons upon moons. Nor have I learned of his visits here; so far north. I returned to be nearer to Mama."

She stared upon his face and counted how, in his blamelessness, she oft awoke and found him curled against her with damp cheeks. That time she counted as innocence, though their habits let her tow no shame for the ways she behaved with him. Now, he offered her reassurance through silent nearness; a trait that also suited him. For this, she nudged Tull's shoulder and leaned against him. "Tell me anyway."

"I cannot believe I missed Judge Gwynne." He slapped his thighs in the same manner as Cameron Lou Fenner, as if driving back a foe or surrendering his hope for joy. "Why . . . *him?*"

The coolness in his pewter irises stole her breath and she looked upon his cheeks, now void of tears that accompanied such a wounded voice. "On the second morn beneath this moon, I received a guest at the tower. This wayward soul offered me a tale for a fee. I believed him unwell, but paid his sum; nothing much—two silver alms—then invited him in. Midway through our first cup of bergamot tea, he told me of Cyril's hand against me."

Tull stopped counting the souls that Mumus plotted against two spans ago and his agitation dwindled since.

"I do not trust the word of a soul who extends compassion or integrity in exchange for alms. Even so, I was warned of an attack and the attack came."

His posture reflected an immediate sense of protectiveness over her.

"Breathe with ease." Her chest rose in a distracting manner and she tested Tull's will as much as she took time afore continuing. "My driver tells me the attacker bore Cyril's face, though I did not see him.

TULL & EBBE

"Charles—my driver—also tells that the attacker's face *changed* again. From Cyril unto that of a creature afore he fled." She gauged his full face for a reaction that he never offered. "The soul who warned me has since proven absent."

All born of the secondkind now towed a beacon near the base of their neck; an identifier that let the judges and chiefs observe the whereabouts of every soul. Thus, a soul seldom proved absent from the judges, the chiefs—or their Guardians.

"You believe me misled?"

"Even if a soul sheds the body, the beacon tends to stay with the bones."

"I suspect this soul used a *false* name."

"Tower security would have confirmed as much"—he spoke in agitation, and not because he believed her unaware—"which lends to the claim."

"And the attacker's false face? Not even your weak-chinned friend's old fathers concocted such a well-made disguise as to convince Charles."

Tull's scowl twisted into a smirk as he recalled memories spent at Sondrea's side visiting movie houses that played the creepy films that made Silas Hendrie Falk—father and son—renowned. He counted few warm memories that excluded the countess. While some counted him as her puppet on a string, he could not deny the influence she held over him.

"You do remember the waxen likeness we saw of Junior *and* Senior?"

The way she mimicked the actual-sized figurine evoked a laugh from him that graced the ears of few souls. In that moment, he never suffered loss or rejection, no creatures warred above or beneath, and no other could divide the time he spent with her. Still, as he admired her and she him, her smile fell, then her eyes dimmed beneath a heavy brow.

"I am shamed, Nelson. I am a scandalous daughter, an ungracious bride, an uncaring mother, and an indecent benefactor . . . as you can tell."

Tull recalled a man who attended the theatre with them. Time made him forget that soul's face and name, but the kindness he received and the gentleness that settled upon the countess made him doubt they toured the displays of waxen likenesses with the bitter advocate of the Archibald Territory.

"Neither have I made choices that reflected well on the territories where I've resided." She ran the pad of her ring finger across her brow and felt no wrinkle after her time in the mending chamber. Still, she remained unsettled. "As you imagine, my retreat to the territory of my birth furthers me from my husband's approval."

TULL & EBBE

She oft spoke to Tull of her family as though he shared some form of closeness with them. In truth, he could not recall when last he spoke with or even looked upon the family's heiress or the judge. Katerena Yvette sounded like a storm of tantrums that he felt blessed to have shelter from. Mumus, on the other hand, occupied two of the Guardian's worst memories and was restrained there.

"We've not spoken of him in many moons, but I believe you still find no good in my husband. If his hand is on this, you will discover the slightest trace of his touch, yet still prove fair in the sight of Yah and in your dealings with him. What I ask of you, is that you would bring your findings to me and no other. What you learn, I decide the course." Her eyes set upon his and did not waver. "Would you, for me?"

"As you say." He nodded, then winced. "But with Edmond's permission."

Sondrea rose, then kissed his face and crown. She squeezed his neck as she leaned upon his shoulders and looked into his eyes. "If you've warmed, I'll show you proof of my words afore you consult him."

How she meant to *show* him proof set the workings of his imagination abuzz. Still, the outfit kept a method of gaining facts and discounting prejudices, deceits, and misbeliefs upon which all—even she—proved subject. "You traveled alone then?"

"My driver—"

"But not Dory? Not Katerena? Not Mim?"

"Take Mim out?" She shook her head. "Charles and I traveled with no other. Katerena has her studies. Dory took the eve from her duties."

"Took the eve or was granted the eve?"

"*Took*. I sought old acquaintances, so I granted her the eve too."

The drifting focus of his eyes hinted at inner suspicions.

"You see a habit."

"As you say." He detected mild agitation when she believed he counted her an elitist. "There is a habit to see."

"I imagine any soul who watched me would see my habits too."

"Is there a chance your acquaintances saw—"

"Gloria."

The name relieved his ego.

"I interrupted."

"Is there a chance that *Gloria* saw the attacker? How they arrived? If they traveled alone?"

Tull & Ebbe

"She hasn't the eyesight for that time of the eve. I was within sight of the tower. I like to see Katerena afore she slumbers."

"You gathered her and came here?"

"I fled with Charles. Dory and Mim arrived the first morn after—with Charles again. Since, I have remained near to these rooms without exception. Which brings us to your return to Ebbe Demesne, where I keep a room for you even now; though, I slept best when I held you."

Such a confession produced silence in him and boasted a mere portion of the power she held over him. Then, with a squeeze of his hand and a tilt of her head, she shifted them toward a different door than that which her succorer led him through.

"Let us sit away from watchful eyes."

The countess had taught him the floorplan long afore; still, she kept a hold of his hand and took him through the double doors at the western end of the parlor, then into a windowless room that was not the room she kept for him. This room, too, held the recessed tub in which she bathed when he arrived by Dory's lead.

She did not open the next set of double doors. In onward stead, she pivoted around her broad-shouldered guest and closed the set of doors they passed through and hid them from the mural of Guardians and the draped windows. Other doors, each slender and identical in height and latch, stood in identical formation; fourteen in all. These closeted cases formed a barrier against wintry gales and listening ears.

Sondrea claimed a seat built into the woodwork and patted the tufted cushion as a soul might coerce a short-legged creature to join them. He took no offense at either comparison, for she crept nearer when he sat further away than she preferred him. She rooted her palm between them, proved rigid from wrist to elbow to shoulder, but drummed each finger as if to tease the slight space she gave to the fall of her shadow; all the while, her eyes never roamed away from his face.

"Are you familiar with the machinations of Holston Lucius Buckler?" She shook her head in apology. "I speak of the inventive *son* and not his *industrialist* father."

For either soul, he shook his head.

She huffed. "You never let me take you to the exposition last gathering season. I spotted so many marvels! I longed a solid moon for the future our era might see."

Tull read many books but suffered a lack of culture. Sondrea enjoyed both, and ensured those she cared for enjoyed the same opportunities as she. Though she extended many an invitation to him, his duties limited his time for social events and what Vic called *whimsy*. Plus, he detested the nearness of the expositions to Mumus Tower and the advocate of that well-to-do territory who claimed her as bride.

"The work Holston's created is *how* I prove my tale to you."

She turned from him at the waist, pressed her nails against the fasteners in the tufted cushion, and plucked from a compartment the rectangular display plate she relied on for the next leg of her presentation. With a few taps and a burst of light that scanned the countess's soft hand, the device engaged while her foot swayed at a lulling pace. Once the device finished, she extended the opposite arm out afore her and sifted through images as though she turned the pages of a book.

"My thirty-fifth winter has irritated my once keen sight." She then laughed at her age. "Don't you believe me old!"

Softer in shape and strands of color, weary but not defeated; never *old*. She wore the span as well as any other.

"Here we are!" She pulled the corners of an intangible image and let the design fill the four corners of the display plate. "This design is Holston's."

An oval-shaped disc balanced upon two copper pins that shared a seamless connection to three copper rings rested upon fins that gleamed like polished jade. Here—in animated form—a single beacon of light shone upon each fin. When the beacon light fluttered, the lone fin changed angles and the craft shifted. As two fins changed angles, the disc turned over and revealed a series of lights and protrusions that reminded him of a camera lens.

"Holston calls this his surveilling craft. Would you believe, the display plate I hold is *three times* the size of this design?"

"A craft"—he struggled for a comparison—"as in an airship?"

"Similar in principle, but more complicated in design. There are no moving parts within this craft. A single burst of pressurized air sent into the central chassis sets the full craft adrift."

"How does he mean to navigate his design?"

"A piloteer uses a handheld like this to set a destination, and the craft determines a path based upon the flow of air across our territories."

"What happens if the wind stops?"

"I believe that may be the problem the builders encountered also. Though, can you name a single territory where the winds cease in full?" She flicked her brow to prove her point. "I read a booklet from the investment offerings. Seems he's built upon the way the winds follow the flow of water down the Loy River and this territory's Villám Fork."

"Can that jot take a direct strike from lightning?"

"Imagine!" Sondrea laughed and sifted through other images. "So few instruments—or crafts, for that matter—withstand the strikes of lightning that enliven Villám Fork."

"I s'pose the soul who decided on the name *Lightning Creek* decided well."

"Less clever than a soul imagines, to be sure!"

In his own cleverness's stead, he offered no further distraction.

"Less clever than Judge 'Chick' Leal. As of this winter, he owns the plot rights from eastern border to western border that offers the clearest basin for winds to travel. Afore his purchase, he worded a law that lets him fine a soul who attempts to benefit from this increase upon his plot. Not unlike the way that Mother Katch wrote a law on alloy mining rights."

Tull looked again at the design that benefitted from mined alloys and wind. He imagined some saw progress, some saw power, and some saw fortune.

"Afore the end of our sowing season, Cyril *invested* in Holston's idea with a distinct purpose. He contracted two crafts be kept; one craft upon my comings-and-goings, and one craft upon Katerena's. He then composed an edict."

"Your friend agreed?"

"Holston values invention over loyalty, but his conscience nudged him toward confessing as much to me *after* he accepted Cyril's alms."

"Then, these crafts *follow* you?"

"The craft is fitted with small receivers that seek my identifier beacon and camera lenses that project my every deed to a display that Cyril can access on a whim any time that he chooses."

"Every deed?"

"As long as my beacon remains detectable. By our one hundred tenth sowing season, I believe he—Cyril—will have secured the purchase of all the glassmaker factories in the Carpenter Territory through his mediary."

The tether between two points escaped Tull's vision amid the many moons that remained.

"I've read drafts of a law that will require every structure in our territories be redesigned; with not less than two glass plates that serve as exterior walls. I believe our judges mean to use these devices to monitor our every action. I serve our judges—including my sibling and my husband—as the first example of the secondkind's future."

"Vic oft says a time will come when we regret that the old fathers threw all their weapons into the sea."

"Imagine the provocation those who take to the skies will find against us. Imagine the provocation of a daughter whose foes can see her every move. Or a soul whose thirst for power, for knowledge, or for control, goes unstifled. How this law will change us!"

Tull then understood her newfound attention toward windows and doors. He felt the burden of not failing double and then triple. As he counted sinister and lecherous misuse of the *crafts*, the strain felt immeasurable. The secondkind did not *need* such right to trespass upon their fellows.

"Now that you understand why we sit in this room, appreciate that, for now, such escapes remain lawful. Keep me from my end, stop my bizarre attacker, and you'll not only protect your fellows, but the whole of the Second Creation as well."

While the burden allowed him only another nod, he forced out a single word whilst she sifted through more information. "Bizarre?"

"Do you remember the Damari law-writer I told you about?"

"She who keeps near to a judge you've not yet named afore your Guardian."

"The same soul keeps near to Judge Marvin Elam Katch."

Tull shivered at what he imagined Katch—a prominent lecher—might do with such designs.

"She obtained this reel from another of Holston's designs."

"'His mind seldom ceases.' As you say."

"Yes! Remember now, for me, that to this device, we appear not as you and I see a soul. Holston uses the *frequency* of every soul to construct a model of our bodies and reads the pulses of our identifier beacons to accentuate those models through the histories his designs collect of each soul's movements."

The image of a coach appeared first in frame and then introduced the skeletal structures of two of the secondkind. Metallic-white light radiated near the base of each neck, and hues faded till the eye observed a resonance of vibration and pulsation through the outermost portions of the body. A glint of color framed each soul's body.

TULL & EBBE

Tull recognized Sondrea's facial structure and shifted as her shape appeared as though poured into clear glass.

She cleared her throat and drew in her torso. "I hinted that he might improve the *modesty* of his results."

Tull looked away from the display plate and from the woman, then felt her shoulder against his arm.

"I do ask you to watch."

He obliged but gleaned the scorn, the frailty, and the outrage that their kind would suffer if the judges set such devices over them. Even he wanted to put a hand upon Holston Lucius Buckler—father or son—and suggest better uses of imagination and time. The immoderacy of observation the device allowed towed an excess of corruption and a forfeit of modesty. Decent souls would be led astray like the thesps of Bel Geddes who forfeited a virtuous purpose for alms and notoriety.

When the imagery proved too telling, she spoke again. "Soon . . ."

She leapt—in both her forms—despite her awareness, and chastised her reaction with a shake of her head. Tull held a warm grin for her viewing, but kept his eyes on the display. He watched with hints of admiration as the attacker crawled upon the coach with little resistance from the momentum or the design.

"Soon . . ."

The faster Sondrea's heart pounded, the brighter her animated likeness's hue burned. A jolt of the attacker's hand against the roof enhanced the definition of her visage by one-tenth. Her driver, purposed also to keep her safe, escalated at a swifter degree of one-fifth. The attacker, to Tull's dismay, increased not one-tenth of Sondrea's one-tenth.

"Watch *him* now."

Tull obeyed, though her tone kept him curious, and then discovered *why*. She thrust a burning star from her hand and the burst of light hurt his eyes once a bulb struck her attacker. His shape then changed afore their eyes and by no trick of the glider's projectors. In the presence of fire, his entire build changed. She paused the reel and kept the hollowness of the creature's eyes on them.

"We have seen such faces afore."

His eyes remained uncertain.

"You do not remember."

"I've never doubted your word."

TULL & EBBE

Sondrea looked upon Tull with confidence, as proud as she sat in Ligurus's saddle on the eve she rescued him, then let the reel continue. As the fire burned her attacker, she who measured a mere eight heads tall gained a sudden height advantage over her attacker. Most souls feared the open flame. None retreated within their husks—except this soul she bested.

"You reacted well."

"See how I shine in brilliant color? Being uncertain of my supernal dwelling place after my end inspired such an effect."

Her guest held his smirk till she rose from their shared seat, handed him her display plate, and rushed back toward the parlor.

"Charles noted that our attacker's gait did not match that of the soul who fled!"

Victor Simon Shannon once informed Tull that a soul of Sondrea's stature neither walked nor moved. He said she bloomed like a ray of light. To watch her, he learned the truth of the keeper's opinion. She maneuvered and drifted with ease, letting pass the effort she spent in her time of mending or the attention she collected across uncounted spans.

He exhaled afore he turned from watching her to look upon her attacker's visage. "I'll see that the outfit makes note of such differences in our patrols."

"I thank you, Nelson." She returned with her grandfather's journal tucked beneath her right arm. "I ask that you read what my grandfather wished us to learn."

She admired his certainty of word and posture and constructed a path with her eyes from his pensive brow down to the weathered boot of his crossed leg. Both he and the boots she had gifted him aged well. She no longer saw the babe she first held, nor the blameless beauty she once took under her arm and into her bed. As he read the words of a Jacobian whose legend he would share, she saw the character of a soul whose worth could not be measured in titles, or authority, or possessions.

He showed no surprise and no agitation over the words. For a moment, she even wondered if she had shared them with him afore. His long lashes batted with gentleness and his jaw remained as firm and still as a slumbering babe's. All her efforts and conclusions, and he never even stirred in his seat.

"Have I turned you drowsy?"

"I have heard such cries and felt the terrane slither beneath my boots."

TULL & EBBE

"You withhold from me?" She gave his chin a playful tap. "I remember how haunted Mama became beneath the same moons. As if she knew and dared not speak. Do you believe that his broken heart changed his mind?"

"No."

She kept a soft spot for certainty. "I imagine Papa knows you've returned. The gates between our wings are set, so you needn't fear him or Saul Ole. Do you recall my cousin, Papa's reeve?"

"I observed a slow-moving tree that smelled of salted meat and hair oil on my patrol this eve; both of which smell better than Mim. I blame his habit of drinking from the millpond."

She smoothed the wayward strands of hair behind his ear. "We remember how Mim breathes to rile. Do we not?"

"I believe his kin wears a badge in this territory."

As she laughed with Celia, she also laughed with her Guardian.

"I tell you, I cannot imagine that we'll receive the help of Chief Guild."

"O, can you not?"

"Ganix broke from tradition and spat *near* the chief's boots."

"With good reason!"

Tull looked upon her.

"A tale for another time." Her grin hinted at her enjoyment of secrets she kept. "Like Father, he comes from our lost territory of Erori."

"I too would bear agitation."

This time, her smile curled the left side of her mouth and added a wrinkle that creased her nose. In all his travels, he saw no other with such a smile as hers. "Remember what I taught you of the shadows in this territory?"

"The shadows are deepest where the scent of lavender turns wasteful."

"Beyond that wasted scent, out near the lodes, past Broken Neck Trail, there rests the Knotted Caves tethered by a continuous fissure. The caves descend unto the Forbidden Sea. If Grandfather's words are true, those caves reach deeper than any overturned settlements that once sat atop this place afore the Accession."

He nodded, but withheld his curiosity toward her certainty.

She leaned toward him and ratcheted down her voice till her hush sounded as if she feared her mother's ear. "When I wanted to be ornery, I would sneak away with friends and see if we could find the bottoms of those caves. We never did."

TULL & EBBE

"Your friends ought to have built better lanterns."

"Well, we seldom brought lanterns or a change of clothes; but, for the sake of your heart, I'll tell you no more."

His lips puckered into an unflawed *I thank you* sort of sneer and he tucked away all he wanted to say to her. "I'll look only for what I can prove. Wherever I search."

"Afore you return to your camp and share my tale with your elders"—Sondrea turned sideways and stretched her legs beneath his as she reached for his hand—"might we have more time? I seek to learn how you are. Tell me. Have you looked after your heart for me?"

EIGHTEEN

Tull returned to camp near the moonset and later than the fruitless patrol that Olley and Harlan made around Ebbe Demesne without a glimpse of Mim. This was the time of morn when all that moved drew the eye toward their place and cast a louder sound than would follow in the bustle. While Asham fussed over the lay of Tull's collar and sniffed the countess's scent, their elders encircled the returnee that he might make known to them all that he learned from she whom they guarded. Given his closeness with Sondrea and knowledge of Ebbe Demesne, he held an insight that rendered the doyen momentary novitiates.

Harlan kept his watch on the sky-fires as Tull gave an account of Sondrea's findings. Edmond, who never upset his wig, and Ganix, who seldom exerted any portion, reacted better to their underling's word than expected. Edmond watched with a sense of sly-eyed amusement all the while Ganix gasped and hissed the remnants of contempt that replenished with every moonset.

In his seven spans of service, the youngest of those four Guardians never asked a favor and seldom spoke out of turn. The hard wind and the smoke off his elders' cigars caused him to scowl, but he did not surrender his foothold any more than Edmond shifted his weight off the elbow which kept him propped against a stack of hand-split firewood. The headship enjoyed the reversal of roles more than he who explained the design of Buckler's surveilling craft. Once he finished, Edmond dipped his right shoulder back and aimed his cigar at the Jacobian.

"Do you believe our success will discourage their plans if they want to set a drove of those crafts above us?"

"No."

"They watch over me"—Ganix registered his complaint—"and I'll prove so vile that they will shelve their soaring imps to preserve their brilliant minds!"

"Buckler is abnormal."

All turned toward the vocal Archibaldian, but Edmond spoke first. "How do you mean that, Falk?"

TULL & EBBE

"The way he enters a room, approaches a soul, and manipulates a conversation." His eyes then roamed the horizon. "He oft seems given to more understanding than he ought to have. I suspect this is why."

"Perks of privilege!"

Tull and Edmond met eyes over Asham's inability to let Olley speak alone.

"Privilege spying on privilege, privilege threatening privilege, privilege taking from privilege to become more privileged. That's all this is about! *Privilege.*"

Edmond righted the conversation. "Would Buckler do as the countess imagines?"

"We Archibaldians have many virtues, Edmond. A desire for doing what no other soul has done is, perhaps, our highest. If Buckler has the idea, he—as an Archibaldian—has an obligation and a need to realize that idea." He gestured toward Ebbe Demesne as though sweeping away an empty cup. "There are no Archibaldians in that manor. He would feel no shame toward any trespass of them."

"How I miss the directness of the Jacobians."

Harlan's remark brought laughter to all.

"You heard her account of the attacker two times?"

"Yes."

"Over tea!" Ganix spat. "Upon crushed velvet or leather?"

"Her details of the attack met what I observed." Tull then prodded back at his territorial neighbor. "I believe I sat longest on crushed velvet atop an ash frame."

Harlan chuckled his unflawed, menace-and-delight-filled chuckle even as Ganix brought a chill to the ear. "But *we* have not seen, have we?!"

"Nor will you."

Afore high-strung Ganix contested, Edmond nudged the account along. "What did you see? Say who our judges sent us to protect her from."

"I saw markings of necrotic flesh around the corners of a mouth that stretches nearer to the ears than our own. I saw a slothful build turned sleek on no more of a dash than we stand from the fruit trees. And, that stature faded—like his disguise—when she doused him with fire and took away the creature's mind for the ruse."

"The Taotáva cannot feel the heat"—Harlan schooled the younger Guardians—"but they hate the light. They process the light of the flame and know that they must protect their husks lest they sacrifice their bounty. Better to use the cold against them. Then, they cannot gauge the brittleness of their form."

"You saw no other marking?"

TULL & EBBE

"The flesh around the eyes looked like the spider bruise Mick bore in—"

"One hundred and two," Ganix confirmed. "The hands?! The feet?!"

"Concealed"—he grinned toward Ganix—"in leather, I believe."

"Or you didn't remember to look! I said all along I ought to have gone! I demand that I see this *reel* afore I engage any further in this farce!"

Without looking away from the sky-fires, Harlan warned, "Let him finish, Barton. His account is enough to be trusted."

Edmond's silence reinforced Harlan's claim and Ganix heeded.

"Sondrea noticed that the way the attacker fled resembled a bird's step afore flight. This differed from the approach. Whilst disguised as Mumus, the steps were heavy. The impressions rose higher up the shin and the cast-off of snow was greater. Upon a second review, I saw that his build changed his gait. He might have stood ten heads high and ran as fast on tender legs."

Olley folded his arms around his chest. "They change every portion then?"

"This soul could. I read from a journal of Zeck's. He learned of the creatures afore Sondrea's birth and blamed *them* on the count. He wrote of standing in the woods and feeling the terrane roll beneath his feet due to their nearness to the surface."

"As have you," Edmond accused.

"As you say."

"They live beneath?"

The Jacobian shrugged. "We've all heard tales of the land beneath."

"Are not all the lands beneath the Jacoby Territory?" Olley teased.

"Only those lowlands across the Loy."

Olley appreciated Tull's jab against his territory and matched his easy sneer. "Then there is truth in this?"

"There is truth, Falk." Edmond paused in perfection. "Archibaldians are the lowest."

The whole outfit laughed.

"Then there are lands alive beneath us?"

"I tell you there are far worse travels beneath us than the nests you've seen!" Ganix's insistence towed a hiss-like scoff and an intensity that made his eyes bulge. "Those who don't dream make a trip beneath and learn the brutality of disturbed slumber!"

"You've seen them?"

"There is less on this isle that I've not seen than have!"

Edmond looked toward Harlan. "See any crafts up there yet?"

First, he shook his head, then, "You've heard every word of the tale that I've heard, Edmond. We cannot keep them from such creatures evermore. What he says sounds as every shape-changer I've seen in true form."

"You've seen them afore?"

Olley's sheepishness drew another of Ganix's ire-filled gasps.

"Must you?"

Harlan waved an arm. "When I was your age, they were as plentiful as the trees."

"Worse, as you neared the lodes." Edmond circled away from Ganix's backside and drew a laugh from Asham. "But plentiful here too."

"We collect them!" Ganix half-spat his complaint. "We collect the trash and the vermin that rolls down from the lodes. Most congregate near the waterways like spiders to a web!"

"I could throw my dullest blade and strike the spot where Harlan and Mick"—Olley patted his friend's shoulder—"and Nelson swatted Gaweł Jolyf Moreau back unto his hiding place. From what I remember of him, that turd didn't roll out the hind end of the lodes. He was pure Shelbian sh—"

"Bah!" Ganix waved Olley away like his own fog. "A brute! A privileged brute and no more! Do not try to tell me of Shelbian history!"

Edmond said of the territory where they stood, "Most of the former lands remain intact"—he looked down and stomped his heel—"here. That changes along the Lightning Creek, where they mingled with our kind—"

"Not our kind in full, Edmond. The *women* of this territory chase after *them*."

"By the north's measure, this territory remains the most twisted by the Accession." Edmond almost let interruption wither. "You know where they nest?"

"More spans fill my shadow than this burdensome lot combined, Edmond, and you ask if I know? Or, do you believe I've forgotten? They refuse to vacate the north, they'll not enter the waterways, but haunt our rails. They must know of properties in the glebe that stave off aging and rigidity. That's why we Shelbians age at a far lesser pace than the lot of you!"

"Then . . . you do not know the way?"

"When last I drew from my wealth you insisted that I lead. I prefer to be counted as a liar this time; I thank you."

Tull & Ebbe

"No other remarks?"

Tull looked toward his feet and the impressions his boots made in the snow. At the time of the Accession, the force of the firstkind's arrival uprooted villages and progress, then overturned them. Those who dug their way free then faced the might of waters as a new sea washed over the territories and surrounded the isle. By the lore of the old fathers, entire settlements remained beneath their feet.

"Not many souls roamed the eve amid a war or winter. Imagine more sank beneath than we've been taught. Sites we've never imagined were wiped clean by new terrane."

"That's how the Behemót Woods were born."

Asham and Olley matched dull stares till the latter asked, "How?"

He pointed toward the northwest hem of the tree line. "There once sat mountains up to the backs of the trees. When the Accession hit, the force ripped them away and cast them out unto the sea. The terrane broke open and the force overturned the groves that surrounded those mountains."

"My father told that tale." Harlan tore ash from his cigar with bare fingers.

"Do we go down there?"

"How would you suggest we travel there, Falk? Archibaldians cannot dig." A proven barb against a territory that built atop of every era afore and upward.

"I'll not attempt! Edmond! I simply will not attempt!"

Edmond patted the air to console Ganix. "Our kind has never prospered from infiltration. Zeck accused Conliffe's magick of infesting the lands beneath like wastewater. Even so, we are not called to invade or attack. We corral"—his gaze sprung upward—"for them. I'm not such a fool that I believe they would defend us if we sought to conquer places the Taotáva keep. We are not near where her coach suffered the attack anyway. We cannot keep the watch over this plot and dig for foes in the Archibald Territory."

"Sondrea spoke of the Knotted Caves on Broken Neck Trail."

"How does a countess learn of such places?"

Harlan's seedy laughter amused Edmond first, then Asham.

"Those caves rest far from roadways with gas lamps and coaches."

"You've seen them, Harlan?"

Harlan looked toward Asham. "I've swam in them!"

"Bears swim?"

TULL & EBBE

"With less trouble than an Archibaldian finds whilst walking in a rainstorm." His eyes sparkled as he riled Olley, who oft roamed with his nose in the air.

"She reasoned"—Tull spared Harlan of boasting-related injuries—"that any of those caves ought to descend further than all the eras that stood afore."

"She ought to lead the way."

"I'd not dare her."

Olley surrendered a chance at barbs. "Is Zeck's complaint true? Did Conliffe create these creatures?"

"Yah created all creatures, Olley."

The Archibaldian scoffed at Harlan's words and drew Edmond's cold stare.

"Do I seem a soul who spends time with counts, Falk?"

"They didn't tell you all the secrets when you took over?"

Olley wondered the same as Asham. Even Tull offered a curious glance.

"You have much to learn of our judges." Harlan shielded Edmond.

"What say you?" Olley gave Tull an audible nudge. "You made your home here."

Tull shook his head. Even now, he would not speak of his former host. Though Sondrea and her mother provided for him beneath Yah's provision, he never forgot how the mere idea of the count loomed over them. Mumus was cruel, but Conliffe made blameless Tull and the women who lived on Ebbe Demesne feel afraid.

"Count the number of Shelbians you see swiping trinkets and glances from this place and you'll see how many souls believe him incapable."

Not even Ganix objected to Harlan's observation.

"How can a soul put a curse upon others that way?" Olley stood aside for George, that he might stand nearer to the fire as he returned from cooing to the horses.

"We've shown you much! This is not the theatres or picture houses of your old fathers! Has your purpose come to you with such ease that you never counted those creatures who've turned the old lands into their home? Your friend stood here and described these creatures aloud. Do they sound like us in any form?"

Once Harlan's growling reprimand stopped echoing, their headship spoke. "Whether Conliffe created them—or Yah—they are our foe now. We sit here as the judges ordered and defend one soul in a territory's stead. We are not asked for more; letting pass how we might teach them what happens when they meddle in our purpose."

TULL & EBBE

Tull remained unclear if Edmond spoke of the Taotáva or the judges who set them on Ebbe Demesne.

"Is my instruction heard and understood?"

"In times past"—Harlan's dignified eloquence rose above agreeable mumbling—"some have followed paths that the judges determined whilst another created a way that benefited the souls forgotten by our judges."

"As you say."

"I never have!" Ganix startled Asham with his outburst. "I've never strayed from our edicts."

"As you say."

"A woman of provenance near to our very purpose has approached a soul whom she instructed afore us; not for her comfort, but from concern for the solitude of our kind."

Tull awaited a third utterance of Edmond's favorite response and even Harlan offered an unnecessary pause. Their headship glimmered in silence as he eyed his friend—once a law-writer of promise—and heard his argument.

"I tell you; I wish only that our wise judges had seen fit to let Nelson cross through the Behemót Woods with us."

Edmond's sneer pulled at the left side of his face and kept him from observing Asham's confusion. "Sad that we had to leave him on the other side of the woods where we cannot keep an eye on his coming in or going out."

Olley proved he understood. "Nice to be away from all his bragging for a tick. You imagine he'll try sneaking up on us, George? Not through the woods, mind you. Not even he is fool enough to travel through the woods alone."

George smiled at the Archibaldian. "I imagine he fears crossing the Lightning Creek as much as I was afraid when we crossed through the forest."

"Which is not to say he's too wise to cross."

"Whether he is or is not wise"—George decided—"he has been taught better."

Edmond accepted the compliment.

"Ah! But I count him blessed, Edmond, for he who keeps to the other side of the woods and away from this plot might never learn of the scheme against our kind or of the judges who snoop"—the Carpenterian looked at his distant neighbor—"while we stay in proper obedience."

Edmond stayed a pillar of unreadable responses. "Ganix? You're in agreement?"

"That's a remarkable accusation!" He then shuffled and stepped nearer to mutter, "Which is not to say I disagree. I dislike this Buckler and his design. But, to agree, I insist upon an invitation to appear unto the countess's manor afore the morrow's moonrise, where the countess will engage me for a chat—in a room warmed by a fire, not a kettle—and no fewer than two cups of tea—a vernal blend, not aged or mingled—served with two fingers of glühwein. I have craved glühwein since Hivi'ern."

The outfit, which included Asham, stood in silence toward Tull's held breath and percolating tremor.

"Agree"—Ganix straightened his neck till the loose skin of his jowl settled atop his scarf—"and I will spin an elegant yarn of my visit to this cursed plot without you."

"As you say." Three monosyllabic words never sounded shorter.

"Tull?"

"I will present the request when next I see the countess."

Harlan challenged him with a prodding smile. "I believe Edmond seeks your *yes* or *no* on the matter."

His shortness of speech held. "I am torn."

"You? Of us all?"

"I obey my judge who was not consulted."

Two of the elders smirked at his knowledge and looked toward each other with proud glances but, where they proved respectful, Olley prodded. "All have heard tales of her . . . sway . . . over you and her many . . . fulfilments . . . toward your needs."

Ganix—of all the lot—hissed. "Stifle such words, Falk!"

"I agree with our Shelbian fellow." Still, George looked Olley in the eye.

"I am the lone orphan here. In that, I sympathize with creatures who've lost all and seek to be counted, but I cannot agree with the wrongheartedness of their methods." Tull's brow then furrowed, and his eyes turned a shade darker. "I've no heart for hearsay, nor complaint over her care of me. Had Sondrea not helped me, I would not have survived my first moon alone. I wish these creatures no harm, but I need no other reason to fight than to fight for her."

"Eloquent."

"Romantic."

"Foolish!"

Tull scoffed and caught degrees of smirks on his elders' faces.

"Falk?"

TULL & EBBE

Olley hesitated and Harlan interceded. "I wounded his pride. I believe he'll not run from harm if harm comes for us."

George put a hand on Olley's shoulder and rendered his ballot. "We will not."

"Gera?"

The Creightonian shrugged. "As you say, my benefactor."

"We'll work on teaching you the power of the vote later." Edmond then issued a clear edict. "None of you are to speak of Tull's deeds here to your scions, your abettors, or any stray doves that roost. That includes journals."

"And our judges?"

"And your judges, Falk. These are my orders."

"As you say."

"I've never needed to teach you much"—Edmond spoke to Tull now—"and you've towed favor for that. I ask you; do you have the resolve to match a soul as twisted as Mumus' or Conliffe's and not embarrass the outfit?"

Tull set his jaw and let his silence be his wiser response.

"Better that he resigns his post and return to the forests!" Ganix half-spat through a billow of smoke from his crooked mouth. "But he proves brighter than Perry and less of a loyalist to the judges than Kemp."

"Then from this tick till we ride on, you're to be a shield to she whom we watch over. Choose your cadre and do your part to keep the rest of us from looking like liars." Edmond creaked as he stood straight. "And should you shame us, throw yourself unto the sea afore the judges come for the lot of us."

Tull grinned till his headship bumped shoulders with him in passing.

Once Ganix tromped away, still ranting over his anticipation of suffering, Harlan set his big hand on the same shoulder that Edmond bumped. "If you feel ashamed, you find us. And *do* avoid steep ledges till then."

Tull acknowledged with a nod and shouldered a swift pat.

"Take some rest! Our moon sets."

He and Olley exchanged glances, for they knew Harlan's ways.

"Take your rest, too, Archibaldian."

"As you say." His eyes—and Tull's—saw the flicker of motion in Harlan's fingers afore he returned to his tent. "Need I locate Buckler?"

"You doubt my aim?"

"After you shorn that Shelbian's crown at the river camp?"

TULL & EBBE

Tull cocked his jaw at the deliberate way that Olley shook his head.

"Whatever you need."

"As is your way."

"Truly!"

Olley's loyalty to Tull rivaled his smugness toward most others. Still, the friends believed in the other's word. Along with George, they proved a difficult trio to defeat. As a defense against failure, the Jacobian approached his tent, backed onto his bedroll, and removed his boots for the first time since afore he and Asham rode for Parantua, and prayed to the Triune for discernment, for might, and for supernal guidance that even a soul of slow wit could not deny.

When he opened his eyes, he found atop a pair of books and a covered glass the same apple that he handed George when Dory arrived for him. The crisp break of fruit between his teeth preceded the gentle removal of the flexible skin that shielded his handheld device, but not from the smack of his hand to the backside of the shell when he expected a swifter response. Another two bites consumed the fruit, and he wiped down his mouth afore the device reached full display. By then, he divided tasks in a plan that would let him follow two paths created by Sondrea's adversaries.

He ignored all the reels that awaited his attention, upwards of ninety, recorded on handhelds or at-home devices and not crafts that navigated overhead, then scoured frozen images of those who kept near to him. In the middle of the second column, he discovered Abettor Valery Leta Koslowski's place and spun the image as the clock turns. When last he saw her, she wore her hair as dark as the shadows. The time afore, wine red—a style the device preferred enough to retain as a still image. She kept no set appearance from eve to morn, and that marked almost all he had learned of his aide in two moons of service together.

"Tull?" This time, she appeared to him with her head shaved down to the scalp from crown to neck on her left. She shook off the confusion, which returned as fast as her hair fell against her right shoulder and corrected her posture. "Guardian Tull."

"A pleasant morn, Abettor Koslowski." He could not see if she shaved the other side but noticed her asymmetrical shape. He also noticed skin irritation that surrounded the silhouette likeness of a horned skull and her nineteenth mark of similar shape along the freckled arm that propped her upright. "Do forgive my waking you."

TULL & EBBE

"I put my head to the pillow a few ticks afore. Last eve marked a feast." She shook her head and stopped explaining her reasons.

"The Feast of Pehdli Nożi'ercuay."

Her pinkened eyelids withdrew from her murky irises, of which he could not determine a color, as though surprised by his awareness of her traditions.

"You enjoyed the prowl, did you not?"

Her smile hinted at fresh memories. "Indeed."

She stooped and retrieved a glass whose contents matched her eyes and took a swig. Her changes in setting revealed her nudeness, yet she made no attempt to keep from his eye. He, like the two souls with whom she lived, and the seventeen remaining *horned skulls* who bedded her, knew too well the start and end points of every tattoo, freckle, and piercing she bore. The tattoo signified the number of lovers and her level of carnal experience with a measure of pride that offended more than Archibaldian elitists.

Her benefactor also learned that the first two marks represented Valery's paternal uncles; whom her father ended afore the judges ended him. Valery became a Partaker by way of her shame but remembered the lessons her father taught her and committed three spans of her time in service to the territories. Tull respected that integrity and her capabilities as his abettor. She further proved that not all Partakers hated the Guardians, despite the claims of judges, Reformers, and other Partakers.

"So, who or what do we seek this time?"

"Cyril Adair Mumus." He then listened to the wind that rose an octave above her hoarse vulgarities and watched as she took another swig.

"My deacons warned me about you."

Those deacons claimed four of her horned skulls and other uncounted marks.

"I s'pose by now you would have smiled if this was a ruse." She squinted as if to see into him but teetered in defeat when she could not. "Onward then."

"I thank you."

"And there you are"—she huffed and cast a wisp of hair astray—"letting those three words land at the right pace."

The way he grinned provoked another fit of swearing and a sneer that belied her sense of orneriness. Then copper scraped pulp as she dragged the display plate off the wooden setting and onto her lap. Tull's view offered the underside of her breasts and a bruise beneath her chin that hovered between her slender fingers as she tapped at keys that showed on her device alone. Partakers had to tow an overwhelming burden of hatred for another soul—or an edict from the judges—afore modesty hid their ways from them.

"I read a poem told from the perspective of an owl speaking to a fox as they watch a coyote hunt the monster who preys upon their forest. The monster was a bugaboo; but the verses were written for another tongue. For them, a bugaboo was named *mumus*. I've never forgotten that, though I cannot remember the title of the poem."

"Néma Róka, Ébredő Róka."

Valery approved of Tull in great ways. That they connected in wit made her smile relax to a well-kept grin as she tilted her crown toward her ink-adorned arm. "What did Judge Bugaboo do?"

"I'm more interested in what he did *not* do. I need to learn whether he sought the means to end his bride."

"Countess Sondrea Ebbe Conliffe." She spoke as one afraid of tainting the magick-wielder's daughter's name, then her eyelids drew together as if in prayer.

"She is unmarred."

His aide sighed and drew a proud breath. "Once, I can't tell you the count of moons ago, though the season was still warm for the windows were open, I saw her. Not up close, but all know her coach, do we not? She passed down an adjacent roadway to mine. I believe"—a word few Partakers voiced—"that she was the most unflawed soul I've ever seen. I'd never felt more hideous or more soothed."

He appreciated her grin as much as her memory. Afore he saw her true character, a ripple of her tendencies drenched the mood and atmosphere. Her words mingled in her throat and surrendered to a raspy cough that provoked a flow of blood from her left nostril. A glob struck the display plate and appeared plum-hued with black spores to the Guardian. His abettor then choked and turned from him, letting her display fall to her feet. The immobile view aggravated curiosities as the intensity of her struggle produced a hollow pang.

Tull sat in stillness and did not speak. Uncounted Partakers across the territories suffered the aftershock of deeds crammed into the dwindling eve when they celebrated the Feast of Pehdli Noži'ercuay. His abettor—who stood a head taller than Asham, as she had boasted to him—invited in more abuse than hope welcomed. Now, till the effects passed, she would suffer dizziness, blood loss, audible hallucination, and an inability to focus due to a rapid twitching of the eyes. Those who mocked fasting Believers proved their foolishness.

"Tull . . ."

He who observed the smear of blood across her cheek and the discolored tears in her eyes splayed his hand till his fingers spanned the diagonal corners of his display plate. "Say no more, Abettor."

When she huffed, her image turned speckled with a crimson mist.

"Mend. My way needn't be your burden."

She flapped her hand and the light and shadow pebbled till she vanished.

"You were created for more, Abettor Koslowski."

The judge he sought—along with that judge's brother-by-law and tepid Judge Elwell—prohibited interference by Believers upon Partakers in keeping them from their celebrations of unbelief. No similar law shielded Believers from the meddling of Partakers. While he considered a prayer according to the tongue of Ministers, another name teased his heart with scraping tenderness—but not for the first time since entering the territory. When his prayer ended, he sent a message across a low-band frequency devised for the outfit and their committed merchants.

Your Guardians camp at Ebbe Demesne. Should you seek to stretch those meddlesome legs I have work for you.

He worked at his wardrobe till he wore neither shirt nor boots and felt the sting of winter on his flesh. That aching reassurance let him settle and detach from his worries. He kneaded the toes scarred by the terrane of Ebbe Demesne and set his thoughts upon the wonderments that surrounded the countess. Then, afore wrongheartedness set in, she who kept him from eternity let her flame take the air from the tent, that Tull might fall unto slumber without idle desires.

NINETEEN

THE 8TH MORN BENEATH THE MOON OF THE MOTHER'S SONG

THE 107TH WINTER SEASON OF THE ACCESSION

IN THE CARE OF THE HELPER, WHO KEEPS SOULS FROM FRUITLESS WANDERING.

The morn—cut brief by the winter—was spent afore Tull emerged from his tent. Having slept from the fifth watch till the ninth, rest refreshed him after he leapt from rooftops, hung from a tree, wore a blindfold, had his eyes opened, kept secrets, and learned more. He heard no more from Valery and told no other of the invitation he sent. Now, he felt his loyalties between purpose and countess tested enough that his silence stood as the greater strength.

The gloom that followed the moonset covered the bivouac and hid Creation's shadow. While dreary to some, this kept the Shelby Territory's foes dormant and let the outfit roam with slighter concern. The light exposed chaos, after all, and made work for the righteous. As for the nearest Jacobian, he saw clearer and listened truer with the light's help, unlike those whose eyes lost their discernment of what was light and what was darkness.

"Tull!"

In agitation's stead, he plunged his crown and face into a brass pot of melted snow, kept hot by an anthracite cell. He kept still and used his hands to wash so the water never entered his ear canals or crept around the nape of his neck. Either risked a bout of heart palpitations, tunnel vision, and breathlessness. All the perks of suffering si'el uni'epotus. Not even Asham's pestering invited him to want that sort of suffering.

The youngest of all Guardians stood with towel in hand and an impatience toward silence. "Olley says you dwelled with the countess near to one span."

"Yes."

Tull & Ebbe

Asham brushed droplets from his hand as Tull patted dry. "He says you dwelled here for the sowing season and one moon afore."

Tull scooped fresh snow and refilled the pot for the next soul while George poured peppermint tea into a wooden cup. The terse Jacobian met eyes with the peace-bringing Westonian who responded with a shake of his head and delivered the tea to him. "A grateful morn."

George touched his chest. "Most grateful."

"I thank you." He blew into the mug and added a handful of snow.

Asham nipped at their heels, intent to agitate the pair. "Ganix says the countess arranged your spot with the outfit."

"When Ganix speaks"—George spoke as Tull sipped—"he oft speaks out of turn."

"One can speak out of turn and still be true. None of the others kept two scions."

"No."

"And Perry selected Shaw—not you."

"Cam chose—"

Asham cut off George's rebuttal with a wave of his hand.

"What do you believe, Asham?"

"I believe I prefer you watching my back than expecting kindness from Ganix."

As for Tull, he gargled his tea, shook the water from his hair, and then raked the wet locks into a passing style.

"She treats you well?" He checked the snow where Tull spat his tea.

"Above any other."

Asham nodded with unusual calmness that felt as refreshing as the breath that followed Tull's next swig of tea.

"Asham believes that *count* and *countess* are not true titles, while Olley insists that our Creightonian friend is a dullard."

"*Rude* and *stupid* were the words he used, George." Asham patted him on the back. "No need to polish his barbs."

Tull rifled his arms through two clean shirts and warm coat sleeves.

"Is there truth that she—"

"Gera!"

Tull cleaned his teeth as Edmond barked the troublemaker's name.

"Go break the ice on the horses' water!"

"My hands are never going to heal. Fire and ice! Ice and fire!"

TULL & EBBE

George offered him a wooden mallet from his tools. "Use this on the ice."

The smile that lit his face proved he never counted another option afore. "I thank you, George! I'm going to have dry gloves now!"

"Best in Creighton, was he not?" Ganix howled, and waved him downwind.

George shook his head.

Tull looked above. "O, how Your sense of humor disturbs Your lessers."

"Your lady"—George spoke with reservation—"took a visitor this morn."

"Known to us?"

"Not known by me, my friend. Olley and Asham gave her—"

"Say no more."

George laughed whilst the Jacobian plucked one-half of an apple roasted with dates and ginger from a tin by the fire. He offered the tin's rest to George, licked sweet glaze from his fingers, and looked toward the manor. Near the western entry, he spotted a barrel-cycle beneath the sheltering branch of a terabinth tree.

"A brave ride in this season."

He nodded and chewed harder as his mouth filled with steam. "Good dates."

"Asham took the pecans." He blew on his serving. "I cannot believe he uses his hands to break the ice."

"Can you not?" Tull craned his neck as another mouthful of steam rolled from his lips. "Near the orchard's eastern hem rests wooden crates filled with nuts off the trees of this plot. Tuck away all the almonds you like. Leave the bitter walnuts for Ganix and Asham."

"Should I leave alms for our host?"

"The magick-wielder cannot digest them."

"Who puts them in the crates?"

"Goblins." Tull offered a teasing poke to the side afore he resumed his duties.

George spoke well of the dedication of the barrel-cycle's rider. A soul required a passion for freezing to mount such a machine this time of season. Tull remembered that his father owned a bulkier model and paused long enough to let this sleek variant produce a vapor-thin memory of Patrick James Tull. Never words, nor a voice. Never a scent. Not even a clear glimpse of the departed soul's face.

"They told me you only smiled for Mom." He mimicked the grin he imagined.

He dismissed the ethane gum-fueled barrel-cycle but not the memory he rediscovered, then traveled the corridor alongside the oblong parlor adorned with ivory-white walls that reflected the snow and fog to near-blinding proportion. He followed the sound of a ripple-less voice that carried feather-like inflections of Shelbian mesmerism and Archibaldian boastfulness with Jacobian calmness and Erorii bluntness as he crossed the threshold without announcement. He believed Sondrea spoke with Dory, till the succorer appeared behind him in the corridor. The intensity of light hid her eyes behind lenses that tinted in response yet enhanced her scornful brow.

Even as the succorer approached her benefactor, she offered another glance at him that changed once she gauged the intensity of his expression; changed by an awareness of mistrust. Dory corrected her path in time, avoided a set of high-back chairs, and went ignored by a rare fair-haired soul who spoke in a hush toward Sondrea. She seemed like a rabbit afore Sondrea's fox. The way she teetered drew attention to legs shorter than the succorer's that must have ached from the exertion of reaching the barrel-cycle pegs.

Sondrea offered her preferred guest a steadying glance that proved her mutual disinterest in the ongoing conversation. She motioned with a flick of her wrist and stepped back from her mother's writing table. Dory then handed the yellow-haired soul a lush sack with an affixed copper button and leather cord. The sack proved large for the receiver's palm, and the sound of loose alms made a distinctive chime as she forced the gift into her rucksack. Without gratitude, she turned from her host and walked an unseen line toward the entryway that Tull and Dory used.

Latter watched former, as if curious to see if he might change or give away the root of his intense expression. The Jacobian proved resolute in a hollow between the shielded mending chamber and a radio from the Era of the Reformers that shared seven-tenths of his height. He minded the windows and the entryway but kept a count of the number of footsteps the rabbit took. Seven spans taught him when souls recognized their Guardians and when the short-legged gait ceased eight steps shy of the doors, with the slip of a heel, she proved her tell. He kept his gaze set out the window even after she recovered, and resumed with an unsettled stride.

A playful whistle, enough to tease a Guardian's ear, preceded an upward scoop of Sondrea's hand through the air and over the opposite shoulder. He obeyed her call like a well-trained pet and approached on one stride for every three steps that her departing guest needed. Dory pivoted away from the gold-trimmed writing table and

TULL & EBBE

chairs that matched the room's brightness and followed the rabbit from the parlor. All the while, Sondrea withheld conversation till they were without other ears.

"All is well?"

"By our recorded annals, neither Guardians, nor scions, nor abettors will make mention of my presence, let alone your request"—he winced afore he honored his orders and shut his eyes as he spoke in pain—"provided you agree to invite Ganix unto your parlor for a visit to include tea made from a vernal blossom and two fingers of mulled wine. You might keep back a finger for your own consumption once he's gone or"—his nose twitched—"too near."

She brushed the pads of her fingers as though a residue formed with the anticipated visit of Ganix. "When I arrived here, I counted the need to have Mama's furniture resurfaced."

That sounded like acceptance to the messenger and he opened his eyes to the sound of a wooden drawer as she retrieved embossed cards and a fine pen.

"You've improved your ability to appear less disinterested than you truly are."

"I thank you." He remained standing, lest he forget his place, and gave thanks that he escaped the heat from the fireplace at the other end of the room.

"I spoke with Mim. Believe me when I tell you that his disregard for you and your title are reflections of his agitation with me. He enjoys being the prized rooster."

"Even the prized rooster feels the stump against his neck."

The forest-dweller's analogy, as much as his dwindling grudge, amused her enough that she ceased from writing mid-word. Then, the sound of the barrel-cycle's engine tearing through the air made Sondrea's eyes cross in disapproval and busied her hand. "That confused little creature might cringe if I referred to her as Constance Ashland Tarry's niece. Better I tell you she serves Noble Joe Massey."

"I prefer the aunt."

"Many do. Noble Joe, with the help of Constance's niece, has taken up the habit of gathering and transcribing the journals of former eras"—Sondrea laughed as if she tasted bitterness and fanned the damp card—"for publication and gain."

"She brought you a copy of their work?"

"No. I purchased these on behalf of"—she gauged his mood as she looked him over—"a fellow. This new era does not understand the ways of the past, and I'll not see my elders tarnished by piety or Noble Joe's sourness."

Tull & Ebbe

Tull accepted the card she offered, then watched as she gathered the stack of journals and tossed seven of the nine onto the fire without reading a single word. "As certain as I am that you have many responsibilities, you might limit the comings and goings of others till we identify all who might have a hand against you."

As she withheld agreement, she grazed her lip in approval of his tone and watched as he read her invitation to Ganix.

He then volunteered, "The outfit will do as the judges intended for them. I will see to the matters you've requested of me. None—Asham uncounted—warmed to the idea of soaring imps following our every deed."

"Soaring imps?"

"To borrow from Ganix, for once."

"And you'll keep from the caves."

"Edmond opposes invasion." He noted a sudden coldness in her and pocketed the invitation lest his interests seem divided. "Have I misrepresented you?"

"No."

She punished him with no further context and organized the books and journals on her mother's table.

"Wherever I go, I represent Cyril. My name is not cited on any official paper. The brides of the judges surrender their names when they wed. In this way, neither of us are here. If the judges keep a record, they will reflect that your outfit handled a matter for the bench.

"This way of theirs I learned after the choice was made for me." She tired of protecting the indefensible and spoke of another time when Cyril betrayed her. "I tell you, as my treasured confidante and agent, that I was not *wed* but *given* to him. That was my father's choice."

A knot formed in Tull's stomach that tempted him to double over.

"When Judge Lane met his end, his driver found him atop his own scion. Whichever soul *ended* the other first is still debated with perverse detail, but they took from all Shelbians their voice on the bench. The most prosperous families nominated their prized stock. Those with the greatest chance of serving sought the endorsement of seated judges."

Tull felt dizzy, but the barb of anger in her voice kept him rooted.

TULL & EBBE

"For a plot large enough to cease the expansion of Leander Jonathan Bromley's timber enterprise and the hand of the first Erorii Guardian's daughter, Cyril endorsed my father's son for the judgeship." She smiled with tremendous sadness.

Tull broke from his leg-locked stance and forced open a parlor window, from which he hinged and vomited. Between heaves, he heard the countess fill a glass of water and approach to stand near to him. He mopped his face and mouth, then righted both posture and window.

She did not judge. "I have never loved him, and he has never been a friend to me. I am the cost of my half-brother's greatness."

Tull gulped without interruption, but the arm that held the glass trembled.

"Nelson." She stilled his arm. "I tell you this because there are souls who will say I turned you against Cyril. That I set a Guardian against our judges."

She took his glass and refilled the supply of water, then gathered a tin of candied ginger—a remedy against nausea—afore she returned to his side. He crunched the ginger with his back teeth.

"I believe your mind swims."

"There's a Shelbian from a nearby settlement"—he finished his second glass of water—"who serves as Ganix's scion."

"Nita Naomi Ozul. She's been an interest of mine since she accepted another's purpose. You call on her and not the scion you keep?"

"Kemp would hear me, swear an oath, and then run to our judge."

"Then you shield Ernie from his fellows." Her eyes sparkled with approval.

"Ganix refuses to retire and let Nita replace him."

"Some souls fear change."

"Most fear not having their way."

A slender smile did not reflect how she marveled over him nor fretted over the sickness she caused him. Still, the walls she recognized in him disguised his weakness through the posturing of a Guardian. "The territory's scion might find travel difficult, should the storm outpace her."

"She arrives afore the peak."

"And Cyril?"

Tull swayed back into stillness.

"You investigate him, do you not?"

"My abettor mends from the Feast of Pehdli Noźi'ercuay."

TULL & EBBE

"Ah! The Partaker with a fondness for showing her"—she glanced toward her chest, stopped shy, and deflected to Tull's shoulders—"*freckles*. The Pride of the Creightonians has a voice that carries further than he intends."

"He's proud of every hint of blush he causes." Tull jostled the candied ginger to the other side of his jowl. "By the eve's moonrise, we'll have set perimeter sensors across every passable route. Then we track the paths of every soul that moves within their boundaries."

"I thank you, Guardian."

Her regard encouraged him.

"Your abettor tends to you well?"

"She believes in service to others; even Believers."

"You've set your trust on her?"

"My abettor—Valery—spoke well of you. She saw you once from afar."

Sondrea blushed. "Another tale I've heard too oft! I am not *royalty*."

"You are beloved by"—he restrained his instincts—"many souls."

"But not in my own home. Or my father's."

"The Forever King told us of this. 'He who upholds finds no adoration among his kind, his kin, or in his own house.'"

"Mama raised me to believe, but I'm not sure how well I uphold." Sondrea stole Tull's breath even as she inhaled and spun. "Lest this dress is less flattering than I remember, I'm no *he*, either."

Tull calmed his tone. "You flatter the dress."

Her head tilted and offset her smile as she gauged the rarity of his flattery. She even recalled how eleven moons passed between this and his previous compliment of her. So special were his words and his presence that she tucked her hands behind her and let the joy she felt keep her on a lightened step.

"You say you selected Dory as your succorer. Do you recall who referred her?"

"I do not." Her eyes danced. "Why your intrigue?"

"Say the travels of short-legged souls intrigue me."

"I'm told Scion Ozul is tall."

He raised his hand to the scion's height, then shrugged. "By a Shelbian's measure."

"And trustworthy? By your measure?"

Tull smirked when she cocked her jaw and let her snarl become a smile.

"And your friend in the Carpenter Territory?"

TULL & EBBE

He dropped his hand to the ball of Sondrea's nose as his smirk rose to match.

Sondrea smiled then reached out and boosted his measure at the elbow. "I'm told your abettor stands so high."

He held his hand at that position but faced her. "And the soul who attacked you?"

She took his palm between her thumb and index finger and lifted his arm till she might twirl on her heels as though dancing with him. "But"—she then tugged at his palm till his fingers caught the breath of her—"this high when he fled."

He studied the line of light that formed beneath her lower lip and ascended her smooth cheeks across the curve of her eyelashes unto the copper pools of her irises and straw-blonde strands that surfaced from beneath the intensity of light.

"I woke this morn with a memory of the way Mama would watch me near her end. Even then I felt as if she lost her certainty—a mother's certainty—that I was hers." She let her chin sink toward her chest as her eyes settled near the location of his heart.

Tull felt he ought to mimic her gesture but was unsure why, so he returned her tin of candied ginger. "I was about to patrol and set sensors but, if you require, I can fetch Katerena and drag her to see you."

Her smile gleamed and she raised her hand to the height of the soul they spoke of now. "You would for me, would you not?"

"Yes."

"Whilst the idea of such rabid entanglement amuses me, better she come stomping and pouting than kicking and screaming."

"Should the countess change her mind."

She scoffed and waved the tin in mock royalty. "Get!"

Tull obliged, but only a few steps. "What you shared afore . . . had I not suffered the restraint of blamelessness . . ."

"Yes?" Her warmest grin held.

"I would have been a heel to their necks." He towed no worry of lurkers or betrayers. "Now that I am a Guardian, no other will suffer such a yoke as the yoke your father set upon you."

"I thank you, Nelson."

TWENTY

Sondrea respected Tull's heart, appreciated her time with him and his attention to his duties, but her mind worked at a pace that exceeded his gait. Though he never browbeat her for information on any matter, he sought enough answers and produced enough barbs to inform her of his suspicions. From his taking on a Partaker as his aide to relying on an unproven scion to respect their host territory, he showed an understanding of the secondkind and an acute need to keep near those souls who would not come too near to him. With that trait in mind, she gleaned from his observations what she overlooked in her own.

Like her would-be attacker, Dory lacked the stature of most—Constance's niece removed from that count of short-legged souls. Then, there was the wardrobe that changed in fit and the lenses that tinted beneath false light. A sure foot, a keen eye, a certain ear, a patient wit, and an above-average height were all common Jacobian traits. Dory Orlean Sevilla possessed none of them. She oft walked slower than her benefactor, muddled her words, and stood two full heads shorter than the countess.

She looked toward the ash of journals in her fireplace. "What mistake have I invited in, my grandfather?"

Tull investigated by his senses and observations, each of which suited his purpose. The secondkind received the same instruction through their first fourteen spans. Then, as they reached an age of accountability and belief, they discovered the purpose for their creation. This was the moment when Partakers took a stand of defiance against Yah in most cases—and many struggled thereafter.

Sondrea never counted straying. With every opportunity, she never needed such consideration. Her father taught her the art of diversion, her mother taught her the recorded history of the Second Creation, her maternal grandfather taught her all he learned about the First Creation, but her maternal grandmother taught her a skill that served her well this morn. Lea Christine Fabray taught her to interpret all that happened between joy and devastation.

TULL & EBBE

Such interpretive skills soothed her when her husband obeyed his purpose. They kept her from anxiety when her daughter wed a corrupted soul. Lea served as a light for her husband, daughter, and granddaughter. Though she met her end afore Sondrea leaned upon her instruction, she prepared her family well and they did not mourn her absence as much as their long wait afore they might see her again.

For now, the countess took a seat at the writing table and took possession of the journals from her purchase that remained unburned. These she held to her breast with both forearms. She then passed backward through her memories—from the visit from Noble Joe Massey's courier, to the time spent alone with her favorite Jacobian, through the reasoning that occupied her mind as she mended in the mending chamber, to the moment afore she sent Dory out to fetch Tull, when she visited with Celia, and further still.

Sondrea retraced moonset to moonrise—in reverse step—from the moment when her succorer arrived at the plot, to the return to her father's side, to the attack by the attacker, and the meeting with her fellow overseers. She remembered tastes of foods and drink, the winter's briskness, and the feel of recuperative gels that aided her mind. Every attempt to coax a loving moment from Katerena surrendered to every opportunity to undo her betrayers. The absence of her husband gave way to books, photographs, reels, and radio tales.

Her legs proved tired as she remembered the exploration of a new, six-storey botanical atrium designed by Deviser Barbara Adal Snow Dove, bride of a soul whose name passed faster than his wandering eye. She and the deviser shared a connection to a certain Jacobian, and she recalled verbatim that exchange of concern and regard without falseness of adoration. A thousand hands, two thousand glances, letterheads, book titles, signs, and then her memories presented again a framed, hand-drawn scape on the wall behind Barbara's meandering husband.

"'*Our Forgotten Othniel.*'" She lifted her head, righted her posture, and took a restorative breath. "'Recreated in our ninety-first sowing season by Artisan Merilyn Harris Sundström.' Her last work of a home she would never see again."

Beneath closed eyelids, her focus shifted from her memory's presentation of the lost territory toward the piercing stare and confident smile of Sutton Robbie Farrell.

"Barbara Adal Snow Dove wed Sutton Robbie Farrell after thirteen moons in wait for another. Her husband specializes in the study of heliotropism and helped her design the lay of glass for the atrium to collect the greatest light."

TULL & EBBE

The letters of his given name, named for his mother's line, reshaped in her mind. *Surobbietton. Rosubibett. Robbsubine.*

"*Sabine*"—she faced the window light but kept her eyes closed—"*Bobbie* Sabine *Sundermann* . . . told me of a soul whom she believed might serve me well."

"I've brought your hand staff!" Dory called out, but did not intrude further. She leaned the slender hickory staff against a high-back chair and worked to straighten the sitting area where she delivered a Jacobian Guardian and a Gierigian rabbit. As she had then, she too worked now beneath the watchful eye of the countess who noticed—most of all—that her aide had not remarked on the absence of her limp.

With inconsiderate habits in mind, she recalled how Bobbie Sabine Sundermann never acted with any regard for Sondrea apart from the recommendation. She recalled no other interaction with the woman that merited her opinion. The more the countess recalled the nature of that moment—the nervous glances and the deliberate answers—the more she doubted the helpful soul's integrity.

"Wilfred responded. I believe he stands as the last soul in the territories to learn that the judges sent their scarecrows to watch over you."

Sondrea's slender grin held, though she despised the nickname given to the Guardians. Why her voice? Why her recommendation? Why was she nowhere in sight when countess and succorer first met?

She watched her succorer thrusting a poker into a log comprised of embers as if afraid. Still, Dory behaved as though the embers warmed her in full. As for the countess, she felt the room's chill in her fingertips and nose. Distracted in discomfort's stead by her mind's measure, she gauged Dory and her character reference near the same height.

"I meant to say *Guardians*. Do forgive."

No, not near at all. She raised her level hand to the height of her succorer whilst she performed the same feat in her mind with the other soul and compared. The same.

As though she heard Sondrea's inner voice, Dory turned and faced her. By then, the countess's hand rested upon the writing table again and her nails scratched at the pulp when the suspicious aide offered the sort of smile that an agitated soul might show toward a hated requirement. Sondrea proved a worthy performer as she unfastened the buckled shoulder straps of her slipover, then fanned her neck as if too warm. With a practiced grin, she then turned toward her reading materials and held the succorer in her peripheral field.

TULL & EBBE

Not a single tick of the clock passed afore Dory, too, peeled off a layer. "I believe I stoked the fire too well!"

Sondrea held her index finger to the display plate's sensor and learned that the room's temperature lingered at seven-tenths of her body temperature. Given the fall of snow and the wintry winds, four-fifths would have provoked her staged reaction. She decided that, in the light, her succorer failed to consider her absent sudor.

"Need I open a window?"

"I'll handle my discomfort." She watched as Dory fanned her non-perspiring throat. "Better we keep the room comfortable afore our guest arrives."

Dory's limber hand formed a rigid fist, which she pushed beneath her arm. "Oh?"

"Charles brings Katerena and he who judges on behalf of all Archibaldians."

Her brow seemed to change in form as her jaw shifted to compress her lips.

"I expect them afore the moonrise."

Her succorer forced a wide smile. "You must be delighted!"

Sondrea let her smile be her answer, for she said this lie that she might test her succorer's truthfulness. "I ask that you tell no other. We dare not put at risk our advocate."

Dory bowed her head with the slightest show of obedience, but the smarmy grin that Sondrea despised never left her face in full.

"I imagine you'll soon slip out of doors"—she looked toward her succorer's feet, then back to her eyes—"for another of your spiced cigarettes."

She could not blush or shine. "Are my habits so foreseeable?"

Sondrea let the light through the windows make clear her distaste. Better she provided her suspected foe the chance to betray her.

"While I'm dressed for the cold, I'll keep an eye out for Mim, too."

Sondrea nodded, but offered no grin in exchange for Dory's sly exit.

"Soon, I'll see you."

"Yes."

That was the last she said. In her mind, however, she still reasoned and judged. She counted a similarity between the creature who served her and the father who played absent host to them. Both—shape-changer and magick-wielder—delighted in confusion. Deception aided them as much as suspicious uncertainty. She detested such tricks.

TULL & EBBE

Her father tormented her mother till his bride counted her own mind as a foe. He directed her toward every cruel misstep and wore down her resolve with ceaseless whispers of doubt. The Fallen First employed the same tactics. Sondrea understood better than most because she regained awareness of those times when he turned the same techniques against her.

"I'll not play the fool for another mingled beast."

Whilst the Guardian took time for slumber, Sondrea read Tarry's writings on *agitators* who haunted the route she traveled by coach. The agitated included her adored Guardian's predecessors who battled but never bested a soul who sounded much like her attacker and the theatrical lots; like a soul from the Archibald Territory who changed his appearance in uncounted ways. In other times, she relied on Tull to glean the truth from his secretive fellows. On this matter, those bested included the full count of the first and second eras of Guardians.

"Better I seek this creature without you; though I doubt he and my attacker are the same." Her gaze drifted from the corner of the room that met with the three-storey atrium and connected to the wing where her father resided to his likeness in a faded mural. "You boasted so oft! Did you not once tell me of this creature with your own odd turn?"

In rare times, when her father's heart for bride and daughter calmed the beckon of magick, he offered them brilliant retellings of his bravery against frightening creatures and malicious spirits. Her blameless mind could not conceive a creature daring enough to stand against him. Then she felt the darkness in their home; a learning darkness that made her open her eyes and see. There, in his most terrifying tales, she discovered that he presented his deeds as those of an upright and gentle soul.

"All the while, our territories feared you most."

That fear worsened without the Guardians present to contain her father. In his longest-lasting—and last—season of decency and brightness, he installed gates at the mouth of every corridor from the manor's atrium. Though the adornments seemed extreme, in the seasons that followed, he gave his family reason upon reason for gratitude toward those bars and locks. With those restraints in place, she still remembered a sense of ease when her father's fellows visited Ebbe Demesne.

The pair from whom she bore no genes—and who proved more forgiving than her grandfather—stood in the atrium with cloaked gear in tow and represented two of the last guests they received afore his magick overtook his heart. Randolph Herford

Wylie's blonde hair turned snowy by then, but the ornamented jacket he wore beneath his riding cape still gleamed with medals and ribbons. She focused now on the shape they formed in her mind and turned to the array of shelves that kept the book she believed held a similar illustration.

"There was a soul in the Era of the Reformers"—she plucked an oversized white spine with gold stencil letters and sifted the deckle pages within—"who hid face and name from our territories' elder Guardians."

She found detailed recreations of the territories as they developed throughout her grandfather's and grandmother's era. This was a collection of the isle's first seventy spans in the Accession. So precious was this book that her mother never allowed her to turn the pages on her own. Now, none remained to help her.

"No two witnesses ever agreed upon his face or heard his voice."

She recalled that hers and Charles's attacker never spoke either. Now that she counted all that she remembered from the warning of the attack, the reference of her succorer, the indistinct voices of the unnamed visitor to the tower and Bobbie Sabine Sundermann escaped every memory too. Still, she recounted a flow of details from other reads.

"When he vanished, he vanished with full anonymity intact."

This confusion lent to many likenesses, which lent two pages to a subsection on lore and legends and proved her memory for the many books at her disposal. The constant detail amid composite illustrations was a shaped light that formed a staggered, triangular chest-piece like those of the medals on Wylie's jacket.

"You inspired many souls, Guardian Wylie. Your foes too?"

In three of the illustrations, each from a different artist across two territories and two eras, the high collar of a topcoat framed a bloom of light beneath a balaclava like those worn by her grandfather—and now Tull—along with the secondkind's many protectors. Around the hem, where the face held the fabric in place, a gleam of light cast the eyes in deep shadow.

"Paladin?"

Her brow creased in a humored manner that lent to the return of a wrinkle once removed from her visage. She owed her confused response to the memory of the Guardian's make-believe foe in the maligned film about her parents and grandfather.

"I believed this book merited and favored."

TULL & EBBE

With a hint of disgust, she cast the book upon the wooden desktop of her mother's writing table and pressed the pads of her fingers against her hips.

"Why would Paladin hound me?"

Controller Gary Adamson Clark swore—boasted, even—that he alone created Paladin; the foe his band of make-believe Guardians faced in *Love Magick*. Most books on the isle received fewer than fifty hand-printings; so, his trickery held. Clark turned the secondkind fearful of Thesp Gordon Wesley Sampson, born a mute and hired to portray the foe to enhance the presence of fear in his scenes. To not learn why a foe targeted a soul needled the deepest fears post-Accession.

"You ought to have struck him harder, my grandfather."

Then, she counted that her grandfather—like her father and their fellows—denied any foe of theirs compared to Paladin. Even her mother made the claim. She gasped with the fright of a child stirred by sleep-terrors and fell to her knees behind the protective barrier offered by her writing desk. What she recalled appeared to her in black-and-white images; as film stock stamped with the logo of Eidolon Pictures and embossed with a whimsical title.

In the film, Thesps Danele Gertie Zuriñe and Ronnie Gerald Knapp portrayed her parents. Knapp showed the count as neither loving nor considerate, but as a soul drunk on magick and lust for her mother. The clash that preceded a screenwriter's depiction of their union let the thesp rely on a light show and dry ice trickery to defeat his costumed foe whilst Danele heaved and fainted. These acts unfolded amid a bland-faced settlement of slight-built simpletons presented in over-the-shoulder glimpses lest an audience sympathize with the wrong lot and fear their hero.

Though she bowed her head in submission to the Triune's revelation of truth unto her soul, another's title arose from her broken heart. "Papa!"

Those Beneath Her

An Interim

The 8th Morn beneath the Moon of the Mother's Song
The 107th Winter Season of the Accession
In the Care of the Helper, who keeps souls from fruitless wandering.

Moses Ian Merill remained in the service of the countess of Ebbe Demesne not due to any sense of debt, nor to a keen ability to do his work well. He evaded his duties, shirked obedience, and snooped worse than most scavengers. Thirty-nine of her acquaintances complained of her disagreeable reeve and his ceaseless offenses. She proved patient—not forgiving—for he was the eldest remnant of her grandfather's tether unto this era.

Afore Zeck met his second bride, defended Hearthfjorden, or was offered the title of Guardian, he traveled with a soul who would be like a thorn to the tender flesh of all whose purposes turned his head in offense or pleasure alike. Mim needed no reason to rile, and few souls who felt his sting ever set out to rile him. He riled because they disturbed his eye, annoyed his ear, or offended him for coming too near.

His sense of trespass was one-sided. He stole more glances, overhead more conversations, and swiped more details than a soul ought to collect in their brief stay on time's plot. To those whom he suspected of recompense, he busted noses, split lips, and crushed fingers. Why Sondrea endured him baffled many a soul.

One such baffled soul who too caught his eye was her current succorer. She he followed the way a bloom followed the light. Even in this, stipulations existed. She must never approach him—being the first—and a barrier of stone or glass oft separated them—being the second. Elsewise, the reeve scattered, for his mind did not prove sharp enough to maintain an advantage without the benefit of tactile barriers.

Tull & Ebbe

There was no trait that stood out about Dory Orlean Sevilla. Heat turned her skin waxen, her teeth seldom showed, her eyes oft appeared dull. The soul she served had the brighter countenance and the eye-catching tresses. The countess, too, kept a figure that—though no longer of interest to Mim's lechery—kept her in the affections of many and overshadowed her aide.

When she—the succorer—stepped out of doors, she took to a path that kept her from the eyes and interests of the pesky Creightonian Guardian and drew the reeve's curiosity over what she sought to keep unseen. In turn, Mim zigzagged from tree cluster to tree cluster to follow her and not earn similar attention from either the pests or the curious creature he followed.

"Hey, brother!" cried out the pesky soul. "Your display plate has been alit with the face of your freckled—"

"Asham. Keep from my tent."

"As you say! I worried that I'd lost my whetstone and wanted—"

"You haven't a whetstone to misplace."

"George's then."

"Where is George?"

The Jacobian whom Mim tormented raised a concern that turned the reeve's spine rigid. Even the succorer paused between three honey locust fingers till the answer of George's whereabouts flowed from the Creightonian.

"You're to shadow him, are you not?"

"He went down to check on the horses. And, I shadow Ganix till the eve." Asham's voice then fell unto a mutter. "Edmond pecks at me still for need—"

Mim lost the rest of Asham's words to the chime of ice crystals that compressed when he leaned his shoulder against the next cluster of trees along his path. Dory moved again too. As long as they moved toward the south, neither needed fear an intersecting path with the Westonian Guardian. No other tracked as well as him, but the way he moved—never disturbing leaf nor casting a flake of snow—intimidated sneaks and snoops. He reminded Mim of Buster Roderick King; a soul who never let him succeed at any of his wronghearted schemes.

The deception of his heart surrendered to the confusion of his mind as he caught another glimpse of Dory as both cleared neighboring hilltops away from still Westonians, loud Creightonians, and ever-seeing Jacobians. Now in place of her ill-fitted belt and cold weather cape she wore a sleeveless surcoat that was the shade of the bark but offered no shed layers for him to steal. She entered the Behemót Woods without fear; not that Mim would have heard her above the heavy beat of his heart or his sharper breathing.

Dory had muscular arms and legs, but with the proper padding and layering, could mimic the flab of Bobbie Sabine Sundermann's limbs. Both women had a pronounced chest; of which Dory's was proudest and better-sculpted. Still, padding and layering altered *much*. A wig and the proper makeup fooled many eyes—Edmond Anson Elragadó proved moonrise after moonrise. Spectacles hid and augmented traits of the eyes and even a blameless soul mimicked a waddle; but, had the reeve noticed the deceptiveness used against their benefactor?

Afore he ascended the next hilltop, a percussive blast chased a hammer strike and the grunt of another soul. Because he had not expected the sound, Mim flung his whole body facedown in the snow. Crystals hung now to his beard and brow, but his eyes watered with mingled fear and curiosity. Then, where he remained prostrate to surprise, he noticed an odd set of tracks: one imprint of a slender left boot and one flat, horned-moon-shaped imprint that covered the right step in full and traveled alongside a set of slipper soles recognizable for their drastic heel impression.

As he was about to reach toward the latter imprint, the next percussive blast renewed his fear. This time, though, a well-known sound of howling laughter drove back the fast-settling stillness that followed a hammer strike. Behind that laughter followed the muddled voice of an Archibaldian. Mim might have heard Olley's boasts toward Harlan clearer had he not rummaged in his ear canals to clear away snow.

Their ruckus put the pair three hillsides eastward whilst the bizarre imprints headed south. Those too led away from Ebbe Demesne; though not alongside the slippery-footed imprints that Dory made. Mim looked toward the southernmost hilltop where the succorer's trail led, half-expectant to find her in wait. More entangled trees awaited and no more. To find her, he would have to shed the sky-fires' light and follow her trail unto the shadowy belly of the Behemót Woods.

Whilst the percussive ripple from the two Guardians dizzied the air, the countess's succorer took hold of a bronze pike with both hands. She pressed with her full might till long teeth with receded gums showed and the corners of her mouth stretched further than the recognized degree amid the secondkind and their collective visage. Dory then sidestepped and let go of the pike, but used the strongest hand to console her weakened left side. A deep-reaching vibration, softer than the hammer strike and pursuant blast, then shook loose a single leaf, which she shooed away as she reached toward a duffel that contained a cast of disguises.

At the top of the lot sat Bobbie Sabine Sundermann, who passed in and out of Sondrea's affairs for three moons afore the countess heard her in a direct manner. In truth, she was no more alive—now—than the soul who visited Mumus Tower and offered suspicions in exchange for alms. Every character existed for a single purpose: to dupe the countess in the hopes that she would return to Ebbe Demesne. That plot allowed for a team of Guardians to follow her there, but the mention of the Advocate of the Archibald Territory set his bride's succorer off-script.

With agitated fingers, the performer clawed at the wig atop her head and removed the full skull from her bald crown. This she stowed in that filthy duffel along with the cape and belt she wore to mimic the countess and appeal to her as being similar. Nearer now to her true form, she kept clean her disguise lest the ever-inquisitive souls on Ebbe Demesne learn of her charade. The countess proved worth a challenge, but Dory had not counted the heightened notes of precision and detail that the Jacobian orphan brought from her benefactor.

She tucked away the remnants of her disguise then drew closed the duffel, which she tucked between trees, for she dared not be undone by the lurking reeve who followed. Her eyes, wearied from the harsh light that the Second Creation lived beneath, kept her from seeing the peculiar imprints even with the tinted lenses she discarded. Those tracks that she crossed with her own feet went unnoticed; as if the light were darkness. Such a trait was common amid the Taotáva.

Her ears seldom failed. This was another trait amid her kind. Boastful remarks, needling laughter, and labored breaths gave away the location of every other rival about her. Still, she bore no fear toward them and stood motionless as she sensed a fifth soul on this side of the entangled forest due to the vibration's sounding one octave lower than the strike she cast. The woods offered plenty of ways to discard a soul who found her there, so she did not fear that trespasser, but the rich scent of oil and alloy confused her delicate sense of smell.

TULL & EBBE

From between mismatched trees—one mulberry and the other elm—terrane flowed outward from the crust of ice and snow; first as two piles, and then one misshapen oval. A pair of muddied hands broke the frozen surface and gripped the overlapping roots afore a sleek head thrust from the glebe. The form that followed—unable to alter since the countess bathed him in fire—spilled outward without need for air or a rush to sweep the filth from his eyes. He stood, still lopsided from injury, and batted saddened eyes toward the creature who shared his lineage.

"Ming, braatu moi'e!"

Dory's manner of speaking changed from breathy snark to coarse huffs of syllables. She embraced the neck of the countess's attacker as though a true part of the secondkind and further alarmed him with her words.

"Moramio ićio kee braatu Noeu. Naaučio saam Mumus putui'ee ovdi'ee stićio ćee dio zaalaaskio mi'eesecaa."

Ming Tovam, her brother, provided more emotion with his eyes than his mouth would ever give. The bronze pike offered greater range of sound than he. Amid those souls who took the brunt of Count Conliffe's magick, he used muteness to his advantage and served as a better spy than all others; till the count's daughter took his purpose the way her father took his voice. Now scarred, he kept to the forest and awaited chances to aid his sister.

Together, the siblings burrowed beneath the terrane that the Second Creation claimed as theirs unto the hidden land where uncounted eras once built and thrived. Places the secondkind now feared. More spoils awaited them beneath than with the subservient lot amid whom they hid for what they sought from above could not be counted in alms. When they claimed that, they would see Yah's favored lot and His First Creation tremble at the mention of their name.

By the time Mim arrived where Dory's path ended, the tunneled glebe had collapsed so he could not trespass beneath. The loose terrane and pummeled ice forged a barrier that he could not break without the benefit of a tool or the sacrifice of his fingernails. When he kicked with his heel, he lost his balance. Lest he wanted the Guardians mothering him, he would have to sacrifice his efforts till he brought back tools.

TULL & EBBE

He did not surrender. The overlap of the slippery-footed succorer's path and the two odd imprints circled around a bronze pike that he could not uproot or jar and a cluster of trees that held between them a filth-covered duffel. This proved of greater worth to him than the feat of exposing Ming's tunnel. The succorer would pay him in alms and favors to have the contents back—and she would pay him again and again.

Mim stooped down and loosened the duffel without guilt. The feel of the wig between his fingers upended him; he could not deny. That unexpected sensation made his heart pound faster and limited his range of hearing. Elsewise, he might have heard metal against wood sooner. In sufficient time's stead, he turned too late. His eyes did not focus in a proper manner, but he made out the swift approach of his blurred visage afore a snow and terrane covered blade struck him across the face and spun his unconscious frame across the duffel he meant to scavenge.

As the mismatched sounds of uneven steps resumed then faded, the creaking of wood amplified and grew nearer. Figures raced above head, unhindered by the confusion of the trees. The Kuusa Si'epä leapt unto the terrane and nine slender bodies clustered around Mim. At full height, they too blocked out the light that fell upon the reeve and covered him with their shadows. They did not, however, stay at full height. As he had attempted in their previous encounter, they held broken branches as clubs to be used against him.

NITA NAOMI OZUL

Nita is deliberate—down to her wolf-like style. Her rivalry with others is rooted in her Shelbian upbringing. Each territory has a distinct personality trait, a specific belief, and some conflict with another. As we spend time with her, we learn of Nita's connection to Ebbe Demesne and her chilly protectiveness of a friend.

Laud & Lament

TWENTY-ONE

The 8th Peak beneath the Moon of the Mother's Song

The 107th Winter Season of the Accession

In the Care of the Helper, who keeps souls from fruitless wandering.

Despite the lore of the surrounding woods and the iciness of the breeze, Tull's fellow Guardians who remained near the camp formed small groups across the grove and watched as he spoke with another's scion. Nita Naomi Ozul, daughter to Edythe Frances Ozul and a father who refused her his name, towed a degree of arrogance that rivaled Olley's, a coolness that made Edmond shiver, and a spirit that kept George more still than he oft proved. The Shelbians raised beautiful creatures, yet she could not gain more than a shallow glance from the Jacobian who invited her. This drew her nearer than was customary between rivaling neighbors.

Tull seemed receptive to the scion's nearness, but the divide between him and Ganix widened with each tick of the pocket watch that the latter clutched in his unclean hand. The host Guardian's jowl formed creases up to the corners of his eyes as he kept his head down and pretended disinterest with the same skill that Olley displayed around Dory Orlean Sevilla. Ganix stared above the rims of his tinted glasses, but if he pouted further, he might hook his lip around the tip of his nose.

Three women served as Guardian in the previous era. The first, who was not Alison Brackett Nance, saw her name stricken from all annals; a feat that cost more alms than the judges admitted to their critics and supporters. Not even the current roster of elders spoke her name—though they served alongside her with Nance and Ember Willows Martel. Nance and Martel flaunted their rareness, but she who went unnamed, defaced in their photographs, and unmentioned in their chatter captivated this era's first female scion.

The way she postured herself within the confines of Tull's frame, and nodded at his every remark, made a soul wonder if she remembered the soul she served. Tull seemed the only member determined to prove her ready to leave behind her long-suffered title. So, when Nita cradled his jaw with both hands and kissed his mouth, no surprise befell their onlookers. Though Partakers claimed the gesture as their own, a kiss stood as a common show of regard and agreement between common and rural Shelbians of all persuasions.

None of the three elders welcomed Nita. In this, they reinforced her loyalty toward Tull, who was fourth in the eldership. The pair might have discussed their preferred jellies and breads, or they might have conspired to oust Ganix. Whatever their interests, they were united in purpose, mood, and gait. By the time they arrived at his tent, their decision resided beneath small talk that none of the others would decipher; though, a fool proved ready to try.

"See you made that wolf call then!"

Nita froze as Asham brushed his fingers through the wolfskin coat that adorned her shoulders.

"Yep! I tell you, Harlan dragged Olley off to lay snares afore he spoke up. That soul does tow a mighty hate for *Shelbians*!"

This time, she turned away to conceal her ridicule but Asham circled to get a look at her.

"I'd have gone along, but the hare cannot mingle with the sloth. And, a soul needed to rile that fair-haired wallop who rode in whilst the Jacobian took his rest."

Tull suffered some wooziness from his visit with Sondrea, so wallops—fair, speckled, or pale-eyed—fell from his concern afore they reached his regard. "Kuti'en i'eotkut ko orete."

Asham found silence beneath the sound of Nita's laughter more than Tull's barb against him. He let the sound of her bristle him. "You keep the scions amused, brother. I am the third Guardian of the Creighton Territory. She falls beneath me."

"In title."

"As you say."

"You say." Tull's posture rose as his tone fell. "You say that she falls beneath you in title alone. By no other measure are we above a soul in these territories."

TULL & EBBE

"As you say, Tull. I am cordial."

The wind passed through the camp as Tull waited on the specific words and shook the battered fabric which drew Nita's touch to his tent and proved her lack of regard for the Creightonian's attempt at offense. For this choice, she missed seeing the change in Tull's eyes that made Asham tremble as if the wind cut through him.

"I ought not have spoken out of turn, Scion Ozul."

"No, you ought not."

Asham's nose and cheek fluttered in agitation.

"Your home betrays you, Jacobian."

"That's Shaw's tent."

With the tone of playfulness gone from his voice, Asham's callousness toward he who advanced because a fellow met his end drew Nita's hands into fists.

"Not that he had the time to unfold or unpack! Cam Fenner called Tull to service so fast that he hadn't the time to wipe the milk off his—"

Nita swung faster than he spoke, connected, and knocked Asham off the heels of his wet boots. Afore his crown hit the terrane, she had deprived him of his consciousness. The Jacobian remained unaffected by his condition. George laughed as he repaired the external fine threads on a soft-metal tripod that held Edmond's field scope and did not speak.

"Arthur George Green, soon I'll learn your secrets well."

George appeared as if he swallowed his tongue and hid his eyes from Nita. He possessed a knack for being singled out in a crowd by those he sought to avoid. She looked to Tull for a non-existent smile and found he placed her gear alongside his tent, though nearer to the fire. Still, another observed her and raised his voice.

"Ozul!"

"Odd hearing him shout another name than 'Gera.'" Tull kept his head down and glanced toward George, who nodded, and mimicked his friend.

"Ozul! Get over here."

In less time than Nita responded to her first order, the Westonian set aside his thread file, covered his work with an oiled cloth, and angled away from Edmond's position. "With her near, I believe Asham might find a friend in Olley after all."

Tull's sneer possessed enough charm to coax a smile from George. "I ought to see to the goats."

"Don't name these."

TULL & EBBE

A handful of snow struck Tull's shoulder and made him prove the gladness he kept. While George hurried away, he who was struck managed a curious eye toward Edmond's ability to fluster Ganix's scion. To Nita's credit, she appeared as stiff-necked as Olley when he collected rebukes. Tull sensed that even the wind settled and kept from risking the bite of Edmond's disapproval. Then, the wind countered with a tart scent for his nostrils.

"Guardian Ganix."

"Your cleverness fails afore your eyes, Tull, and with suddenness that I reserved for an Archibaldian or"—he used the side of his boot to jab Asham.

Tull imagined how Ganix must have crept around Jules, too; admiring with his jittering, yellow eyes the portions she would never offer him. Then, he imagined Vic. How that good soul must have felt when he struck in defense of his daughter.

"If you scheme against me, I tell you I'll—"

"Set fire to my boots? Defile my horse's water? Take credit for my deception?"

A sly grin proved the uneven setting of Ganix's jaw as he took delight in Tull's observational skills. He then read the countess's invitation afore the message bearer for a time that Tull no longer counted.

"Don't you tire of letting others believe you a vandal and a forager?"

"Don't you tire of letting others believe you're at peace on this plot?" He then laughed with a din that set an unnoticed Squire to flight. While he observed the path of travel, he circled the Jacobian and surveyed Asham. "Uncounted moons have passed since you and I last stood on this terrane. Have they not?"

Two hundred three counted moons since Tull's last visit.

"You have forgotten that I was here. They withheld my invitation to see the manor then, too."

Tull appreciated the divulged wisdom but also felt gratitude that Ganix—offensive and selfish—remained an unchanging, ever-reliable presence.

"I confess that I never saw the harm in letting you stay in her care. But Cameron wanted to be the undisputed headship, and all can tell of that fool's monotonous need to prove that he was better than our old fathers." He gathered a woman's hair clip that fell from Asham's pocket and tested the clasp.

Tull watched Ganix pocket Asham's possession, still in silence, rather than give him the satisfaction of failing at shaming him. He flicked his brow over the shared secret and gathered a bundle of firewood. Ganix soiled neither his hands nor his character but strolled along because Tull met his demand of an invitation.

"Tell me, Jacobian, does the countess"—he gasped and circled for fear he spoke her name with more than a hush, then dove toward Tull's side again—"does the countess favor the plums and roses of an Erorii winter or the deepest golds and fieriest reds of a Jacobian gathering season?"

"She tends toward plums and emeralds."

Ganix stopped and blinked uncounted times. "Emeralds, you say? Emeralds?"

"From a painting of Zeck's mother"—he strained to load one piece without help—"who shared her vibrant tresses."

Ganix laughed as if tickled by soft hands. "Yes, they are vibrant, are they not?"

Tull winced and piled on two more pieces of dense wood whilst Ganix folded his arms and pondered.

"I believe I've just the trinket for the occasion." Once he had watched in silence whilst Tull labored, he furthered his complaint. "I tell you; utter confusion looms by bringing that glass-eyed slattern in as you have."

Some barbs proved difficult to endure, but Tull heard more vile descriptors from Nita's lips, so he clenched his teeth. Ganix offended Jules, and Vic righted that offense. If he slighted Sondrea too, then Tull's two hundred three moons of kept sorrow would become his Shelbian elder's ache to bear.

"You believe you do right by her—and I do not believe that you intend to spite me. I tell you, Cameron believed the same when he let in she who I mustn't name."

Tull heard of the harshness and chaos that his elders unleashed across the territories and gauged this measure of Ganix's concern against tales of the Shelbian's chaotic tendencies.

"Better you send her back to Tebet or on to Kërcim afore she sets you against Harlan or Edmond or Falk . . . *versus*. Not that I care! Nor need I feign compassion. But, you are a passable fellow, and who keeps Gera as anticipatory as Falk does?"

"I thank you for withholding your praise of him till he's not around."

Ganix's laughter never drew sound but proved evident in the way his entire body jostled even as he traipsed back toward the fire. He let a spark of adoration smolder and then his tone turned as smooth as his singing voice. "Reassure your Carpenterian dove and her father that I meant them no lasting insult. My ways are upon me and I do enjoy making scatter even the gentlest of souls."

He then paused and looked upon Tull's hands.

"But, most of all, I have no desire to spend the rest of this moon shitting my teeth." A speck of light entered his eyes and then scurried as he drew a much-needed breath from the exertion of momentary decency. To salve his lacking fortitude, Ganix let a groan from Asham serve as a reaction to his crude remark.

"Was I down?"

The way that Ganix smiled at Tull troubled the Jacobian in that he felt the same expression crease his own face.

"Say, Tull?"

The Jacobian wearied beneath Asham's precursory warning of yet another intrusive or ignorant word. Ganix offered him the hair clip he swiped and nodded, as if to tempt him into using the trinket as an anvil against the Creightonian. Tull considered, then shook off sinful abuses and flung a piece of wood upon the fire.

"Tull?"

"Not even for the eves he cost you in Parantua?"

Tull flung aside the rest of the firewood and held out an open palm, which Ganix filled with the stolen trinket. Though he asked Yah's forgiveness for not protecting Jules from Ganix's offense, he too thanked their Creator for the moment of sincerity with the Shelbian. He then knelt and set the hair clip upon Asham's left shoulder.

"Dare I sigh for him to fall mute?"

The Jacobian leaned forward on the weight of his knee, then instructed the mouthiest of all Guardians. "When you repent with sincerity to each of your fellows, Ozul counted, for your constant offense and neglectfulness, you will find your way from beneath your bind."

"Nelson, I—" Asham's attempt to disprove Tull's capacity ended with an abrupt collapse.

Lest a fool suffer the elements, the intentional Jacobian stoked the fire and added the choicest pieces of wood for Asham's benefit. By the time Ganix's scion returned to the *lesser* end of camp, a mighty flame raged.

"This fire turns immense."

The Jacobian stared as though she nicked him with a barb.

She side-eyed the agitative soul she struck and the trinket upon him, then drew on all that was proper according to her purpose. "Forgive me, Guardian Ganix, if my anger against my Creightonian Guardian brought you shame."

TULL & EBBE

While as clever as any soul in the outfit, Nita had not spent the time with Ganix required to learn of his disdain for praise from those he deemed beneath him. Such lessons, Tull imagined, came from a teacher whose bark sounded like thunder. He peered toward the tents of the elders and felt unnerved when he found that same teacher watching him again.

"I will save my frustrations for the next foe."

Ganix shooed her with redirection. "Do you seek a blizzard, Tull? The wrath of that blaze! A soul might believe you pulled down the sky-fires to heat this camp!"

Even when Ganix, who oft complained of freezing, enjoyed a sight, he found a way to sound displeased. In his defense, the ridiculousness of heat that arose from the fire proved how Tull worried over his invitation to Nita, his bond with Ganix, his hand against Asham, and the disapproval he would face from his headship if he failed. Still, he relied on well-practiced disinterest. "Snow blows from the mountains."

Ganix checked Tull's observation and retracted as if he spotted bizarre creatures descending on them from the distant peaks. "Ozul! Ozul! Gather some wood and set a stack near my tent."

"Once you've stacked that wood, join me on a sweep of the east plank." Tull then added for Ganix's benefit, "Should our elder Guardian approve."

"Fine! Fine! Saves me the trouble of making work for her."

Tull watched how Edmond let the others congregate around him, as if to test him. Their headship sealed the distance with a sly grin and returned to his tent without barricading the heat. In the confines, removed from unfamiliar eyes, he took the hat and wig from his head, then mopped his brow. The Jacobian gathered a bundle of wood, in the absence of the Larsonite's scion, and approached their headship's tent.

Edmond's socked feet swept upward, cramped and twisted from his many seasons and undiscussed defeats, as he stacked the wood without the offense of racket. He went unaddressed whilst Edmond rested on his crated bed, worn journal in tow, and observed how he used his teeth to unfold a pair of spectacles. Even if he enjoyed his headship's trust, Tull felt he owed him the proper show of respect in approaching with a willing show of obedience.

"I've not seen you build a fire like that since you cleaved the head off ole Judge Taft's best cow."

"In due fairness, I had never swung a scythe afore."

"In due fairness." His smirk held to the right corner of his mouth.

"Ganix clinched at Nita's praise."

"Which end of him?"

Tull brushed at the ball of his nose. "I believe I ought to show Ozul the perimeter afore the moon rises and teach her to set a sensor."

Edmond made a note in his journal, but with a wave of his hand proved how well he mimicked Ganix. "Fine, fine. How fares the countess?"

"As I imagined her." He deflected Edmond's curious glance better than the barb her secrets planted in his heart. "Her visitor enjoys Noble Joe Massey's provision."

His headship's exhalation seemed as harsh as Ganix's expulsions.

"She's also niece to Thesp Constance Ashland Tarry."

"You don't say! I sat in the shadow of Ott's Playhouse back, oh, my thirtieth span or near, and saw her give what they called a play for the crowd." He scoffed. "She was so liquored that she slurred through much of the second act and teetered halfway out of her dress and through the back door with the accordion player holding on with all his might. I can't tell you most of the crowd noticed, though. That accordion player's bride, to be certain, did. He was the best one-armed music-maker at the Playhouse after that."

"They hosted many?"

Edmond raised his hand and wriggled four fingers. "All righties!"

Tull's grin matched his and he sensed that Edmond would tell him no more about the memory. "Asham will remain on his face till—"

"We can all handle rest from that dullard. Remember! Our purposes are contrary for now. Let Falk try his hand at corralling him." His belly hopped when he laughed, and his toes curled on his right foot. "Ozul laid Gera out!"

Tull ducked his head and checked Asham's proximity as the whistle-like sound of Edmond's laughter rolled from his tent like steam from a kettle. A satisfied grin spread across a dour face; enough that the newest recruit took sheepish notice. Rather than draw her eye onto their headship, he averted his eyes onto the snowy terrane and set his hand against the stump where Edmond rested his boots.

"Nelson." Edmond drew his attention and rested his journal. "Do remember we travel in *her* territory. The ways of these souls, however kind we treat them, are not like ours."

"I'll mind her hands."

"And her teeth. And those ceramic tips. You remember the old prayers?"

"Some."

"If you hear so much as a repetitive incantation, you cut tongue and throat, then get back to this camp and stay near to that fire till the wicked lot feasts on her."

"On your orders."

"Mine and no others." Tull's elder shifted on his cot and reached down to massage his knotted arch. "You fall, and I'm stuck training Kemp! That's *two* who've kept close to this territory. I thank you, no. Is Falk to be a problem?"

"I'll ask him not to be."

"Keep him afraid to disobey you." Edmond let out another whistling laugh. "That spirit-infested cow cooked up nice on the fire, as I remember him."

"I remember the same." Tull nodded in lieu of a formal exit.

TWENTY-TWO

Sondrea stared at the gated mouth of the corridor that led to her father's parlor in the furthest setting of the opposite wing. Photographs framed in broken glass created a tapestry of chimes, due to how the winds blew against the outer glass wall. These panes let in the light but kept those who lived indoors obstructed from those who spied on them. That was her dilemma. From daughter to spy.

Due to her proscriptive relationship with her father and the expectations that Cyril instilled in Katerena, Sondrea's awareness of the conventional bond between father and daughter proved tarnished. The most famous instance when her mother kept a secret from her grandfather resulted in her birth. She never learned of the joy or the strength found from the simple act of running unto her father's arms for safekeeping. What her father taught her kept her aware of every word, sound, and act as if each choice threatened his approval and provision.

Her half-brother and male cousin learned the same example and enacted far worse upon their daughters. Her mother spared her from such despicable relationships. Gloria Bea Greer—whom she counted as her eldest friend—suffered beneath a violent father. Even Nelson—whom she counted as her most cherished soul—suffered from a father who put his mother's whims above the needs of his son.

There was never a habit of paying a visit to her father afore she gained his approval. Even this visit hinged on his sending her cousin, Saul Ole Ebbe, out to unbolt the doors of the manor. The threat upon her soul failed to trouble him enough to console her. So, the idea that she could approach he who was responsible for her mother's phenomenal lie required another act of disobedience.

"Not that he can take your title from you."

She bore her title because he sought to humiliate her mother in the eyes of the entire Second Creation. Maia deserved the marvel affixed to the title of countess of Ebbe Demesne. She suffered. She abandoned her purpose in Yah's plan to be a bride to a magick-wielder. The count coveted but never appreciated her sacrifice.

TULL & EBBE

He placed the title upon their daughter and paraded her to wound his brides. In this, he took away her purpose in Yah's plan too. His cruelty set Sondrea in the scope of Cyril's gaze. Now, the attention of a bad villain from a despised film turned toward her. No other could ever speak to her about heaping too much disdain upon another's creative work.

"Yet, none of that sets you on the other side of these vile gates."

That same set of keys that Cameron Lou Fenner handled to unlock her bolted bed chamber—that she then used to gouge Nelson's taker's face—rested again with Saul Ole Ebbe as a reminder as weighty as his mighty hand. As Tull described him, he was a slow-moving tree. As she had warned Tull, he also bore a heart surrendered to magick and other depravities. Without embellishment, she oft imagined a time when she would have to defend her next breath against him.

"Not afore I have my answer." She drummed the brass-plated iron bar that held the brass-plated iron rods that kept her from exiting her mother's wing and entering the foyer. "Not afore Nelson hears that answer."

She cast off discouragement, for she benefitted that the glass-encased wing came after the original builder completed the manor and, upon her return to her parlor, traced her fingertips along the white-and-gold trimmed mantel. Due to the placement of the fireplace, a gap existed between the historical home and the addition where she spent her blamelessness. In that time, she discovered a slender passageway between the aged stone of the former exterior and the freestanding ornamental trellises that provided this wing a skeleton.

With the removal of a pair of loose bricks at the fireplace's side and the undoing of rickety copper screws that spoke to her frequent travel, she sprang from the proper lay a section of insulated planks that held back the trapped air between structures. Time dulled her memory of the stench of that air but the way her hand covered her nose again reminded her how she basked beneath that welcome then too. Now, the flexible tubes and brass lateral carriage gears of her mother's private mending chamber blocked the corner in the passage from north to east. She would need to pry at the innards of plaster and wooden slats to gain access to the octagonal foyer.

"And not tear the old skin."

She still bore the lessons and values her mother instilled in her toward respect of possessions and what was not theirs. The manor belonged to her father now. If she damaged the walls or made obvious her hidden passageway, she would prove

TULL & EBBE

disobedient to her mother's teachings. She weighed her concern with the flexibility of her mingled leg and retraced every other option that led to her father's parlor.

She stepped over the ductwork to the mending chamber, but there her travels required a sharp turn. What once offered her plenty of room from south to east no longer seemed hospitable to travelers. Her crown now collected a garland of cobwebs whilst her breasts and backside upset seclusion's dust. The snugness lodged her afore she completed her first step, though she felt her toe scrape at the stone of the adjoined floor.

"Twenty spans ago? Yes!"

The echo of her voice mocked her.

"You warned me, Mama, not to tire of my slim build too soon. Did you not?" She huffed for reprieve and cast away a ribbon of cobwebs. "Of all the times when a soul might benefit from the advantages of being a shape-changer."

With the foot that found no rest, she pushed against the furthest adjacent stone and pivoted back around the bundle of chamber tubes without marring her clothes in dust or soot. Her mingled limb proved competent. Even when she sidestepped out unto the parlor in retreat, the muscle and foot responded as well as her complete leg.

"A soul ought to speak to you about passageway design, Inventor Putnam." She shimmied her narrow waist and fussed with the straightness of her shoulders. "All Holston Lucius Buckler—the second—considers is the best way to better amplify a woman's habitus. A barb I now wish to pluck!"

She unfastened the knit outer coat that kept her from a chill and offered an unheard compliment to the soul who invented the well-proven adornments that corrected her leg. Diane Lowell Putnam earned the respect of the countess, who was ten spans her junior, for the way she oft took the heart that the First Creation poured out upon the secondkind and bettered their routines. Her index finger traced the blunt lights along her femur with a humble awareness that she ought to have been an amputee.

"Truly, you are an underappreciated friend to me, Gloria, for your persistence."

She folded the knit coat, which she took with her once she reset the false wall, then hurried through the adjoining rooms. The coat she tossed upon the bench seat she shared with her cherished Guardian but elected to use the parallel bench as her path continued—from the lift of her head and the arch in her back—upward. For this, she unfastened the cuffs from the sleeves of her blouse.

TULL & EBBE

"If I had back the alms I spent on clothes I later soiled with plans like these"—she set the cuffs atop her overcoat—"*I* would own Ebbe Demesne."

A riskier method remained, so she bolted the doors to the parlor and double-checked every curtain. She might have concealed the eyes of the mural of elder Guardians, for another lesson that her father taught her was his ability to see unto places he never set foot. That she wed a soul with similar interests ought not to have surprised her. She asked forgiveness from mother above Creator, then moved toward the unintended entry of the next passageway.

Her sigh made her reconsider her corseted high belt, which she rid from her waist without debate. Where that fell, she did not see, for she set her focus on the wooden cabinetry of the windowless room that offered smooth passage with a clever turn. A forceful tug at the trim on the outer and rear corner revealed a mechanized hinge that drew narrow slats from their upright and recessed lay unto a narrow ladder. She offered a downward thrust of the trim and set them in a locked position for the balls of her feet.

A crawl space above the room let the panes shift according to the season. This same space allowed for placement of pipes and wires amid any creature that sought a forgotten place in which to nest. On the other side of a slide-away plate awaited her second-best route to her father. With a hesitant will and marginal bravery, she hoped no other creature awaited her there and climbed the next rung to confirm that hope.

"See, Mama? Our Creator still smiles upon this plot."

Sondrea hurried, lest smugness mar progress, and ascended the next three wooden rungs till her fingers reached enough of the ornamental trellis that she could climb using the strength of her arms and her whole leg. With these three limbs, she protected her mingled limb and traversed the length of the wing toward a triangular-shaped outlet that divided the height of the second-storey of the original structure and offered narrow passage unto a place where all guests felt like intruders.

The three-storey, three-wing manor at Ebbe Demesne hosted forty-six rooms filled with handicraft and furnishings that pre-dated Sondrea's birth. Whether she changed her father's heart toward a home filled with the sounds of children or magick took him so far from his plans, the place withered beneath cold and staleness. The longing creak of the neglected floors invited her to trespass. She took this as a sign that no other stood against her.

Some mild hammering with open palms reassured her of her belief and let her remove a hand-carved wooden vent cover that enabled moderate air flow from above her mother's wing unto the second storey. Once she kept the cover from falling, she crawled through the triangular passage minus the use of her left leg or the elegance afforded a countess. She felt like rivals Hawwah and the Liar as she pressed through the opening and slithered across the dusty floorboards of an empty bedroom decorated for a son who was never a brother.

There were three rooms that matched; each with the same bed, the same desk, the same books, and wooden blinds. None fit the tastes of her mother—or her—and she passed through the room in disapproval. The door slid open with ease and she set foot on a patterned runner sewn to fit the open foyer that led unto the atrium above the third storey through a series of open stairways with identical runners.

Beneath her sat the foyer and gated mouths to the other wings. Then, a peculiar pattern demanded her attention. Wet imprints of a slender left boot and a flat, horned-moon-shaped imprint that covered the right step puddled on the jade-and cobalt-hued foyer floor. Sondrea's rump still tingled with pain from a cruel whipping that her father used as punishment for her forgetting to wipe her feet at the outer door. His laxness now seemed as unforeseen as the bizarre step of the responsible soul.

Even so, she had hoped for better observance from the other Guardians. She had heard no vehicle nor approach of a horse, and the foot size proved smaller than those of her cousin and still her father's aide. Sondrea leaned outward to see if the wet tracks went beyond the gate. That she found proof spoke to her failure to hear the newcomer, whom she might see if she moved onward with her own travels.

While she bypassed the gate on her wing, she would have to travel further through the original build to find a way around the gate that defended her father. From here, she counted two paths. Neither offered better chance than the other. In point of fact, both offered barbs and promised bruises.

Sondrea chose the furthest stairwell, with access to the third storey. From there, she would climb to the atrium, pass through the broken observation windows, and cross the peak of her father's wing. There rested a hinged access that the magick-wielder retracted in times when he sought to harness magick outside his own. She needed only to engage the counterbalance and force the gear lock free whilst keeping her balance and not getting pinched, whilst also avoiding her cousin's reach and not suffering the brunt of her father's magick.

TULL & EBBE

She reached the third storey without incident or boasting. The floor contained two oblong chambers down the northern and southern walls void of occupants in this era. In the gaps at east and west sat the rooms that proved of interest to her. There she hid in times of game-playing as a blameless soul and when her father's magick frightened her; after those who called him benefactor sought alms from other hands.

The eastern joist of the northern chamber offered the clearest passage unto the atrium since the direct stairwell buckled and tore loose from the foundational wall. This separation occurred in the same season when Nelson James Tull sought to run through the Behemót Woods. While she never connected the two events afore, she now wondered if he sensed her father's true character even then.

She entered through the second sliding door of the chamber, beyond the vast open floor design, and traced the wall that disguised reinforcements for the atrium and an attached chimney that led to the small fireplace. After her failed return to the hidden passageway in her mother's wing, she dared not attempt a climb through the old chimney. The reinforcements held a simple wrought-iron service ladder that ran to the ornamental vents of the former observation terrace. During a snowy morn when her father played as though blameless too, he coaxed her into hiding in the tray of that vent whilst he convinced her mother that he made her vanish.

The pulley and cable that held the roll-aside door in place snapped since her last foray and required more of the countess's shoulder afore she created enough space to pass through. She disapproved of the many reminders of tight fits and the perceived glide that moved her between resting points acquired an obvious, if not pouty, stomp of her left foot. Her sole comfort rested on the lack of strain she put on the service ladder as she climbed. She had no disillusion that she would still tuck away in the vent tray, but she wondered why Yah reminded her of times afore her difficult-to-reach father turned against her.

A mouse that nested upon the vent tray met her at eye level and made her shudder to the point that she required the sturdiness of both legs to keep from tumbling from the service ladder. Even so, she shut her eyes and thrust against the vent cover with her full forearm because blindness toward an unpleasant creature made that creature cease to exist. Her mother swore by such a lie. She squealed first, though, and breathed in a cloud of fine dust.

The vent broke loose and she climbed without challenge from the tray's occupant. Toward the narrow entries and passages throughout the manor, she cast a bombardment of memories of the designers and dressmakers who oft sent gifts that boasted her figure and fattened their purses. Still, nothing encouraged rigid posture and vaulting leaps like the rodents whose best roosting place was within the veil of magick.

"You'd best not be the disappeared Reformer that Papa complained about so oft!"

Either way, she returned the vent and faced the view from the ramshackle observation terrace. She could see the livery but not the Guardians' bivouac. With a sweep of her fingers across the twisted body of the corroded telescope, she imagined the way her ancestors lived afore the Accession. In that time, a village sat on the opposite side of the Behemót Woods. Now, that village sat beneath.

"Is that why Paladin intended malice?"

Entire settlements, already ravaged by warring, were lost. In love or fear of the Triune, she comprehended how a soul might turn against Their perfect plan. As she acted in defiance of her own father's rules, she understood how a foe's pain wrecked the heart. She then drummed her fingers against the telescope and touched what Their hand touched.

"Fear and awe seem too light."

She hoped she, too, proved light as she slipped her right leg over the collapsed rail that once stood between the terrace and the recessed library. To pass the telescope, she had to walk across the top of the bookcases built against the terrace's foundation. The atrium roof collapsed against the rest of the floor—she reasoned—from the might of the Accession or soon thereafter. Her father never explained why he kept the atrium in this mangled form and the last time she pestered him for an answer, he terrified and humiliated her with his punishment.

He taught her to maneuver with a soft step. That step she tested against the bookcases and appreciated that both remained upright and unspilled. Her sideways stride proved best when she added a shuffle of feet. Still, she heard the whine of the rail when she tested the rigidity with the might of her upper body. Less, and the atrium's former copper peak would have sliced her crown or shoulders.

Her ankle then struck a corroded flowerpot that still bloomed with blue monkshood flowers. Such an arrangement sat at the four corners of the former floor design. According to her father or mother, she forgot which, the soul who built the manor and buried both his sons set the pots there afore he brought about his own end. The flower grew wild across much of the territories, yet she never discovered another room that showcased such an arrangement.

"Better that I turn my mind opposite the mind of he whose curse let in every upsetting thing." Her face then went pale. "Not spiders, Papa!"

This was no random fear that she blurted. No sooner had she swung her left leg across the potted monkshood and across the broken setting of atrium windows than she noticed a swath of ascending eight-legged pests. She bent her right leg at the knee and raised her heel from their path. As though their pods burst at once, enough spiders to cover the entirety of the accessible routes toward her father's wing now overflowed. Each appeared to share the breadth of her wrist, which she felt tremble with their ascent.

She believed with her whole heart that her father toyed with her mind even still. This was the sort of agitation he relied on—a slight that agitated and suggested that he could not be bothered to offer greater deceit. Even so, her body reacted in contrary response to her heart. Soon, both feet were back upon the bookcase and her hands clutched at the observation terrace's safety rail.

At the same time that she uttered a willful curse against her father, she attempted to relocate her confident right foot. Whichever displeased the Triune, she did not learn in time. The boards beneath her heel crackled and plunged her headlong. Afore she had her audience with her father, she fell through the brittle floor of the observation terrace and unto the floor of the third storey.

TWENTY-THREE

"Then, you haven't actual proof worthy of your mistrust toward the succorer?" Nita's briskness, agitated by her pristine Shelbian accent and unmarred appearance, made the falling snow crystals flutter away from her hyper-critical perch. She watched the jarred limbs and the slithering Kuusa Si'epä that cast down the snow but let the creature retreat into the shadows above head rather than deny her curiosities. "You subverted the—"

Tull swung a mallet and struck a pneumatic pipe-ram that injected a three-pronged, all-weather sensor into the frozen glebe—as Olley had spent his morn with Harlan's aide. Beneath ordinary assignments, the less-exact soul loaded the sensor and held the ram whilst the soul with the better aim swung the mallet. He had invited along a scion. If the sensor failed, the outfit could not cower beneath her blame.

So, he loaded and cast fourteen sensors without aide as an example for her to watch and learn from his technique. As sculpted as lean muscle made her, the idea that she possessed the might to swing a mallet with the necessary force to inject the sensor rendered the lesson a chance for her to watch him weary his upper body whilst she wearied his mind. Already agitated by Sondrea's tale of courtship and new information he received from Valery about Mumus, he glanced at the persistence of an idle accuser who resembled her mentor more with each unwanted barb.

"You subverted our judges for the pleasure of long-towed memories?"

"Have you not listened?" Tull tossed aside the mallet, gathered a crossbow—also percussion-fueled—and fired a bolt that struck the branch where other bothersome creatures perched. A satisfying cry rang out, but his amusement remained veiled by his balaclava. He then traded his tools again and continued to the next station along the northwestern line of the Behemót Woods.

"I have heard, and I have listened. The territory has plenty of tales about what terrors go on here. I've heard of the ways the countess of Ebbe Demesne *cared* for another woman's son."

Tull missed his fifteenth bolt. "Then you've listened and not heard."

TULL & EBBE

"Long have you heard these peculiar stirrings and abided by them!" Nita leaned on the ball of her right foot and tapped at his chest with a glove that bore retracted ceramic talons and coaxed the undivided attention of the Jacobian. "Never have you disobeyed the orders of the judges or meddled in the purpose of those you guard. You ask me to believe you would act on this for any other soul in this territory?"

"When I prove grievous"—he brushed away her hand—"I find we suffer."

"That would provoke not even a guilted soul's conversion."

Tull ended her debate with a single admission. "Since I boarded the judges' steam tram, I felt a stirring to invite you here. Better I ignored that?"

"Reformer Burghardt Seth Paiva might call that the voice of the Helper."

"I haven't the dreams of a Reformer."

"Dreams, visions, prophecies, *stirrings*. All are a Believer's hopes! Give them to a Partaker, and we would hunt them down for their wickedness."

"Has your heart turned?"

A smile arose as she met his challenge and opened her wolfskin cover as if to tempt him. "Dare to touch my heart and decide?" She released the lapels of her coat and shook away the confusion in her mind. "This *belief* is enough to sway you?"

"Not mourning my friends is enough to sway me."

"Is this why you invited me? You believe I'll vouch for your stirrings and lead the lot of you unto the caves?"

"Better to ask George and watch him stand in a heap of his own droppings? Or Asham, and watch the lot lose their wits over his asinine curiosities?"

"His wit might bring him the judgeship of his territory."

Tull exhaled his disgust.

"Your friend the Archibaldian must have an opinion."

"He declares a lacking imagination."

She groaned with sympathy and let the words flow from her lips without regard for insult. "At least he's handsome."

"Don't fret. He's mindful of the rest of ours' *affliction*."

She prodded his midsection. "I said *handsome*, not *beautiful*! And, if I said you displayed that notorious Jacobian sense of piety, would you not take that as offense?"

"Is that our reputation?"

"What *did* the countess do to you all those moons spent together?"

TULL & EBBE

Tull mopped his brow and waited for her to settle as she sauntered back and forth. "I tell you, once you know Olley, you'll understand him. Till then, he means you no direct offense. I say this as his friend."

"I was taught that Jacobians kept distant from souls that trickled down from their bluffs unto the lowlands across the Loy. Is that not so?"

"Our kindness betters them."

Her laughter threw her off-balance, but she spun with the eloquence of her rebuttal. "Why call upon me? Why invite any Shelbian to this place? All the moons you made this place your—"

"I could have Kemp or Marko relieve you; should you prefer."

"You wouldn't dare! Dainty Marko Glenn Stran?"

His masked grin flickered with orneriness. "While I'd not count him as my first choice, Marko does not brim with the faults so many apply to him."

"And your abettor? Does she brim?" The scion made an impression of her boot alongside a print in the snow of the Kuusa Si'epä's clefted limbs.

He counted what she gleaned in a few ticks of the clock's hand whilst he stood in Sondrea's presence that morn. "She proves deep with ability."

Nita dusted away her inferior print. "I've heard that about Partakers."

"And who will serve you, scion"—he circled—"when you serve this territory as I serve mine? You sit amid Partakers and souls who would prefer to take than serve."

She turned against the clock's hand and kept her back toward the line of sensors. "I know better than you who and what Shelbians are."

He offered her the pipe-ram, that she might teach him. She sneered and accepted with a non-committed grasp, which he cinched harder with his coarse hand. "A light hold will let the air within determine the course. Lest you want the prongs of the sensor to pierce your foot, commit as much of your weight as you're able."

She proved her form minus a single fault.

"Do mind your crown and shoulder." He waggled the mallet at her.

"Is that not why they describe this as senseless labor?"

"We cannot patrol, delve, and remain present afore the souls we defend all at—"

"I counted five Guardians seated near the fire. Could you not have divided—"

"Two souls returned from horse patrol at the moonset. The younger soul tended the horses whilst the authoritative soul tended to our judges"—he swung on the pipe-ram's anvil and launched the sensor—"and the next two went on patrol."

TULL & EBBE

She clutched the groaning tube with both hands as harnessed air forced the projectile downward.

Tull steadied her shoulder. "And I spoke with my abettor after I met with she whom we guard."

Nita's elbows twitched and the ceramic tips of her gloves scraped at the oil-rubbed tube.

"You may take the pipe-ram away now."

Seven.

She huffed as though his suggestion fell behind her intention, but her eye still inspected the results.

Six.

Beneath the surface of ice and snow, a copper-and-quartz dome no broader than her palm responded to her nearness with a pulsating chirp.

Five.

"Even now, Edmond monitors our progress."

Four.

"If you please him, he'll set the field to recognize your identifier beacon as a welcome reading."

Three.

"And, if I fail?"

Two.

Tull held up his left index finger. The scion then fell onto her side and convulsed in a manner that hinted at a sensation of intense pain versus internal ailment. Nita writhed and grunted worse than the creature that he pinned above head; who also reacted to her wails with a shrill wheeze and the fanning of mire-scalded limbs.

"Her squelch"—he spoke with a raised voice as the newest and nearest sensors emitted an alarm at a stomach-churning audible pitch—"will fill you with a mighty urge to expel the contents of your gut by way of your body's weakest outlet!"

The eager-to-critique scion's convulsions continued though she tried to voice another barb.

"Most souls lose their wit and vomit. Olley struggled with his trousers for two eves; though, George and I suspect the second eve was for his indulgence. Asham spilled his bowels like an overfed runt." His eyes drifted toward the peaks in the east.

TULL & EBBE

"Harlan suffered no response. A point he's proven through sixty-three willful reenactments."

Nita swallowed her barb as her jowl shifted and she covered her ears with the palms of her gloved hands.

"Do mind those talons, scion!" Tull set the ankle of his boot at her tailbone and broomed her toward Ebbe Demesne and the racket ceased. "Not that I would tell another soul of your response."

Her convulsions ended, too; still, she glowered when he claimed the pipe-ram again and reset the anvil.

Suspecting her revolt, he also took his hammer. "I'd heard tales of Shelbians who abide in the dark. Has no soul taught you about an interrupted circuit?"

She coughed and spat in lieu of a response.

"Other than Harlan and the firstkind"—he delayed as he tucked beneath his arm the hammer and reached beneath the hem of his coat—"and, of course, any creature who trots, barks, mews, or slithers—a soul whose identifier beacon interrupts the circuit field of our sensors betrays their own plot. So, we drag them away, bind their joints, and hose them down."

Her chilly irises showed even less warmth when he stooped and shook his canteen in front of her. He set the drink offering into a snowy cleft made by the Kuusa Si'epä rather than tempt her to extend the ceramic claws on her gloves.

"We allow a passable threshold at the main entry, which is why a soul or two remains posted at the bivouac within sight of that point. We wouldn't want the countess's driver or the count's chef suffering for their purpose."

"I possess a spirit of letting her reeve spark for a prolonged tick as recompense for his hoisting you unto the overturned trees the yester morn."

Nita spun when she heard Harlan Bottin Vosburg speak and found him in the slender silhouette of trees till all she identified were his vaporous breaths alongside Olley. She looked back to the soul who taught her about circuits and, though dizzied, paired the Carpenterian's words with the frayed leg of the Jacobian's trousers.

Olley blew on his hands. "I miss the fire."

Tull cast him with a scorned stare, as if the Guardian somehow knew of the size fire he built. Olley proved unaware, as evident in his off-guard and curious stare.

"Work at your own pace, then. I'll thaw with the bud."

TULL & EBBE

Harlan took hold of the pipe-ram and followed the line of sensors. Tull then swung and injected the next sensor. "I thank you."

Nita trembled and turned her head away, but set her heel in the encrusted impressions left by the Kuusa Si'epä and slipped afore she stood.

Olley laughed at her expense. "She knows nothing of proximity, I judge!"

"I believe that's not why she trembles."

"Not this . . ."

She sat so near—and at the same level—as Harlan, who pulled forty-six Shelbians from a pool of burning mire afore he slayed the three brothers—husbands of the forty-six—who sought their mass sacrifice. On ceremony, and with a hint of personal fear, she rolled onto her knees and elbows in his presence. "Guardian Vosburg!"

"Again?" Olley huffed in a manner that tickled his elder and barbed their underling.

"Let the Archibaldian whine, Ozul." Harlan tapped her shoulder and offered his hand to help her stand. "He chafes from all the perceived attention he lacks."

She touched his hand and he hoisted her onto her heels in a way that made a Shelbian blush.

"I tell you, less than twenty of those brides were of this territory. There were two—not three—brothers, and a nervous horse set loose the hay rake that pierced the slowest of them."

"I have met some of those brides, Guardian."

He splayed hands as wide as her face. "A mere attempt to diminish the legend of the bear."

Nita stared at his battle-weathered hands till a smile lit her face.

"Seems Ganix's scion has found her gut again."

"And her balance."

"I s'pose that makes you feel justified for inviting a lowly Shelbian?"

Nita recovered with greater rapidity than either imagined; which she proved best when she pivoted and landed a left hook across Olley's smart mouth. The Archibaldian fell afore her grunt ceased. She then cracked her knuckles as she pressed her fist against her side. Her feet stopped shy of her arm's ability to touch Tull. "I thank you for a lesson I'll not forget, Guardian Tull."

TULL & EBBE

"And, I thank you." He tilted his head and protected his jaw. "For two spans I've tried to teach Asham that"—he prodded Olley's limber shin—"suffers a weak chin in more ways than appearance."

He reacted when Harlan slung his canteen and Nita saw that their elder waggled the pipe-ram, which he reloaded with a mighty thrust of his hand. She took the tool from him and knelt nearer to the Carpenterian's feet as he retrieved a worn mallet from his coat pocket.

Tull disregarded the scion's response toward their elder, stooped, and then patted Olley's face till his eyes opened. "How goes the thaw?"

"I believe that Shelbian struck me."

He awaited the end of Harlan's howl. "Better you count this as a lesson in proximity."

Olley looked past Tull toward their elder, who swaggered in a manner that a peacock—even an embittered Archibaldian—might recognize. He prodded away Tull's hand and fumbled back to his feet with a chorus of grunts and an off-tune huff. "I'll give you a silver alms if he hasn't bedded her afore the next moon."

Nita purred when Harlan struck the anvil and shielded her face by tucking toward his thigh till the percussive blast ended. The pair set two more sensors whilst the Archibaldian and the Jacobian ignored her cooing and injected sensors of their own. The soul who despised Shelbians then changed his footing and kept an unapproving eye on her whilst Tull reset the anvil.

"Did she fawn over you?"

"She might have"—Tull winced—"had she ceased from correcting my every remark."

"That's a Shelbian's gratitude."

"Better you have an eager Shelbian on your side if you're to go into—"

"Is she to be your recompense?" Olley spat against the wind and boasted as though some particle struck Nita. "None blame you for your ailment. We don't need a stand-in and we don't need another—"

"She isn't the soul who broke you." The Jacobian discharged the anvil with a well-timed strike, working alone as he had with Nita whilst Olley sulked. "Archibaldian."

Olley turned toward Tull's calling.

"I meant you no insult."

TULL & EBBE

He spat again, this time away from the wind, which prompted him to rifle a hand through his hair. "There's been no offense between us that I recall."

"A tick?"

"As you say." Olley stepped back toward the worksite, then the two friends extended the mechanical perimeter, though not out of range from Nita's ear. "You turning territorialist on me? Have I chipped deep enough to make an impression after all these spans?"

"I seek your wisdom."

"I have much to spare!"

Tull's expressionlessness held. "How long since you've seen your judge?"

Olley's eyes sparkled with intrigue and released a smile that dazzled. "I imagine the trouble you'd find were your abettor not half-withered from her kind's carnival of thirsting and thrusting."

"*Festival*. Your meetings?"

"Not that I believe you unclever alone." He winced. "I made that remark on a whim . . . *thirsting and thrusting*. A whim!"

"Olley."

"I cannot say."

"We meet our judges—"

"I uphold custom as well as you." He glanced toward their elder as if to break some arrangement. "I do not see my judge in those times."

"At all?"

"Remember when we agreed against discussions of him?"

Tull's eyes warned against Archibaldian difficulty.

"These past ten moons, I have met with Wilfred Doppelt Gesicht—"

"The researcher?"

"My judge's mediary"—he set his thumb beneath Tull's chin lest he suffer another interruption—"that he may inform me of his expectations."

Tull arched on the balls of his feet and escaped Olley's pin. "Mediary?"

"One who serves—"

"His expectations till when?"

"I did not ask. I don't much care to be in his presence, as I cannot lie to him as I might to you. Not that I do lie to you. Lest I do." His smirk proved an unflawed barb.

"Do you not count that arrangement as an odd turn?"

"Nelson, I've traveled with you long enough that many oddities seem outright simplistic to me now." He then took a deep breath and rubbed his still-cold arms. "I happen to enjoy the arrangement, as I happen to enjoy our arrangement."

Tull looked at his friend in cluelessness.

He shook a finger. "And to savor that look, I'll not tell you why."

True to his word, Olley then set his desire for warmth above Tull's observations. Within the past ten moons, by the Jacobian's count and a confirmation from his leave-permitted abettor, Mumus set projection gliders over his bride and daughter whilst also appointing another soul to keep watch over the Archibald Territory's third Guardian, yet the judge and his scion planned a visit to Ebbe Demesne. He believed Valery, letting pass her ailments, but he never doubted Olley.

He could not yet see where his cycle of detection separated from his opportunity to take apart a foe. None despised Mumus more than he—yet he sensed no inner nudge toward suspicion of the Archibaldian judge's hand at work against Sondrea. Tull's history proved that the judge knew the way to Ebbe Demesne. He needed to learn more from Sondrea now that he better understood what to ask of her.

"The way he speaks to a friend"—Nita sowed contempt as she took the canteen Tull offered her afore—"and you believe he cares for another soul?"

"Aside from his mother, his uncle, his cousin, her mother, Harlan, George, me"—Tull poked the canteen with his knuckle and cast water down her chin and chest—"and the seventy-six thousand Archibaldians he serves?"

"You're rather glib when you remind a soul of their foolish barbs."

"An attribute of my heritage." He then felt her return his canteen to his hip. "Till you're settled, my tools and provisions are yours. Speak against my friends again, and you'll learn my jaw is sturdier than Asham's or Olley's."

She proved she blushed but lost her barb when she saw Harlan tromping through the field a few hefty strides behind Olley.

Tull enjoyed a sip from his canteen. "We've much work to complete, Scion Ozul, and I wish to get back to the manor. What say I show you the method I was taught when forced to load a pipe-ram anvil without a helper?"

She accepted the offer with a nod lest he club her for speaking against his authority.

"Do you favor yellow to green apples?"

"You are giving, Jacobian. Have you either?"

TULL & EBBE

"George has each, if not more, I suspect."

"Then you are giving with George's provisions?"

"In no way. I bet him an apple that you would strike Olley afore you took your first meal with the outfit."

"O, did you?"

He smirked as he cleared the ice and terrane from the cradle of the pipe-ram. "Hence my offer to let you pick which apple we share."

"How giving!"

"One wearies of constant piety."

"Your smile is not unpleasant, Jacobian." She handed him the next sensor from a soft satchel. "I ought to tell you that another whom I count as close to me as a sister promised to lend me her set of pre-Accession wine goblets to use for the Feast of Gratitude if I bed two Guardians afore then."

The silent Jacobian provoked the tomb's envy.

"By my measure, only our Guardians from the northern territories count as worthy lovers."

The unblemished snow admired his modesty.

"I presume I could take Harlan as my *second* with ease."

The anvil sprang from his grip and the pipe-ram flopped to the glebe. Outspokenness resided throughout the half who held the greater number amid the secondkind's population—and those concerned by the dwindling number of potential mates. So, afore she laughed at his expense and boasted over her ability, he offered a counter-barb. "I've no doubt that the smell of Ganix will have washed from you by the time she seeks to reclaim her wine goblets."

TWENTY–FOUR

Sondrea padded her waist afore she cinched her corseted high belt with all the tightness that a bruised wrist allowed. The restorative gels in the mending chambers needed another full purification cycle afore she reentered—well after the moonrise. As she waited, she draped her knit outer coat over her sullied outfit and her shame-tucked tail. Her attempt to gain an audience with her father proved fruitless and she crawled—in the proper sense of the word—from the third storey to the outer door of the foyer.

Her feet still ached with cold from her hunched passage through the main door of the manor to the entryway of the wing where she retreated. From the knees down, snow-drenched fabric stuck to her legs. In all that time, neither her mistrusted succorer, nor intrusive Mim, nor Saul Ole, nor any of the celebrated Guardians found her. She created a spoor of clues, but proved most injured by isolation.

"Do I keep you from slumber?"

"No." She brushed a tear from the corner of her eye and sought the face of the lone voice that brought her comfort. "Sit."

Tull claimed a seat on the bench that she used to ascend the collapsible ladder toward the service panel and crawl space. His hand even clasped at the nearest rung as if to prove his awareness of her choices. Even so, he withheld criticism.

There were times when Cyril toyed with her so well that her sole comfort was to weep in Tull's calm presence. A blameless soul held great sway. Even now, with a teary-eyed glance toward his monkshood-like pewter eyes, she felt comforted. "Might I trouble you for some tea?"

Because he was not dim, he discerned when to be still and when to obey. This moment fell nowhere between. Cyril wounded them. Since she spoke to him of the conditions beneath which she wed, she saw the return of hurt that surfaced in his irises as specks of lavender.

He steeped two cups of tea, prepared each as they preferred them, and returned without more disturbance than the clacking of a spoon against the rim of a cup. Not because he sensed her wounds, he offered a hand and helped her sit upright. This kindness could not dull the sharpness of pain which slowed her reaction and let slip another tear and her first sniffle. "I thank you."

With enviable and limber ease, he crossed his leg and let the steam rise from his cup. Since his first visit, he did not eat or drink afore his host. This was a trait amid Jacobians that she of Jacobian descent learned too. Still, he provoked an angular brow when he scoffed and shook his head. "I remember a time when Olley and I called upon an elder who saw the Era of the Reformers and who offered us a meal for our remembering her. Olley—as Olley is—complained that she served soup steeped with water and not broth."

Sondrea proved solemn as the lightheartedness faded and revealed the gleam of his eyes.

"This provider of three eras broke down crying in apology, for she had nothing *finer* to offer her Guardians." He too let a tear fall. "A soul we were sent to honor sat ashamed in the home she kept, for her Guardian did not understand that she loved him in such a way that she shared the best of what little she had rather than send us away with nothing."

Sondrea's release of a pent and pride-filled breath filled the silence.

"I've remembered that elder's tears amid every soul whom we've defended who has shared what they have with us even when we have more than they." He then offered an ember of his former grin.

"What does Olley say to that?"

"He oft remembers my pitiful response to the habits of a Partaker from Othniel."

She chuckled at his admission even as a tear reached the crease in her cheek.

He let his gaze wander from her covered feet and knees to her belted waist, her defeated breast, her fallen shoulders, then to the hands that made her cup tremble, and the inquisitive curl of her upper lip. "I've learned that . . . the Judge of the Archibald Territory . . . does not sit upon his bench these past ten moons."

"*Eight* moons." She set aside her tea without buckling in pain. "The first two he spent on preparations afore the gathering season settled."

"He set his purpose upon his mediary."

"Wilfred Doppelt Gesicht."

"A soul whose works trouble many."

TULL & EBBE

"The judge's scion remains too young to shoulder the duties of the bench. In such times, there are provisions that allow for the naming of another to serve in an unnamed capacity in their stead. On those matters that Wilfred decides, our annals reflect a judgment by Cyril's rule."

"A soul who took a bride as he took you would be the sort who would devise a crime against her whilst he remained tucked away."

"Lest you afford me unmerited favor, I do confess that I used sources you trust in order to prepare you for all I've withheld. Better they confirm his absence using their methods than my telling you."

Curiosity shielded the lavender flecks in his irises.

"I further tell that you convinced me to suspect Dory is not who—perchance *what*—she claims."

The fall of his gaze landed upon the padding that cushioned her bruised body.

"Do you remember the film of my parents well?"

His teacup chattered on the saucer.

"My next confession is that I let my hatred for the work replace my memory of the work, for I've learned who—or what—seeks me."

"Danele Gertie Zuriñe's spoiled career?"

She struggled to withhold her laugh, for she knew of his fondness for the actress in spite of the role she first remembered her in. "Only if her career dresses as Paladin."

"Paladin?"

The way his face contorted made her turn loose her pain and laugh. "I blush at the mention of my fourth confession to you—especially to you—but I proved my abilities foolish when I sought my father's ear."

"When?"

"Since our visit this morn." She shook her head in disappointment. "I allowed my resolve to share my fear of spiders."

"That would explain the adornment of webs in your hair."

"What?"

He set aside his cup and reached to pull the spiderwebs from her hair that she wore since her trip unto the hidden passageway near the fireplace. "Have you noticed that the hiding places we once valued have lost a portion of their worth with time?"

"Much of this peak! Believe me when I tell you I hide my embarrassment and my disgust in equal portion beneath this outer coat of mine."

TULL & EBBE

"And a padded hip."

"I returned to the observation terrace and touched the telescope."

"By way of the buckled stairs?"

"By way of the service ladder beneath. I then saw those spiders and fell through the floor."

"*Through* the floor?"

"The floor on the third storey proved sturdy."

"You lost the light?"

She nodded.

"And the time?"

"I leave my devices to keep the time for me." She shooed away his concern. "I took a thorough look in the mirror when I returned. All remains where I last found them."

"How long afore you return to the fish tank?"

"You needn't fret that I'll spurn my invitation to humble Ganix."

If ever he conveyed the feelings of his heart, that moment now swam in the depths of concern in his eyes.

"I will mend afore most Shelbians slumber and long after the moonrise."

He cocked his jaw and tilted his head in a manner that proved his attempt to keep the words from his lips.

Because she counted an idea of those words, she squirmed in her seat and stroked the blush that crept from her face toward her neck. "Nelson?"

"Are you sound enough to tell me why you believe Paladin hounds you?"

Her gaze remained unfocused, but her jaw provided both a pleased grin and a discernable nod. "There is a book on the writing table in the next room that shows likenesses of a shape-changer as described by multiple witnesses in varying eras and territories. Each of them bears the look of Paladin."

"All have seen that—"

"The book predates *Love Magick.*"

"Only a fool devises such a title as that."

"All the while, I credited that same fool with the creation of Paladin." She glanced from Tull's shoulders to his backside to his hands as he retrieved the book. "Nelson, how did you get past the bolted door?"

"I entered through the door to the chamber you once shared with me."

TULL & EBBE

She looked toward the doors at the opposite end of her former bed chamber and saw the staff of light that passed because he had not closed the door behind him in full. With some effort, she then twisted on her seat till both shoulders and the back of her head rested against the adjoined closet wall, then hummed to dull her pain.

"None have repaired the latch in all these seasons."

Her eyes followed the sound of his warm voice till she watched his return from boots to hips to chest, but never ceased from humming as he knelt beside her bench. She then studied his expression of amused annoyance as he compared the renderings of the shape-changer and held the book for her to see, too.

"You count your succorer amid the Taotáva's lot?"

"Do you not?"

"I can tell you that she never spent a tick within sight of Taft Bluffs. She missteps too oft to have survived the winds there." He twisted the book to get a different look. "Do you imagine the soul who approached you with this tale was another of them?"

"If not the same. I suspect you must share my suspicion."

He shrugged and drew her eye toward the breadth of his shoulders.

"In all our time, have you heard me speak of Bobbie Sabine Sundermann?"

"No."

"Yet I trusted when she referred Dory to me."

He placed the book on the opposite bench. "The name sounds Perlinese."

She heard his words but withheld a response, for she caught his obvious second glance upon her as he settled.

"Your succorer braces when she moves." He patted his forearm as he mimicked Dory. "She overburdens the limbs on her right to accommodate those on her left."

"You are observant, even for a Jacobian." The countess pursed her lips till they appeared as slivers and shook her head. "I am unsure of the root. She arrived at Ebbe Demesne with the stitch you've observed. Arrived from where? I've not asked."

"We do better by not . . ."

"Observing?"

He traced the spine of the room with his gaze. "In the second moon that Jules spent beneath Otto's benefaction, she spoke of frightening changes to his character."

Sondrea listened even as she took the pressure off her left leg.

"That same moon, Deputy Inspector Rusty Wade Guild stopped Otto's brother, his Partaker bride, and her Partaker sister from harming their novitiate."

TULL & EBBE

Sondrea considered the baffling tether that held Celia Freyja and Elsie Ilona Kind Hand. "Otto Meynell Chessy has a twin brother."

"Does your succorer?"

The countess could not answer.

"I'll ask Edmond to watch her. We should learn whether she does by the next moonrise. Sooner, if he involves Asham."

Her gratitude toward his decisiveness showed in her expression but gave way to a hint of confusion that she seldom showed any other. "Names sound Perlinese?"

"Those of wilting dispositions."

Her mouth twisted afore she found the tea cooled enough to consume in a few sips. Still, she saved some for fear that an empty cup might signal a time for him to leave. In favor of avoidance, she set her rampart aside, then softened her posture, her gaze, and her humming voice to keep him near.

"Might I . . ."

She turned her ear toward him but never let her eyes stray from his lips. When he hesitated, she let the brilliance of her smile warm him and draw him nearer. "Yes?"

He glanced toward her throat and shook his head. "That tune."

"'A Bluebird Visits the Terebinth Tree.' That's the only tune I remember Papa dancing to with Mama. He looked so proud of her and she of him. I believe they were in love then." She watched his brow furrow. "Their romance disappoints you; or does blame for that expression rest on my humming?"

"I believe you used to calm me with that same tune." He blushed as an impure memory of her arose.

"Your belief is right." Her smile proved this beyond her words and added a necessary pause to draw him nearer. "You hated the bath because of the water's pull on your heart and breath."

He looked toward the opal void of the sunken tub in the corner that seemed to him without bottom when filled with water, then recalled a gleam of moisture upon her flesh and her hair piled atop her crown.

"I would keep you in my arms and sit with you in the bath." Her eyes sparkled till the room seemed brighter. "How I loved to feel your racing heart grow calm whilst I kept your heavy shoulders against my breast. To sense that you were soothed by my voice and nearness to me brought me the deepest peace!"

TULL & EBBE

Tull felt a strand of heat course through him swifter than any fire produced. In admitted fear, he looked toward his exit from the room, not for signs of an attacker, but for the projection glider that Cyril Mumus set upon his bride. The visage of a displeased Minister seemed possible too. He then noticed Sondrea's bare foot slide through his peripheral field afore she took hold of the threadbare balaclava around his neck with the breadth of her thumb.

"You wear this as well as my grandfather and better than I whose fearlessness rests on the readiness of a healing chamber."

"I've much to accomplish afore I can be called deserving." Still he sat as her thumb's hold let loose of the gift from Zeck's belongings that linked them and rested on his shoulder, where she still reached to brush his jaw.

"Cyril is not guided by morality—as my grandfather was guided and moral. As you are guided and moral."

"A fear of Yah's wrath oft gets mistook for morality."

"My grandfather told me how much the secondkind accomplished with the help of the Ministers. By the time I heard this, the blameless who became our parents had invited rot unto the territories if for no other reason than to hurt our grandparents." She soothed him in word and teased him with a touch. "I've focused for so long upon fine souls like yours, like Law-writer Kind Hand's, and a handful of others, that I've forgotten those—like Scion Ozul—who will need grooming to offer support to those who will lead better than these judges."

"I imagined the Reformers would've claimed power over the judges by now."

She smoothed his sleeve. "Would that settle you?"

"Reformers cannot rule *through* law. They must be an example of the Law and ever obedient. They cannot have our flaws in their way."

"You have traveled these territories—as I have—enough to see that there are shadows drifting nearer; waiting to consume us." The countess reached beyond his shoulder and traced his furthest collarbone. "And who would seek to manipulate those shadows but our judges?"

"Yet, believing this, you sought your father?"

She withdrew her hand and tapped his chin. "I sought to learn why we were deceived about Paladin. In that, I may learn why he hounds me now. Those renderings prove he existed, and that we have not remembered him. Renderings of the eye and confusions of the mind are high amid my father's delights."

TULL & EBBE

"And, what does your succorer tell you?" He isolated her wrist to preserve his focus. "By now you've tested her."

"As you say." Her inhalation borrowed from his breath. "This answer invites yet another confession from me. I afforded her a chance to sneak away after I informed her that the judge of the Archibald Territory travels to Ebbe Demesne with scion. I've not seen her since; though I have kept busy."

"The judge of . . ." He grated his lip. "She does not know?"

"My succorers have never enjoyed the privilege of my kept secrets as you have." Her tone softened as her focus sharpened on him. "Perchance the next will."

"When does the judge arrive?"

"Guardian Ganix may have a tea he never forgets."

"I cannot promise that Olley will keep from this matter."

"My invitation comes with only a promise that I'll arrange an introduction between the two of you. He has heard many tales of our fourth Guardian from the Jacoby Territory."

"He is not Jacobian."

"We mustn't hold the shortcomings of others above their grasp." She pinched his hand in a playful manner but conveyed her desire that he hear her. "We have a limited time—you and I—where we might make tremendous advances. Better we keep Wilfred understanding than suspicious in the five full seasons he has still to serve on the bench."

His eyes proved his curiosity, though he stirred. "I should tell Edmond."

"You may; though, there is much more for me to tell you." Her hand slipped through his till she took hold and gained the leverage to stand again. "Much that affects your heart. Much that affects Cyril's judgeship. Much between us."

He offered Sondrea a simple, agreeable nod.

"What I offer is meant for you and no other." She angled her crown toward her former bed chamber. "Would you bolt the door as I once taught you?"

When he agreed, she turned toward the opposite door nearer to her sunken tub. As she moved toward that end of the room, she settled her own heart whilst he kept them from every intrusive creature and every unsuspecting soul on the isle. In this, she furthered her step along the path that Yah intended for her. Her intention, like Tull's obedience, did not mingle without provocation, however.

TULL & EBBE

In times throughout the history of the Creations—First and Second—Yah's plan surrendered to their determination for suffering. As neither Tull nor Sondrea turned away from the other, but let their hearts grow nearer than was meant for them, the Triune set a new command upon she who watched over the Guardian. In this, the sky-fires dimmed, and a steadfast Minister hid her fiery eyes. Enke'loi withdrew, with two similar flames, then a third, followed again by a fourth, and the wrath of their trains jarred branches and twigs along the Behemót Woods and took away the storm.

In Time for Tea

An Interim

Still the 8th Peak beneath the Moon of the Mother's Song

The 107th Winter Season of the Accession

In the Care of the Helper, who keeps souls from fruitless wandering.

No other ran as Nita ran. She had an elegance and swiftness that the Guardians of other territories stopped and admired; which proved why Tull referred to the source of her speed as meddlesome. Even slim George, who walked twice as much and ate half as much as the next-fastest Guardian—Asham—could not have kept up. How Harlan Bottin Vosburg understood this mattered not, though. The Carpenterian entrusted her with a purpose no Guardian could complete: stop Mim. She did not even know what a "Mim" was; only that she dared not fail.

The setting betrayed her. Not the depths of crusted snow nor the momentum-wasting hills. Behemót Woods betrayed her. She ran her hardest, her most cunning, and never lost sight of bald-headed, side-waddling Mim for longer than was required to sprint from hilltop to hilltop.

Her emotion betrayed her. She was not an emotional soul. Few seldom showed emotion less oft than her. Mim ran as scared as a soul who feared their end and found a Guardian in mad pursuit ought—but she was not a Guardian. His fear had nothing to do with her and that made her nervous.

Still, the mix of nervousness and agility helped her reach the other side of Behemót Woods. No creature kept her from passing through. The trees did not take her from the terrane. The sky-fires shone in full splendor above head and the Loy cried out as her waters flowed against the ice that capped her surface.

TULL & EBBE

Advocates Elwell, Gwynne, Conliffe, Mumus, Lael, and Katch betrayed her. Their mandate refused her the right to pursue another soul across territorial lines. Rage coursed through her veins, carried on the rush of adrenaline and the hammering sensation of her heart, and devoured her other emotions. A sense of irony mingled with the increase of anger.

The lone judge who voted against the mandate—who welcomed all travelers—represented the Jacoby Territory—where Mim stood in wait and taunted her. Judge Ernie Purcell Bliss would not fault her for pursuing the reeve. The other six judges would see her punished in unimagined ways. She had to let Mim go. Any show of disobedience reflected on the outfit and those who helped her learn the laws of the judges. She had to let Mim go.

The tramcar that belonged to the house of Judge Cyril Adair Mumus passed her by, with Ebbe Demesne their intended stopping point. She dared not pretend she went unnoticed; not even on precedent. Now, she faced a new dilemma. Could she race back through the Behemót Woods and alert the outfit of Mumus's nearness afore he walked unto the gut-wrenching blitz?

Her hoarse, searing breath sounded as weeping where words failed. This would be her last deed as a scion. She needed air and strength. With a resistant shake of her head, she let Mim go. She was letting Mim go.

Nita pivoted on her heel, ignored Mim's laughter, crossed her forearms, raised them as a shield, then raced back unto the Behemót Woods with no regard for her name, her purpose, or her soul. Tull deserved this risk from her. Harlan would see that, for he valued loyalty unto other Guardians. In the spot where she had rested, a mash of bloodied impressions marked her nearness to the territorial line and now she followed a similar path back unto Ebbe Demesne.

~

BEACON 090.01.302 RECOGNIZED AT 191 TAUROG ROADWAY . . .

IDENTIFIER CONFIRMED—KATERINA YVETTE MUMUS.

OBSERVE AT ALL TIMES BENEATH EDICT NO. 112009-11B.

TULL & EBBE

An occasional research partner, occasional rival, and friend of twenty-seven spans took a tremendous chance on Wilfred Doppelt Gesicht's character. Cyril Adair Mumus entrusted him with many secrets, unending wealth, and greater power than a soul deserved. Now, Gesicht served as mediary advocate of the Archibald Territory; a title that belonged to two souls since the Accession. Even so, he faced no sight as unnerving as the sight he found in his first visit to Ebbe Demesne.

The dryness in the air tempted a minor arc of static to ignite and robbed his nostrils of the metallic tinge he identified as blood. On a warmer peak, from what he saw in his first glance, the air would prove rich with the smell. So stained was the brilliant snow that numbness that cut deeper than the biting wind overtook him. Skin pulled from the pads of his fingers when he let go of the door handle to his friend's custom-built tramcar, known for the marbled burgundy skin and narrow windows that no soul could see through lest they sat inside.

Distinct footprints, marked by saturations of blood and varying shape, created a visual flow of blood that made him consider if the glebe bled out of the lands buried beneath his feet. This path he followed, away from the entry door and the tramcar. There were no sounds greater than the oscillation of his heart in his ears; not even from the Behemót Woods. Gesicht divided his focus between brilliant, crimson footprints and the entangled trees of legend; should those terrors within the woods also watch him.

"Uncle!"

A cold grip—even draped in suede gloves—took hold and shook him from his stillness. He believed he heard his heart stop for a tick and touched his chest. He then faced the culprit: Novitiate Katerena Yvette Mumus. Three spans since her blamelessness ended and she risked not reaching four.

"Why aren't you moving?"

"Remember that you agreed to wait with Charles in the tramcar?"

"Remember that you agreed you would learn what happened?"

"Your mother—"

"The entry remains bolted. She would tell me to stay near to you!"

The mediary who had no authority over the absent judge's true scion tried his best to appease her. She was the reason he served as mediary, after all, and no other soul on the isle called him *Uncle*. Though she was not his niece, he took a bold step onward. Her hands did not slip.

TULL & EBBE

They continued away from the doors to comfort, pursued by their own reflections, and aware of their steps along and never atop the stained snow. Katerena's breath sharpened along with her grip. By then he learned why. He craned his neck and sought a sign of breath, which came after a trickle of blood pattered from a torn sleeve unto the snow, from a fear-stricken soul.

Asham Benjamin Gera looked younger in person. Gesicht watched reels on all the Guardians and read enough reports that he felt well-prepared for looking them in their eyes. That changed with far less preparedness. The youngest of the Guardians sat hunched with his knees twisted beneath and his right hand cupped against the base of his neck.

"Guardian Gera, I am a friend." Gesicht led Katerena in his mind. She who never met a well-to-do soul who disinterested her might have disagreed. The Creightonian held what appeared to be his first real wound, minus an odd, lattice-shaped abrasion against his chin and brow. "I represent the bench of the Archibald Territory."

Asham covered his brow and widow's peak with his other hand but could not shield his vacant eyes. From the dried blood beneath his nostrils and his stained collar, he looked as a soul struck from behind ought. Gesicht checked on Katerena, gauged the discoloration of snow, and then checked the pattering of blood from the Guardian's raised arms.

"We're moving onward, Guardian, but I will send help back to you."

The many remarks—constant remarks, even—regarding an incessant need for chatter seemed misapplied. This trait, mingled with the stillness of the Behemót Woods, made Gesicht suspect of all he had learned about the outfit. Then, an intense sound of a woman choking for air echoed across the open field. He and Katerena shared eye contact and she backed away that he might lead.

"I will send help back to you, Guardian."

"The millpond's over that way."

His ear failed to follow the path of her voice. "Which way?"

This time she let her manners slip and pointed. "Away from the blood."

"Away from your mother."

She had no response.

Gesicht shivered, for she reminded him too much of her insipid father. "You ought to be in the tramcar."

"And not you?"

"Your father would expect more than this."

"Papa would never let him set foot here."

The distraction of blood took away Gesicht's worry over visiting a magick-wielder. His forehead turned to a mass of creases and his broad chin turned gray as his lips drew tighter against his teeth. For the first time, he realized he might face his end because some magick-wielder lost his hold on actuality.

"Are we going to the millpond?"

"We are, Katerena."

She pointed a second time and he side-eyed her. The peak of the roof of the mill that fed energy unto the manor sat in idle wait. The visiting mediary might never have lived such a distance from other souls, but he possessed greater knowledge of structures and land patterns than a novitiate. Then, once his eyes focused, he saw why she pointed that second time.

A woman's wardrobe—minus wearer—sat discarded. He had torn clothes afore, so he recognized the level of agitation that ripped three layers free. Beyond that heap of ruined fabrics, he saw a tract of amber-hued snow and, further through the drag marks, a headful of hair—minus the head.

"Stay—"

"That must be a wig. No?"

"I've never seen such devices up close."

Katerena ran toward the site without fear of what else awaited her on the plot. She took hold of the padded crown and swung the snow-embellished mane as though a pendulum.

"I fear we ought—"

Another echoing round of gasps and a vulgar, wet cough startled a soul enough to throw down the wig. Gesicht raced past Katerena as he heard a distinct, feminine tone to those sounds.

"Countess!"

"She hasn't mulled-rose hair." The heiress spoke through teeth clenched by agitation. "The soul who wears such a color is—"

"Countess!" Gesicht reached the brim around the millpond and discovered a nude woman turned facedown. Her flesh was pink with cold and her legs bound by the arms of a bear-like soul who also cinched her wrists. "Guardian Vosburg!"

TULL & EBBE

Another soul turned, recognized Gesicht afore being recognized, and uttered a salty curse—a habit of Olley Hendrie Falk's.

"Is that—"

"Dory?"

"Guardian Falk!"

Gesicht's thunderous bark frightened Katerena enough that she teetered and sidestepped away from him. That she wielded the wig as a defense proved to all how unschooled she remained. Her father's mediary reached for her neck and kept her close afore he shouted at the soul who reported to him the past ten moons.

"Guardian Falk! Explain what I find here! Where is the countess?"

"She keeps from harm now!" Both travelers then heard Olley speak toward the bear-like soul. "He is the soul I spoke of afore. My judge's mediary."

"Pull that soul from beneath, Guardians!"

He might have represented the bench of the Archibald Territory, but the tone he used implied that he was not intimidated by these souls or their titles. Harlan offered him a wild-eyed stare and an agitated smile, then his face reddened with color. He pulled the countess's succorer from the waters of the frozen millpond broken open with a mallet that a mediary could not lift. Whilst the tortured soul coughed and vomited water, Gesicht followed a collar and chain that stretched her neck and pulled her toward the surface.

"What has this"—he noticed her facial features and dared not call her *woman*—"this"—even *creature* seemed wrong—"this is beyond your purpose, Guardians!"

"Goe vo'erio laez vi'er?"

She struggled beneath Harlan's hold but could not slip free. Her right eye remained open and a widened mouth proved an array of teeth that exceeded what the secondkind possessed. Her nose, now slight and blackened around the nostrils, flowed with plum-hued blood.

"I say to you, 'Tell him!'"

She trembled and sputtered beneath the roar of Harlan's voice, and then her iris warbled in the socket.

"She failed in her purpose! You are proof of that, Mediary!"

The half-drowned creature—as all *are* created—spewed words that made no sense to Gesicht's ear and frightened Katerena. He blamed the suffering and extreme cold but found no remorse in the Guardian who maneuvered her.

TULL & EBBE

"Whom have you failed?"

She pursed her widened mouth and her nose shrank in an expression of refusal that no longer awed those who controlled the scene. Harlan then let the weight that rested at the unseen end of the immersed chain pull her head beneath the icy water again. Her screams churned the water and recoiled along the millpond's ice belly. How she endured without breaking limbs or spine confused even a sound mind.

Harlan's voice bore a comfortable tone when he faced the Guardian at his side. "She will give to us a name afore my arms lose the might to heave her."

On those words, Gesicht stomped toward a scene that overwhelmed him. "Pull her out, Vosburg! Pull her from the water! What have you done?"

"I? I tell you, Mediary, of a scheme. If a Guardian suffers their end, the judge who is meant to visit is kept away. A judge who sets foot on this plot spoils that scheme."

"Who is this you punish?"

"She who passed herself off as succorer to your countess." Olley turned his head at a sharp, eastward angle and stretched out an arm that was more developed but not stronger than Harlan's. "And here comes her brother."

From the direction that Olley pointed, the headship of all Guardians approached on a well-paced, even step. With his left hand, Edmond Anson Elragadó clutched the chin and lower teeth of Ming—who attacked the coach of the plot's countess. In the other hand, he held the reins to his horse. Atop her back, Gallant carried Ming's soulless body.

"Guardian Elragadó!" Gesicht then remembered his own fellow traveler. "Don't look toward him, Katerena."

The novitiate meant to disobey, then cringed when the Guardian from the Larson Territory stepped from the withered orchard. His boots and trousers were speckled crimson and he bore a similar streak across his chin. This was, by most standards, the most disheveled he had appeared afore any authority in more spans than those that Katerena had aged.

"Guardian Elragadó!"

The calmed soul flung Ming's head toward the millpond and struck the heel of his old friend's boot. "Let her gaze upon that face when next she surfaces. If her mind holds, her jaw will loosen."

Gesicht felt the chill of aftershock and gasped.

"Mediary Gesicht, you ought to have stayed back. Has the warning not gone out?"

TULL & EBBE

"Not as of yet." Olley was right to serve as mediary to his judge's mediary; even toward his headship.

"They count their words better than we, Edmond."

"Better than some of us!" Edmond countered Harlan with a bonus wry smirk. He then looked their eventual judge over. "This is no place for a refined soul, novitiate. My soul despairs that you have seen us in our labors."

Dory convulsed in Harlan's grip till he strained to raise her from the water. This time, Olley lent a hand and took control of her forearms. Her wet screams and a thirst for air held no bearing on the calmness that all three Guardians emitted. Even when a plea rose from Dory's lips, none bristled except for Gesicht.

"Conliffe! I curse you!"

Olley proved cruel when he flung her headfirst toward water or terrane. Neither seemed to matter to him. Even when the succorer struck hard enough to snap her collarbone, she showed no hint of sorrow. Rage contorted his face and he used the heel of his boot to force her cheek against that of her brother's head.

"You must stop this, Guardian Falk!"

He remained unaffected from outward appearance, but Harlan rose in intervention toward Gesicht after he flung Dory's feet yet began with an apologetic tone. "Mediary Gesicht, I ask that you consider your audience."

"Then you consider we who are not Guardians but have long heard tales of cruelty from your fellows. Be the merciful—"

"This soul you have pity on tried to end all that you are." Harlan stifled the prestige that Gesicht's title held and attracted the attention of a novitiate with his soft-spoken, poetical tone. "She invited this and, I tell you, she ought be terrified. Lest she speaks the truth, I will give her over to the water and what is beneath."

Katerena looked upon the millpond's broken surface with terrified eyes.

"You will find no other soul in these territories who wishes for another way than we who have sullied our hands too many spans; but believe that we abide by a rule that protects every soul, regardless of the laws they compose."

Edmond added steadiness when he spoke without fidgeting. "These two ended a Guardian. He whom I ended attacked your mother's coach, Novitiate Mumus. He is the reason that she returned here."

"You speak to me, Guardian Elragadó, as I—" Gesicht scampered again in surprise.

TULL & EBBE

From the brim that bore his tracks, Nita fell to her prayer bones with enough force that she almost toppled. Her gasps for air matched Dory's, as did the mist that arose from her skin.

Undaunted, Harlan sought her report. "The soul who snared Nelson?"

That was all the greeting she attracted. Even as she scooped snow to her mouth for relief, none offered her their canteen. She shook her head, and Olley scoffed at her failure. He then set his foot across Dory's back as though she served as the returnee's substitute.

"Ozul! You'll help cover the pane that his bronze bow mocked."

Nita nodded in response to Edmond's command as though fit for fire to burst from her nostrils and ate more snow.

"And, I'll find you a proper canteen for your efforts when I return to Conliffe's Landing on the morrow."

Gesicht glanced toward the body in Edmond's tow and counted two arrows but no sign of an archer. Dory wretched and convulsed beneath Olley's heel and further distracted the mediary. Between vomitous fits and brutal coughing, her body changed from recognizable form to a shape he could not describe without more time. He then looked back toward the latest arrival. "We saw you near the roadway on the other side of—did you pass through the woods?"

Nita responded with a nod of her entire, doubled over upper body.

"The reeve witnessed the countess's attacker's end. He squealed and fled toward the Behemót Woods. Seems he outran . . . her."

Nita conserved breath that would have been wasted on Olley regardless.

Gesicht chuckled from nervousness. "Why did you not pursue on horse?"

The Shelbian lifted her head and stared him down with feral annoyance.

Harlan marveled, and offered a veiled retort. "You speak to a Shelbian, Mediary."

The reader of reports shook his head.

"A Shelbian would sooner lay with a horse than ride upon him."

Gesicht cringed at Olley's remark and spoke above the snort from Katerena. "Where is Guardian Ganix?"

A bear-like arm crept around Gesicht's shoulder and Harlan walked him past Nita up to the brim around the millpond. With a splayed hand, he motioned along the stained path that the mediary abandoned and toward Arthur George Green, who wrapped Ganix's head in cloth and kept the watch over bloodied Asham. In the distance, an easy walk from the Guardians' bivouac, Ganix's soulless body squatted at the base of a bitter walnut tree. As Gesicht hemmed together the clues, Nita vomited from the intensity of her run.

"Why Ganix?"

Olley crouched and scooped Dory's form backward by her bound throat. Gloomy eyes, a spot that consumed both nostrils, and a pale mouth as thin as a papercut identified her face. "Better that the water ruins her mind. Her ignorance is fatal."

"Guardian Vosburg?"

"They ended Ganix because he was the eldest of our camp."

Gesicht, Harlan, and Olley looked toward Edmond.

"In their culture, the eldest lead till they breathe no more."

Gesicht shared Olley's curiosity toward the Larsonite's knowledge.

Edmond scoffed at their dimness. "They ended Ganix in my stead."

A voice then rang out, as though from the sky-fires, above all other sounds and commanded an immediate stillness.

"ON THIS, THE EIGHTH PEAK BENEATH THE MOON OF THE MOTHER'S SONG,
ALL SOULS ARE ASKED TO PAUSE, THAT WE MAY GRIEVE THE LOSS OF
GUARDIAN BARTON BLINKEN GANIX, NOW TAKEN FROM OUR COUNT."

"Gone with greater swiftness than came this announcement," Edmond reported.

"GUARDIAN GANIX SERVED THE SHELBY TERRITORY
FOR TWENTY-FIVE AND THREE-FIFTHS SPANS."

Harlan confirmed, "Longer than any other soul by six moonsets."

"A TIME OF MOURNING GUARDIAN BARTON BLINKEN GANIX
WILL BEGIN WITH THE MOONRISE."

"Not that you'll see," Olley threatened Dory with a tug at her arm.

"WE THANK THIS SOUL FOR HIS SERVICE TO THE SECOND CREATION
AND ASK EVERY SOUL TO REMAIN SAFE."

"No mention of Ozul."

Gesicht sensed his territory's Guardian's dislike of the Shelbian and followed Olley's line of sight toward the hunched scion.

"Then again . . . why would there need to be?"

The Archibaldian mediary folded his arms in agitation and confusion.

"At the end of the three eves set aside for Ganix's remembrance, any soul with the courage to claim our new Shelbian's purpose will have set a petition afore the court. Should she wish another purpose, she'll ask the judges to name her replacement and thus be granted her leave."

"I've not heard of that law."

"A northerner's custom."

"Is that not how you came to be called Guardian, Harlan?" Olley smiled, though Harlan would repay him for his teasing.

"You are without fault, Mediary. Much time has passed since a woman stood as Guardian. The men who serve are not given the same opportunity."

"Are they not?"

"Not even Falk, with all his gentle loveliness."

"And what he spoke is true? Is that how you came unto your purpose?"

"The judges had him in mind when they passed the law!" Olley stooped toward the water and heaved at the chain that kept Dory beneath the millpond's surface.

"That was their lone salve to keep him from challenging their rule for evermore."

Gesicht looked toward Edmond as details settled in his mind and waited on the headship's goading laughter to end. "We have seen Gera, Vosburg, Falk, Elragadó, Ganix, and Green."

Gesicht's count remained incomplete due to the second broadcast of Ganix's end. Like Harlan, the mediary turned in the direction of the Saki Signal House, identifiable by the mast of a copper beacon lost in the haze between the trees of the Behemót Woods. The secondkind constructed signal houses that cast frequencies and a sweeping lantern to other potential survivors of the Accession on isles they imagined but never saw. As of the current season, their efforts proved fruitless. So, the judges declared another purpose in the design, lest their souls fail: mass communication.

The echo of the final statement still rippled as Gesicht sought the answer no other volunteered. "Who guards the countess?"

TULL & EBBE

Harlan looked toward Edmond. Nita looked toward both elders.

"She rests since mending." Olley disregarded all three and proved less tactful than even his muddied hands suggested. "She took a spill from the observation terrace, but she mended whole. Tull keeps the watch over her now."

Had Harlan the reach, he might have swatted Olley and restrained Gesicht by his collar too.

"Tull and his bow remain outside the Behemót Woods by order of the bench." Gesicht stepped toward the blood-speckled elder. "Does he not, Guardian Elragadó?"

Harlan proved better at interference and chivalry. "I will lead you to the manor to see how the countess keeps if you'll follow me now, Mediary Gesicht."

Gesicht measured the lack of apology in Olley's expression as a miscreant who brimmed with pride for going against orders: first the judges', now Edmond's. He needed a moment, too, to sort whether and how Olley went against him. "Lead us from here, Guardian Vosburg; but I will expect a complete report from you afore the eve settles, Guardian Falk."

Harlan led the well-dressed pair toward safety and comfort. He neither challenged Edmond nor scolded Nita for not bringing Mim back. Silence condemned as well as a harsh word. The regard felt for a legend faded too.

No other served as scion longer than Nita served Ganix. Her patience suffered refinement upon refinement. She trained longer, studied broader, learned discipline, laws, and tactics; all without application at her benefactor's side. Now the judges forced three more eves in wait upon her, that she might consider the worth of her preparedness for a purpose that she claimed from a soul too vain to accept Yah's need for him.

For every season she spent in wait of being named a Guardian, of doubting her revised purpose, she hated Ganix more. Her Guardian—seasoned and fragrant—was gone. The Guardian of her mother and friends was gone. They and those amid the territory who doubted Ganix's withdrawal would require her safekeeping. Now that their shunning and ridicule made her numb, she received her due.

TULL & EBBE

That same unifying voice—though never identified—poured from twelve signal houses situated around the seven territories a third and final time. By now, the souls of the Second Creation from every point on the isle heard. That the voice emanated from on high crushed the spirit with an implied barb of a failure that created a wound as harsh as any suffered. Even Edmond sighed in defeat and turned from those who followed him.

This was Nita's time of declaration; not defeat. All who heard understood who would complete the outfit and that set her apart from the older, seasoned Guardians' failure. All would keep her name on their lips. From this belief, a pleased smile took root and bloomed. As of this peak, and unlike their misshapen foes, she would be remembered. Nita Naomi Ozul, second Guardian from the Shelby Territory and third woman counted amid all Guardians—though four served.

"Well"—Olley groaned as if the moment drifted from his heart and wrapped a muddied chain around Dory—"Ganix never set foot unto the manor."

She would be honored.

"I suspect he'd enjoy letting every soul who learns of him believe that he shunned an invitation to tea and hot wine from Tull's countess." He then wasted the water in his canteen to rinse his forearms whilst Nita suffered from thirst. "His disgraceful end is still the end you bowed to."

She would be feared.

"And you, Shelbian, can be a spectacle these next three eves whilst imagining how you'll adorn the truth that your lone merit for being declared Guardian of this territory is that your forebearer had an obnoxious bowel."

He laughed at Nita as if no other pleb brought him more joy.

"Imagine the invitations to tea that you'll receive so others might hear the tale of the second Guardian from the Shelby Territory!"

And What Communion

TWENTY-FIVE

THE 10TH EVE BENEATH THE MOON OF THE MOTHER'S SONG

THE 107TH WINTER OF THE ACCESSION

IN THE CARE OF THE HELPER WHO KEEPS SOULS FROM FRUITLESS WANDERING.

Missions had suffered tremendous failures afore. The Guardians deviated from the rule of judges, the outfit amended their purpose whilst beneath a foe's attack, and souls proved lost and irretrievable—all afore. There was but a single difference this time: Mediary Wilfred Doppelt Gesicht. No judge would risk harm to their rule but a mediary was finite.

Gesicht was not wronghearted when he ordered that Edmond keep Tull from the bride of another. No Believer would argue for Tull's justification. Now Harlan led whilst Edmond and Asham took Ganix's head and body for preparation, surrendered the weapon used on him to Chief Guild, and found time to have Asham's wounds mended for no rescue medic would approach Ebbe Demesne. None berated Asham this time for there was no fault in he who proved apologetic.

Harlan relocated the Jacobian's tent to the side of camp that housed the most-senior Guardians. He then awaited the mediary's decision on their defiance of the judges' order that Tull not set foot on Ebbe Demesne. Harlan appreciated the composition of the law and the beauty of structure and proved eager to learn the outcome even at the expense of Tull's reputation. None doubted that he too hoped to argue on the Jacobian's behalf—even the mediary.

Gesicht served in a judge's stead and was privileged to the same authority. No other judge—Conliffe's son, for example—appeared at Ebbe Demesne or made inquiries. Then again, had Gesicht stayed away, there would have been less urgency toward an attack. Harlan reminded the mediary of his sullied hands, too, for his decision to be counted as unafraid. Since then, Gesicht and Katerena kept close to Sondrea and the manor.

All now mourned as a unified body; shunning resentment toward the ended soul or each other. Mediaries, Guardians, Believers, Partakers, countesses, and common souls stood for the Triune and the firstkind to see that they were not undone. The outfit gathered on the furthest side of Ebbe Demesne, further from the Behemót Woods and nearer to the eyes of all who sought to see them even in their shame. In this way, the secondkind soothed the displacement they suffered at the time of the Accession, when an entire world was scattered, isolated, and reshaped.

Almost all. The transition from scion to Guardian proved Nita selfish. In a time for remembrance of Ganix, she arrived last—and with a swain in tow who might level two of her four counterparts with a single swat. The distraction drew Olley's attention, which made George shuffle as he stood between Archibaldian and Shelbian. The former's posturing annoyed Tull enough that he ceased from utterance of the third verse of eulogy and scolded Nita with a sharp glance that inspired Olley.

"That's not the same creature she strolled from her tent with yester eve."

"And that matters to our memory of Ganix?"

Olley still grumbled, and Tull resumed mid-verse whilst Harlan and Nita offered them curious glances from either end of their line. Since the announcement of Ganix's end, Shelbians tested their fears of Ebbe Demesne and ventured to leave alms for she who would serve as their new Guardian. Nita took every gift and invited a few souls who caught her eye to spend time together in her tent.

"I cannot recall the name of she"—Olley resumed his gripe—"she who served me when I advanced from scion. Only that I wanted no other at that time. Can you remember the dove the Jacobians sent to you?"

Olley flustered Tull enough that he strained to follow the proper flow of words to honor Ganix. Tull never spoke of such moments, nor did he encourage others to tell of deeds not meant for the minds of others. Olley riled all when he felt riled. The Jacobian counted the words spoken over Ganix and his eyes veered toward the countess who stood ahead and to his left. There was no moment when she sensed him watching or looked his way on chance but he and the mediary traded an unsettled glance.

"That is four."

TULL & EBBE

Tull nodded at Olley's count of the times Gesicht looked their way.

"Two less than yester eve. Has he spoken to you?"

"No."

Then Sondrea knelt in prayer afore all who gathered along Taurog Roadway. The act filled Katerena's pale face with color and made Gesicht rigid at his prayer bones. This was why many esteemed the countess. The mere gesture proved scandalous, amid a territory that brimmed with Partakers, but she proved she was unafraid when harm sought her and inspired others who knelt with her.

Olley kept near to Tull; whose observational wit kept him postured even after the gathering for Ganix ended. He looked toward the Shelbian in their presence and spoke loud enough to offend. "Shelbian Believers and their prayers."

Nita took her revenge by making an affectionate display with a soul of sturdier build than the Archibaldian whilst George ducked their reaches and sought time amid a less-demanding flock.

"Truly! They pray not to the Triune but to the Ministers." The Archibaldian saw a glint of annoyance in Harlan's eyes and hushed till their interim headship ventured halfway between their place and the mediary. "They are fools."

"All are." Predicting a rebuttal, Tull challenged afore him. "You prefer they bow to the Fallen First?"

"I tell you; this is all fruitless." He sought Tull's interest, checked Nita's disinterest, but withered with impatience in between as none approached to honor them. "I believe we were born in the Pit. Our prayers are unheard. There's no hope for us."

Tull pleased another trio with a kind grin but Olley batted them away with his next claim.

"We're trapped down here. We believe we defend in obedience"—he waved a hand toward the First Creation—"but we obey our jailors. We climb too high, too near our escape, and they swat us down."

A soul across the roadway looked upward in search of proof of Olley's words.

"Elsewise, we might see above the brim and see where we are." He looked toward the gathering as if he expected applause. When he received none, he noticed that most looked to Tull for his response. He turned too. "I listen."

"Our words—spoken and elsewise—*are* heard on high. This eve, your words make the supernal perches drip with weeping."

Two souls across the roadway, plus Nita's lover, looked upward.

Tull & Ebbe

"The Triune hears us. They see us. We are not clever enough to surprise them. The pits I fall unto are pits I found in my own disregard for Their laws. Had I not proven stubborn, They would have kept me to my way."

"Yes, well, I will never mourn a Shelbian!"

"Then I must add a prayer for your heart's behalf." Tull made others scatter as he turned from Olley.

"I told you I—"

Tull patted the air between them and hushed his friend. "I must ask our Creator to be gentle when He humbles you."

Tull turned his back on his friend, avoided Harlan and Gesicht, allowed George his solace, and bypassed the trail of impressions back to the camp to create a cleaner path to Maia Espe Zeck's wing of the manor. Yester morn's snow hid the stains between the orchard and the millpond, and drifted snow blew from the broken windows of the observation terrace in the atrium still. He never counted spiders on the atrium or looked toward Count Conliffe's wing for disturbances, for the wooden drapes upon the corridor outside Sondrea's temporary residence stole his attention.

"Forgive my aim, Merciful Creator."

He splayed his gloved hand and touched the varnished covering. Though all felt solid, he heard the sound of the glass that the arrow cast from his bronze bow shattered. His aim saved George from a flint dagger and kept Sondrea's attacker from reaching her a second time. He never even set foot out of doors.

"How I ought to have shown greater mercy."

Jacobians, Carpenterians, and Westonians viewed the end of their fellow kind with a regard that the other territories dismissed. They prayed for a soul's safe travels unto eternity, they grieved for absence and the death of purpose, and prayed for a heart that never forgot the lost. This included their foes. Now, that included the Taotáva. Tull added the grief of not entering eternity to his repentance.

"I have cost another of Your creation their chance to enter Your courts."

He turned from the evidence in shame and veered from the doorway to the wing without regard for the obviousness of his path or the remainder of the walk for the countess and her companions. In those moments of reset, he learned to sense Enke'loi's nearness. This was not that. He felt her absence, an absence of peace, and a lingering of doubt greater than the disapproval of a mediary.

"Will Your perfect plan keep my kind from mourning me once more?"

TULL & EBBE

He would undo the claims that Olley made against their existence and the lovers that Nita took as the impression of how she might serve. George's grief, the abuse of foes, the loss of Ganix, and the wounding of Asham proved worthy of his re-hemmed journey too. Most of all, he would suffer another end if that would undo learning the secrets that Sondrea shared with him and the rage that burned in his heart since. To undo that ache, he would suffer his end and volunteer another.

"How would I explain my path had I been born an Archibaldian?"

Those from Olley's territory held no belief in resurrection. Twice Enke'loi kept Tull from his end and, in turn, kept his friend from ends of his own. His fellow heard Tull's claims but lacked the imagination—the *faith*—to believe such possibilities.

"Better that I'd been born a Shelbian?"

A chill moved him as he found wooden crates once filled with nuts and fruits that now held Ganix's possessions courtesy of George's tidying hand. None of his resets preserved the Guardian they now mourned. Ganix seldom stood in harm's path since Tull, the bivouac's caretaker, and Olley began their purpose. They, with Hector, Edmond, and Harlan, shouldered the load. Even one-legged Mick proved more reliable.

"His purpose was his undoing. Mine will not undo me." His eye found a possession amid Ganix's many that offered him direction away from his inward moping. "By Your grace, Yah."

Olley liked to tease Tull for every time a Jacobian wept with bitterness for the souls of their beloved and their despised. The Jacobians wept too oft! Neither a tepid Archibaldian nor an indulgent Shelbian perceived a kind of joy where souls spent eternity with those who made them miserable *down here*.

"Weep for what joy we have lost and those souls that we failed to turn in time." A grin then disrupted his placidness as he pocketed the possession of his found in Ganix's stash. "I thank You for Your patience and Your guidance."

Tull set the crates of possessions near the stack of firewood at Edmond's tent, that his headship might decide upon them, then created a clean path from the bivouac to the millpond house. No tongue called to him. No foe stood against him. If Yah hid him from all others, he would have proven the least surprised for his feet had not just an assured step but a purposefulness that he could not have counted as his own as he lacked any intention other than to reach the door.

TULL & EBBE

To prevent Olley from heaping cruelty and scorn upon she who infiltrated Sondrea's confidence, Gesicht ordered Edmond who instructed that Dory be kept from her end and chained about the trusses of the millpond house. Her last blessing was not that Olley bore no further interest in her but that Mim had not returned to the place where Sondrea made him sleep. In point of fact, the callous and irresponsible reeve had not returned since he fled.

In the yester eve, a group of Partakers who learned of the Taotáva arrived at Ebbe Demesne, that they might use her for their pleasure. They were the lowest portion of the lot for they saw no creature that they would not attempt to know in a sensual way. Harlan, Olley, and Nita taught them a brutal lesson. They fled, too; wounded for other Partakers to see, fear, and brutalize in Dory's stead.

Tull found, when he arrived, no snowy footprint on the steps that led to the door, so he left some. He felt, in a word, *compelled* to check on she who blindfolded and led him, as if this gave them a bond. Dory's visage appeared nearer to the face that she used in her role as succorer, though the brow turned heavy and her shoulders drooped when Tull brushed open the door. She hid her eyes from the light and covered her face from further reveal.

The open room bore a dampened chill and no comforts other than a window that looked upon the watermill. A heavy wooden case protected the levers, gears, and connections that generated Ebbe Demesne's operational energy. There were no tools, no broken planks, and no sharp edges to benefit her escape. For all she suffered in the millpond, the desire seemed as absent as the comforts she enjoyed afore her arrival.

She drew her limbs and face unto a covered position, knotted tighter with each step that he took across thunderous planks that calmed the groans of ice on the watermill. Tull stopped at the mark that George drew on the floor in expectation of Dory's reach; though none learned the true length that a shape-changer might reach. He felt no fear of her, but kept his boots shy of the mark and flung a folded blanket that landed on the side of the room she faced.

"I'm told that the cold is keener to you than me, so you ought to keep covered."

Her body trembled, but she did not reach for her much-needed provision. The millpond's mud still flaked from her skin and from beneath an odour like rotten fruit rind marked the place where she laid for too long. Tull raised a hand to his nose and breathed in the residue of mint leaf from the kettle of tea that he, Harlan, and George finished afore the second mourning. This calmed his twitching nostrils and reminded him of the spiced cigarettes she smelled of in their first meeting.

"I cannot punish you more than you've suffered. Accept the blanket."

Her fingers jutted without movement of her arm, and drew the duvet close to her face and chest. With her next breath, she reacted as though taunted. "The stench!"

"That cover belonged to the soul you helped end. Be reminded with every breath of the reason you rest here but be warm in your grief." He moved toward the wall nearest the sky-fires that he might see the light cast over her to observe her reactions, gestures, and the mark he believed he saw. "You have clothes and shelter because she whom you plotted against shows you undeserved kindness."

"Why bother?"

Tull reacted to her temperament and seized hold of the pail that held her supply of water and a blunt ladle. He pushed open the door with his boot and tossed both unto the porch where they bounced and spilled down the staircase. "If you seek a more difficult time, then I'll instruct the rest of the lot not to bother with your needs. Will that include Ganix's blanket?"

"The smug lout from across the river is better at proving his threats true." Her ear changed in shape and grew toward the sound of his nearness. "You are of no regard to me, Jacobian."

"Olley will soon forget you."

"Praez noi'e glaev!"

"Do you bear hatred toward the countess?"

"I might have ended her more ways than we have moonrises! I never set my hand against her."

His eyes remained on her now that her anger made her sit upright. The corners of her mouth fell unto necrotic pits and her nose eroded unto long grooves that made her upper lip droop. He doubted she could see him for her eyelids turned swollen and marred by black webbing and a milky, thread-like build-up that flowed across her cheeks from the tear ducts. This let him confirm the imprint pattern on her arm caused by a circular instrument that mimicked the needle pattern of the mending chambers.

"We obeyed when I ought to have used her trust for my gain."

This was not the first time she spoke of the soul who kept authority over her. Perchance the reason for Tull's unease? He increased her unease when he kept still.

TULL & EBBE

"You ought to have ended me as you ended Ming Tovam!"

"Ming Tovam . . . Sevilla was your twin. Was he not?"

She proved her stubbornness till he set his hand upon the staff that powered an array of kettle lanterns and covered her in false light. "I led him from the womb of our mother but all Taotáva are brothers. All are sisters. We do not isolate this soul from that soul because of their descent."

He took away his hand and let the room dim. "Then you practice greater charity than we show our own."

"Your kind heaps pride upon your young and disregards—"

"Nothing else you say"—he crossed the floor toward the door—"short of an apology toward the countess, interests me."

She pursed in refusal and pits appeared like the bruises on the skin of an apple.

"Why you are as you are is an answer meant for another soul." He glanced at the mark on her arm as proof. "I will take your brother's soulless remains to the Knotted Caves, so your ways are honored."

"You do not know our ways."

"I know that your blameless will accept their fallen elder. You told me as much."

Her expression proved as unsearchable as her visitor's till she laid back down and flung Ganix's blanket away.

"Because I do not believe you will survive this place, I will arrange for a Reformer to visit you afore you're turned over to the bench. You've lived long enough to learn of the Triune and are thereby accountable. Your soul is no longer declared blameless. Lest you repent to Them of your deeds, you will suffer a despair that will not cease."

When his silence proved troublesome, she turned to criticize the Creator but found that she was alone again with the door opened that she might watch her drinking water freeze because of her rejection of mercy.

TWENTY-SIX

The tenth rising of the Moon of the Mother's Song was not to be as bright as the fourteenth, but her brilliance still mingled with the sky-fires to turn fields of snow unto an explorable illusion. Those who warred above volleyed and created trails like flaming arrows that cast streams of light across the glebe. Even the path toward Broken Neck Trail remained well-defined. So, once Tull informed Harlan of his talk with Dory and took a meal to George in the pasture, he headed toward the stable to saddle Blizzard and return Ming's soulless remains.

The odor of straw, flayed apples, and horses seemed amplified by the cold. Even so, the swiftness of his progress pleased him; in that he believed Yah favored his choice. As for his heart, he mended by piecing together the puzzle-like memories of a time afore slab walls seemed shorter and the stalls narrower than when Sondrea brought him there in his blamelessness. He saddled a horse better now and fed Blizzard by hand to coax him toward the load he would soon carry.

Blizzard enjoyed a second helping of tender grass whilst his owner made the rounds with a wooden mallet and broke the ice from the water for all the stabled creatures. Each received a mix of grass and hay, some oats, and an apple wedge; cut from the supply that Ganix hoarded away. Tull brushed the mane and legs of the horse whose rider was no more; but not so much that Blizzard turned resentful. Then, the surprise of a familiar and changed face drew forth a smile that the Jacobian discarded at the end of his blamelessness.

"Say! Is that you, boy?"

Tull's alit expression drew the eye of an old stallion who approached without alms of grass or apples. Even his walk remained as regal as what a blameless soul committed to memory. The former pride of the stables, now adorned with feathers of white amid his faded coat and a silver mane, trembled with age and cold but showed no hesitancy toward the returned guest. For this, the Guardian soothed his neck and rested his brow upon Ligurus's crown as he pulled a blanket across a proud, old back.

TULL & EBBE

Such time passed since the horse towered over him, yet he still remembered their travels together.

"Do you still trot through the waters afore the thaw holds or ride beneath the lowest branches to scratch your back?"

"He has mellowed; or, his rider has."

The sound of the countess's voice warmed both creatures.

"I believe he remembers you."

"I confess, I imagined he saw his end by now."

"You were far from as rough on him as you might have convinced your heart that you were. He and I set many trails across our territories afore you, as my grandfather had afore me."

Sondrea approached Ligurus's opposite side, offered two purple carrots to him, and brushed the stallion's neck but kept the Guardian in her fond gaze. As for her, the time in the mending chamber made her look younger still; enough that no eye would believe she held eleven seasons over her favored Jacobian.

"I heard from my friend Gustus, who was swift to complain that Mim arrived at his station at the Zatopić Lock and Dam half-frozen and bloodied. He is terrified that your outfit will blame him for Dory's trickery and hunt him. He's asked to stay away till I end my time on Ebbe Demesne."

"Once we turn Dory over to the judges, that end might be declared."

"Perchance then they'll send you on to that matter you coveted to address."

His grin proved agreeable enough, but his eyes softened her.

"I've missed that wide-eyed soul who once hung on my every word." She rubbed the underside of the stallion's jowl and felt his ear against her cheek. "So has Ligurus."

Tull swept his hand along the back of the horse she rode when she rescued him from the shadows of the Behemót Woods fifty seasons afore.

"I caused your eyes some dimness afore."

Twice.

"More than once in our visit."

"I need time to"—he shook away his remark—"I must learn what to do about what you've told me."

"My counsel remains yours, Nelson."

His hand settled against Ligurus's back.

"I believe you know that I'll do what I must to ensure that Wilfred sees you in the best light."

"I'm told he believes his Guardians are monsters."

"He's dwelled in the presence of a monster for so long that he's forgotten what should frighten him."

"'What we lift as our god becomes our devil.'"

Her nose crinkled when he cited her. The joy proved short-lived as angular creases as shallow as an Archibaldian returned when her brow furrowed at the disguised cargo that awaited Blizzard's back. "Is that him?"

"He was named Ming Tovam Sevilla. Twin of your former succorer."

Her mouth hinted at her curiosity, but she withheld her voice.

"I seek to return him to the Knotted Caves, that his kind might prove forgiving."

Her eyes fluttered from horse's back to horse's back. "You travel with no other?"

"I'm to remain judge of my own heart."

"Is that safe?" She reached beneath Ligurus's neck and took hold of Tull's forearm. "My regard is not fleeting. Broken Neck Trail earned the name."

"She claims she obeyed he who employed her to play the infiltrator and that she has never sought to harm you. I believe her."

"Then this gesture lets you gain favor from her, as well. That you might learn from her who sent her?"

"Since you told me of"—he disliked the knowledge so much that he dared not repeat her secret—"Mediary Gesicht's arrival"—he tried to keep her gaze—"I've sensed that there is more that we have not yet faced."

"Papa's magick oft lingers. Not that I believe you've forgotten."

"I've faced worse than magick-wielders."

She brushed the hem of his cuff with her gloved hand and held to the fabric. "This soul whom you show favor does not ask that you seek harm for her."

"Good! If you had, I would lose all sense of slumber."

"The smells remain as awful as I remembered!"

Katerena Yvette Mumus's ability to enter a room—or stable house—needed some polish, but offered the pair time to put more than Ligurus's breadth between them. Even as the novitiate stared at Tull with opulent, green irises and lifted her proud chin to reveal a flowing neck adorned in rich-black tresses, he remembered her from a time when she slobbered, jabbered, and rested upon any surface that supported the weight of her round head. In hindsight, she seemed manageable then. Now, even Ligurus stomped a hoof in protest and retreated further into the stall.

"Hush!"

The demanding heiress of three established lineages, eleven moons younger than Jules Baker Shannon, possessed the calming nature of a serpent and all the horses whinnied and stomped in protest of her order to their elder. The veins showed through her pale skin, which made her eyes appear unnatural in volume. Olley once noted the resemblance between her smile and a horse's mouth, though Tull tried his best not to make any comparisons that offended Yah's four-legged splendors.

"Ignorant beasts!" She then proved Olley true when she set her eyes upon Tull a second time and added a smarmy smile. "Withhold your offense, Scarecrow. I speak of the horses this time."

"Katerena! I told you to stay—"

"If you sneak, I sneak, Mother."

"I am the countess of this manor and all her plots. I needn't sneak."

Tull patted Ligurus's back and turned toward Blizzard.

"You go?"

He stooped toward Ming and checked the binds on the fabric that concealed their foe. "Harlan fidgets when we run later than we ought. I told him I'd return from the caves by morn . . . to mourn."

"Is he not to look upon you when you speak to him, Mother? Would he dishonor my father in the same way?"

Tull smiled at the ideas of how he would dishonor Judge Mumus and hiked the remains over his shoulder. He let the saturation of fabric that followed serve as his warning against Katerena's needling. "Does the bench object?"

She who misunderstood his previous boast shook her head. "I believed you decided against such travels. Was I in err?"

"Only with regard to my penchant for seeking harm." He delighted in their eye contact and Katerena's inability to look away from Ming's spill. "I prove harder on my purpose than most."

He slipped the body off his shoulder and across the lay of blocks that bore the load of the stable and formed the dividers between stalls. These stood mid-height and showed that Ming's slightness mimicked Dory's.

TULL & EBBE

"As easy as his load proves, I ought to be able to see the Squires play like fireflies on my ride in."

"That confidence led to your upset in Küzdellom; lest I'm mistaken?"

Even Blizzard huffed in response to Sondrea's fine memory.

"And, your attempt at throwing"—she tapped her hand staff against the hard footpath between stalls—"spears."

"I have learned much since then about balance's pull on aim."

"Yet other Guardians carry throwing weapons and you do not."

When he mimicked Blizzard's disapproval, Katerena offered a noise that sounded like a shrill whinny as he set a duvet across his mount's back.

"I tell you, Guardian"—Sondrea performed a visual inventory of bridles, duvets, saddles, and lanterns—"as countess of Ebbe Demesne, upon which you'll spend well-nigh half of your travel, I must insist that I ride with you."

He dared not scoff. She remained a better rider than most of her Guardians. Even Katerena withheld a barb of the slightest prick.

"I can still teach you the trail, and I believe I deserve to see my defeated attacker returned to his kind."

"Defeated?" Another shrill whinny cut through the cold air. "Our Guardians cut away his head, Mother!"

"Mind you, Katerena must join us."

Both Guardian and novitiate offered soured expressions.

"Katerena, I'll not leave you alone at the manor nor have you troubling the Guardians. Besides, the time out of doors will remind you of the many blessings and comforts we forget too oft."

"I'll not saddle Lucy on my own!" A lingering huff punctuated the complaint. "Where is Mim?"

Sondrea glanced at Tull and tipped her head toward Ligurus, who oft bucked a pest, then patted his neck to tell she too had a sense of humor. Tull grinned, then resumed his work lest the countess prep both horses rather than delay his purpose. The countess detested idleness as much as he and, he believed, would feel offended by such an offering.

"Do not set the buckles too tight!"

"I assure you that I know how to set the buckles."

TULL & EBBE

Katerena's Archibaldian father promoted the idea that other souls sacrifice their purpose to appease the heiress's whims. This same spirit moved through the outfit beneath Cam's guardianship and, with Ganix's end, was, at last, no more. Except for jest, he never heard Sondrea raise her voice in pettiness or laziness.

"I see you remember how to set the buckles too."

"He waddles when I cinch too tight."

"I suffer the same trouble with some of my own adornments."

Katerena groaned from another stall, though not because she paid the pair any mind. Sondrea sighed in a manner that regretted and apologized for her decision to include her.

"She is a competent rider."

He glanced toward the heiress between checking Blizzard's shoes. "Can she keep up with a Jacobian?"

The countess proved amused by his slight against other territories and offered no unnecessary defense of Katerena's ability.

"Let another Archibaldian travel along so her reputation avoids suffering."

Tull righted his posture at the sound of a new voice and stood a full head taller than Mediary Gesicht, with no exaggeration.

"No need to appear sullen, Guardian, I'm competent enough that I'll not slow you down." He then proved the opposite as he marveled over the corral of horses. "Firefly. Salmah. Cuss."

"He keeps to a schedule, Wilfred."

"I'm informed of such." He folded his arms and did not flinch when George's horse, Salmah, stomped a hoof in the stall behind him. "I've withheld my determination this late. A ride might afford me a better understanding of your ways, Guardian. Is this not Ganix's horse?"

"If each of us travels with him, whom do the other Guardians defend?"

"They have plenty of work. Besides"—Gesicht stroked the horse whose name might provoke offense, then claimed a saddle from the rafter joist—"if every Guardian stands in individual service to fifty-five thousand souls, then the three of us ought to ease our Jacobian shield."

Sondrea offered a shrug of surrender toward Tull.

Gesicht looked upward at Ligurus. "Whose is this creature?"

"That is the last stallion owned by my grandfather."

TULL & EBBE

"Zeck's last stallion? Tremendous!"

"Mediary." Tull winced for his sidekick's benefit. "If you are to travel with us, I feel obliged to offer you my horse. He is the best adapted for the terrane and the lacking light."

Gesicht proved detached and pivoted afore he pointed back at Tull's offering. "Blizzard! Your first purchase as a Guardian."

"He looks nothing like the snow!"

"He wasn't named for the snow, scion. Our Jacobian Guardian raced unto an ash storm in the Creightonian lowlands—"

"Truly! I do not care why he chose the name."

Tull scoffed. "He will not wander, Mediary. If you know why he bears his name, then you may trust my claim."

"Am I responsible for"—he pointed toward Ming—"too?"

"Ligurus will carry him." Sondrea set her hand upon Tull's shoulder and leaned on his strength versus her hand staff. "Should you care to take him out once more."

"He has no saddle, Mother."

"Your grandfather never allowed his stock to bear a saddle."

The mediary's claim made Tull bristle.

"Lest that's changed for you?"

"No."

"Then we are set, are we not?"

"I believe we are."

"Leave your gear with your horse, Guardian. I'll not harm what is yours."

"I thank you." Tull scratched beneath Blizzard's jowl. "When we ascend Broken Neck Trail, I'll go on foot. You needn't do the same. He'll hold you."

Blizzard snorted and drew a sympathetic pat from Sondrea's hand.

"Say that again and you won't see another green apple till the thaw."

Gesicht grinned at the exchange but, like Tull, watched as the countess mounted a tan mare named Agnate. She covered her chest with her riding cape and secured her left leg in the stirrup using her hand. If any held a concern over her ability to make the ride, none spoke; and not while she strapped her hickory staff to the saddle beneath the other leg. Till Katerena led the charge out of the stable upon her speckled mare, all seemed content with the silence.

"Nice boots, Scarecrow."

TULL & EBBE

Tull looked upon his feet as though shamed by Katerena's disapproval of his marred old boots. He then side-eyed the mediary who surveyed alongside him.

"Currie Leland Kirke. I'll bet those were tremendous in their time!"

The Guardian fidgeted at the mediary's knowledge and looked upon she who gifted him his second-most expensive possession.

"I have two pairs of his designs too."

How the Guardian smirked made Sondrea chuckle. Gesicht laughed with her, though he missed the joke. He then mounted Blizzard and chirped when the horse trotted without instruction.

"He'll not throw me, will he?"

Tull shook his head and let out a heavy sigh as his chances for a peace-filled ride seemed exhausted.

"Not that I would keep such happenings in mind!"

"He teases, and Katerena puts her anger for me onto you."

"She's as gentle as I've remembered her."

Sondrea reached and scratched beneath his jowl as she passed. "Come along, Guardian, and do make your territory proud."

Her drifting laughter masked his groan as he hoisted Ming upon Ligurus's rump and climbed the stable wall to mount. The stallion drifted sideways, then righted his stance. Tull settled, too, and held reins in his right hand and a twine lashing from Ming's covering with the other. He then tested both his core and the stallion's as he whispered in his ear.

"Worry not. I'll pray this eve proves tremendous in ease, old friend. Let us ride."

Ligurus responded to his purpose and led the Guardian out with the poise deserving of Beau Itzal Zeck's last stallion. Sondrea appreciated the sight and offered a smile. Gesicht chuckled and shook his head, though Blizzard proved ornery enough to jostle rider and replacement. Then Tull offered another clack and sped their path through the orchard toward the caves in the distance.

TWENTY-SEVEN

<u>ON BROKEN NECK TRAIL</u>

ABOVE THE FOOTHILLS OF THE CARPENTER TERRITORY.

HIGHER THAN THE REACH OF ATKINS AND SAKI SIGNAL HOUSES.

"Tremendous!"

Gesicht's outburst marked the third time he had distracted the seasoned riders from their progress. Sondrea and then Tull indulged the mediary as he marveled on the brilliance of the sky-fires from their elevation. Blooms of violet and lavender filled much of the canvas, but a glimmer of gold and silver cords framed the view. The Crater of N'Ach Shi'an captured remnants of white across the moon and the Valleys of Mechh'täva were rich with hues that matched the Jacobian's irises. Only Katerena huffed in displeasure and scowled at her makeshift uncle.

"I reasoned that we might see a storm. I can see further than I imagined now. The Ministers must love warring if they cannot stop in awe of such presence."

"We've crossed unto the Carpenter Territory."

"Then we've not slowed you down, have we?"

Sondrea's left cheek creased with a subdued smile as her eyes followed the Guardian. Once she kept time of his and Ligurus's pace, she explained his remark to Gesicht. "You're unfamiliar with the teachings of Ivar Calvin Peeters."

"Is that an inventor, a chronicler, or a Reformer?"

"He's a Reformer who was once a Partaker and who has performed chronicling, too, of the lessening expanse of the sky-fires above the Shelby Territory."

"How is that now?"

"Ivar believes that the vastness we behold of the firstkind's perches relates to the purity—the cleanness—of our Believers. The Carpenterian soul is a good and noble soul. The Shelbian soul increases in unbelief. With the number of Believers who abandon her, he believes that a near entire covering will divide the Shelbians from our Creator's field by our one hundred twentieth winter."

TULL & EBBE

Gesicht watched for a crinkle or a smirk upon the countess's face and then looked toward the Guardian. Though Tull kept his lower face masked, his eyes reflected the sky-fires and no humor.

"All that you marvel over and you doubt that such a veil exists. O, you disturb me, Wilfred." She cooed at Agnate and glanced at Katerena, who followed on Lucy and proved the claim that she was a competent rider.

Gesicht's laughter disturbed an unidentified creature in the woods that drew Tull's passing interest. "Do forgive my low Archibaldian wit."

The mediary watched as the pair led the way. Tull, in practiced silence, slipped from Ligurus and massaged the stallion's jaw. He gave a firm tug on the reins and the stallion responded with a nod. Then, he addressed his own horse with two clacks and a swift, sideways nod. Blizzard whinnied and obeyed with a soft trot, letting pass Gesicht's perceived control over the loaned horse.

The Guardian then brought up the rear as Sondrea led the way along Broken Neck Trail, named for the staggering incline that made the neck twitch if a soul stared too long at the peak. Ligurus moved well beneath a lightened load and Blizzard proved steady enough to not sense Gesicht's bothered nature. None spoke, and they soon made up for the moments lost on talk of beliefs and veils. Still, Tull's smirk changed the lay of his balaclava the two times when he observed Gesicht's glance toward the sky-fires.

Tull no longer doubted the secondkind's inability to process the scope of their Creator's possibility. If Yah's plan and Enke'loi's determination to make him of use continued, he believed he might see an era when Shelbians looked up and saw nothing but dark clouds and thick haze.

"Uhmmm"—Gesicht broke the comfort of silence—"Countess, are you making that sound to needle us?"

Katerena snorted and shook her head so that the flowing ribbon of her hair shook like Lucy's tail.

"Countess?"

To those who knew her, Sondrea showed an unsettled sense of humor. She mastered the art of reproducing noises in the woods, of gliding through dark rooms without a sound, and—by the eve's demonstration—mimicking the tune of the pylon's song that oft filled the harbor between the Archibald and Jacoby Territories, where the winds passed through the remnants of Forgney Bridge that once offered passage from the bluffs of the Jacoby Territory to the harbor in the lost Gierig Territory.

Gesicht twisted back at Tull. "Do you hear that sound?"

"Mother!"

Katerena's fourteenth overuse of the title made Tull inhale with a sharpness that oft complemented deliberate aggression. He never liked the heiress's use of the cold moniker—never mom, mama, mommy, maw, or any variety that suited a tender heart. The name was as odd to his ear as Gesicht's overuse of the given name she seldom used or his declarations toward the tremendous.

"Even the scarecrow riles!"

A grumbling from Katerena's lips bothered Tull and drew him a step back. Ligurus whinnied and sidestepped but allowed the Guardian to keep him near with a static arm. The winds picked up, the tangled branches scraped and tangled, and the Guardian lifted his head toward the sky-fires. Katerena's steed pecked at the terrane with her rider's impatient tone but Sondrea circled as if to defend their rear.

"What, Mother?"

"Is there a matter?"

Sondrea grabbed the reins from hands that had never labored and bared her teeth as she spoke with a low hush that made Katerena stir and keep her gaze downturned with her chin pointed high. In this, Tull recognized an Archibaldian response to scolding.

"What do I not see, Guardian? Because she calls you Scarecrow?"

Tull led Ligurus till he stood at Gesicht's heel. "Her grumbling approaches blasphemy. If the Squires respond, we risk being struck by flaming branches or a washout. In that, I fail my purpose, and the heiress becomes recognized as malleable to the Fallen First."

"Let us avoid that." Gesicht's smirk proved a gentleness he withheld. "You do not address Katerena as the countess' daughter."

"Do I not?"

"Are you not above jealousy?"

"Have you heard me call our host by her title?"

"Countess?" He shook his head and expressed an inability to answer. "Why?"

"Till his teeth returned to him, our Guardian called me *Counteth*," Sondrea teased. "He calls me by the name my grandfather cherished."

TULL & EBBE

"A simple curiosity"—he offered Tull a glance—"Guardian. I meant no offense."

"Nor I, if I unsettled you, Wilfred." The countess established her rule. "I sought to remind you of the sounds of home; so far from Sevier. I pledge to prove my soberest behavior till we reach the caves. If the two of you prove ready?"

Both agreed to resume their climb, but the mediary voiced some doubt toward Tull's former explanation. "Flaming branches and washouts? For grumbling? I'd like to hear about this claim. Guardian?"

A slyness overtook the Guardian and he egged Blizzard with a heavier step. "I witnessed a Squire pluck Francis Ferndale McDougal mid-fit and not disturb a kernel from the bushels set around him. His hair ran white afore the next moonset and two full seasons passed without words—without sound—crossing his lips again."

"I'm unfamiliar with Francis Ferndale McDougal."

"As you say."

"He spins a yarn, Uncle, and you are his loom."

"Then you can name for us every soul that shares the isle, daughter?"

Gesicht laughed. "A fair point, Countess."

"Go to the cottage at 1948 Lees Grove, heiress, and ask for the counter if you doubt my word. Ask to see the unmarred imprint of brass fingers upon his lips." Tull patted Ligurus's front leg and retrieved a fallen branch from his path. "Squires haven't an ear for grumbling. The sounds mingle too near to their offense and—"

He snapped that same branch. From the front, Sondrea chuckled and offered a glance from over her shoulder as Katerena gasped and made her hair sway with refusal. Gesicht maintained a curious gaze upon the teller of tales but proved silent lest he be judged.

"Then the Squire rises away."

"You spend time near the storehouses, do you?"

"Even your Guardians contribute in the gathering season, Mediary Gesicht."

"I have never contributed to field labor!"

She who received scolding still proved her contrary nature.

"I cannot remember counting Cyril in any field, either." Mumus's stand-in then inhaled and shook his head. "My!"

"Let me." Tull stated rather than asked and took hold of Blizzard's reins.

The air thinned high above the low-set waterways around Ebbe Demesne and limited the range of Gesicht's breath for the Archibald Territory sat lower. Still they climbed. The orchards throughout the southern territories offered slight hills. Even those from the lode region of the Carpenter Territory proved too gentle in their step to navigate the coastal bluffs that elevated the high northern territories.

"The air does not"—he covered his mouth with a fine scarf—"trouble you?"

"He is Jacobian!" Sondrea called out from beneath a covering of her own and hesitated that she might cinch Katerena's scarf afore she rode past.

"I do remember"—Gesicht coughed—"his territory."

"Better we keep our breath from here on."

The northern Jacoby Territory, home to his mother's line, shielded the lowlands from the altitude and harsh winds that necessitated a stout breath and sure foot. Tull led the mediary and two horses without slowing whilst those beneath his guard held fast to the bridles and leaned nearer to the necks of their horses as they ascended. When Lucy's rump swayed and her hoof slipped, Tull mingled Ligurus's and Blizzard's reins and patted the covered wrist of the overindulged heiress.

"Hold to her neck with gentleness and I'll guide her."

Sondrea looked back to see that Katerena obeyed without argument. "Around this bend, the ice surrenders to the glebe. The roots of mighty poplars weave together and offer a foothold."

"Much higher"—Tull called back—"and we trespass on the firstkind's perches."

"And we've climbed but one-third of the face. Better we spare the horses and go the rest on foot. We'll head north and away from the Loy. The caves are not far from us and the way proves kinder."

"I don't mind this path."

Tull's ear heard the contrary from the spoiled soul as he and Gesicht helped her from her saddle. "Around the stretch then? The winds off the Loy abrade, but—"

"Mother?"

Sondrea understood his humor and scolded him in equal measure. "We'll stay to the trail I've oft traveled, Guardian. I thank you."

"As you say, Countess."

"Now your hand."

Tull obeyed without letting go of three horses and helped her dismount whilst he kept his eye on Gesicht's face to gauge expressions. The mediary nodded with approval. Then, Sondrea's sigh and a trade of her grip from his hand to his shoulder let Tull know she stood on both feet.

"My hand staff."

He reached over Agnate's back, unfastened both buckles, and never dropped the reins. Once she held her walking aid, she made a hollow sound as she bopped his crown. She and Agnate forged a path with Katerena and Gesicht behind them. Tull kept their order intact and let Lucy, Ligurus, and Blizzard protect the rear while he watched both sides.

A winding path took them between segregated slopes where the snow retreated and a floor of hardened stone echoed beneath the horses. When the trail ledge narrowed, Tull crossed first, secured the horses, and returned for the other travelers. At the first sighting of their destination, Sondrea claimed Agnate's and Ligurus's reins, then handed off Lucy's and Blizzard's reins to their riders. Tull plucked a soft case from the hind of Blizzard's saddle. What he cast aside revealed his bow and quiver; which was all he took as he advanced ahead and from their sight without instruction.

Silence loomed amid the threat of shadows, then three reverberating knocks preceded three blooms of amber light kept in tubes fitted to certain arrows. He drove an iron bolt unto the rock and then shot a fourth arrow toward the furthest bloom of light. A sound of an unspooling tether followed, which he plucked for tautness afore he hammered the iron bolt deeper. Each watched as he prepared a path for them, and the countess used her hand staff to collect the soft cover of his bow from the terrane.

"See, now, why we fare better beneath the care of a Jacobian?"

Katerena remarked to offend, "'A Shelbian would sooner lay with a horse than ride upon him.'"

"Katerena!" Sondrea drew her breath and shrank her core. "I believe we're near enough from your mouth."

"I repeat what words I overheard from our *Archibaldian* Guardian when I arrived."

"Our Guardian sets that line for us to find our way back to the light if we're pulled unto the shadows." Sondrea tapped Katerena's chin. "Better you hold with both hands and less lip."

"You prove your aim well, Guardian!"

"And you your breath, Mediary."

"As you say!" Though airy and waffled, Gesicht's laughter returned.

"The line will hold, Countess." Tull then offered each soul a handheld orb aglow with matching amber light, tossing the third to Gesicht.

TULL & EBBE

"I thank you." Sondrea removed the covering from around her cheeks and patted at her nose, mouth, and chin. "I thank you."

Gesicht gripped the orb as Tull held his bow. "That's a tremendous weapon."

"Only a Jacobian can bend a bow of bronze!"

"I can name another."

"Your fondness for the Poet King inspires you still!"

"I see no rareness in him!" Katerena's shrillness returned. "Even you could pull back that weapon, Mother."

"I tell you, I cannot. I have tried."

"You allowed that?"

Tull looked toward the mediary. "Not in my care."

"My grandfather offered me the opportunity when I approached my grandmother with a nature not unlike Katerena's."

When he heard the heiress scoff, the Guardian held out that same bow as an offering for her to prove her greatness. An arrogant expression stole her beauty and she squirmed as if no barb came to mind.

"On my lone attempt"—Sondrea warned—"I ruined my boots and trousers."

When Katerena looked away, as if the test meant nothing, Tull withdrew his offering.

"Wilfred?"

The mediary raised his hands in defense and reminded them of his orb. "If trouble awaits, I prefer that he who has earned a name for that bow keeps a hold and not me."

"Your wisdom humbles us." She chuckled and squeezed Tull's arm. "I tell you I hear the memory of my mother warning me to keep far from these suspect caves."

The Guardian and then the mediary joined her and studied the impressions along a butterscotch-hued lesion that grew beneath the exposed roots of fifty-eight trees. A series of mouths as blackened as their foes' mouths sat disguised by brushwood. Above them, jagged icicles shimmered with the amber blooms of false light. If the quality of each arrow held as well as previous uses, the light would keep till the moonset.

"Do you see the mouth that has the shape of a lamb's head?" Her description drew Tull nearer and turned Gesicht away from watching Katerena's step. "See, the ears?"

"Yes."

TULL & EBBE

"That mouth, and count two to the right, and then four more further right, were oft my preferences."

"You visited this place oft?"

"My friends and I dedicated well-nigh an entire sowing season and part of a gathering season to learning these caves."

"Then you found what you sought and stopped?"

"No."

Tull heard as solemnness limited the range of her voice but another soul proved oblivious. "Were you frightened, Mother? My father would not fear a hole in the glebe. Neither would Papa! Why, Papa would make every creature afraid with—"

"Katerena! Enough. His magick is not an answer for every dilemma."

"You were afraid. No?"

Tull loaded an arrow, drew back as he pivoted, and fired above their heads and the segregated contour that shielded them. His arrow struck with a whine, then a flickering light drew the sound of buzzing. A mist of bitter smoke poured from one of Inventor Holston Lucius Buckler's two projection gliders that followed them since Ebbe Demesne. Then, that glider dropped.

"Guardian Tull! What was—"

"Rest at ease, Wilfred! Our Guardian shielded us from Cyril's"—she glanced toward the archer and recalled his phrase—"soaring imps."

"Not his gliders!" Gesicht's agitation stirred Blizzard. "Do you know the cost of your actions, Guardian?"

"Less than the cost of such intrusions upon creatures we ought not rile."

"That will set our gain rearward."

"Mediary Gesicht"—he shouldered his bow—"however vast the sky-fires prove, we do not sight-see here nor offer covert tests of gadgetry with no use to us, and whilst I am purposed to be a shield, I do not uphold the selfish decisions of our kind. Even those of my betters."

"Guardian!"

"Yes."

Sondrea recognized that the pair might argue evermore and tapped at the bow with her hand staff. "Let us leave the other's decisions alone."

"This is not forgot—"

"And let us leave him to his purpose, Wilfred."

TULL & EBBE

The calmed mediary settled atop Tull's horse. Sondrea offered a sharp nod toward Ligurus's rump when she caught her fellow Jacobian's smirk. His expression rumpled, but he surrendered to her direction and retrieved the soulless remains without setting aside his bow. As a show of gentleness, he did not approach the nesting place of their foe's kind with his quiver in tow this time. When Sondrea counted this as a shortness of hands, she leaned upon her staff and reached toward the strap.

He brushed her forearm with the curve of his bow and shook his head. "If you lose sight of me, and if I am not he who returns, then those will serve you well."

"Soon I will see you."

"I believe this scarecrow is afraid, Mother."

"You've forgotten how you once never let him stray from your sight."

"I never!"

Tull sensed that both watched him now. Still, he lingered along Blizzard's neck till the horse accommodated him. He spoke hushed words unto a tickled ear and ended with a tender brush of brow and jowl. His eye then found Gesicht's, but the two did not speak. The next sound heard was the break of ice-petrified grass as he stepped toward the caves with his offering.

"What did he say to his horse?"

"'Aenna vi'hoyai saemme syödä valittaei'ean kui'n i'eohdaet kaksi muutae.'"

Katerena shrugged. Though Gesicht shared a basic understanding of the firstkind's tongue, he offered no translation. Even so, he crossed his leg atop the saddle and settled with an easy smile. Once Sondrea gauged his reaction, she draped the quiver across her breast and held to her hickory staff with both hands where the sky-fires kept back the shadows.

Tull felt a warm breeze, like a breath of satisfaction, and paused till that breath blew over him. The three blooms of amber light increased as his eyes adapted to discern the shadows from the feathered slope of the floor beneath him. Across the mingled terrane, he followed the impressions of more feet than he could count. None bore as much definition as his feet. Still, he discovered enough detail to prove that a creature who moved on two feet also crushed the grass afore the winter settled. Then, the center of the three arrows he fired burst and cost a bloom of light.

"All is well!"

TULL & EBBE

He calmed his mind, settled his heart, and resumed his path. His feet followed the curve of the floor and did not slip even where slicks of ice tempted a fall. The leg that supported the shoulder that held Ming then burned. As he dwelled on the muscle pain, his mind betrayed him with a memory of Sondrea revealing her mended thigh to him. The bloom that rested between him and the countess then burst.

"All is well!" His eyes drifted toward the depths of the sky-fires. "Yes?"

His left ear heard a hiss and then the third bloom, nearest to the caves, went black. The floor beneath vibrated and he stopped when a roar from the bowels of an unidentified cave proved sullen enough to increase the rate of his heart. Tull felt overwhelmed by an urge to fall to his knees. When the desire seemed as heavy as the soulless remains, he cast away all that he towed and bowed whilst a moon's count of prayers rushed through his inner chambers.

Stillness then comforted him. This was not the stillness of comfort, but the stillness of preparedness, for he knew in his heart what to expect next. The air turned bitter and a high-pitched sound of scratching grew louder. A flicker, like sparks afore flame erupted within a cave, spread to two mouths, then to three. Tull had time for a shallow breath and pressed his hands against the cold terrane.

Then, the creature who embodied that roar burst from beneath and turned two walls of limestone to rubble as three caves were reformed as one. A four-legged beast with the feet of a falcon, the body of a lion, and the head of a Minister emerged as if from a Reformer's sleep-terrors. Soot burst from nostrils as coarse as the glebe, and eyes adapted to the dark squinted as the creature's rage burst upon another roar. Talons like opal razors scrawled the terrane, rivaling Katerena's distant shriek, and a guttural tremble brought the head of the beast low.

A brilliant, red plume spread as the torso twisted and the segregated belly raised eight times. As the creature's back rolled, a pair of blackened wings flung ash and mire onto the unblemished wall. The front feet rested upon talons alone and still the sound of the beast's rear talons clawed from the depths of the cave. Though Tull saw none of these details in the darkness, he shouted a name known well to the Fallen First.

"Hyl ki'ö!"

The creature called Outcast roared and the horses that remained visible beneath the sky-fires whinnied and stomped. Agnate tore her reins from Sondrea's gloved hand whilst Lucy bucked enough to make Katerena mimic her neigh. The commotion attracted the wrong attention, and Tull reacted with the urgency of a prophesier who foresaw a terrible end. With no more than a knife from his boot, he roared back at the outcast and charged. In that moment, he felt his legs increase in weight till his gait became like a chore and labored his breath.

Gleams of light, like descending whisps of open flame, proved the creature's shape till Ligurus raced around his rider and blocked him from harm. A shrill cry rang out, but the old stallion never yielded. The gleams intensified and sparks created puddles of fire upon frozen, incombustible terrane. The sound made by talons atop stone whilst in fear made Tull nauseaus.

"Run back to her, horse!"

The Guardian lacked time for a better plea. The stench of abdominal mire stung his eyes and stole his breath like the altitude stole Gesicht's breath. The outcast creature, fearing them, leapt. Though Tull hurled his knife, Ligurus stood ready to suffer the brunt and Tull could not move him, even with the might that bent bronze.

A sound like thunderclouds shook the branches of the trees above the caves and caused a sudden, short-lived snow shower. In the belly of thunder, gleaming creatures of fire and brass vaulted toward the outcast with a swiftness that exceeded any arrow and stopped the creature from inflicting harm by ascending upward without slowing—a knife buried in a brilliant, red plume. More glints of light fell, not unlike fireflies, and passed through the misshapen mouth of the three caves. Afore their ascent, those caves collapsed so no soul might enter them again.

Behind them, yet another team of Squires—less than one-third the size of those that took the outcast—gathered around Ligurus's hooves and head. Another patted his flank, and the arthritic hip that slowed him rehabilitated with completeness. This drew praise from the Squires, who stroked his mane and sang. When they set their eyes upon Tull, pools of immaculate flame brimmed in the sockets. Their heads tilted back and, afore he batted his lashes, they raced back unto the sky-fires.

Though Tull laughed, he soon fell to his knees and wept. Ash as soft as feathers fell like snow and rinsed away the creature's spilled mire. Around every puddle of flame, the terrane cracked whilst flowers regarded for their nourishing berries and healing properties bloomed from the openings. Such were the events that the Shelby Territory turned from.

TWENTY-EIGHT

"Nelson!"

The Guardian patted Ligurus's nose as he nudged him toward the countess's call for him. He gathered the stallion's reins and marveled at the flicker of firelight in his eyes. As he led the way through soot and ash, he proved his identity. "'Yah, our perfect Creator, makes war in my name!'"

Sondrea chuckled and her figure took shape as she moved amid the ash.

"I say, 'Yah, our perfect Creator, makes war in my name!'" He emerged in front of her with his hand against Ligurus's jowl and breathed peace as they reached a stop.

"'So I must keep still.'" And, still she remembered words long unspoken. She brushed her beloved Guardian's face with both hands, but also patted at her grandfather's last stallion when he nudged her for affection, too.

"You're—"

"Unmarred?" His grin soothed her. "All remain well here?"

"I've not enjoyed such silence!" She looked toward their silent companions, who kept their gazes fixed upward.

"The two of you ought not to sneak further!"

Gesicht and Katerena, who stood behind Sondrea and the horses, looked toward the other in embarrassment. Then, Tull looked toward a location other than theirs.

"An Archibaldian need not *sneak*!"

The mediary leapt as Olley arose from a squatted position behind a cluster of boulders. Then Katerena gasped when George stepped from behind a slender and upright tree. Both brushed their trouser legs and drew their horses unto the open.

"I tell you, we stood at the ready."

"Nelson? Nelson, how did you see them?"

"He oft turns that way after"—Olley motioned upward toward the Squires' path—"wink at him. A renewed sense, or so he claims."

"A renewed sight."

"As you say, George. We prove accustomed to him, Countess."

Tull & Ebbe

"And he to you?" Olley's acting judge spoke up. "Guardian Falk, we did not hear you. We were taken by Guardian Tull's . . . predicament."

All settled as the mediary looked harder at Tull.

"Are your clothes brighter?"

"Such interactions are odder than they read on the page, are they not?"

Gesicht nodded and returned his gaze upward. Then to Tull's outfit. And then upward again.

"You missed the Westonian's bolt." Tull awaited George's bright smile. "You took my third bloom."

"He swore he saw a figure creeping along the trees. Even blamed him for taking the first two blooms."

Tull grimaced as that conflicted with his belief of Who took those same blooms.

"I never saw!"

"Yet you're sure the tree-creeper was a *him*." Sondrea called Olley's bluff. "Your friends prove troubled over your traveling without them, Guardian Tull."

The smug lout who upset Tull at the last mourning grunted. "I blame George! He noticed Blizzard's hoofprints were off and proved he's a bigger nag than Salmah."

"His hoofprints were different?" Gesicht marveled at the claim and shook his head afore doubt fed his laughter.

"George could track you across the territories and tell you how many alms you spent on your journey afore he rests his hand in your pocket."

The Westonian leaned out and patted Blizzard's hind as he addressed his true rider. "My friend, we saw Hyl ki'ö returned to his Judge. Harlan will not believe us."

"I suspect not." Tull nodded. "Who agitated you more? Olley or Nita?"

George pointed at the Archibaldian and smiled for all to see.

"Countess! Your grandfather's boot knife ascended in the breast of that outcast."

"Better the knife than you."

"Edmond will agree! He told us to get up here and collect you so you're back in time for the third mourning."

"Edmond returned?"

"In time to see Ozul broom away another—"

George nudged away Olley's gripe and reminded him of his manners with a glance toward Katerena.

"Dust bunny."

TULL & EBBE

"Guardian Gera returned too?"

"With a lump he'll show to every soul who passes his way."

"He's earned as much."

"This time."

Sondrea followed their remarks from Archibaldian to Westonian to Jacobian.

Olley scratched behind his ear. "Edmond made an awful direct point about punctuality, I tell you."

"Our route to Ebbe Demesne will be slowed by our descent"—Sondrea spoke in Tull's stillness—"but I suspect we'll arrive in time. We might even see more fireflies."

As if he understood her words, Olley's horse whinnied and drew his rider's rebuke. "Hush."

Gesicht laughed. "Because his name is Firefly."

"Well"—the Jacobian tightened his gloves—"I've another purpose to see to first."

"You lost another note from your pocket?"

"I was kept from my purpose for traveling here by the outcast."

Olley stared toward the Knotted Caves. "Are we not close enough?"

Tull nudged him backward a half-step.

The Archibaldian took another lest he surrender a last word or deed.

"I shed Ming and my bow afore the beast appeared."

"But, Nelson, the Squires sealed the cave . . . and your heart." Sondrea's eyes crept away from his when she sensed and confirmed that Gesicht watched. She said no more and, like Olley, stepped further from her beloved Guardian.

"There remain plenty of mouths. Better that I unfurl him and brush away the fires, lest his kind believe he was good to stand against us."

"Nelson." Olley shook his head in protest of his own heart. "I believe George might tow less regret if you took him along this time."

All took a moment to marvel over his compassion till George patted his shoulder.

"I am not without care. I see the worth of not carrying a burden."

"Your lacking regard toward the Shelbians does not go unnoticed." Sondrea scolded a Guardian for his crassness but saved her disapproving glance for Katerena.

"My lacking regard remains; though, my offense was meant for none but the Shelbians, Countess." He then took a breath that renewed his pride. "I'll keep the watch in the light. The two of you skedaddle. I'll not suffer Edmond's heel for you if we're late."

TULL & EBBE

"I'd worry more about her hand staff." Tull smirked and offered Ligurus's reins to the staff-wielder. "Soon I'll see you."

"I expect so." She swatted his rump with her staff.

His grin held till the shadows cloaked him and then he and George appeared in glimpses as they passed from drifting flame to drifting flame. The smug Archibaldian pushed against the hem between light and dark but kept his word. Still, the sound of creaking leather as he pulled at his sheathed saber drew the countess's ear. Though she offered him a steadying glance, she let Gesicht's approach occupy him.

"Guardian Falk, what do you gain by volunteering the Westonian to go too?"

"I needn't gain."

The remark went against what most Archibaldians professed and shook the mediary and she who called him uncle.

"George mourns a soul's end."

Sondrea recognized the heart in those words and tested him. "All who have souls do mourn."

"Not like my friends mourn." His eyes found hers but searched harder for those he regarded. "I've traveled these territories at their side since my fifteenth span and I've not witnessed their hearts turn cold toward any—not any loss—of fellows, friends, strangers, or foes."

"You speak as though you admire their tenderness!"

"Their hearts intrigue me, heiress."

"Your purpose requires—"

"My purpose requires that I stand out here for that's proper, by the law."

"Elsewise?" Gesicht studied him in expectation of a revelation.

"Better I fall with my brothers than live to mourn their deeds."

Katerena scoffed as a soul without siblings might, but Sondrea looked upon Olley with a sense of esteem.

"George goes because—by his measure—his reverence to us cost Ming his head."

Sondrea turned toward Gesicht in confusion. "Guardian Falk, I was informed that Nelson's bow ended our foe."

"No."

Gesicht crossed his arms in restraint, but Olley no longer withheld.

"Tull shattered the glass of your father's manor to change Ming's path, but he aimed only to keep George from his end." He set his hand upon his shoulder, then his thigh. "Two arrows struck to hinder. Edmond then tracked the spill and took that bastard's head for what happened to Ganix."

Sondrea stepped nearer. "Then why does Nelson sacrifice his bow?"

Olley reacted as though the countess threw cold water on him. "How oft he proves me unaware."

Katerena giggled when the Archibaldian cursed against his friend.

"Lest he seeks to be a shield for Edmond"—Olley set his jaw and fumed—"and presents his bow with Ming to tell them he alone is to blame"—he shook his head in disgust—"and proves Harlan right when he warned that he'd gone too far."

"Guardian Tull has gone too far?"

"No, Mediary. Harlan spoke of our headship."

Sondrea watched the way Olley fidgeted with his fingers to the hilt of his saber and his teeth against the skin of his lip. She then looked toward Gesicht, who appeared to study him as if learning of tells he might mimic and exploit. "How tremendous is your ability to imitate he whose seat you fill."

The remark stopped Gesicht and confused Olley. For these reasons, their hands did not reach for her when she ran unto the shadows. Both Ligurus and Agnate whinnied, but neither followed. She ran on bruised limbs from flame to flame, evoking the route Tull and George walked, and her leg never betrayed her step.

In the darkness, though, the lights from the sheath that helped mend and recompose her bone drew a peculiar hand. Small fingers that lacked texture and range patted at the oddity of her limb. Those lights, much like the light of every identifier beacon in the neck of every member of the secondkind, were harnessed from a source shown to them by the firstkind. The hand that slowed her belonged to neither.

She looked from the soft hand to an opaque arm that curved as though without a skeletal system to hold form. Her eyes adapted slower than Tull's, but she discovered a dull, undeveloped face not far from her hip. In response, she lifted her arms away from her sides. The creature who patted her proved a decent mimic and held the same pose. When the countess smiled, the same expression formed on her mimic, but extended nearer to the lobes of two tiny ears.

At that moment when her heart overwhelmed her sense of reason and she stooped as if to pick the creature up as a mother held a child, a firmer hand met her shoulder. She recognized the fingers and forearm. This time, she lifted her eyes and found a fellow Jacobian afore her. She covered his hand with hers and corrected her posture but looked toward the other who captured her attention.

"Nelson, are they not wonderful?"

"Once their heels leave the terrane"—he glanced backward and directed her attention—"they prove ornery."

Sondrea erupted with laughter at the sight of George, who stood as a tree whilst others who resembled the bairn at her side climbed his limbs. Another daring member straddled his shoulder and pulled at his ear. Even so, the locals' plentiful numbers made Sondrea cautious. "*Oooo*, Nelson. This isn't the welcome I imagined!"

"No."

Her hand brushed the crowns of the plentiful runts. Then another swatted her rump with cupped hands and made her chirp in a manner that drew Tull's ornery chuckle. Though she calmed him with a glance, she hid her dislike of such greetings and looked upon another. In those cupped hands, the berries that grew from the aftershock of the Squires' visit sat upon stained palms.

"Cloudberries." He chose a bright orange berry and ate. "Good for—"

"Nelson, I taught you about berries."

She ate too and set her gaze upon the oversized pupils of the offering-bearer.

"I see no soul taught you of comity, but I thank you for the alms."

As she bit half and kept the rest between her fingers, she hurried and caught the juice afore her fingers bore a similar stain. The creature watched and mimicked. This produced a sound of smacking lips and a purr.

"They're learners, are they not?"

"I believe that's engrained."

She brushed their crowns in approval. "I see now why my succorer grew, well, not *grew*—"

"Turned?"

"*Turned* inhospitable toward all that stood above head or reach."

Tull remembered offending Dory well, and gauged that all the creatures who ran around them stood no taller than four heads high. "None that I've seen bear a face like the offering of remains we brought them, either."

She finished her berry and looked toward the creature who offered nothing. To further Tull's theory, she took and offered another to the first who approached her.

"None even bothered when we presented him."

"Share." She then ate and purred. "Perchance they feared him too."

The diminutive creature mimicked her and ate.

"Good." She nodded and watched a similar reaction. "Do you believe any recognize, well, me?"

"I believe we ought to leave afore we let them."

"They seem blameless."

"How oft did you get into trouble when you were blameless?"

The countess blushed.

"Do you keep the orb I handed you?"

"In my hip pocket."

"I learned about manners. Might I ask that you . . ."

"Fetch?"

"I believe they will."

She proved willing to test his idea. With a hand as sly as her father's, she retrieved and returned the orb that contained soft amber light and did not spill a beam through the exchange. Tull accepted and watched as she took another berry for the first who approached. He then whistled three sharp notes and two flat, which prompted three flat notes and two sharp from the overcome Westonian.

"When I cast this—and if they chase—we'll return to the horses."

"And if we entice them more than a rolling trinket?"

"They won't go beyond the hem imposed by the light."

"Lest they tunnel beneath."

His confidence wilted.

She sighed, reclaimed the orb light, and stooped to roll the glass sphere across the terrane and away from George. The two who amused her copied her motion, which cost some berries, but others responded to the fast-moving light and the rolling chime. Natural flaws in the floor made the orb skip and flutter, which drew even more attention. Still, the two at her hips did not move from them.

"Nelson?"

"We go anyway." He took her hand and whistled.

"I am away from them, my friend!" George called out as he passed.

Sondrea minded her step as much as the curiosity she felt toward the two small creatures she met. The creature to her right fumbled with berries and the other repeated the way she had raised her arms when they met. She counted them as bright, giving, and adorable; far from the threats she feared might harm her or overtake Tull in the darkness. When the time came that he delivered her across the hem between shadow and sky-fires' light, she tested his theory of boundaries that their hosts lived beneath.

"Your leg?"

She shook her head, for he suspected she fell but remained on her right knee as she knelt back toward the shadow. If these were the same terrible creatures many claimed lived in the shadows, then she would spend her time going to every fool and correcting them. First, she wanted to prove another's brilliance. "Will they be hurt by this?"

"May the Squires be swift if they are."

Katerena nagged and Agnate whinnied. Even Ligurus huffed. Sondrea held her place and turned that the lights within her leg might make the little greeters remember her and pursue like the cast orb.

"See?"

"See what?"

"Do not panic." His hand steadied her shoulder as he crouched.

Olley cursed. Then Gesicht. A smile spread across Sondrea's face; not exaggerated like the faces she observed in the dark. More than two, and closer to twenty, approached the furthest point of darkness.

Purring and chimes rippled through them as their pear-shaped figures pushed against each other. Their eyes reflected the sky-fires, but they did not let that light shine on their faces. Even Dory proved sensitive to abundances of light; supernal or false. But, once the swiftest body reached the front, a small hand reached unto the light.

"Mother!"

Sondrea did not tremble. She cupped her hand and reached toward the shadow. The undeveloped, webbed hand opened and Tull's orb fell unto her palm. She proved a good catch, but was not swift enough to pat the hand afore the limb retreated.

"I thank you, little dove." She watched the eyes decrease. "Nelson, might I . . ."

He nodded. She then set the orb on the frozen terrane and rolled the trinket back into the darkness to gauge how far the sound might travel. When the sound kept going and the padding of feet followed, she rose with satisfaction. Even so, he kept her shielded.

Tull & Ebbe

She shared all she wanted with a glance at him and avoided Gesicht's offering of her hand staff. The Guardian accepted on her behalf, buckled the aid to her saddle, and then offered his hand to her. Gesicht turned away and the silence loomed across the others. Sondrea squeezed Tull's fingers as she sat upon the saddle and corrected the lay of her riding cape; even covering her crown with the hood after she hid much of her face with her scarf.

Tull received the orb back from Gesicht, but the mediary withheld his gaze from Sondrea. The Guardian, proving a good mimic, then offered that orb to the shadows with a single farewell: "Share!"

"You're giving away orb lights as toys now, are you?"

"I needed to distract the Archibaldians."

Olley's chin struck his booming chest and unfurled a lock of his wavy hair. "You surrendered a fine bow."

Tull turned toward his friend. "I defend a fine lot."

"What I said at the mourning—"

"You meant." His eyes drifted toward the unkempt lock of hair; for all in the outfit laughed over the Archibaldian habit of preening, which fell second to boasting.

"From depths I cannot gauge." Olley smoothed his hair as some polished metal.

There ended all apologies. "You'll guide your mediary?"

"I'll not laugh when Blizzard tosses him aside." He folded his arms in a manner that broadened his impassible nature.

"Another matter proves troublesome."

"Your nearness to my judge's bride?"

Tull's face went as blank as those creatures in the shadows.

"Or my judge's bride's regard for a stubborn and self-sacrificing Jacobian?" His nose twitched and he remembered Tull's concerns. "You spoke of troubles!"

"Only that these creatures cared more for an orb light than remains or the sacrifice of my bow."

"We have encountered deceitful and untrustworthy foes afore."

"None that climbed George as a tree or shared berries with trespassers."

"As you say." He checked to see where his mediary and she of Tull's regard awaited them. Then, he shielded Tull by turning his back toward both. "We seem to be a spear's head for interests less revealed than our own."

"You've only now noticed?"

Tull & Ebbe

"No other in the territories appreciates the Jacobian manner as I do."

"Which interest leaves you suspect?"

Olley tapped his shoulder with the fingers that pointed toward his mediary.

Tull cinched the ends of his unbuttoned collar between his fingers and scraped at the unshaven whiskers between his chin and lower lip. This signified the headship's manner of fine dress and the triangular patch he paired with a moustache. "And a soul marked our prisoner with a precision instrument like those found in the mending chambers."

"What type of instrument?"

"Circular with an array of needles."

"Larger than a copper alms?"

"Within measure."

"George saw the same mark, but there was none when Harlan and I—"

"Tried to drown her?"

Olley shrugged but bore no shame. "She is our foe."

"She obeys another foe. Unnamed for now."

Olley felt Tull's burden. "One more odd turn . . ."

The Jacobian arched his brow.

"The countess believed your bow ended her attacker. Lest your habits have changed, I believe we know who informed her."

Tull stared across Olley's shoulder at Mediary Gesicht. He then tried to remember every word told to him by Sondrea since the outfit arrived on Ebbe Demesne. Had she invited Gesicht or had he nudged? He heard her tale of Mumus's repose but who—if not he who forced her to wed him—told of Ming's attack or sought the outfit's Guardianship of her? The count? Her half-brother? Her husband's mediary? And which of them, if not Paladin, worked against her?

"She remarked that he imitated her—the judge—well . . . and then she ran unto the shadows to be nearer to you."

"*Imitated.* That was her word?"

"I cannot recall ever saying the word afore, so, yes, the word was hers alone."

Tull weighed the interest of Mumus's research partner, shape-changers, the mark on Dory's arm, and Sondrea's choice in words. Of all she knew, she seldom wasted. He then counted a phrase written by her hand in the journal where she kept a record of Judge Mumus's peculiarities: *lu'qem atoaen si'el*. That is, *the myriad soul*—a single soul who wore many disguises, many faces, and many titles.

"A silver alms from my sachet to yours if he does not attest to our need for you." Olley glanced toward the mediary upon whom Tull stared then ticked side to side, but brought no shame to his coiffure. "I cannot gauge if he means to bolster your name or pin every shortcoming upon you. You ought to have kept his—Mumus's—imps adrift."

He hesitated when Sondrea turned toward him and offered his most peace-filled gaze in idle talk's stead.

"You are a soul who seeks his punishment in finest form, Nelson."

Tull stepped backward and made space for George. "All is well?"

"I believe our horses will soon need water and the novitiate unsettles me."

"Nelson and I were in discussion of those who manipulate us."

"We forgot the soul who corrals all creatures who roam on four legs."

"Manipulative and decent."

"And soft-spoken."

"We ought to upend him."

Both Guardians looked upon the serene face of their friend afore they conveyed their unspoken accord. Tull shook his head, and Olley shrugged over their inability to rile him.

"Have you noticed any peculiarities on this side of the shadows, George?"

"You were correct when you compared your judge's daughter's smile to—"

Olley swatted him whilst Tull laughed. "Toward our purpose."

"Only that the mediary asked to carry the pall of the remains we leave here."

"Now why would a researcher have interest in that?"

"I believe—"

"He knows why."

George looked toward Olley, who nodded. "This is why Asham oft feels confused by you. Your words and your character are in conflict."

"'The simplest way to suffer a simpleton is to make a simpleton suffer.'"

"He uses another of his mother's roles to increase his wit?"

"The same role."

"I fear I can perform her role too after this much time with her son."

"I can recommend a simpleton to you." He and George looked to Olley.

TULL & EBBE

The less-humored Archibaldian stomped his feet like the horses. "What do we do? You're of highest seniority here."

"If Gesicht works against us, he'll want to be rid of us."

"Provided he sought proof of our foe."

"Provided."

"And now he is . . . provided." Olley's glance toward George held. "One of us ought to take back what was not his to give away."

"One of us ought not to challenge an advocate or his mediary."

Olley's disbelief flared as he looked toward his only other friend. "You do speak with irony?"

Tull shrugged.

"One of us ought to tag him afore we get back to the manor."

"I agree."

"Nelson?" Sondrea kept her grin for his eyes alone. "All is well?"

He counted his simplest lie. "We debate the best source of water for the team."

She accepted his answer and patted Agnate's neck.

"George has the slyest hand."

"Second." Tull tipped his crown toward the magick-wielder's daughter.

"Dare we enlist her?"

Tull shook his head. "I'll mark him."

"You are the least sly"—Olley protested—"so I will mark him."

"I believe I—"

Sondrea huffed loud enough that she calmed the Westonian. She nudged Agnate and reached out her hand as she approached them. Olley hanged his head and George ducked away, lest he stand between scorn and Tull. Even Ligurus shook his head. So, Tull reached unto his pocket, retrieved the tool, and obeyed her order.

"She hears well."

"Yes."

The trio watched, with some rotation in their gathering, as she rode alongside Katerena. Whilst she instructed, she raised her hand and swept a plated rod fitted with an internal reader along the base of the neck; where all wore an identifier beacon beneath the skin. She tucked the device between her fingers, patted her daughter's back, and sidestepped Agnate to approach Gesicht. While she performed the same trick a second time, Olley practiced behind a shield of friends.

TULL & EBBE

"Rest your hand." George warned Olley.

Sondrea tossed the device to Tull and leaned between his fellows. "Now both are marked and ready to be followed by your abettors. Might we go soon? I find the chill unkind."

"George"—Tull offered a glance—"will you guide the heiress's way?"

"As you say."

"Lest you want to return and gather a friend."

He waved off the idea and shrank away from Agnate's presence with equal certainty.

"Forgive me, Countess, if I withhold the same offer from you."

"I remember our route." She cast a displeased look upon Olley and watched him slink away too.

"Odd turn."

She watched Olley appease Gesicht. "The fleeting bravery of lowlanders?"

He unwound Ligurus's reins and warmed his back. "That the creatures we met never appeared afore."

"My friends and I sought what we might achieve, Nelson. You sought amends."

"I thank you for your kindness and your help, Countess."

She sat prouder. "The best and nearest water source is the warm spring at Moselle Foothill. This time of winter, the water refreshes and does not freeze."

"George has spoken of the wells."

"I would appreciate the comfort of a friend. You'll ride alongside me?"

He nodded in proof of his ability.

Olley called out, "We ought to beat the moon to her rest!"

"Edmond's heel will be pleased." Tull noticed an uneasy ripple through the lot. "George, let us stop for water at the foothill nearest Violet's grandmother's farm. We'll travel to avoid a spill, but rest with confidence. Your Guardians have trained upon this rock beneath moons of every season. We'll see you returned to Ebbe Demesne."

"I imagine a seat alongside the eve's roaring fire." Olley spoke to invite information. "You will join us, Mediary, will you not?"

"From there, I must travel to Sevier for I have much work to do." Gesicht looked toward Katerena and did not see how Tull or the other Guardians doubted his character through their suspicious glances. "I can take you along lest you—"

"I'll travel with you."

TULL & EBBE

"With your mother's approval."

Sondrea, who observed the trio's exchange of glances, made clear, "I'll let Gloria know of your return to the tower. Wilfred, I thank you."

The mediary nodded from a position ahead of her and did not look back.

She then spoke in a hushed tone. "Nelson, I must warn—"

"Guardian Tull?" Gesicht interrupted without apology or acknowledgment of Sondrea. "Might I . . ."

Tull's eyes apologized for their interruption whilst his hand pocketed the tool that recorded identifier beacons. He then checked the shadow's nearness and the slopes afore he approached Gesicht on a backward gait that boasted Ligurus's greatness and pestered Blizzard.

Gesicht seized Tull's shoulder afore he rode past and, for a brief tick, made certain souls unsettled. He then raised both hands. "In case the horse slipped."

Tull appeared calm, but an unwavering eye challenged the mediary.

"You were wrong in your disobedience to the bench, but you respected the structure of your outfit and obeyed the order of Guardian Elragadó. Blame falls upon him for . . . much. When asked, I will make clear that the countess would have suffered beneath the judges' orders to have you stay uninvolved."

In his peripheral, Tull saw Olley reach for his alms sachet.

"I believe my friend and judge would see that his bride and his daughter benefitted from your protection."

"He can show thanks by not sending more gliders. Lest I cease their flight too."

Gesicht cocked his jaw. "I believe this confidence is why Cyril riles at the mention of your name."

The Jacobian was surprised when Mumus's research partner offered his hand.

"Guardian Tull."

"Mediary Gesicht." The pair shook hands.

"Lead us away now."

Sondrea observed both souls—stubborn and esteemed in ways that set them apart and made them alike—and prayed for a peace-filled return to Ebbe Demesne. She determined enough from the suspicions and mutterings of Guardians Falk, Green, and Tull to discern why Gesicht might seem duplicitous to them. In a way that did not betray him, she meant to ensure the trio realized that they traveled with a respectable soul who also sought to abet a soul he cherished above all others.

Beneath the moon, those who departed from the Knotted Caves remained visible even to those who stayed in the shadows. With every tick of the watch, that shadow took the distance from the light. Though Tull, Sondrea, and the others faced only the challenges of their descent, their unmet foe gained advantage over them.

Noeu emerged from the trees above the mouths, cloaked in a manner that the secondkind had not yet perceived. As he moved, the tree behind him moved, too, in appearance. When he leapt down to the floor where Ming's soulless body and Tull's bow rested, his feet and legs appeared as the rock, along with the hand that supported his balance. This was the most prestigious of traits in the Taotáva's array.

He cared not for the show of remorse or honor, for such traits were not a portion of his character. He lurked behind veils and raged without contest. As he cried out in a show of that rage, he made the smaller, gentler creatures flee unto the darkest caves. The abandoned orb lights no longer mystified amid an unchallenged soul's tantrum or cruelty without end.

Noeu seized Tull's abandoned bow and pulled, that he might undo the string. He failed to bend the bronze limbs. In function's stead, he turned the weapon into a hammer and beat the offering against the rocks broken by Hyl ki'ö. His tirade lasted till he freed the jagged limbs from stock and grip. Once he tore away the bowstring, he held the limbs and imagined them as weapons against the countess, her Jacobian Guardian, and those who trespassed upon the plot he ruled.

Akin & Arcane

An Interim

THE 10TH PEAK BENEATH THE MOON OF THE MOTHER'S SONG

THE 107TH WINTER SEASON OF THE ACCESSION

IN THE CARE OF THE HELPER, WHO KEEPS SOULS FROM FRUITLESS WANDERING.

191 TAUROG ROADWAY

THE ADDRESS OF EBBE DEMESNE.

NEAR TO THE SITTING ROOM AND A ROARING FIRE.

Returned to temporary comforts far from the caves of the Taotáva, Sondrea awoke from peace-filled slumber with a sense of clarity that kept her a protective step ahead of her favored Guardian. With Katerena safe at the family home atop Mumus Tower and without the meddling of Cyril's research partner, she believed the worst had settled and devoted her energies once more toward the eves that awaited.

Though she had not known what to expect at the Knotted Caves or time spent amid the personalities of certain souls, she found joy in her travels. The time spent with Katerena warmed her, but she learned much more from the interactions between Wilfred and Nelson—and Nelson with those two Guardians who joined them. Their mutual regard, she believed, proved the goodness of the Second Creation in the balloon-shaped eyes of the Taotáva. Still, her heart purred for the inchoate creatures and the gentleness that brimmed amid them and inspired an idea of returning there in warmer seasons and without worrisome travelers.

As for her third appearance of mourning fallen Ganix, she found amid her mother's closet a dress from a time when that beloved soul still turned her father's head. A soul seldom allowed for luggage whilst a foe pursued so, the differences between mother and daughter aside, she pieced together each eve's wardrobe from tastes that were not her own. She altered the flow of another dress amid memories, allowed for some boasting of her corrected thigh, and took away a ruffled collar that hid her bustline; which benefitted from her frequent dips in the mending chamber.

Such work, whilst a distraction from fruitless agents not on Ebbe Demesne, drew her nearer to her mother, with whom she oft passed the time creating new fashions from old wardrobe. In these rooms, they hid from the uncertainty of her father's magick. No arrangement or object changed lest they changed them. Outside, all fell subject to his manipulations. There they toiled in fear for spans till they realized he no longer cared enough for them to squander magick or time upon them.

Where the count's hand lessened, Cyril's rule increased. He structured his home by the laws he composed and composed laws by the way he wanted his home structured. His seven seasons of slumber, taken every forty-eight seasons, were all the time to herself that she experienced. In those times, she sought to reclaim her way.

When she heard the latch of the outer door, she suspected those daunting souls heard her unspoken worries and halted operation of her mother's sewing machine. She then returned to her fingers four large rings. Sondrea had sent for a Guardian and prepared a bottle of orifice-cleansing, eye-stinging ginger vermouth. A Shelbian favorite, the bottle told to whom she extended her hospitality.

"How the time passes from us, Mama . . ."

Footsteps ceased but no body appeared, to which she hanged her head. Their influence aside, every soul took pause in the presence of that cursed mural.

"I must"—she pushed the machine unto the cabinet—"receive guests through the furthest door"—then draped the eve's dress from a hanger—"if *I* am to be feared."

She exited the room where she bathed, dressed, and entertained pewter-eyed Jacobians whom she used as her succorer to retrieve her present invitee.

"Which of them inspired you, Guardian Ozul?"

A razor-sharp brow held less of an edge than the icy flicker of light in Nita's honey irises as she found her hostess. She who appeared prickling and sharp at every edge then spoke with the same tone. "You expect me to name Buster Roderick King because he and I share—"

"I expect to learn which of your predecessors inspires you." The corner of her smirk matched Nita's brow. "I care not about what you may share with them."

TULL & EBBE

Nita's expression froze, and she heeded her mother's warning that she never speak ill against Beau Itzal Zeck. All had their faults and merited their punishments. Zeck, according to Edythe Frances Ozul's stern warnings, deserved more than a soul could offer—his granddaughter did not.

"Your mother remains in Tebet, does she not?"

"She does."

The countess appreciated certainty, even brevity, but briskness wore her thin. She had heard the suspect tone in the voice of others who distrusted being alone with a magick-wielder's daughter. "I visited with your mother seventeen spans afore."

That air of contempt swelled as Nita sized up her hostess from foot to crown and trembled as her hostess looked upon her with similar eyes.

"In this same room." Nita's silence bordered on a refusal to speak, and Sondrea felt gratitude toward Katerena for the many seasons of preparation that let her heart remain at an unbothered pace. "In that time, I sought her as nursemaid whilst I—"

"Jacobian women oft prove"—Nita looked over the soul who relied on mending chambers and privilege to slow time's grip—"confused"—and who used her figure as an advantage—"over the purpose of their breasts and unable to tend to their babes."

"As you say." She let Nita boast a lilt of victory that formed a crinkle in her face from nostril to lip. "Though, nursing proves difficult for any soul whose womb has not opened for a babe. We Jacobians do not have the Shelbian desire for suckling every open mouth that passes."

The countess meant to jar the smugness from her guest and from the rush of color from cheek to neck, Nita proved jarred. Her pale irises gauged the pertness of Sondrea's breast, the smallness of her waist, and the setting of her hip all afore she managed to receive explanation from she who jarred her.

Afore Sondrea lost her guest, she softened her posture and swept a hand toward the seating arrangement and the mural. "Your unapproachableness comes from your father, as my arrogance comes from mine."

Nita's silken complexion turned waxen.

"One eve during the sowing season, not long afore Nelson's bereavement, Cyril entered our home with a chubby babe in his arms. Whether he sired her, bought her, or stole her, he has never said. I was presented this shrill green-eyed creature as if he meant to keep me further removed from all the souls for whom I cared."

Tull & Ebbe

Her guest stood and watched as her host kept her back to the mural; a statement of the power that remained behind her every breath and deed.

"I learned after how well he plotted; how he spun a tale that I bore her during the winter and remained too frail to present the babe so all might—"

"Why tell me of this?" Nita looked as though another's admission of pain and humiliation offended her.

"I tell this to you as we both suffer the cruelty of judges whom we cannot escape. I tell you as you are my niece."

Nita struck in response and turned her aunt's head.

Sondrea kept her hands at her sides and did not smooth her hair nor reach for the reddened flesh on her cheek. "That disadvantage you received from him too."

"I am not known to you."

"Your father stares at me through your eyes. He was cruel when first I met him, and he has never warmed to another soul since."

Nita held her tongue and let her proud chin speak to her resolve.

"He now grooms your half-sister to be as monstrous as the men of our line whilst he denies the fruit of uncounted others whom he—"

"I have not come here seeking a lesson in histories or reunion."

"No, you've come because I sent for you."

Nita froze, for no other spoke to her in such a manner besides her mother and Guardian Elragadó.

"Now sit and listen, my niece, for I have much to tell you; some that might reshape your purpose and ease your burden."

In rigid protest, and not a spirit of obedience, Nita took a seat beside the seat offered to her.

Sondrea recognized the test. In response, she withheld the offering of drinks that sat in blatant readiness. "Your ascension goes against your father's plot. He, and not Guardian Ganix, expected to keep you from realizing the purpose you claim."

Nita assumed—even guaranteed without proof—as much. Still, she hated that another saw through her with such ease.

"Your mother wrote to me in your stead. She told me how you cherished the heart of another in Tebet and asked if I could speak to your father for her afore you made your bold declaration." She drew out her pause, as if she withheld the cruelty of her half-brother's disregard for Nita's heart or mentioning how that soul she loved proved devoid of gratitude for her sacrifice.

"You seek to be recognized by him who would rather see you fall as a Guardian than declare you as his daughter? How you must abhor joy! Yet, here you sit with a soul who has not wronged you; despising her."

"You are the fruit of a temptress and a magick-wielder." Nita kept a measured breath but let go afore her voice returned. "Still . . . I listen."

"By now, you've learned that our advocates make lavish and cruel demands of those beneath their rule—the Guardians above most."

"We're the Guardians of the secondkind, not the advocates."

"You lack the reputation of the moody soul from whom you borrowed that barb. He would not trespass to tell you that my half-brother will call on you if only to prove his cruelty. He will delight in the beratement and humiliation that his laws let him heap upon his daughter."

Nita had no words nor expectation of kindness from the father who denied his sin and her existence.

"Accept that you advanced further than any of us imagined and then step down from your borrowed purpose this eve. Should any soul learn who your father is, you will never have peace in your role. This I tell you from my own pit."

"You don't do this for my benefit."

"Why I do this would be a burden to you."

Nita laughed from her taut belly and sank her nails unto the cushion as though she still wore gloves with ceramic tips. "I find you as cruel as my father."

Sondrea laughed too; contrary to her own preparedness. "You what?"

"You and your brother"—she delighted in another borrowed barb—"'share that disadvantage.'"

"I've been forthright with you—"

"Not toward me; you are no more a portion of me than he is. What you do to Tull is your most wanting cruelty. You keep him near enough that he cannot forget you and distant enough that he wants only to return to your side. He will take root with no other soul while you keep his heart and shape his memories."

"You wish that he would take root with you?"

Nita scoffed. "I would crush his sensitive Jacobian heart in a moon's passing, and he would heap praise upon me evermore."

TULL & EBBE

Sondrea's doubt for such claims caused her stare to freeze.

"If you were kind, truly, you would cease from this"—the newest Guardian looked her over with hatred and disgust—"*vileness* that you mistake for *affection*. He was blameless and intended for your care! But what did you do? If you continue, I tell you, I and those who see as I see will believe there is no honor in your line. I will then be certain that you are your father . . . and I will ruin you." Nita rose and pricked at her own chest. "I am Nita Naomi Ozul, second Guardian of the Shelby Territory, and daughter of she whom Judge Dale Marius Conliffe violated! And you will suffer your end in a pit lower than the whores of Perlin."

Sondrea sat speechless.

Nita rounded the seat she no longer wished to fill. "Keep your ginger swill. You'll need strong drink once your heart turns cold."

The countess of Ebbe Demesne remained still, though her brow arched, and waited on the sound of the outer door slamming as her distant niece left. Once achieved, she too passed the bottle and glasses. With unfettered poise, she ventured toward her writing table where she collected the true reason for requesting Nita's company.

A bag of alms—trinkets and wealth that belonged to the Conliffe tree—required both of her hands to lift. She heaved the entirety into the fire with the unfulfilled letter from Nita's mother and the same shortness that insult merited then watched embers rush across the floor like those tiny creatures she and Tull met in the shadows. For them, she sighed in satisfaction.

"We Conliffes prove a short-tempered lot evermore, do we not, Papa?" She offered a sly glance at her father and once she turned from the mural, a smile lit her face as though a soul who witnessed a creature that she adored take their first unassisted step. "I was right to refuse her mother's plea."

NOEU THE TAOTÁVA

This tale was created on a three-word synopsis: "Musketeers versus Magua." Another character from childhood inspired a change in our villain and turned a single foe into a line of wondrous creatures. Noeu—who shares Nita and Sondrea's tether to Count Conliffe—corrupted what was within and then tried to devastate what was around him when he found himself unsatisfied—also like the count. That is the spirit of monstrosity and villainy.

Trust

Twenty-Nine

The 11th Eve beneath the Moon of the Mother's Song
The 107th Winter Season of the Accession
In the Care of the Helper, who keeps souls from fruitless wandering.

191 Taurog Roadway
Along the northernmost edge of Ebbe Demesne.
Standing against an icy wind.

At the final mourning of his Shelbian counterpart, Tull offered in tribute to Ganix a scarf sewn from gentle thread and given to him as alms by Sister Suzanne Tifton, whose gift would be noted by chroniclers. He pinned to the scarf a handwritten and favorite lyric from a song that the wearer of many scarves sang most oft. Ganix's singing would be missed. He believed a time would come when even Jules spoke a kind word of the fallen Shelbian.

All any soul on Taurog Roadway paid mind to—for now—was his new storm coat. Made from darkened leather and lined with the fur of a forest bear whose coat proved large enough for four storm coats that reached to mid-thigh. A high collar bore another lining, visible when turned upward, and significant to the Jacobian's favorite balaclava. That shade of red also matched the leaves of maple trees that populated Minder, the settlement where Tull spent eight spans in blamelessness.

Copper buttons on the shoulder straps identified him as the eighteenth of all Guardians and the fourth from his territory. These buttons matched those at the cuff, along with a hem that matched the collar. No other identifiers drew the eye on his, nor the other members of the outfit's, coat. In point of fact, no other but Nita stood out as different, for she found no storm coat tailored to her fit. These came as a gift from Edmond, who ordered the handmade winter wear long afore Ganix's end.

Nita's character suffered not. She who adorned herself in snow white trousers, matching boots, and flowing wolfskin—sans blouse or additional cover—stood apart for all who gathered along Taurog Roadway for a glimpse of their new Guardian. Soon, few would mention Ganix at all. Even so, Asham returned; no worse for wear, and as pride-filled as Nita due to his wounds. They stood again as an outfit undivided yet incomplete by the headcount.

"All of his fussing"—Olley whispered for Tull's benefit—"and Edmond doesn't bother to join us. Doesn't bother to appear with us at all in three eves?"

"An odd turn."

"No odder than Ozul amid this lot."

Tull watched as Nita returned from offering her tribute. At the same time, he noted a specific mourner who kept his focus trained on them.

"Marko claims the heiress arrived late."

Neither Olley's abettor, Marko, nor Abettor Koslowski found behavior worth noting as each tracked Katerena and Gesicht on behalf of their territory's Guardians. Whilst the Archibaldians kept the watch over their judge's fruit, the Jacobians kept a tally of Gesicht's time spent at Zavar Advancements as the mediary, first a researcher, had not reported to his home since he departed Ebbe Demesne. The one hundred nine thousand nine hundred ninety-eight other souls they kept the watch over provoked no offense worthy of a Guardian's meddling. Still, Tull set his gaze upon that mourner of sizeable girth who hid brow and eyes beneath a brim that mimicked his build for he stood out the most—and reminded Tull of a slumbering judge.

"Your abettor must dispute with you over technologies and advances." Olley veered away and then teetered nearer, but never saw how the mourner's eyes followed. "I doubt she's able to keep clothes upon her frame long enough to tend to her purpose—as we must—without her devices."

"Insight such as yours brings to mind a Creightonian wit." He sensed another's eyes upon him still and offered a lopsided grin when he found those eyes beneath Harlan's heavy brow.

The brawny Carpenterian tested the seams of his storm coat and dripped with sweat due to the thick lining. Tull rid his face of any grin for his jaw's sake lest he offend his elder. Each recited the farewell prayer, then the two who stood at either end of the line—Harlan and Nita—stepped ahead of the others to gather Ganix's tributes. As this marked the end of mourning, the remaining lot formed a slack circle around the straight-legged Jacobian.

"You"—Asham slapped Tull's arm—"look as sour as Edmond's scion."

Whilst Tull counted mourners, Olley nudged Asham away. "You saw Pine?"

"Pine delivered our coats." The Creightonian straightened the button on his shoulder strap so he alone might read the number three. "Edmond kept us apart."

"A blessing to Pine!" Olley asked George, "How long since you saw him last?"

George shrugged.

Olley then faced Tull. "And you?"

Tull dismissed the mourners. "What of Dory?"

"She remains unable to reshape her head to slip the bind from around her neck." When Tull bristled, Olley put up his hands. "I needle! She remains agitated and bound at her hips. I set sensors beneath the floorboards should she try to burrow beneath."

Tull shook his head.

"Is that what you would have done?"

"The choice of her restraints was never mine."

"Not what I asked."

"I misheard you perchance."

"You told Harlan of what you saw in the shadows?"

George nodded.

"What does he believe?"

"He believes"—George gauged their second-in-command and Asham's nearness and blocked him with his shoulders—"what Edmond expects him to believe."

"Do you believe that?"

"I do not."

"You?"

"We follow Edmond's rule in this outfit." Tull's doubt dulled the pale lavender strands in his pewter irises.

"Your eyes don't match your tongue. Did he say what the judges told him?"

"If he had, he would not say to me."

"Come now!" Asham intruded. "You are right hand to our headship's right hand. That must lend some privilege to you."

TULL & EBBE

Olley nudged him away again. "Speak useful words! Even you must have witnessed a sight or heard a word that benefits us."

"I mended in a warm bed, took two hot baths, and ate my meals at Edmond's side. Well"—he buried his hands in his coat pockets—"I watched me that reel on the count's discord. By my measure, the countess is loftier—and her tits are in finer fettle—than that chipper set Danele Gertrude Zuriñe showed for every soul on the isle to see."

A jubilant sneer lit Olley's face and, as he stepped aside, he felt Tull's hand brush the hip pocket of a dual belt he wore beneath his storm coat. Rather, he felt the pocket flap fall back into place. Then, the draft changed and Asham groaned as an untied boot fell from his bare foot. His coarse tongue fell unto muddled pleading as Tull tethered him—not unlike the way that Olley had bound him to a tree—to the angular pike of a copper likeness of the count that stood in the yard of Ebbe Demesne.

The spool that rested near Asham's breastbone ratcheted and limited the depths of his every breath due to six lightweight, high-tensile lines meant to restrain the limbs and wings of fallen messengers. Tull took a knee and restrained the crude soul's ankle in the same manner. His wrist suffered identical restraint, though further bound around his upper arm, afore the Jacobian ceased. He then rummaged through the pockets of Asham's bespoke storm coat till he found what he wanted.

He side-eyed the smirking Archibaldian and flicked precious alms his way. "Compliment your armorer in my stead."

Olley applauded such brashness as the watchful mourner remained in silence across the roadway. He then watched as the Jacobian took the bulk of Asham's alms and approached those who lingered in wait for their attention. George picked up the discarded sachet, which he tossed to the applauder. The most foolish of all Guardians grumbled, but the Archibaldian silenced the noise when he pulled at Asham's tresses till a bulging eye fixed on him.

"As is oft your way, you say too much. Any fool—each of whom I count as wiser than you—knows that Danele *Gertie*—not Gertrude—Zuriñe portrayed the *mother* of the countess. You've now offended this outfit's objective, her mother, my friend, and the memories he keeps of his mother's favorite thesp." Olley tugged at the restraint and found no slack. "Lest you chew through your binds, at the expense of your teeth, you'll not be freed by his fellows."

With that, Olley and George stepped from Asham's line of sight. The talker whispered to the listener, who nodded and circled wide around the plot and toward the camp. He who boasted saw a chance to increase his name—once more—and leaned upon his best friend's need for modesty. As he watched Tull's kindness with Asham's alms, Olley took a long sidestep and addressed a trio of blameless admirers.

"Remember"—he patted Tull on the shoulder—"that there are no Guardians more giving than our Guardian Falk here."

The freckle-faced soul who stood nearest to Olley shrank away in confusion without picking up his feet.

"Guardian Tull is my favorite!" claimed another, and stole the nearness of his confused friend. "Are you him?"

"I dare not boast. Do tell your young mothers—or your older sisters—of my own kindness, and my brave, enduring friend—Guardian *Falk*—though."

"We will!"

The boaster stood so Tull, and no other, might hear his agreement with Asham. "Even a Believer must confess that the countess has an unflawed set of tits." Olley stepped from his reach and laughed. "You have learned this long afore the rest of us."

The scorn softened, but the strands of lavender flourished. When he glanced away, he noticed the watchful mourner had moved too. So, he offered two of Asham's last alms to a scrawny soul who stood no higher than those he had met in the shadows at the Knotted Caves. "Your Guardians ask that you go be warmed now and pray to Yah for Guardian Falk's soul."

"I hope I'll see"—Olley waved off the blameless soul who took Asham's last alms and further challenged the giver—"you fight for an idée fixe you truly want afore the territories mourn me, you accursed and stubborn Jacobian."

His eye then found she who waited for him. "I'll find you at the bivouac."

"Do take your time." Olley confirmed Tull's reason with a glance toward the countess. "What possible future does this hopeless lot have in my absence?"

The third-in-standing shook his head in dismissal of the fourth afore he took place at the side of she who exchanged icy glances with the newest Guardian. Since afore she injured her leg, he had not seen her dress in such a manner as she appeared on this eve. Though Jules oft defeated him with her eyes, Sondrea possessed no inferior traits—letting pass her relationships with a wicked father, an obscene brother, and a cruel husband. She dressed as no other soul, and the act of looking upon her produced the truest sense of fear that he experienced since Enke'loi first kept him from his end.

TULL & EBBE

As for Sondrea, she heard the accusations of her niece when she looked upon the first babe that she held who now made Believers and Partakers alike take notice of his presence. Her mind wandered, as did most, but she imagined how all might marvel when he ruled as their headship. The lone complaint to such a notion was mingled in her desire to keep him for her delight and no other's. She then realized such a feat would make her like Cyril and her father, yet the way he looked upon her made such a forfeit less displeasing than imagined. "A mournful eve, my Guardian."

She perfected his grin. He glanced toward the collar necklace that warmed her elegant neck yet withheld honeyed words. "May he have his rest."

"May he have his rest." She followed the contour of his upper lip. "Your elder's absence proves . . . curious."

"As you say." His brow furrowed in response to a chime of his display plate and word from his abettor, which he read as her eyes followed the shape of his face. "Mediary Gesicht also stands uncounted. Consumed by his purpose, I imagine."

"Nelson." She stalled as she looked into his eyes. "You tow the wrong impression."

His smirk needled her even as she lost his gaze.

"When I told you that I made a promise to Wilfred in regard to you—"

"An introduction to your Guardian?"

She nodded. "There was more that I offered him. In name? A chance that he might gain proof of the Taotáva and their ways."

"The pall?"

"He seeks a discovery that is as important to him as you are important to me. We do him a great favor by letting him use my attacker's pall whilst Cyril is not in his way. When he succeeds, I believe he will seek the guardianship of he whom I trust above all others."

He swallowed his doubts and focused on the gleam of her lips as the gas lamps along the roadway ignited and lit her copper irises.

"Do not judge him by his unsettling fellows." She tilted her head in adoration. "Even he might stand in admiration of this *tremendous* storm coat."

"The collar agitates." Much like confusion and riddles.

Without request, she reached toward his neck and made an adjustment to the seam as an excuse to prove her care for him. "You'll remember what I told you, will you not?"

"As you say."

Her grin appeared softened with relief as he took on another secret. The slightest graze of fabrics, the shared warmth of bodies, and the undeterred chance to admire kept them near enough to draw speculation from all who observed: the innocent who adored heroes, Olley, and even a mourner whose impression did not match his girth.

"Might I ask of you?"

His formality made her laugh. "Yes, Nelson. Evermore you may ask of me."

"Even about . . ."

"Cyril?" She nodded.

"Do you recall when first you met him?"

Her fingers stopped and a glint of curiosity mingled with the eve's settling light to boost her admirer's heart. The lay of slender, handmade feathers that covered her breast drifted when she exhaled with emphasis. She resumed work, closing the gap between them by an intentional half-step. "I learned of him in my blamelessness."

"Through encounter?"

"Through accounts. The same as many learn of their judges"—she teased his earlobe—"and their Guardians. Why?"

"I wondered when he and your father began their acquaintance."

"Ah!" Even when he blushed, he delivered a barb. She made note and finished her adjustments to his collar. "But that is better framed as when my father first met Cyril."

He remained unfettered as she fidgeted.

Her hands fell away, and she then folded her arms against the sash of her coat. "I remember he visited the manor once. Afore Mama and I were moved unto another wing. That was after my grandfather returned to us. Yes! That long ago.

"I did not speak to him then, short of acknowledgments, till I was told that I would be his bride." Her eyes calculated and her posture shifted so her shoulder hid the wing where the count resided. "I remember little else of him. If my father would see me, I would—"

"You seek him still?"

"His confusion of spiders and my fall did not take that desire from me."

Now his smirk brimmed, his shoulders broadened, and his voice sounded as though he boasted an advantage that she did not hold. "A Guardian has access to the opposite side of every door, gate, plank, or bridge in the territories."

"Well!" She raised her hands as though surprised. "Mightn't I have kept from the humiliation and sought you in my stubbornness's stead?"

TULL & EBBE

Now he reached and held to her wrist without concern for whether another soul took notice. "As representative of the bench of the Archibald Territory, Countess, I serve you above our host; if not by preference, then by law. If you seek an audience with your father, I am required to glean that audience for you."

Her mouth turned so small that her face became as expressionless and innocent as those creatures they encountered in the shadows as he took away any sense of what she might say to him. As proof that she believed his word, she nodded, then allowed him to lead her across the plot of her title. He proved his knowledge of comity and extended his arm, that she might take hold. She showed gratitude with a nod and never let go as they walked unto the manor together and beneath many a watchful eye.

THIRTY

A breathless whine preceded a crackle and finished with a creaking gasp as the gate that prohibited entrance unto the count's wing of the manor fell victim to the Guardian's devices. The gate remained cool to the touch and teetered with a nudge of Tull's hand. This feat impressed the count's daughter and made her cock her jaw leftward as she suppressed a smile. Her escort proved certain in his work and truth-filled in his word.

Tull kept on his pair of heavy leather gloves, which shielded him from the handheld wire arc that eroded the gate bars without odour or ash as he tucked the device back unto a wooden box that fit well within his storm coat pocket—as Edmond intended the design. The same tool sharpened the tips of arrows and let him form new tips. Then, he who delivered on his claim hoisted the remnants of the gate that weighed, by her estimation, as much as him. This too increased her esteem.

Once he placed the gate on the floor, he observed that Sondrea's topcoat rested between the bars of the gate of her mother's wing. The work had preoccupied him, so he had not heard her step away or make the change. Now, he could no longer avoid the sight of her in a sculpted, white velvet dress and a corset belt with a silken purple ribbon. From her neck, an uncounted bloom of blackened emerald feathers draped from a collar necklace that made an immodest flaunting of her breasts less blatant.

"I am impressed, Guardian."

Even when he tried, his doe-eyed peripheral acuity did not let him avert his field of vision and the teeter of her smile proved that the dress achieved the response she imagined. So, he nodded and sighed. "As am I."

"Are you in no way daunted?"

"Not by your father."

She took what seemed a compliment but let him have a moment to hem some definition to his remark. When that failed, she ushered him nearer that she might lead the rest of the way. "Then let him see that he could not divide us."

TULL & EBBE

The nearer they stepped toward the parlor's double doors, Tull noticed that the damage to every picture frame worsened. Composed of a less durable material than the wing's exterior glass panels, the thin framed plates held the aftershock of a percussive blast that originated from his host's destination. This, too, was trickery; a design of the magick-wielder meant to let foes and visitors alike create a fear of him in their minds afore they stood in his presence. The effort felt wasted on a Guardian, and the impact the corridor made on him in his blamelessness drifted like the snow cast from ornamental trellises.

Tull had forgotten so much of the place—the land—through time and resets. He had forgotten the veil that formed there; comprised of dimness and palpable air. The count managed to convince his pesterers that the elements conspired against them; that he held power over the flow of light and their next breath. The magick-wielder gave his heart to corruptness and sought to corrupt other souls that they might esteem him with the awe intended for their Creator.

The Jacobian saw as much in the eyes and expressions of those souls whose visages remained behind the fractured pieces of glass. Not even those that were twisted and dreadful exceeded the expressions of the Fallen First. At times he wondered if Sondrea realized the souls that her father's magick broke, or how he turned an entire territory from Yah. He swore—uncounted times—that he witnessed the count take the breath from his own fruit; but he oft denounced his blameless imagination.

"Nelson?"

The horrid screams from deep within her body haunted him but also made him brave in the face of the Fallen First. Any shrill sound, unnerving sight, rancid scent, or pain-filled touch reminded him of how the count hurt his firstborn daughter because she fought for an orphaned Jacobian. Such memories remained as certain and tangible as the thick webbing that draped between frames.

"Nelson, I tell you your heart does not slow."

Tull felt her hand upon his chest and her nearness caught him unaware. "I will not fail you."

"When have you?" She slid his hand beneath the bloom of feathers draped from her necklace and kept the back of that coarse hand against her breast whilst a cloud of anxious breath swirled around her lips, fed by the laughter that robbed her of deep breath and the coldness of air outside the closed doors. "My heart challenges yours. I cannot tell you the time that has passed since I stood afore my father with a soul I revere in tow."

"Two hundred three counted moons."

She tilted her head as her grin rose against the clock's hand. "I believe so."

In conversation's stead, he responded to what she did not sense and reached around her waist to pivot them into a different position, where he stood between her and the doors. Darkness crept from beneath and hid his boots even as she sought her balance and kept his hand against her. Then, a silhouetted form appeared as the door opened and a soul of towering build and soft girth set a cold hand upon Tull's neck. He then turned the pair and stooped toward Sondrea so near that the breaths from his broad nostrils upset her Guardian's comfort.

"Much time has passed, my cousin." Sondrea released Tull's hand, then leaned upon the balls of her feet and set a kiss upon his heavy brow. "Worry not, Nelson."

"Nelson?" When he scoffed, the feathers leapt from Sondrea's breast and made her shiver onto her heels. "This runt is Nelson? Why, I reasoned for many moons that they must have buried his little bones spans upon spans ago."

"No." She joined her cousin in sizing up the clinch-fisted Guardian. "I tell you, he has grown strong and shun fear."

"Still keeps at your tit, does he not?" He set his barb in the same way he prodded Sondrea's left breast with two large fingers.

Tull reasoned that Olley or Harlan at his side might have made Sondrea's cousin more obliging. He imagined *both* might be best should he prove a betrayer.

The count's reeve seemed to know Tull's concern and snickered. "Both souls plus the Shelbian! She sets a fire!"

"We must speak with Papa, Saul Ole."

His jowl swayed and shook his entire head in refusal.

"Saul Ole . . ."

"Your brother, my cousin, made clear to me the expectations of my duties. No outsider sees Uncle Teddy."

Uncle Teddy. Tull scoffed at the gentleness of the name and the unusual ease that simplified the count's legend.

"Dale Marius would whip me in the roadways if I broke that rule."

"Saul Ole, our hosting judge has never had much of a swat."

TULL & EBBE

He chuckled in agreement, but prodded Tull's chest with the same two fingers and set him backward a full step. "He's to wipe his boots afore he crosses the inner threshold."

"As you say, my cousin!"

"And you won't take him to Gutefiel."

"Nor will I bring Gutefiel to him."

"As you say, my cousin."

Sondrea, whose turn for another barb arose, offered a pleasant tilt of her head, then looked up at the silent Jacobian. "Wipe your feet, my Guardian, we step inside my father's parlor now."

Tull obeyed and *let* Saul Ole Ebbe laugh at his expense. As he leaned upright, he discovered his reflection in the last portrait to reach the threshold; a study of a crying child. Though void of color, the fiery curls and copper irises of the subject shimmered through inexplicable heartache. He glanced toward Sondrea, and found her inside her father's wing on a brim of shadows that consumed much of their guide.

He who lost his parents wondered why a father chose that photograph and why that chosen image, but none of the others, bore an unbroken frame. This busied his mind whilst Saul Ole Ebbe led them through a maze of decorated corridors. Where most displayed beloved kin and friendships, the count draped bizarre paintings of creatures and photographs of splayed bodies. As the passageway toward his parlor darkened, the grotesqueness mimicked. Then, after passing seventeen identical doors along four meandering turns, they reached an entryway with no more barricades.

A wheelchair-bound soul's eyes appeared crushed by the weight of his wrinkled brow and a crown that turned bulbous due to disheveled locks as white as the snow. His eyes, hair, and skin bore no color, and even his lips seemed gray to Tull. Were there not a pencil-thin mustache upon his upper lip, the man's identity would have invited the Jacobian's doubt. Count Theodore Reaume Conliffe no longer appeared fit enough to tend to his own needs, let alone be the same magick-wielding Guardian who oversaw the northern territories. The soul afore him appeared too distraught to recite his own name.

"I agree with Katerena."

His relatives turned from the count and looked around the parlor.

"A Shelbian *would* sooner lay with a horse than ride upon him"—he recited Katerena's barb spoken during the trip to the Knotted Caves down to her smarmy tone afore his smile turned ornery—"but a Jacobian would wither trying to remember which end of himself to feed and which end to—"

"Papa!"

The elder Guardian rested his chin on his slumped shoulder and fixed his colorless eyes on his guest as if to let Tull bask in his host's darlingness. He then mimicked his seed with a taunting sway of his head. "Papa! Papa! Only two doves in this land call me by that name. Where is the fairer, daughter?"

"She gives us rest." Sondrea stooped and ushered his focus toward her beloved Guardian. "Papa, can you recognize my guest? This is Nelson James—"

A sickened sound in the count's laughter unnerved he whom she presented as he watched their elder tease the bloom of feathers with a breath that made her shiver.

"Papa . . ."

The count laughed and swatted his daughter's backside with the same manners that the little Taotáva showed her and made her jiggle in misstep. "'Even a Believer must confess that the countess has an unflawed set of tits.'"

Sondrea turned from her father in embarrassment and felt ashamed in her mother's dress.

"Count Conliffe!" Tull's authoritative tone drew tear-filled copper irises onto him. "Is this how you seek to be remembered by she who keeps Zeck's blood in her veins? Your daughter is the last remnant of our great elder Guardians of the North."

The disgraced magick-wielder tried on trembling arms to push himself upright and feign an air of the former distinguishedness that he had cast away. As he trembled worse, he cast a worried crease upon his daughter's forehead. He proved himself still proud, though, and pursed his lips rather than cry for salve.

Tull set his tone on gratitude. "I humbly thank you for allowing me into your home and ask that you hear your daughter's every word."

"A . . . *noble*"—the count trembled and struggled against an unseen foe as he forced his tongue to obey his mind—"line . . . made their home in the . . . Jacoby Territory. You are . . . my . . . honored guest."

"Soon, we'll leave you to your rest, Papa." Sondrea wrapped an arm around him, kept him from collapse, and whispered words of encouragement in his ear. "I wanted to see you after my long absence. I never get to see you."

In the frigidity of the parlor, a horse's scent seemed sharper even than the powdery-sweet scent of clematis terniflora that Sondrea introduced to the setting.

Tull recognized both, let his eyes stray from the countess's reunion, and sought a source amid the tapestries of darkness that hid three walls. Then, from beneath the dust upon shelves and brasserie that he remembered from his previous stay, he detected a faint odour of rotted fruit rinds; less ripe than the scent of Dory.

"I believe Paladin, or another of his kind, was once his honored guest too." His gaze remained on the looming darkness as the sky-fires shone through the blotted panels of the glass roof. "Was he not?"

Not even the sound of Sondrea's sudden breath disrupted the stillness that fell.

"Did you seek to corrupt him as your magick corrupted you?"

The count uttered nervous laughter that made oily sweat gather across his high forehead.

"Were you noble when you drove beneath those your magick created? Were you honored when you destroyed all that they salvaged so you could betray a brother and steal from him his daughter?"

"Nelson?" Sondrea's confusion multiplied as a gasp ascended and caused every light in the room to flicker.

Tull cocked his jaw and rested his accusations, for they had not come from any lesson found in previous lands. Another—a Helper—spoke many words through the Jacobian and his time as scion and Guardian. These words proved true through a rancid odour that seeped from the count's pores and sickened the stomach just as the count's magick sickened his soul.

"Is this true, Papa?"

"Say that you regard your daughter more than your character."

In that remark, the countess heard Tull's heart.

"Say that you would take her place"—the Jacobian taunted his elder—"as a father ought to defend his seed from every pain. Say that you are not so lost to your magick or blind to the certainties of Yah's wonder that you cannot remember how her nobility comes from her mother's tree *alone*."

The oddities of the old Guardian—from his pompous manner of dress in moth-bitten garments, to his conversations with absent bodies, and his hiding from the Triune's light—hid beneath a withering body's trembling and lobbing eye contact.

Tull looked toward Sondrea as the count withheld. "I believe you've heard his silence well."

THIRTY-ONE

"Guardian Tull, I tell you to remember your elders better than we deserve."

Edmond, who wore a horsehair wig and brimmed with talk of histories, emerged from the pebbled shadows with a wry smirk on his face for the way the Jacobian snapped rigid but remained unapologetic for his accusations. Beneath the murky-green hues that filtered throughout the parlor, the adhesive that kept the Larsonite's false brows, mustache, and soul patch in place added a shimmer of sparkling yellow flecks upon his skin and drew the eye toward the handcrafted pieces he wore as his own. He said no more to chasten Tull. Neither had he wiped his boots, according to Saul Ole Ebbe's rules, and left behind puddling forms of slipper soles with a drastic heel that elevated his height and delivered his temper to two of the Jacobian's fellows.

He then looked upon the countess. "You lack his surprised eyes."

"No other conscript made sense to me."

"Did they not?"

"Not surprised." Tull spoke of the look Edmond saw in his eyes as he realized how all in the manor then had outsmarted him and looked toward Sondrea. She who never wasted a word spoke of Edmond's absence from the third mourning of Ganix. Now he looked her in the eye as if she might reveal with a glance when she set her suspicions on his elder and headship. "Disappointed."

"Gentle steps, Guardian."

"Wilfred believed Nelson's aim delivered my attacker to his end."

"There's no harm in letting the territories believe that a Jacobian and a Believer fought so well for all our sakes."

"He does."

"He's still a runt!"

Sondrea reacted to her cousin's interruption. "Saul Ole, we must learn to edify."

"Keep swinging him from that tit, my cousin, and—"

Edmond frightened all but the count when he smacked the reeve across his mouth. "Remember who your Guardians are."

TULL & EBBE

The reeve trembled in rage and shame, then sulked away from twofold admonition. The headship then confirmed that Sondrea's cousin exited the parlor afore he batted an eye at the soul he disappointed, who in forgiveness's stead stared at his headship's boots and then at the yellow-flecked residue along the rims of his cheeks and near to his sideburns and brows but withheld a reaction. Sondrea looked toward Tull but could not discern his focus.

"Give him the time, Countess. He decides if I am like your father or your attacker."

She offered an audible swallow and stepped nearer toward her Guardian. Her father, ever unsettling, goosed her and prompted her to chirp like a duckling then strike his hand like a serpent. The magick-wielder cackled and, in response, yanked his daughter onto his lap and held her as though she were still in her blamelessness.

"Have I ever visited you—or those you keep near to your heart—with harm? Ever once? Have I not sought the best paths for all our feet since you met me?"

The magick-wielder kissed his child's face and blew against her feathered necklace. "Listen, daughter, as we speak of creatures of old to you!"

Tull found the count's voice irritating and trusted he meant for a multiplication of the Guardian's confusion as he attempted to discern Edmond's aim.

"There once roamed the terrane three creatures. The first was named Róka."

"The Fox." Edmond's translation kept Tull's stillness.

"The second they called Prérifarkas."

"The Coyote."

"The third, who sat above, they called Bagoly."

"The Owl."

Tull's fists tightened as he felt agitation over the way the count recited a portion of a conversation he shared with his abettor. He believed Edmond played the spy for the count's benefit and offered no fear unto magick. "Do you believe we came to hear a poem?"

"I cannot imagine a reason that might keep you from following her."

"Shall I forgo my tale then? Is my audience not grateful?"

"You were about to tell of the bugaboo"—Edmond shifted in his stance and looked away from the countess—"*Mumus.*"

Each of Sondrea's joints restricted as if she hoisted armor against his unexpected barb. Her mouth shrank as her breast rose with offended breath. Her father took notice and delighted; still, he chastised the heritor who stood against him. "Hear me well, Jacobian, for I speak of the seed Paladin trampled."

Though curious, Tull lacked an interest in comity with magick-wielders. He offered his hand to Sondrea and set his boot against the wheel of the count's chair to keep him from mischief. The former accepted his help and the latter let her go.

"If you wanted a ride, too, Jacobian . . ."

Sondrea moved on steps silenced by her father's cackle but drew Tull's curious eyes as she immersed her hand in darkness and took long, slow steps away from him. Tull made use of the moment and knelt to entice the magick-wielder, too, in a hush lower than her step. "Prove untoward to her again and I will call down more Ministers and more Squires than your cheap devilry can perceive."

"*Mmmmm* . . ."

Edmond kept watch on Tull while the peculiar count bantered in an inaudible voice and spoke with a hush of his own. "Soon you will see this as the way."

"Here!" Sondrea pulled at a lamp chain and burst from the darkness with an age-worn journal embossed with a gold leaf reproduction of a crest from an empire that no other soul in the territories visited. She made a wide arc around a twisted, emerald bulb that emanated from a copper band in an immovable floor setting and furthered that arc away from her father's reach. "All his involvements from the seventy-second sowing season are found in this journal."

"Not"—the count laughed as if he heard a joke—"*all*, as you say, daughter. I was busy much of that time"—he winked at Tull—"delighting your mother."

"That's impolite, Papa. You once despised a crude tongue."

Tull opened his palm to receive her offering. "This gets us closer to Paladin?"

"He hasn't an ear for tales!"

With a wave of his hand—and afore Sondrea swatted the materials from Tull's grasp—the count made his journal burst into flame hot enough to consume the ash and knock two Jacobians off their feet.

"You'll learn nothing from me!"

Edmond pulled the soul he cared about to his feet.

"Like Zeck, you are an indignant fool! Reliant on an unseen deity and Jacobian arrogance!"

Tull and his elder both helped Sondrea to her feet.

"When my daughter sees her end, you'll have yourself to blame!"

TULL & EBBE

Tull stepped afore her as a shield and sword.

"Pray to your Triune, poi'kai! Beg! They'll not resurrect her soul!"

"Pysy poi'essa ai'atu ksi'ani i'a tämä nai'onen"—Tull pointed at Sondrea—"en li'i'an, paho lai'nen!"

Though the magick-wielder mocked him with shrill laughter, Tull grinned and clapped his hands. In the echo, a silent prayer of certain belief unbound the cords that kept light from entering the room. Tapestries unfurled from hooks and swung toward the middle of the room, dragging across the old filth of floors and wiping away trails of feet and wheels. Beneath the unrestricted sky-fires, the count's paleness looked like white candle wax and made him conceal his brow with bony hands.

"Olko ni'in."

The broken and disappointed heart resurfaced in Sondrea; though, not for her sake. "He deserved so much better from you, Papa. You've never once cared what he means to me. You've never cared for another above yourself. You were blameless then so you could not remember my father as he has been evermore."

Tull remembered, in rightness, a monster.

"When my grandfather struck him, he changed a portion of him that has never returned."

The count waved off her critique. "All that seeps from Zeck's line is awfulness."

Edmond braced for a show of due wrath. The Jacobian, no longer blameless, learned enough of Conliffe to find no honor dwelled in him. So, he struck once. A swift uppercut set his knuckles against the underside of the count's jaw with a measure of strength that spilled magick-wielder and wheelchair onto their backsides and revealed the dirty soles of Conliffe's boots. A crystal orb bounced from beside Sondrea's father like a soft-boiled egg and produced a dimple in the pristine surface.

The magick-wielder's distant eyes reflected Tull's silhouette as the young Guardian stood over him with fists still clenched and the sky-fires behind him. "Old mate?"

"Remember your foe's name. I am Nelson James Tull, the fourth Guardian from the Jacoby Territory. I am the proud grandson of Judge Juanita Gene James, and the son of Reckoner Kara Doe Nelson and Mechanician Patrick James Tull, once kept from all harm by the Countess of Ebbe Demesne . . . and your neglected bride . . . and your betrayed fellow. Rile she whom I revere again"—with might that exceeded a created soul, he set his heel against the dimpled crystal and produced a sound of terrifying thunder that reduced the orb to clouded rubble—"and no other soul will see you after or evermore."

"Guardian Elragadó." Sondrea turned her back on her cackling father. "As you boast your friendship with my father, you no longer keep my trust in the matter that brought the Guardians you lead to his plot. I will send word to our judges and ask that they convene to decide on furthering your purpose; far from this territory."

"That isn't a concern you need tow, Countess."

"As representative of the bench of the Archibald Territory, I assure you, the concern is my pleasure! By proclamation of Judges Rogers, Burton, and"—she twisted toward her Guardian—"*James*, a Guardian is granted two moonsets' rest upon attaining their purpose. I'll ask that Guardian Tull arranges my travel from Ebbe Demesne, though that be his time for solace, and will pray that my father has not offended him so much that he'll refuse me."

The creaking of Edmond's boots spoke to the loss of integrity he suffered against her as he swayed side to side but held his tongue. In a room so still, all heard his curse-like breath. Over this, Sondrea grinned, yet she soon looked upon the parlor with utter disgust. Fifteen spans after he inflicted his greatest betrayal upon her in this same setting, she turned from her father in full and faced he who led her away from darkness evermore.

"Guardian Tull. Please lead me from this place I no longer care to recognize."

Tull glowered at Edmond through his hurt and offered his arm to Sondrea. Together, they headed toward the nearest door away from the connivers; now revealed beneath the return of light. This time, in an undoing of forty-seven seasons of hurt, Tull passed through the door where Cyril Adair Mumus once awaited and departed with the judge's bride. None called to him, followed, or forbade the pair.

"Nelson." Her use of his name went unheard and she called to him with commanding breathlessness, "Beloved Jacobian!"

He froze mid-stride and felt her hands steady him as he teetered. She stood between him and the stable house and took a calm breath that he might see and keep his heart from darkness. Still, he trembled with anger. "I'll not express shame for striking that—"

She hushed him with a shake of her head and a pat of fingers to his lips. Her hands then splayed like spider legs and she pulled him nearer to kiss his mouth with all the intentions of a grateful lover. A harsh wind took the brilliance from her copper irises as she loosened her hold, and her playfulness lacked warmth when she tapped his chin with two slow strokes of her index finger. "Since my grandfather's end, you are the first who stood in my name. I thank you."

The blood in his veins churned in his ears. "Your belongings . . ."

"I have many an acquaintance who can retrieve all that I want from this or any other plot. I no longer need look to the past to make sense of all I see."

"As you say." He struggled through a calming breath but led her further from her father. "Tell me why we did not enter through the parlor's outer door?"

She looked over his shoulder toward the stone wall. "There is no visible door from this side. Another of his spells."

The Jacobian rolled his eyes but did not look back. "I have a trick door of my own."

"I listen."

"There is a plot in the timbers where I can protect you, but that requires a ride."

"Wherever we must go . . . this plot is no longer a part of me."

"The place where we go lacks the comforts—"

"You will be there, will you not?"

"I will."

"Then I tow no complaint toward my Guardian."

THIRTY-TWO

No complaint arose between them, but Tull remained ever curious of the sway that a poem held over his purpose. Once he made certain that no other soul twisted by a conniving spirit lurked in the stable, he took from his coat pocket his handheld device and sought insight. Sondrea, all the while, brushed Agnate's jaw and made no attempt to manipulate the brooding Jacobian. Rather, she craved his lead.

A crackle of sound and a man's distant shouting preceded the slamming of a door and a sharp inhalation. "Guardian. A pleasant eve?"

Tull's brow answered in place of his mouth.

"Brecht"—his abettor pointed a thumb at the door behind her—"my lover still purges from the feast."

"And you, my abettor? Are you mended?"

Another brisk inhalation. "I feel the limits of my appetites."

"Once we end this conversation, I ask that you send a thorough surge—as we used in Clive—against every device on Ebbe Demesne."

"As you say?"

"Focus on the manor."

"The manor?" Her enthusiasm waned. "As you say."

"Valery"—he checked the opposite entry and the entry behind Sondrea to see again that no other interfered—"remind me of the poem."

"Néma Róka, Ébredő Róka?"

"Yes."

"I too learned the poem," Sondrea offered with a modest shrug.

"In the original tongue?"

Sondrea shook her head and gathered Agnate's prim saddle.

He watched his abettor peer toward the edge of her device, as though this might let her see to whom he spoke. "Abettor?"

She peered up at him, offered a lopsided smile, and adjusted her posture. "The poem focuses on three characters; first is the youngest brother, the fox. He appears as the first threat."

"Ming."

"No, Róka. The poem is titled for him."

"Believe me, I speak of Ming. The next character? The owl?"

"That's Bagoly. She who hears and sees and knows all."

Tull and Sondrea spoke at the same time. "Dory."

Confused, she who suffered hallucinations of all kinds stepped further from the screams that filled her home. "Did you not say you've read the poem?"

"My mom started to read me the Believer's translation afore she"—he held his breath.

"Indeed." Valery hesitated till his silence held and let pass his insistence on names. "There are characters in that version who do not appear in the original text, and contrariwise."

"How many characters appear in both translations?"

"Four. The fox, the coyote, the owl, and the bugaboo."

"They called the coyote 'Prérifarkas.'"

"He is their elder brother—what they refer to as a brother."

"We've not met him yet."

Sondrea shook her head even as she fastened Agnate's saddle.

"That leaves the bugaboo." Valery wasted no time. "In every translation, the fox and the coyote hunt down and devour Mumus. All but the eyes! The owl keeps the monster's eyes because that's how the monster sees in the dark. The poem ends as the owl ascends to become the moon so her brothers can hunt all who showed them wickedness evermore."

"That's a terrible story!" Tull stood baffled. "Who writes that to a blameless soul?"

The speechless Partaker had no answer, as the poem circulated since the first era from an unnamed creative.

"Go and prepare Blizzard and Ligurus." Sondrea took Tull's display plate and faced his useful aide. "Abettor Koslowski, I thank you, and he of contrary disposition thanks you."

Valery blushed and bowed her head with a lilt of modest cooing in recognition of the countess.

TULL & EBBE

"We must get. Do mend well from your feasting! Our territories need you." She ended the relay, then shook her head. "Nelson, does she ever cover?"

Tull looked at Sondrea's wardrobe and removed his storm coat that she might be protected from the eve. "Not that your dress brings to mind a horse ride."

She ripped the slit up to her hip socket and rid his face of all expression. This made her grin, and she accepted his offering with a pat to his cheek as he retook the display plate. "Do hurry! I prefer my eyes remain in my head as we live beneath enough moons."

"You aren't Mumus." He adjusted his saddle atop Blizzard.

"By law, I am he." She laughed at the irony. "He wrote the law that way."

"Eyes might mean identity."

"Or they mean access to all I see, and access to a shape-changer would undo our kind when mingled with the weight of Cyril's bench."

Tull appreciated now that she returned to the place that wounded her and fitted the bridle. "If Edmond ends this, I can ask that a soul go to Sevier so there is a presence of Guardians. Olley or Nita—"

"No, not Guardian Ozul." There were still secrets that Sondrea kept from Tull, so she borrowed from a simple fact. "Katerena bares no respect for Shelbian women."

"As you say. Is this your father's hand against *him* while he slumbers?"

"Do you believe we might convince him to tell us?" She awaited a shake of his head. "Then let us get!"

"You pursue her too?" Olley shouted as he entered from afar with his saber and pack in tow.

"'Her too?'"

"Dory has worked loose." He set aside his gear and slung a black saddle over Firefly's back. "George discovered odd tracks toward the millpond house. He never found Edmond."

"Edmond sits with the count." Both stared at the other. "'Odd tracks?'"

"'Edmond sits with the count?'"

"You're down the line of succession after Nelson, are you not, Guardian Falk?"

Olley nodded and answered Tull over Sondrea's prompting, "A slender left boot and a flat, horned-moon-shaped imprint."

"I discovered similar tracks in the foyer." She looked to Tull. "Prérifarkas?"

"Could be."

Olley looked as though overcome by a splitting headache. "Prérifarkas?"

"My foes seem intent to act out—"

"A poem! I remember." Olley glanced at Tull. "My father played Prérifarkas in that atrocious film. And, they are *our* foes, Countess."

"The count had a journal that must've told more than he liked, for he waved his hand and reduced every page to ash afore I learned the content."

"And sullied your new coat." Sondrea brushed a mark on the elbow but that was the least of her woes so near to her father's continued betrayals.

Tull shielded her even from Olley in her state of hurt, for less seemed callous. "We ride for Appledash Road."

"A fine plan."

"I had hoped to have you return to Sevier to check on the heiress."

"Another *Mumus*. I'll ride with you to Desard Bridge."

"I cannot ask that of you now."

"And I cannot say I sought your permission."

"Permission for what?" Harlan appeared behind Olley. "George told me of Dory. I saw Nelson and the countess running from the manor. Rather, the manor *wall*. And I believed I might see no magick on this plot."

"I am told that Edmond is on the other side with the count."

Harlan looked toward Tull for confirmation.

"My purpose has not ended. I intend to take the countess from here."

The Carpenterian gave Olley a glance.

"I go with him to see that Scion Mumus remains safe in Sevier."

"Believe that I will end any soul who stands in their way."

The collective turned toward the sound of Edmond's voice. Tull, who identified his place first, swept Sondrea behind him. She, not a soul intended for shooing, stepped around him again and nudged his arm with her shoulder as she took his wrist in hand.

"None of you need fear me."

"They tell troubling tales, Edmond."

"Does the truth not exist, except to shake us?"

"Why, Edmond?"

"I, like Ganix, tired."

"Then you betrayed us?"

TULL & EBBE

The eyes of their headship found Olley the accuser. "I betrayed my purpose. I might even have betrayed a territory that despises me. But never believe that I betrayed any of you."

"I can name a soul who might disagree."

Edmond accepted Tull's scorn.

"Why end Ganix?"

With Harlan counted, three Guardians turned against their headship, who took an unsteady breath. "The soul you seek—Paladin—is called Tai'bu Kaas. He keeps a home above the Chrisman Sweets Shoppe in Readick."

Sondrea recited the details in a whisper soft enough to tease Tull's ear and turn his head toward she who kissed him.

"That's where Mick and I put him—by arrangement between Judges Conliffe and Elwell—the morn afore Mick set the outfit beneath my rule. Conliffe salved his father's thorn and Elwell let Paladin set his hand against every soul who terrified that portion of the Weston Territory. Who would believe if they saw? Who would talk if he let them keep their breath?"

Silenced by facts, Olley glanced toward Harlan, who seemed as schooled as he.

"The mute—Ming—was not his, nor was she whose face you scrubbed off in the millpond. *Twins.*"

Sondrea bristled at the mention of Dory.

"What of the coyote?"

Edmond's eyes sparkled again toward Tull, as if honored by and responsible for the Jacobian's wit. "*Noeu.* I tell you, he is an ornery bastard. He exceeds the lot in all his ways and traits. Their elders fear him—Paladin, too. Like me, he has hunted too long. Like her, he is as much Conliffe's seed, though not born because of him. Your daddy ought not have accepted this plot after your great old father and Saul Ole Ebbe's old father fell. His magick mingled the creation in ways he never . . . counted."

Harlan turned his head till his beard mingled with the collar of his preferred bear skin coat but did not set his eyes on the intended recipient of his orders. "Take the countess, George, and Olley. Ride from here."

"Do what he tells you, boys."

Tull stared into Edmond's eyes. "I take Nita in George's stead."

"Don't you trust me to fight alongside my friend?"

Tull's smirk held the same dazzle of Edmond's eyes.

TULL & EBBE

"As you say then." Even as Edmond spoke, he sensed George arrive behind him. "You've all earned your say."

"Olley . . ."

"I listen."

"As the territories lay."

"You lead, the countess stands as the Loy, and I to the rear. I can manage the wicked rear as well."

"And I the wicked front. Manage to let the Shelbian ride at the countess's blessed hand too. George . . ."

"I will not betray my purpose, my friends."

"Harlan"—Tull spoke with softness—"would you send Blizzard toward me?"

The Carpenterian led Tull's horse by the reins and swatted his rump to set him on a swifter gait toward the Jacobian. Olley claimed Ganix's horse, still fitted with a greasy, discolored saddle that none liked to touch.

"Settle." The Jacobian took hold of the reins as they swung toward him and Blizzard obeyed. "We get."

"Remember . . ."

All looked toward Edmond.

"The coyote never stops being sly; not even whilst he slumbers."

"Is that all?"

Edmond felt Olley's cold tone. "You boys never displeased me."

"Soon we'll see you, Harlan, George."

Edmond barked toward the horses, "Get!"

Tull took Ligurus's reins and led both horses in a rearward step without trampling Sondrea as she mounted the saddle on Agnate's back. She clucked her tongue twice and Ligurus matched her mare's trot. The two Guardians followed, neither surrendering a step nor looking back to see how Harlan and George dealt with Edmond. Nita, ever the runner, ceased from a path she created out of the millpond house and breathed through her mouth.

"Mount this, Shelbian!" Olley flung the reins of Ganix's horse at her. "We ride toward a decent place."

She shied away from the reins and Olley, met Sondrea with disapproval, and addressed he who invited her. "You intend me to . . . ride . . . this beast?"

"The mare's name"—Tull drew the eyes of aunt and niece—"is *Scion*."

TULL & EBBE

Scion whinnied but Olley interrupted the offended breath that preceded Ganix's other scion's next remark. "Get on that horse or I'll drag you behind mine."

Tull did not defend Nita from such harshness. "We await you, Guardian."

She responded to his impatience with an ugliness that no Shelbian ought to flaunt. In point of fact, her effort to mount a saddle made the others and their horses cringe. She appeared clumsiest as her foot hovered above the terrane and her hand offered the saddle horn a vise-like grip. The round-and-round betwixt horse and rider nary proved the barb that the count repeated about Shelbians and horses.

"If you require a steady hand . . ."

"You do, and I'll see you in a mending chamber."

"Consider my hand withdrawn."

Even Blizzard mocked her and circled in a contrary direction to occupy a place on the other side of his owner and the countess. But, as Olley chuckled at the horse's cleverness, Nita proved successful.

"Listen well, Guardian Ozul." Tull asserted his authority. "When a Guardian betrays their purpose, they betray us all—every soul of our kind and the firstkind. The nearest soul who holds the utmost authority stands as judge of that soul."

"You speak of Guardian Elragadó? Elragadó betrayed . . . us?"

"No, not us."

Nita ignored Olley, saw how Tull patted Ligurus to keep them moving onward, and bounced in the saddle to get Scion to follow. "Guardian Vosburg would end him?"

Tull withheld that answer even from Sondrea.

"Guardian Falk?"

Sondrea adhered to Olley's dislike of Shelbians and spoke toward he who led her. "When did you learn of his working against you?"

"A tick after he stepped from the darkness in your father's parlor. After I smelled his horsehair wig above your perfume."

"I'll not hem my belief to that remark! Consider again and tell me *when*."

"Since the onset of winter"—Tull watched the play of the sky-fires' light upon the drifts of snow that surrounded the northern and western sides of the orchard—"he practiced needless cruelty."

"Cruelty is never needed," Nita hissed, and made Scion misstep, "amid Guardians."

TULL & EBBE

"He kept from us"—Olley ignored the outfit's newest member but waved toward still-bound Asham as he minded the shadows that crept from the orchard branches—"in presence and in word."

"He toiled alms as a soul who no longer feared a time without them."

Olley reached another conclusion. "As a soul who expected to be found out."

"Or *intended*"—Sondrea hinted—"as he intended us to find him aligned with my father."

"And Guardian Ganix?"

Tull led them around a blackened spot in the snow where the shadows conspired against the sky-fires. "Edmond would not burden us by setting us beneath Ganix's headship."

"Ming—Ming took Ganix's head."

All three looked upon Nita till she felt small.

"Did he not?"

Olley tossed an orb light upon the conspiring shadows and bat-like creatures flew away till only the snow remained. "Ming sought to strike George."

"I struck Ming."

"Edmond then chased Ming toward this end of the count's plot."

"Where Ming fell in two parts."

"He never passed beyond the manor."

Sondrea followed the map they constructed. "Nor entered your camp."

"Yet Edmond returned from the orchard with his accusation on him."

Nita's audible swallow drew no ire.

"And let in the coyote."

"What coyote?"

TURN

AN INTERIM

THE 11TH EVE BENEATH THE MOON OF THE MOTHER'S SONG
THE 107TH WINTER SEASON OF THE ACCESSION
IN THE CARE OF THE HELPER, WHO KEEPS SOULS FROM FRUITLESS WANDERING.

191 TAUROG ROADWAY
IN THE STABLE HOUSE OF EBBE DEMESNE.
WITHIN REACH OF THE BEHEMÓT WOODS.

"You took Ming's head, Edmond!"

"He . . . saw."

Guardian Arthur George Green looked toward the former law-writer turned interrogator, for he did not understand his headship's claim. Harlan Bottin Vosburg, who once demanded and achieved the removal of a judge from his territory, now cornered his truest friend on the cusp of the forest that destroyed him. The defeated headship took off his pristine, white hat, his horsehair wig, and the kerchief around his neck. With the latter, he mopped the oily sweat and residue from his bald crown.

"He saw . . . my love."

Harlan scowled and shook his head in disbelief. "No."

Edmond's gapped teeth showed as he smiled and nodded.

"No!" Harlan's thunderous rejection made the remaining stable whinny and stomp. "She's kept to the mountains since Benest and Shelley's reclusion. Our judges saw to her!"

"I tell you, she does not keep to any mountain."

The Carpenterian breathed in a way that made the branches creep nearer.

TULL & EBBE

"I have cared for her since afore he whom Cam took from here and whom we brought back was given unto our kind." His claim sharpened the wintry breeze.

"There is no way. I tell you; I have monitored her place!"

Edmond laughed with a sense of sickness. "Another saw to that ruse . . . for a fee against our souls."

Neither George nor Harlan grasped the meaning behind his actions when he reached behind his head and teased the base of his neck with his soiled kerchief.

"She will never be where those who maneuver us believe she keeps."

"Then you brought her here?"

"She has followed us since our Westonian fellow procured his farm."

"Forty-nine moons."

Harlan looked toward the Westonian with a sharpness in his eyes that none had witnessed twice. "I warn you, George. Never tell of what you learn from him now."

He who kept the most decent path amid all Guardians wavered as he weighed the burden hoisted upon him.

"Listen to him, George." Edmond peeled away his false brows, mustache, and soul patch. "There is no greater burden than that of destroying the trust of a friend who treated you as a brother."

"Who am I wicked enough to betray, headship?"

"Tull cannot keep the countess from what comes for her. Nor should he. If he recalled what she . . . she might be the worst monster on this plot."

George saw Harlan's agreement in the way the Carpenterian hung his head. He considered all that he had learned in tales of the countess and her intentions toward his Jacobian friend and his stomach stirred. As those tales mingled with the deeds of those who led him, he rushed to the doorway of the stable house, fell to his knees, and retched.

Edmond patted his shoulder and offered him a pristine kerchief. "I sought to shock her sins from the shadows of Tull's mind, but on that eve when he stood and told us of his visit with her, I realized my fault."

"That was not your sole fault in this, Edmond."

"My love will scour those faults—and the countess—from this forsaken plot so no other blameless soul is turned. So no potential mother betrays her purpose again."

"She will not stop there."

TULL & EBBE

"Will she not? I alone have kept her on her path. I have kept her safe so she can have this."

"You have never kept her. All this while, she has kept you."

"Truly!" Edmond laughed as a tear fell. "I am proper in my scheme. He mustn't become me."

"He never would." Harlan's words were so soft that they failed to ripple across other ears.

"That arrogant succorer! We had . . . a fine plan. She and her mute twin forced your hand, too, old bear, but you proved your pluck against her . . . against me." His sigh flowed from his gut as if he towed no secrets and had no need for lies. "My love suffered offenses too. The mute saw how she could not leave Ganix to my hand."

"Or to your heel?"

Edmond sneered even as he turned from Harlan's barb toward the Behemót Woods. "This plot destroyed me twice. How right that my headship ends here!"

His truest friend reached between the hem of his storm coat and his belt and unsheathed a bone-handled knife with a blade that might pierce a body from front to back. His clutch proved so determined that his arm shook. "Face me, Edmond."

"She waits for me there."

Harlan would not stab him in the back, yet Edmond held his breath in wait.

"Let me go to her. My end should not be your burden. Let me go to her."

Still, he approached with knife in hand, took hold of Edmond's neck, then cut the straps of his weapons from his storm coat. "He who turns from his purpose has no claim to such weapons. Go to her and make yourself our foe."

"I will miss you most, old bear. Let Mick tell you all that is useful of Tai'bu Kaas. He is not what he seems." He traced his fingers along his face with such pressure that he left trails of blush upon his pale skin. "And he is not an orphan like our Jacobian fellow." He then wept. "Better this than becoming prey to the boys."

With these words spoken, Edmond Anson Elragadó turned from his purpose and fled unto the darkness of the Behemót Woods. His fellows did not pursue him.

FALL

THIRTY-THREE

<u>POINTED AWAY FROM THE BEHEMÓT WOODS</u>
NEAR THE NORTHERN HEM OF EBBE DEMESNE.
WHILST EDMOND TURNED FROM HIS WAY . . .

Beau Itzal Zeck's last stallion raised up on his hind legs but did not spill his rider. When Ligurus's front hooves touched the frozen glebe, those behind saw a gathering of creatures blocking the roadway; figures who resembled Ming and Dory in form crawled from holes burrowed in the frozen terrane of Ebbe Demesne's hem. Muddied hands wiped faces stained with plum hues from strained muscles that bruised the flesh and eye sockets pitted with webbed veins. Each stood on uncertain, everchanging limbs as they sought to frighten through imagination those whom they could not intimidate through wit.

"We'll see to you in a tick!" Olley brushed them off with a wave and leaned in his saddle to deliver a hushed barb to Tull. "Even now I count no coyote." And then looked toward she whom they protected. "Another sort of count."

The impulsive Archibaldian loved to nudge. His eyes lacked warmth and his tone seldom mingled with patience. Yet, his heart for their friendship and his devotion to keeping Yah's Second Creation from harm oft proved unshakeable. Why he discredited such esteemed portions of his character bothered Tull. In the same manner, the habit inspired the mindful Jacobian to change how he spoke for their foe's ear.

Olley leaned upon Firefly's saddle horn. "Not the time for lengthy prayers."

"I speak to he whose kind does not claim him as kin!" Tull said this for Edmond called Noeu a bastard. His eyes watched not for interest but for stirring wrath, for he recalled the anger of being an orphan. "I speak to he who hunts the wicked for the wickedness that he has suffered."

From this remark, a recollection of the poem, he narrowed the possibilities down to six souls.

"As the Third Creation has snakes, so Yah's Second Creation too has those who live best upon their bellies."

"Cowards!" Olley spat.

Two laughed and narrowed Tull's count. "I speak to he who believed a coward's lie. For those who hide their fear and cruelty behind magick are cowards."

Sondrea's concerned sigh drew her Guardian's ear but his eye spotted how one amid the four waved a hand in disinterest and turned away. Another stole from the pocket of the Partaker at his side.

"All of Yah's creations have failed! All have inflicted unkindness and cruelty upon their brothers and their sisters. Even worse, we have inflicted such indecency upon those we deem as less than us."

"I doubt this lot grasps the words you say!" Olley's complaint drew Nita's ear. "Each appears dimmer than a Creightonian."

"We—those who are the secondkind—defend our pain with a coward's tact—with barbs and crudeness. Like an orphan despises a whole family or a proud soul despises all who are of the same territory as the attacker who humiliated him."

Nita looked toward Olley with softness even as he neared blasphemy.

"In our suffering, we inflict for we fear more suffering. I believe none of us sets out to inflict further pain. I ask what you believe."

The leanest of the two remained agitated and uneasy in his step. Still, he would not advance toward Tull's position.

"I speak to the Coyote. Prérifarkas! Kojot! Koi'eot!" He set his eyes on the agitated soul he suspected. "Noeu!"

He whom Tull settled on wilted with anxiety and looked to other gatherers, as if confused by what to do. This confused Tull. Then, the sound of clapping hands divided the cluster and a black felt hat with a wide, round brim floated nearer to the front. As more moved aside, the overweight soul who watched Sondrea and the Guardians at the third mourning stepped out afore the others.

"'Coyote' must hold another meaning in their tongue." From behind Tull, Olley reasoned aloud and dismounted Firefly. "That pleb looks more like an overfed rabbit."

TULL & EBBE

Afore those of Conliffe's tree criticized Olley, the soul of hefty girth pointed in the manor's direction but did not turn the heads of the elder Guardians. Nita twisted and confused her borrowed horse whilst Sondrea peered from the corner of her eye. A blinding light intensified from beneath the sunken atrium—as if the lantern that struck Ming—and the full adornment burst. The crushed telescope and weighted stand, the leather armchairs, the withered library, and the potted monkshood mingled with glass, copper, wooden floor, and ornamental frame to become fodder in Noeu's plot.

This was the closest to an act of war that the secondkind observed in their time, for the firstkind turned the elements into weaponry. Never afore had Sondrea or Nita witnessed an effect as crude or destructive as cannon fire. Tull proved less enthralled over the destruction and pulled the countess from Agnate's saddle lest she be struck whilst observing the fall of her family home. In her stead, once he held her close and knelt as a shield to her, he watched Noeu's wrath surface.

The horses that belonged to Tull, Falk, and Ganix responded to the threat by laying down as a barrier around the foursome. Ligurus and Agnate did not. Sondrea gave her mare a swat and sent her back toward the stable with a scream. Ligurus still refused to budge and proved ornery in the face of trouble; like the countess's grandfather.

Tull took hold of the old stallion's reins and, with no more than a flick of his wrist, coaxed him to mimic the others. Ligurus squatted onto his hind legs and let his front legs stretch outward. The Jacobian patted his neck for this but felt the same chill from the snow that the magnificent creatures felt. For now, they faced other problems.

Explosions along the high peaks created pools of fire that rippled across the shingled faces and shattered windows. Whilst Olley marveled but shielded the pair, Tull wondered how a foe with charges snuck past and entered the home that betrayed the count's daughter. The humiliation of failure seemed too much.

"This is falseness."

Olley blanketed Firefly's rump with his storm coat. "Say again?"

"I said this is false! No way they get past our beacons or our patrols to lay charges in a house that we could not enter."

"Elragadó!" Nita accused as she squatted opposite the trio.

Olley pushed her away with a hand. "He would not!"

"My father!" Sondrea called out.

TULL & EBBE

"I don't see him."

She elbowed away the first to speak. "I do not approve of my father's magick, but I believe he will keep back any threat to his intentions."

Tull could not argue, nor could he agree with such swiftness. The count proved insane, but Tull doubted that even he would destroy his hideaway or let another drive him out of doors to stand beneath the sky-fires. He then looked toward Noeu's legs. "The coyote has feet."

Sondrea confirmed the same. "Is this not Prérifarkas?"

"Another must bear a flat, horned-moon-shaped imprint and a slender left foot."

The countess looked toward the glow of light beneath the flesh of her left leg and furrowed her brow as if she faced trouble upon trouble. She then looked upon the gentle profile of her beloved Guardian in her truest desire to keep him and to keep him from harm. "I tell you, we ought to move onward."

"Would you prefer we pass through the Behemót Woods?" Olley needled.

She then gave no other explanation.

Olley nudged Tull, this time with a hand to his shoulder. When that failed, he seized his knee and pushed him till he pivoted on his right heel toward what unsettled the Archibaldian. Both formed a shield to Sondrea, who felt Nita's cold gaze. Once the pair traded barbed glances, the judgmental Shelbian looked in that same direction as her fellows.

He who stood between both sides removed his winter coat and tossed away his hat, which covered a knife-shaped patch of hair and a forehead of stone-like pallor. From behind his ear, he tore away a pulp-filled mass that burst like crushed fruit and soiled the snow as his head proved misshapen in form. Startled Nita sank her ceramic nails into Tull's shoulder and made him grunt as the figure pierced his own jowl with long, bony fingers. He then tore away what appeared to them as a cosmetic, flesh-hued disguise; the sort employed by thesps like Olley's father and grandfather.

"Theatre gums and fabrics?"

"No, a second skin."

"As a snake sheds? Plus an ability to change shape?"

"I too am disappointed."

"None wondered, Shelbian."

A slender, pointed jaw hid beneath. As a bony hand shoveled away the flesh of one visage, the horrid mouth of another face took form. The corners of his lips reached to the hinge of his jawbone, that every tooth might be revealed and able to work as a weapon. That trait, though grotesque and bizarre, explained away his canine-related moniker as he tore at the other side and regained a shape nearer to symmetrical.

"So, the rabbit becomes a coyote." Olley took a breath of consideration. "I heard of a similar change once."

Aunt and niece shushed him with identical pitch and duration and drew a glance from Tull. Then, Sondrea nudged her Guardian to look back to their foe in time to see the reveal of cheekbones higher and broader than any soul who moved on two feet. These protected deep-set eyes that swam in puddles of bruising and veins. Between, a long nose reached to a point so low that—in sight—the ball almost touched the cleft of the lip.

"Yah made such a beast as this?"

Nita's Shelbian tone bristled Tull. He still noted the vulnerability that Noeu displayed with bravery. Whether he intended the same, the Jacobian rose to his feet and kept his hands visible. Noeu stripped away a torso's covering of flesh that stained the snow and turned the gut. Beneath, he bore a muscular frame spotted with plum-hued bruises where muscle pulled across bone. With a roll of his shoulders, his ribs changed in shape to carry the taut flesh.

Sondrea then stood behind Tull, but visible to those who blocked the cordial exit from Ebbe Demesne. "'Yah, our perfect Creator, makes war in my name . . .'"

"'So I must keep still.'" He maintained smirk and timbre.

"Do the same, Shelbian"—Olley joined the pair on their feet—"and you might be remembered by your territory come the morn."

As Nita rose, too, she took her first glance at others amid the group whose bodies jerked and tremored in an unsettling manner and whose ripped flesh spoke to a rare segregation of the populace. "They are the Infested!"

Those souls who upset Nita were Partakers who invited in the wayward spirits of the Fallen First and offered them a home. That home was their created body; meant for a single soul's occupancy. The spirits that overtook oft destroyed the intended soul, broke the body, and sought to act with malice toward Believers. Their truest goal, though, was to upset the First Creation who still warred beneath Yah's command. They seemed to upset the Kuusa Si'epä too.

Tull & Ebbe

Amid those of the First Creation, whose disloyalty led to their fall, existed a rivalry. Those who once served in the court of the Most High despised those siblings who proved too weak to retain their own forms. The wayward spirits sought to agitate those whose dwelling place went from a supernal throne room to the muck of an entangled forest. If the Kuusa Si'epä attacked the wayward spirits, then the Guardians would have to defend the Infested whilst fending the attacks of that lot. Noeu's poise hinted that their efforts to weary the Guardians bolstered his scheme.

Olley fitted a tasseled blue balaclava across the bridge of his nose and cinched a corded bead that held the fabric in place. "We ought to send the Shelbian for Harlan and George . . . if she runs so fast."

"They settle other matters."

"There's no way we get through the Behemót Woods. By now"—Olley heaped on another barb—"I imagine you regret not keeping your bow."

"Do I seem unsteady, Archibaldian?"

"I do not see Dory amid the lot."

"Would we recognize her again after all she suffered?"

"I imagine not." The countess sensed the looming nearness of the Kuusa Si'epä and offered an ear toward the impact their cleft limbs made against the glebe.

"Yah on nopi'ea. Yah on ar moll i'enen."

"Why do they stand idle?" Nita huffed in fear. "Why do *we* stand idle?"

"We are no longer Guardians serving our judges." Tull said no more till he remembered the lack of preparedness that stayed with him in his first season and how that made him forget their ways too. "We are travelers. We cannot attack lest we suffer attack."

This time, Nita looked toward Olley and his heartfelt disgust over her or the trespass of the Infested. "Flee? These souls look to me now."

"And, they will bury you with Ganix. Better to wait them out. See if they truly wish to be feared and risk being hunted down by a mob of those who do cherish us."

Nita's curse drew Tull's ear but no Squires or Ministers. "This is your territory, Guardian Ozul."

"I am aware of my—"

"I believe"—Sondrea interrupted, but delayed as the Kuusa Si'epä became visible beneath the sky-fires—"he refers, in his way, to the law of invitation. As host

Guardian, even in resting, you may call upon your fellows to help you sort a concern till such a time that a superior directs you elsewise or calls for a judge."

The newest amid Guardians stared at her without blinking and then faced the creatures to their rear.

Sondrea looked at Tull. "Do you not?"

"'In my way.'"

Nita fidgeted with her ceramic-tipped gloves as false light from around the manor struck the waxy, discolored eye sockets of a creature. "You've my invitation."

"I thank you." Tull resumed the lead in the new Guardian's stead. "I count seventeen mingled foes from this side."

"Sixteen!" Olley corrected.

"The soul atop the gas lamp."

Nita looked over her shoulder to see.

"The gas lamp on your left side."

"Yes."

Still, the Kuusa Si'epä drew nearer and Tull paid them no mind.

"And the slip of a soul beneath he who clings to the fallen tree east of that lamp."

"Uhm . . ."

Sondrea sighed. "That's a terabinth tree from my mother's first home."

"Nelson?"

"The Archibaldian has yet to learn his differentiations."

The odor of the forest wafted off the husks of those creatures in Nita's path.

"So, there are!" Olley watched the rutting pair a moment then revised his count, for their eyes held no reflection of the sky-fires. "Seventeen."

"Nelson!"

"The rear became yours again when you set your charge upon him!" The bitter Archibaldian growled. "Born in the Pit, I tell you!"

THIRTY-FOUR

Olley swatted Nita aside and took a stance to provoke those who dwelled in the woods that haunted him. He drew his saber and scabbard, as blade and as club, then swung each from right knee to left shoulder. The blade made a clean incision against two limbs whilst the scabbard knocked away the husk in broken clumps. Afore that same beast responded to the loss, Olley stabbed backward and severed the tail-like membrane that extended from between the lowest limbs and once served as a chalice of pristine light.

The severed chalice turned to sludge atop the snow. That sludge burned the eyes and drew pain from the next creature, who struck the remains and roared. This attacker Olley kicked sideways, which took down another. He then cut away limbs on the left side of each and took a knee. A fourth member of the Kuusa Si'epä leapt over him but, in landing's stead, fell into the arms of a Squire.

Two more Squires followed, took two siblings in hand, and vaulted back unto the sky-fires. Those fallen beasts that remained lunged, tumbled over the glebe, and made easy targets for the kicks and swipes of the Infested. Even as grace departed from them, so too did balance and skill. Both sets of foes spent more energy on missed opportunities than any blow landed. In this, Olley found reason to enact swift strikes.

"Too accursed and too weak to hold onto their own bodies."

Tull cinched his red balaclava around his nose, lest their foes steal his form. This custom—a rule amid the outfit—Edmond impressed upon them. He acknowledged that with a glance toward Olley, whose covering tucked into his vest and protected him as he dodged the mist of spirits cast from the body of the latest Infested he wailed on. Olley then tossed Tull the second of his twin, curved-blade knives he kept sharpened to such a fine point that the tip appeared unseeable. Tull accepted and knelt to slice away a swath of fabric from the countess's gown.

"Too accursed and too dumb to use ours."

The Jacobian arose to find she who shaped the dress for her frame with arched brow. "Hide your ears, nose, and mouth, lest the Infested share their spirits with you."

TULL & EBBE

Sondrea obeyed, as all heard the tear of fabric as Nita ripped away the belly of her outer cover, but backed away as Tull offered her the same knife.

"Should a creature let you see the absence in their eyes"—he offered her the knife a second time—"make them regret their nearness."

"I"—she took the blade and pursed her lips as she felt the weight, then looked each Guardian in the eye—"I thank you all."

Olley swung backward and proved that he possessed enough upper body strength to lift off the terrane the Kuusa Si'epä that took his blade unto the midsection. With a bend of his arm, he turned the creature head-down and dropped with the might to open the skull as if a seeded vegetable. Nita made the sound of the first syllable nearest to blaspheming when Tull took the breath from her lips with the force of his thrown blade. As her vapor fogged the broad edge, the blade cut the limb of a creature who almost seized the newest Guardian by her throat.

The creature screeched as Olley struck the stump. Afore he stood, another Squire plucked and ascended with the screecher. The Archibaldian offered an upward nod of his chin and Tull took notice how, from the safety of the road, Noeu watched unscathed. He used the time his foe remained still to retrieve a leather-wrapped cylindrical cannister, no longer than the blade that the countess held and no broader than two fingers, from a saddlebag. Of similar tastes, too, both countess and niece appreciated the sight of Tull as he bent toward Blizzard's ear.

"Vi'en hänel'lä, i'eolla on li'ekt huksi'eolla, merk tystä maelle, todellaenen yustäväno."

Both admirers looked in opposite directions as he pivoted toward them. He paid them no mind but ran gloved fingers through Ligurus's mane and bent his right knee to speak to him and no other.

"Omi stajasi neuvoa saenua paremmon kui'ene mi'enä voi'esaan. Si'elti maeonun pyydettävä, että todo stat i'ehtä valpas i'ea nopea kuin mättini, i'eonka muistan, i'ealo yustäväno." Tull wrapped the strap on the cannister around the fastener of his suspenders and eyed both horses. "Oltae molemmatte oasa Yahin i'eulpei'että."

In response, Blizzard and Ligurus whinnied and stood.

"What did you say to them?"

"He warned them against Shelbian lusts." Olley landed another barb.

Tull helped Scion rise but awaited the glimmer in Sondrea's eye. "I told them not to bite back at the Infested."

TULL & EBBE

She puckered her lips and shook her head as he winked in jest.

"The others must have heard . . ." Nita stared toward the stables. "Why would they not run to us?"

"None told them we remain."

"Do you not fret for your father, Countess, or your family home?"

"You judge me for the emotions you do not see. You know little of those I do not show. I wish no further fight with you, Guardian Ozul. My home, wherever that rests, remains open to you."

"After these fall!"

Olley's growled tone drew the focus of aunt and niece toward Taurog Roadway, which Tull approached without them. With no weapon in hand and no fellow in sight, he proved reckless to those who did not understand the soul.

"Fools take many forms"—Olley rolled up his sleeves—"but we are not to be fooled."

Out of his hatred toward all Shelbians, for reasons Tull aired, the smug Archibaldian created a commotion that upset the uninfected Partakers and cast them away from the Infested and the Taotáva. Like the tip of a dart against a balloon, two rival flows of chaos needed a place to impress upon; either to pierce or to resist. That place came where an orb light fitted with a percussive blaster landed. The shrill song that burst from the device scattered every sane—though depraved—mind.

As those who stood amid the blast turned their hearts away from patience and peace, and with the Kuusa Si'epa submitted beneath the Squires, the Guardians' demeanor took on new form. No longer did either ratchet down their rage or devotedness. Like Olley, Tull's eyes declared and his musculature proved that he would stop the hand of any who sought the countess's harm.

"Tull!"

The Jacobian spotted a peripheral gleam and dropped to his snow-covered right knee in response to Olley's voice as his hatchet passed behind him and struck the thigh of a charging man with ruptured, mended, and re-ruptured flesh. He fell and laughed as though delighted by the suffering. Elatedness was the Infested's most chilling response to agony for they invited brutality.

Tull remained solemn; unbothered that Olley invited a fight. Even so, he spoke an admission to Sondrea that she could not hear. "Chances are keen that I'll not be the same soul who returns to you when this fight has ended, but I will return to you."

TULL & EBBE

Olley screamed above the blast of his orb. "What?!"

One amid the cluster stomped the noisemaker.

"I thank you!" He looked again toward Tull. "What?"

"Our foe lets others fight his battles."

"Cowards oft do."

"I do the same. The difference is that whilst his find strength from beneath, ours brings theirs from above."

Tull unscrewed the tethered cap on the cannister and jostled the contents within as a devious smile spread across Olley's chiseled face. What sounded like chimes were the broken shards of an ornamental kettle lamp that belonged to his grandmother; or so the Reformers told him at the presentation of alms. Two moons in the mountains proved fatal for the gift, but he found another purpose for the tattered pieces of mustard yellow-hued glass adorned with hand-painted sparrows in flight.

He found a glass piece with smooth edges, the size of two fused copper alms, and brushed the trinket's cold face. As he gauged his belief, an Infested screamed in rage and ran toward him, hand raised above head. Tull blocked the attack with his shoulder. At the same time, he entwined his arm with the lowered arm of he who charged him and, with their combined weight, drove his shoulder down and flung that soul across his back. The attacker landed with a thud, and Tull set the broken glass piece upon his breastbone.

A vile laugh escaped the soul's coarse lips. Then, when he tried to stir, his body wriggled beneath the weight of that small trinket that proved immovable to him. His fume-like breath turned to gasping, and the sound of grinding from robust weight against bone preceded a sharp howl of pain. The glass sank against a recess in his breastbone and Tull stepped back in soberness.

This act provoked a response from a second foe. Blessed with longer legs and a leaner build than the first attacker, he gained a swift lead. Tull plucked the next glass piece and ducked a swing of that soul's fist, but rammed that foe's midsection with his shoulder, then flung him. Afore he slipped from Tull's reach, the Guardian pressed that second piece into the palm of his hand.

The attacker fell—hand hardest of all—and cried out. The shape of his hand, as slender as the rest of him, broke through the frozen terrane. He tried to toss the glass piece but could not. Nor could he shift, pluck, flick, or lift what Tull set upon him. So, he cried for help from his kindred.

TULL & EBBE

The nearest to him, however, set his sights on the countess of Ebbe Demesne. She, who proved a worthy detective and a wise teacher, learned of a surprise in the name of self-defense. While she bore no desire to use a knife, she planted a knee against the underfed mid-section; her left knee. The meat of her amplified thigh struck him hardest and cast him across the slope of the yard, past Tull and Olley, then toward Taurog Roadway and Noeu.

Both Guardians took notice and watched the distance the fool skidded. They looked at each other in confusion then turned toward Sondrea. The breeze caught the slit in her gown and bared her thigh. In the eve's veil, the soft lights beneath the flesh drew the momentary attention of the Guardians. Soon enough, she covered her thigh again and swept both hands toward them, as if redirecting them back unto the fight. Her well-pleased smirk never faded all the while.

Olley swung his way back unto the defense whilst Tull's gaze held till he recognized the sounds of running. He, too, possessed sturdy legs; which he proved when he tackled another of the Infested. While this foe snapped at him with broken teeth, the Guardian pulled a third glass piece from his dwindling collection. He set the piece in the divot between the tormented's collarbones, which bore the knots of multiple breaks, and subdued the threat.

As Tull ran deeper unto trouble, he bore no fear that those he pinned might rise back up and resume their attack. He took down four more, never inflicting permanent harm or maiming, and set a single glass piece—by Sondrea's count—upon every foe. She did not perceive what she beheld. All she learned of his unceasing bravery in seven spans' time, his expertise with the bow, and his wisdom of the firstkind; yet none told of what she now observed.

"You turn accustomed"—Olley declared afore he imitated a battering ram and buckled another of the Infested backward—"or so he insists!"

"How does he . . ."

"When I've asked"—he twisted the rammed soul's arm till he dislocated both shoulders—"he has said 'belief' and no other word."

"*Belief?*" Her brow creased and her mouth turned small as she watched Tull stop another along the side of the roadway where Noeu had stood. "Truly! He is—"

A dozen of the handmade feathers on her collar necklace fell away as a slat of jagged bronze—from Tull's bow—pierced through Sondrea. As she dropped to her knees, she revealed that Noeu had burrowed up from behind her and still held the weapon in his bony hands. Olley screamed and frightened Nita. When the countess's Guardians observed his triumph, Noeu released the makeshift sword and let her fall.

When Nita, who had no reason to feel warmth for her father's half-sister, saw her aunt, she swiped a claw-adorned hand across the face of he who sought to end her. The ceramic tips cut to the bone. She applied a second, upward swipe and drove her heel with the might to fracture the jaw she struck. Both she and Olley then ran to the countess's aid.

The sounds of chaos turned Tull's head, by which time Olley wrestled with Noeu in a match of equal strength whilst Nita retracted the ceramic tips on her gloves. Her hands trembled, visible even from two hundred paces, as she lacked the confidence to remove the piercing limb of the bow. Tull's blood ran cold at the sight of Sondrea, fallen whilst beneath his protection. His purpose—his survival—then meant little.

From the opposite direction, in the shadow of the burning manor, Harlan led George toward the fight without sign of Edmond. Tull reached Sondrea whilst she still had breath. Olley fared no better, as Noeu slapped him away with a broad forearm, set on ending what he started.

The Taotáva oddity was struck by Ligurus's charge and spun like a top. Nita buried her head, her narrow hind end toward the commotion, and shielded the base of her neck with her arms as the horse leapt over her. Tull showed no doubt in the horse's prowess and cradled the stallion's owner. Neither sought Noeu.

Injured to gruesome extent but kept alive, Sondrea did not perceive that Tull bore her blood on his hands. She reached toward him in shock, and he struggled to hold her still. The elder Taotáva, letting pass the innocence shown at the Knotted Caves by their blameless lot, bore a cruel streak—as did all creation. Noeu laughed when the next jolt of pain that Sondrea suffered made her shudder as she coughed for breath.

"Gloria . . ."

"Gloria?" Tull struggled to hear as Olley growled and bones broke.

". . . Verenitku Route."

A soul who matched Tull's breadth charged with a broken length of timber in hand, certain to break him, but Harlan leapt upon his back and took him down. What he made of the timber, once in his hand, proved how he defended those beneath him. He and George then helped Olley recover and took turns against Noeu. The Guardian who abstained from the fight, all the while, proved of steady hand and prayerful lips as he sought to treat Sondrea.

Tull & Ebbe

"Pocket . . .—she batted her fingers toward her hip—"Pocket . . ."

Tull remembered the tool he tucked away and hurried to retrieve the handheld wire arc that cut away the gate to the count's wing. He packed snow around the wound on her chest and fitted the device to his palm. In no time, he cut a clean edge on the copper limb of the bow he gave as an offering of peace with the Taotáva.

"Gloria . . ."

"Nita." He removed both pieces, from her back first, and then from beneath her collarbone. "Go into my saddlebag and find the cleanest linen."

She obeyed his instruction as George swatted Noeu across the shoulders and neck with enough force to snap his throwing staff into three pieces. Olley crouched and buried his fists in their foe's midsection, and Harlan struck Noeu's peculiar jaw. He proved malleable—unbreakable—at their every attempt. As slow to learn as Tull oft proved, they mopped their sweat, changed their stances, and tried again.

Nita returned with a wrinkled blouse and sliced through the shirt with her ceramic tips. Tull peeled back his storm coat to expose Sondrea's wounds, which he packed again with handfuls of clean snow. She trembled from the sensation of cold and pain then pressed her crown against Tull's chest. He kept his prayer internalized but reassured her with a gentle hand as he turned her onto her unwounded shoulder. Nita understood and gathered the softest of spare bedrolls from his saddle to use as a pillow for the injured's head.

Tull removed and unfurled his red balaclava then bound the wound till even Nita winced. "Will you watch over her in my stead?"

"There is a mending chamber—"

"I'll be a tick."

"—in the manor." Nita shook her head as he ignored her. "Truly! These souls prove as slow to hear as to learn."

"My niece . . ." Sondrea's words drew Nita's attention and her eyes drew her near enough to hear words softer than a whisper.

Nita sat upright and gripped her thighs till her dusky hands bore pale knuckles and her eyes turned pink with tears.

The countess tried to speak again but pain silenced her.

THIRTY-FIVE

Noeu paraded without disguise, a boastful laugh on his misshapen lips, for he tasted victory over the magick-wielder's daughter and the secondkind's best. Tull wanted to tear the plum-blotted flesh from his twisted bones. In a time when his heart ought to have burst with rage, he remembered in his blamelessness how Sondrea wept over her inability to console him when he mourned the loss of his father and his mother afore him. Her heart broke for him even then, and she begged his forgiveness for not knowing what to do to make his way gentler.

The Jacobian tossed aside a glass piece no larger than the bead of a child's teardrop and struck his proud foe's calf with a stomp from the boots that the countess purchased for him. A thunder-like snap of the leg bone sickened. The Taotáva's cruelest fell in pain, but swiveled at every joint to snap his teeth at he who struck from his weakest side.

Tull then swatted at the hinge of Noeu's angular jaw, beneath the bony shelter of his cheek. When a misshapen hand cradled the hinge, Tull isolated the elbow and delivered a knee to the crater-like armpit beneath his foe's bruise-speckled shoulder. This act cast Sondrea's attacker sideways and exposed the leg that brought about his fall. Tull seized the cold ankle of that tender leg and twisted till a wail of surrender rang out.

Around them, other souls of Noeu's kind backed away, for they had not heard such sounds from his lips. The scent of fear made them salivate, though, and most drew nearer despite the threat. He who led through fear made enemies on both sides of his cause, after all. His jaw snapped again but found no part of Tull to take. Afore he called out for support, his mouth suffered yet another strike that loosed the setting of the overexposed teeth on his left and shocked the airway.

A wheeze for First Breath followed Noeu's yelp and Tull clasped his hand around the wrist stained with Sondrea's blood. That he broke too. Noeu needed breath like the flame needed air, but Tull offered him no rest. He glanced toward George, who backed away, and furthered his onfall; no longer with the purpose of a Guardian but the rage of a soul who lost too many of his beloved.

He rounded Noeu's bare feet, as oblong and malformed as his hands, and immobilized his foe's other arm. Rather than inflicting another break, he pulled him onto his right shoulder, as Sondrea also lay, and struck Noeu's jaw. The flesh and bone reshaped and held the form of his fist. Each punch he landed impressed the same change upon him.

"Surrender." Tull could not believe the first word that departed his lips nor those that followed. "Admit your hand was turned against us for another's gain and let your kin prosper beneath a new beginning with my kind."

Teeth fell from Noeu's mouth on a torrent of blood. "I will drape your head from a branch alongside the magick-wielder's daughter."

His voice was softer and less indifferent than Tull imagined. Even so, he fished two glass pieces from the cannister and pressed his shin across Noeu's chest. "Cry out to Yah."

"Your Creator fears me."

"No."

Those two glass pieces Tull forced against the peculiar structure of his foe's canine-like cheekbones till the flesh consumed a sharp edge of each and shadow-darkened blood trickled from the created wounds. Noeu howled and snapped to no avail. His fiercest attempt to shake Tull loose bore no success and his hands wrung at the air for salve from his pain.

The Jacobian then made an example of Noeu and proved why so few of the other territories riled them. He pressed a glass piece beneath the flesh of both shoulders and both of his foe's feet and watched fright bloom in moss-yellow irises. In coldness, he then looked upon those who followed Noeu. The Taotáva backed away till their eyes appeared as specks of light in the orchard's darkness.

Noeu's howl of pain made Sondrea groan. Tull kept his back to her, lest she heard his words, and crouched near their foe's ear. "If you seek rescue, you must surrender. Elsewise, you will not be moved from this place except in portions."

Pursed lips said much about a soul's refusal. The Infested had laughs as pleasant as the icy winds that blew off the Loy and abraded the skin. Even they proved silent. Appearing unaffected by the change in them, Tull flicked a seventh glass piece upward that all might sense of how weightless the alms-shaped piece felt in his palm.

TULL & EBBE

He then checked the progress of fellows and friends. Olley overpowered a creature that made Harlan seem frail. Harlan mashed the crowns of two more. George bound the wrists and ankles of another Infested—his sixth—and Ligurus stood guard over Sondrea and Nita. Tull jostled the trinket he held from hand to hand and decided to return the piece to the cannister. In mercy's stead, he retrieved his axe from Blizzard's saddle and made his steed whinny.

"You ought to have kept from this place, and you ought to have kept from the soul you've wounded." He ignored the glint of fear in Noeu's eyes and drew his axe as if to swing.

Harlan seized his arm and plucked away the weapon. "Look to me, boy."

Tull saw the hollow despair that filled Harlan's eyes.

"This is not your way." With that, he kept hold over the axe and returned to his own fight.

Tull fell to his prayer bones with an immeasurable weight that mimicked the hold that burdened Noeu. The ice of the frozen glebe cracked, even beneath the Guardian, and raced beneath the fallen soul. Flakes of snow tumbled toward him, as though on a downward slope. The weight of Tull's belief and Noeu's refusal to repent pulled the Taotáva foe beneath and no rescue visited him.

Noeu's rage fueled his scream and echoed throughout the orchard and unto the cavern created by his prison. Water from beneath the freeze line flowed upward and pooled at the mouth that held his form. Though the secondkind mourned every end, Tull offered no prayer for his foe and drowned out every sound except his unsettled breathing. In this, he let down his guard—and his Creator.

"We see you, Son of Mighty Maidens!"

Shrill laughter, like beads of water consumed by frost, teased the back of Tull's neck. Enke'loi and no other called him by that name. Filthy, pungent feet—deprived of shoes and socks—pattered through the snow, blood, and fire toward him. As he looked upon the body that hosted uncounted voices, a filthy arm swung a hand wrapped with Nita's shed glove at the pewter-hued eyes that reflected the sky-fires' brilliant light.

Three ceramic talons scraped to the bone of Tull's face and dizzied him afore his blood flowed and his skull suffered tooth-jarring pain. A chorus of screeching voices from an unaccompanied mouth rippled his flesh and disheveled his hair when the Infested surprise mocked him. This made his vision pool with thick tears as blood and swelling further affected his left eye. The unsuspected threat was no more than a stray with underdeveloped arms and a plume of unkempt, mud-colored hair.

George flung the mingled creature away and knelt by his friend's side. "Be still."

"I must get her to Gloria . . ."

"No. Keep still, my friend." A passing sound of hammering feet against the terrane changed the pace of George's voice. "See that he steadies. Do not leave his side!"

"Me?"

The sound continued, then came a shrill scream and more hammering feet. George yelled and wood cracked against blunt objects.

"See that you stay steady!"

Recognition of Nita's panicked voice took a moment, and Tull better spent his effort on propping his weight onto his right knee and forearm. From that same side, his ear filled with the sounds of striking—metal to stone—and grunts of exertion. The scrape of Olley's saber put him between the orchard and the manor.

Tull struggled to plant both feet beneath him and took an intensified breath that smelled of horsehair. The blood in his eye met with an onyx field and a coarse huff. As he reached out with a shaky hand, he touched a bony surface that led from velvet-fine hair to a long, silver mane. "Help me stand, Ligurus."

The stallion nudged him jaw to shoulder and Tull moved with uneven steps, an arm draped across Ligurus's back. He mopped his unmarred eye with the sleeve of his shirt but relied on his sense of smell to find the powdery-sweet scent of clematis terniflora that improved the horse's odour. A smudge of dull fire guided him onto one knee, and with icy fingers he touched the countess's hand and wrist. Sondrea groaned, but he could not hear her soft words above the shrill screams and continued hammering of rushing feet as his fellows contended with the threats around them.

He pulled her by the shoulders of his storm coat and walked backward till his heel struck Ligurus, who knelt in wait. The Jacobian patted with an open hand, identified an unsaddled back, and swung his right leg over the well-trained stallion's crest. He tugged Sondrea nearer, each time costing her a whimpering breath. By the time he supported her in both arms, sweat and blood mingled on his brow.

Tull then swayed from side to side as Ligurus accepted his weight and rose. Creatures on uneven limbs raced toward trouble whilst others ran from the same trouble, but none stirred him. A cluck of the tongue set the proud old stallion in motion as Tull kept the reins in the hand that held to Sondrea's side. The other patted till he found the hip pocket of his storm coat where he believed he kept his handheld display plate, as stowed by his fellow rider.

"Please." The feel of slender glass against his wet palm drew a sigh. "I thank you."

He maneuvered his left hand's grip on the device for the stronger other and kept Sondrea from tumbling with his chin to her crown as he clenched the display plate and plotted his words with deliberate concentration.

"Instruction. Guardian Nelson James Tull requests connection . . . with Abettor Valery Leta Koslowski"—he clenched as Ligurus's rear hoof broke the rim of a burrowed hole and jarred him—"for single-frequency . . . relay. Passcode: Traveller Zero-Eight, Zero-Eight Abide."

"INTERFACING. SEEKING AUTHORIZATION . . ."

Tull could not read the screen through bleary eyes but saw the change of colors as the words formed across the plate. He heard the stallion's front hooves strike cobblestone and tugged his rein to turn him toward the Jacoby Territory. Ligurus responded well. When strands of his hair no longer tickled his throbbing wounds, signs that he faced the westward wind, Tull loosed both reins.

"ACKNOWLEDGING . . ."
"CONNECTION CONFIRMED . . ."

The stallion jostled his hindquarter to settle those he carried. Tull, who remembered his attentive companion, swept his ankle against Ligurus's belly with affection. "I thank you."

"Yes"—Valery gasped a mouthful of smoke and strained to see the face beneath the torn skin and sheeted blood—"Guardian Tull?"

"My abettor . . ."

"What has happened to you?"

"I forgot my way." He cinched his hold on Sondrea. "I forgot my way. I seek Gloria . . . Bea Greer. I've forgotten her address."

The Partaker still sat in shock of his new face and low, dizzied voice. She then sought the whereabouts of the name he gave to her. "She is Othnieli, but keeps a plot along the Jacoby-Shelby border."

TULL & EBBE

What felt like upright posture to him proved a slump of his right shoulder and a contrary angle of the neck.

"Your eye weeps too much for proper focus. Might I guide you?"

"I must travel fast." He turned the broadcast light from her freckled skin toward Sondrea's face.

Valery withheld her blasphemy but cursed the way that the wind turned harsh. "Is there time?"

Tull offered her no answer, for his mind failed to process her concern.

"If you can ride so far, you will find Greer keeps the Gyddingford Chamber House on plot seventy-six of Verenitku Route. I extend a second tether to inform her of your approach now."

He slumped even as more screams rang from Ebbe Demesne.

"Tull!"

The Guardian did not respond to his name but prodded Ligurus with a squeeze of his thighs and the stallion responded with a heavier gallop. Like his grandmother afore him, Tull raced along the roadways designed for tramcars and rigs on horseback. He recited his portion of the verse that Sondrea made him memorize in blamelessness; that she might hear how he continued for her sake. Still, as he rode with her in tow, his request for her safekeeping trickled into his recital.

The trustworthy stallion cut off passing coaches and foot travelers alike in response to tugs at his reins according to Valery's audible prompts. The trio moved slow enough that the abettor tracked them by Tull's identifier beacon and mapped out a safe course for them where his sense of direction failed. She who suffered for her devotion to a Guardian and Believer never faltered. When challenged by a forgettable wageworker at the chamber house, she proved her convictions.

"Now you listen well, for I am the unworthy abettor who serves a noble Guardian, truly, but far worse for you, I am a well-worn Partaker. My name is known with delight amid my kind and not with the fear that my Guardian's name brings to the battered lips of those I magnify. I am she who turns paths and upends those ways that the Creator I defy commands. I am why you will grant my Guardian access.

"Do not, and I will visit not that den of poison you uphold. No, I will see you in your home"—she drummed the transparent keypad and read the result that bloomed—"at plot sixty-four of Nanovic Way, two settlements from where I sit. And, you may believe, I will not travel to your door alone. I will bring those who defile the soul, and I will make them drunk on tales of your acts so you might see them defile every soul dear to you till you cannot look upon your mother or hear your son's voice or remember a time when your bride was beautiful in your sight. How will they keep you in their hearts then?

"We will learn, for you I will keep for myself; that I may remind you without end of the shame you brought upon them when you set your purpose above their unspottedness. You, I will preserve. And when I tire, I will give you to the mob of Shelbians who—Believer and Partaker alike—thank the Creator for she whom my Guardian seeks to mend."

Then, silence guided them. The stench of three fuels told of their nearness to Ezra's Trust Chapel. Partakers set fire to the place on three occasions and still did not burn the church to the terrane. Amid sounds of terse breath and fluttering voices from within his handheld device, he redirected Ligurus to the north and listened for the softness of the glebe and the pooling of fuels that still seeped from those failed attempts.

"You've reached the point where Taurog Roadway crosses Verenitku Route."

"My grandmother slept on this glebe"—though the church sat thirty paces to his rear—"after the second fire failed."

"My grandfather told me the same. He helped cut the wood that the Partakers used for torches."

Partakers of that era abided by a form of law. They burned symbols, but dared not murder for the sake of their defiance. Their children held less regard. Now, their grandchildren relied on each other as Partaker watched over Believer and tracked his progress across snowy hillsides by way of visible markers.

"You are near enough that you ought to prepare for the sharp turn that awaits when you reach the gas lamps that resemble a cluster of olives. They mark the beginning of Boone Roadway and eastward passage to Gutefiel."

Tull offered no response.

"Guardian Nelson James Tull. Do you hear my voice still?"

"*Mmmm.*" He seized hold of the reins and Ligurus slowed to make the turn well.

His abettor did not repeat herself or congratulate the horse. "You near Gyddingford, and I am told you have obtained permission to approach. Afore you reach the place, you'll cross over Channel Spine. The magnetics that are generated beneath will end our linkage. I'll not be able to guide you further. You must try and keep your eye clear so you can trace the amber fog that leads to her hem. Do you understand my words?"

"Magnetics."

"Yes. The magnetics will sever our linkage. I'll track your identifier beacon, but I'll not be able to guide you. The countess will need you to set aside your pain for her. Use your senses to follow the amber fog and the smell of sour milk. May your heart guide you, though your vision fails."

"My heart is . . ."

Valery sat in silence as the lone Believer who trusted her pushed onward. Ligurus's hooves provided a soothing rhythm that no voice dared interrupt. He took the wounded Jacobians past Shepherd's Trail; the last smooth stepping-stone afore travel required climbing a narrow hill onto a winding, cobblestone path that Harlan called "the place from where you could look down and see Hector Geirolf Picadura's discarded heart." No marker set the spot where the connection with Valery ceased; but, the stallion never ceased, and Tull never let go of the darkened device, the reins, or the countess.

THIRTY-SIX

76 Verenitku Route

The Gyddingford Chamber House.

A concealed place for mending.

Aided by the brilliance of the sky-fires and the wisdom of Ligurus, who seemed to perceive Valery's direction better than his rider, Tull felt their race slow whilst two plots shy of their destination. Fog that bore an amber hue and the tart odour of soured milk met them there. Both vented from the furthest side of an unassuming glass structure and, in their way, brought to mind memories of Barton Fredrick Ganix. The recirculation of breathable fluids used in the mending process cast out the impurities of disease, wounded flesh, and other rot. Such offenses and oddities proved small, given the benefits.

The Gyddingford Chamber House rested beneath a grove of camellia trees that obstructed the tart stench and sat in the cleft of a rolling hillside that offered a fort-like defense from the wind and the dregs of Villám Fork, whose ice groaned through the surrounding woods. Had Tull the pain-free acuity, he might have considered rumors of private chamber houses across the territories reserved for judges, celebrities, and other elitists. Letting pass his growing legend, he would never belong to the echelon where Sondrea dwelled or find acceptance to reclusive mending places.

This proved most evident when he directed Ligurus to the doorway of the single-storey structure comprised of dual panes and a visible, decorative iron frame. The outer layer kept back the elements, which included fog and odour. The inner layer kept hidden the happenings within. Even so, an isolated soul watched the approach of the wounded souls on horseback and spoke through a display plate that reduced his true size by three-fifths.

"This house is not open to you."

"I am Nelson James Tull . . . fourth"—he shook off and worsened his dizziness—"the fourth Guardian from the Jacoby Territory. I protect—"

TULL & EBBE

"This house is not open to *you*, Guardian."

He stomped at the display plate with the same force that raised his voice. "I guard Sondrea Ebbe Conliffe, Countess of Ebbe Demesne, bride to Judge—"

"Guardian Tull! Guardian Tull! Stand aside, Greeter Banks. Guardian Tull! I spoke with your abettor. Your access is granted. Please"—the threatened administrator swallowed—"Please, enter. We *will* accommodate you."

The defiant soul who refused Tull turned sweaty as the anxious soul whom Valery threatened fidgeted with a series of unseen controls. Auxiliary bulbs hummed as light flowed and the secretive happenings within the chamber house became visible from out of doors. These same bulbs revealed how the fog swirled and coiled in wait. Such disturbances proved common near the places where the secondkind mended, for they were the disembodied spirits of the Fallen First who sought hosts.

Four technicians stepped unto the gap between the exterior shells and stared out at the new arrivals. More than that cluster of souls hid from sight when the outer doors opened. Ligurus stooped and the Guardian followed his lead as they entered. Metal on metal clacked in time with a harsh puff of air as an anxious tech hammered the control that shut the door behind them.

"Pi'en aelepo, Ligurus."

Tull gave the order, and Ligurus obeyed by lowering in stature. Even with the benefit of a well-trained horse, the art of dismounting proved harder given his corrupted field of vision, impaired depth perception, and blood loss. Add to that the weight of the woman in his arms, and his plight intensified. His fear of falling and hurting her worse kept him seated longer than any expected, given his prior outburst.

"Let us confirm you by your identifier beacons."

Even as a cold hand turned down the collar of his shirt, a slap at the exterior shell of the house sent a ripple of sound through the holding place. Tull ratcheted his hold. He then counted beats of Sondrea's heart afore the next strike. *Six*. When another six passed, a strike landed with the force that caused the trellises to creak.

"The countess's identity is confirmed. Her breath is light."

"We ought not to have accepted him."

"The countess has suffered a piercing wound to her shoulder."

Tull turned toward his right in time that he heard a condescending response from the left. "Our faultless scarecrows know more than we do."

A sharp gasp joined a squeeze of his shoulder. "Truly! You are Guardian Tull."

The condescending voice that caught his ear once murmured a second time, "He was so beautiful."

Then, the voice that spoke from behind shushed them. "The spirits have bombarded us since the Feast of Pehdli Noži'ercuay began."

No remarks followed.

"They sweep and rumble without end."

"If the mist coils with them, put away the light." Tull's voice seeped like the fog; low and slow of pace. "If the mist slithers, light torches."

A moment passed and the lights dimmed.

A soft tug proved no match for Tull's hold. "We must move her, Guardian."

"She's no bother."

"As you say. Should you lose the light—"

"I will not."

He who confirmed Tull sighed with regret. "Let him."

"Ole lae vosha, moatta tarkkai'ea, i'ealo yustäväno." His voice echoed as he commanded Zeck's last stallion to stay afore the locks set and the group led Tull and Sondrea to the mending chambers. He then spoke to the unconscious soul whose head rested on his shoulder. "Not even Mim riled him. Do you remember?"

The technicians swarmed and circled but played more tricks on his perception of setting than his ability to travel. Fingers pried and instruments pressed as voices from blurred faces barked findings and recommendations.

"She was pierced by the brunt end of a bronze limb. I cut apart and removed—"

"We don't need to know, Guardian. I thank you." A breathless soul steered him as another stripped the countess of Tull's storm coat, her gown, and adornments, then prepped her for mending. "Our equipment will tell us all."

He bowed in wait as a nearness of two bodies lifted Sondrea from his arms. Then, another near to his elbow spoke out of turn again.

"Let her seek mending in the territory of her mother."

Tull reached on instinct and set his bloodstained hand upon the complainer as an elder steadied his shoulder with a clinical touch. "You could use help too, Guardian."

"Moving her into our fourth chamber!"

"I suffer from si'el uni'epotus. I cannot enter the tanks."

"I am aware. You don't know what we do here, do you? We have methods that other chamber houses cannot offer. We can have you looking—"

TULL & EBBE

"Please take your hand away and help her." He heard how Sondrea whimpered when the seven barbed needles required for mending pierced her abdomen. "She—"

"All know her, Guardian." A gasp of sealed air began, but another slap from the wandering spirits made the lights flicker and tricked the ear.

"She"—cold sweat fell as he trembled and the elder ceased from interruption—"is your lone patient."

He who tried to counsel Tull then called over his shoulder, "You forget to send alms for the utilities?"

"Mend well, sister." A woman spoke from the same direction. "Soon we'll see you."

A mechanized voice issued an alert in seeming response:

BEACON 072.19.434 RECOGNIZED . . .
IDENTIFIER CONFIRMED—SONDREA EBBE CONLIFFE
RECUPERATIVE PROCESS STARTED.
MENDING TIME: 8 WATCHES, 7 TICKS.

The harsh lights in the room turned copper and filled the room with a fire-like flicker as breathable, recuperative gel flooded the chamber and adhered to the skin and hair of the countess like an extension of her. This reaction proved her whereabouts to the injured Guardian, too. He remained still, joined by the elder, whilst the sounds of circulating fluids and harassing spirits filled their silence.

"I asked"—the elder spun in surprise—"Oh!"

"I heard what you asked. I've not forgotten my duties in twenty-two spans."

"I believed you hadn't. I sought only to distract you from your burdens."

"And that kept you from treating your patient?"

Laughter preceded excuses. "Perchance he'll listen to you?"

"As well as you do, I am sure."

A warmer hand replaced the clinical touch on Tull's shoulder and a figure of smaller build than the elder took his place.

"I am Gloria Bea Greer. I've known the countess more spans than you've seen, cub; though I have learned plenty about you too. You might keep the heart I've heard her claim that you have—again and again—but I expect you to also keep from looking upon her."

Tull bristled with offense and sneered at the knowledge she claimed to *keep*.

TULL & EBBE

"Will you let me wash your face?"

"All seven lines function at optimal flow."

"You don't want to scar, do you?"

He failed at his test. The technician's mention of lines turned the Guardian's head toward the abdominal disc worn by all who entered the mending chambers. In response, Gloria turned him from the source of the room's copper light.

"How she mends is not meant for you, just as what she lets you see when she's not in my care is not meant for me. Here, you abide by my rule."

His right eye produced humble tears, and he offered an obedient nod in response. "I want only to see her well again."

"Then let these souls who obey my word uphold their purpose. You've upheld yours! Simmer now. We'll see to her. Let us see to your—"

Tull dodged her nearness. "I won't leave her side lest my fellows relieve me."

"I can tell you from which side of your tree that stubbornness takes root." She matched his unpolished stare till a pane of glass outside the room cracked and Ligurus whinnied. Then, Gloria sighed and hanged her head in defeat. "Just when I might have talked him unto mending."

"Open the door."

"No."

"I must defend her."

"What good can you do when you cannot stand any straighter than you are?"

Another pane shattered and provoked Ligurus to stomp his hoof. Tull circled, no longer sure where the door stood, and backed toward the source of light that marked Sondrea's chamber.

"Ole hyvä, Yah, oi'ea kättäni."

A second hoof strike came as he bumped the glass tube that comprised the body of the mending chamber.

"Varo näi'etoa si'ela."

He mopped the sweat from his new face as the seal on the inner room's door broke and the fog flowed inward.

"Ole hyvä, Yah, syntani'e aenti'eksi."

Ligurus struck his hoofs, as if to alert the Guardian, and Tull felt his heart and temples pound. Lest he pace his heart, he would lose the light afore he learned the lay of the room. Then he could help none of them.

TULL & EBBE

"Esi'el halua koorjata. Hänen puole staan kaersi'ene kui'en mörkete."

To remain alert, he took the knife from the sheath on his boot, which kept sharp the pencil he stowed there, and pointed the blade toward the prompts of hoofs.

"Kaennä sydi'emaesa minua köhti häntae."

Sondrea raised her head and opened her eyes from within her chamber. What she saw made her push away from the tube, but as she screamed Tull's name, the pain of lifting her arms and agitating the wound made her lose consciousness.

"Pranoa hoaentä."

Then, as a fire reacts to the taste of fuel, so an unseen presence reacted to the threat. Cold vapor hissed unto steam as a lake of purple-tinged flame rolled across the floor between the bloodied, blinded Guardian and the uncoiling fog. As light shines and chases away the dark, the flame withered the vapor. In an instant, the threat fell to a residue of grit and the fog around Ligurus retreated.

Tull listened and kept his knife aimed. None of his lament mingled with his physical wounds even as he repeated his prayer. From the fire, a figure took shape and cooled till the eyes of the Second Creation no longer witnessed the arms that consoled the tattered Jacobian. A voice that spoke to the unstifled soul heard the groaning of the defeated heart. In the consumption of the pain, the rejection, and the fear, a Minister of purpose different from Enke'loi's offered comfort.

"You are slow to learn, cousin, but so loved! Rest. I will stand the watch over you now as so oft I must."

Tull surrendered to the pain and slumped as he lost the light. Si'an-Drosa'ahn, who watched over Tull since he took his first breath, swelled with delight and filled the place with warmth that matched the light from Sondrea's chamber as he consoled the Guardian. Gloria Bea Greer muttered over the scorn she would suffer when Sondrea next saw the new face of the stubborn and devoted Jacobian she adored; a matter for another comforter.

Still, the greatest ramifications awaited.

Stricken & Scuffed

An Interim

The 11th Peak beneath the Moon of the Mother's Song

The 107th Winter Season of the Accession

In the Care of the Helper, who keeps souls from fruitless wandering.

On the No. 9 Steam Tram

Having departed Monkshood Station.

In passage toward the Carpenter Territory.

On the morn that followed the mayhem at Ebbe Demesne, Sondrea Ebbe Conliffe faced an assortment of broadcasters, chroniclers, law-writers, and Reformers who towed alms ranging from well wishes to prayers to an uncounted number of invasive concerns. This distinguished lot spoke of concern, yet kept the countess from the rest that they stacked their concerns upon. She proved their better and never complained. In point of fact, she offered more hope for the hearts of the territories than they—or the judges and interests who employed them—sought.

~

"Does the count remain on Ebbe Demesne, Countess? Is he well?"

"I thank you, yes. He is"—she remained giving and clever even in well-chosen words—"himself."

"Will we see him again?"

TULL & EBBE

She looked upon a chronicler younger than her. "Have you seen him afore?"

"Will you speak to us of the disappointments in our Guardians? Will you speak to us of what unraveled them?"

"I am in no way their judge."

"Will you speak to us of your trust in them now after they failed you?"

"I am in no way failed."

"Forgive us, Countess, but have you not come from a chamber house?"

"A consequence of my own choices and, I will attest evermore, the truest of sacrifices from our Guardians."

"But your family's home—"

"Have you spoken with Judge Mumus about—"

"Have you seen Guardian Tull?"

"I am reminded of a matter, heard on the heavy voices of our noble Guardians, of terrors that afflict the souls whose names go unspoken amid this circle. I am reminded how each of our Guardians desired that they might share their vast insight and their considerable ability to make safe again those forgotten souls."

"But, Countess, they destroyed your family home."

"I cannot remember your presence on Ebbe Demesne, Chronicler McGee. We saw not a single face of concern like any of yours. How I cannot imagine the workings of unlearned minds that turn against those who sacrifice for us. Perchance, do those who offer you alms seek to arouse doubt in our Guardians?"

Another arose in defense of she whom Sondrea challenged. "Countess, has your benefaction of Guardian Tull not given him—"

Her laughter drifted against the wind. "Your fascination toward my reach is as limited as the reach that fascinates you, Broadcaster Irvin."

"Were the Guardians in mending on Ebbe Demesne?"

"Where might you mend?" Their silence responded. "I imagine that, with some effort, any soul in this setting might learn where

TULL & EBBE

you go in retreat. If we believe that all share equal reverence, ought we not approach every detail of how you spend your time with the fervor you show toward our Guardians?

"I will speak to the heart of those Guardians whose hearts toward us do not cease. My father and my dutiful family have agreed that in times such as these, where a soul identifies a need, we have a responsibility to ease the suffering of those who must live out their purposes amid such fear and aching. My father, the count, and my brother, the Shelby Territory's advocate, have indicated to me their intent to provide abundant alms—alms from the Conliffe heritage—to their afflicted brothers and sisters in the southern territories."

"Well"—one interrupted—"we have heard no such—"

"And who ought to have an ear for their voices? A daughter and a sibling? Or a chronicler?"

Though she struck back at the family who manipulated and plotted against her, as much as those who upheld dishonest gain, she added, "I am to blame for what befell our Guardians, for I believed our friends—these same Guardians—safe on the plot of our first Guardian and beneath the rule of my sibling-judge. Even the inspectors shied from their duties, believing their purpose unnecessary in light of our Guardians' talents. Yet, you rest fault on our Guardians?"

Their buzz sounded like the swarm of insects till a piercing voice shouted above the racket, "And what of Guardian Edmond Anson Elragadó? We are told—"

~

"Guardian. Your judges require your audience. Rise now and follow me."

Having put Ebbe Demesne behind them, and having returned to Monkshood Station at Conliffe's Landing, a new gathering of souls watched he who rose with the slowness of a weary bear. None prodded him. Those who looked upon him stepped away and spread thin their frames lest they bristle him. Such was the processional march of Harlan Bottin Vosburg, second Guardian from the Carpenter Territory, and now fourth headship of the contemporary outfit.

From forearms to fingers and knees to boots, he remained caked in mud. His filth and the mingled stench showed no regard for those who awaited his audience. Most who heard his slow step blamed the wind for the creaking of the frame of the judges' steam tramcar. Even more wondered about the bolted copper bell-shaped apparatus that he towed with straps that pulled on both shoulders and wearied his knees.

The Fabulous Guild Trio observed too. Even they proved bright enough not to rile him; not whilst he had the judges' ears and the power to sway the operations of every chief and deputy inspector across seven territories. Harlan would face the judges in shame but not without his dignity. His choices would keep safe or upend the Second Creation till such a time when the next soul—no longer an even match between Tull and Olley—claimed his authority.

When called to appear, he stood alone. He let no other join him. In this, he proved that he would lead in a different manner than Edmond; of whom, Harlan imagined, much would be spoken. He would shoulder the burden and bear the judgment of the bench whilst sheltering those he led from those who lauded authority over them. Such was the heart of this headship.

He knelt afore Mediary Gesicht and Judges Katch and Conliffe—two of whom savored the undeserved gesture—and offended each when he cut away the straps of the bell-shaped apparatus that buckled him more than their presumed reverence. When he stood, he swayed as if he felt lighter than remembered, but recovered better than the drunken lot who caroused out of doors and within sight of those souls on the steam tram. This same bench, and others who withheld appearance there, paid alms for their esteem to the lot who criticized Guardians and challenged countesses that they might increase their rule.

Gone were the advocates' scions and the law-writers who heard every word and ruling. No testimony and no verdict would be committed to record. When last that happened, the Guardians denied the existence of a member and how the judges' authority destroyed a settlement. In short, they sought to hide their hand in the mayhem at Ebbe Demesne. By this, Harlan understood the judges' position afore they set their attention on him.

"Remain standing, Guardian. This appearance will be kept brief."

TULL & EBBE

Harlan obeyed the word of the oft compromising Judge Marvin Elam Katch and imagined they feared the idea of having to clean mud from their furniture.

"You were informed of your responsibility to appear afore this bench this morn?"

"I was so informed."

Katch focused on the globs of mud that soiled the Guardian's bearskin coat. "And yet you appear in this manner?"

"I believe we might overlook the Guardian's appearance this once," Mediary Gesicht protested, "if we are to remain brief."

The compromising judge nodded, true to form, though his eyes never wavered.

"Many unexpected turns between this and our previous visit, Guardian Vosburg."

"As you say, Mediary."

"You might imagine that none of us expected an outcome of this consequence. I'm told"—Gesicht glanced toward the judge on his left—"that the manor is beyond rebuilding."

"The fire burned even as we traveled to make this appearance."

"Without sighting of Count Conliffe?"

"I never set eyes on him afore the blast. I had no reason to believe I might see him following."

"And you've no explanation of what caused the fire?"

"Partakers. The Infested. The Taotáva. Or, his erratic magick."

Katch scoffed. "Your purpose is to put down such nuisances, Guardian."

"I thank you for reminding me of my purpose. As I dealt with other matters that kept me away from the manor, I cannot—"

"What matters?"

Harlan had not, by then, spoken the words.

A sneer twisted Katch's face. "He speaks of Elragadó."

"Rather"—he swayed for reasons other than weariness—"I do not have the words to speak of him."

"Shame. Shame was his fruit."

Harlan sighed and lost a portion of his stature.

Gesicht looked upon Katch in disbelief of his cantankerousness and then once more upon Harlan. "Who found Guardian Elragadó?"

"Guardian Arthur George Green."

TULL & EBBE

"The Guardian described how he found Elragadó soulless with a blade near hand"—Gesicht learned afore—"and his throat cut?"

"As you say."

"The images of tracks around Elragadó... I see one distinct boot and... a shape I cannot define."

"They were all about the plot." Harlan glanced toward Judge Conliffe. "But we found no soul who would tell us of their root."

Gesicht followed Harlan's gaze but refrained from looking upon the soul who kept the family's secrets.

Katch then spoke with a gust, "You followed these tracks? They led to nowhere?"

"They led to a wall of Ebbe Demesne."

"A wall?"

"An exterior wall of the manor with no door and no window."

"And there they stopped?"

"Yes."

"An odd turn, Guardian Vosburg."

"As you say, Mediary. Will I be permitted to see to Edmond's remains?"

"The Larson Territory claims Elragadó's worth"—Edmond's judge, Katch, spoke with the regard shown toward stock and crops—"less what goods he kept in travel. Those shall revert to his scion."

Harlan worried so much over the current roster that he had not even added a scion unto the fold of his responsibilities.

"Elragadó and Ganix are to tow the blame for the destruction of Ebbe Demesne and the injuries to Mumus' bride; as is appropriate due their seniority. Better to let the territories believe the disappointments end with them."

The third judge, who stirred beneath the darkness that masked his identity, drew the eye of Katch. Without a word shared between them, the judge who spoke added to the severity of his ruling.

"Though... the lot of you... will feel the weight of this bench upon you these next thirteen moons and unto the thaw of another winter. This will not be a gentle season for you, Guardian Vosburg, but you Carpenterians abide, and we will endorse your headship of this... disappointing... lot for we act in your interest."

Harlan's eyes bore an agitated flare as he set his stare upon Katch. "In what way?"

TULL & EBBE

"The reports we've observed prove you are unsettled. From our faultless concern for what you might do, if led by your wit alone, this bench must restrain you."

Restrained. Jailed. Kept. Caged. "And, of those who rose against us?"

"They are no—"

"The Shelbians have earned a rest from reckless and disobedient Guardians." At last, the third seated judge spoke with the arrogant lilt of the Shelbian tongue and the rage of vile insult.

Harlan remained bristled, even as he offered a bow of his head; a show of support for the false compassion that Conliffe heaped upon his rotted territory. "All the while, two of my boys remain uncounted."

"Guardians are trained to survive worse obstacles than abandonment by their fellows." The callous Shelbian needled; lest he reveal his hand against those already afflicted. "Are they not?"

"Which two?" Judge Katch sounded anxious for his own well-being.

"Gera and Tull."

"Guardian Tull . . ." If cadence equaled blasphemy, then the Squires ought to have rained fire upon Conliffe. "The culprit of this travesty!"

"How can that be, Judge, when members of this faultless bench excluded the Jacobian? Your own laws have stated that no Guardian can shoulder the blame once a member of the bench excuses them—afore, amid, or in aftershock—from their purpose."

A gleam caught in Gesicht's eye that drew the eye toward his amused grin. "I remember this same law."

"You say you traveled to Ebbe Demesne"—Katch applied a condescending tone upon the name—"Mediary Gesicht. What say you of this bench's concern?"

His face turned as unremarkable as leftover pudding till he forced out his lower lip and shook his head in denial. "I cannot say that I set eyes upon Guardian Tull on Ebbe Demesne; though, I believe we might have passed him whilst riding horses on the surrounding terrane."

"You believe?"

"I have heard how oft he is mistaken for Guardian Falk; my fellow Archibaldian. Perchance other souls, though wise and though keen, made the same simple mistake."

Harlan let his beard hide his smile even as the sit-in for Cyril Adair Mumus looked to him for support.

TULL & EBBE

"Am I misinformed, Guardian?"

"You are not, Mediary. He indeed confuses the eye of many."

Katch scoffed, not out of hard-heartedness but because he proved wise to their scheme. He then offered a wry barb. "A confusion that I'm told will wither now and never again be repeated."

"You speak of the wounds he suffered to his face?" Harlan ratcheted his waist with a deep breath. "Yes. This is further proof of the dangers that congregate so near to the Behemót Woods."

"And what of Gera?" Gesicht showed true concern. "I'm told he mended from the attack that cost Guardian Ganix his—"

"Head?" Katch smirked. "Yes. What of the Creightonian?"

"I've learned nothing more of him except that he went missing amid the confusion. Neither have our scions nor his abettor heard from him. We will find him."

"Do take better care of your new Guardian, as I believe he might help to remind those who remain of their purpose." Katch threw another barb and then raised his voice. "Bring us the Larsonite!"

Advocate Scion Madár reappeared on Judge Katch's command, for Katch kept no scion, as pompous as afore, and more offended by the appearance of Harlan. Not even the filth-covered Carpenterian recognized the smooth-faced soul who followed Madár and who served as Edmond's scion, for the Guardian who fell tucked away his successor from the whole outfit. Aged as long as Asham, give or take two seasons, he towed a dim semblance of Olley's conceit, the agitated woundedness that hid in Tull's eyes, the suspicion that George regretted, and none of his predecessor's vanity. Elsewise, nothing of him seemed notable.

"Scion Robbie Rudat Pine, you are now recognized by this bench and your judge as second Guardian of the Larson Territory." Judge Katch peered across the cut lenses of his eyeglasses. "Serve us well till your end, Guardian."

"I thank you for the opportunity, Advocate. I am certain that I will contribute much to the outfit and bring other souls to see your wise counsel."

"Yes, well, we are certain to have time to consider that."

Judge Conliffe moved them along with a stern grasp of authority. "You will be assigned your abettor by this bench upon completion of your third complete moon. Till such time, you will rely on your training and our determination of your purpose."

"A way I prefer, Honored Soul."

TULL & EBBE

Harlan shook his head. He had misjudged the faintness of Pine's conceit. The steam bowels whistled as they neared the next station. He inhaled his complaint as he recognized that the judges held no interest in recognizing the merits of those they sought only to punish. He set his heels against the steady, bell-shaped apparatus behind him and braced his knees and hips as their speed of travel waned.

"Have you any alms for us, Guardian Vosburg? Any show of appreciation for the bench that endorses your ascent and rewards you this eager Larsonite?"

"Guardians Ganix and Elragadó were due alms from the previous moon's service."

Harlan raised his brow and felt the mud on his hands crack as instinct formed fists against Conliffe's tone.

"I claim those, in full portion, in the name of the Shelby and Larson territories."

"By your rule, Honored Souls." Harlan believed them adjourned and turned toward Pine to let him lead their exit because Katch set aside his eyeglasses and collected his journals as the steam tram reached a full stop.

"And"—Conliffe further needled—"what of the seat of the Archibald Territory?"

Gesicht shifted in his actual seat and waved off the implication. "The Archibald Territory remains prosperous enough. We do not require—"

"Nonsense. Such is Guardian Vosburg's honor."

"My honor?" A laugh like a lobbing rattle stirred in his throat but never reached his lips. "My honor."

"We recognize your good work, Guardian. We do not diminish that; though, Guardian Pine proves favored to lead your outfit." Such a barb rivaled the suggestion that Asham proved a better Guardian than Olley. Conliffe sought to provoke; which was his true hope for ascent to the bench since his beginnings. "Lest you believe the inspectors will welcome you without this bench's endorsement."

Gesicht spoke up. "Guardian Vosburg, you were once a law-writer. This seat would benefit from the perspectives of a soul who served two honorable capacities. Perchance a journal filled by your hand might serve as your alms?"

"Forgive me, Mediary, but such writings fall well beneath this bench." He drew a breath and coughed like the thunder. "I am told of your interest in the . . . pieces . . . of our foes."

The barb against Gesicht seemed strange, though Harlan spoke in truth and from the wealth he learned from his three most-trusted fellow Guardians. He spread his hips and crouched toward the bell-shaped apparatus and wrapped the straps around forearms that rivaled the biceps of every soul in the tramcar with him. His face turned red and his teeth showed as he hoisted the apparatus then swung till the container landed upon the sturdy bench with a force that shook loose the dust between the joints.

"Let this serve as my alms to you and to a territory whose fondness for expositions is unrivaled."

The three judges cowered in silence with agape mouths and wrinkled brows.

"A trinket I dug up for this very occasion."

Still the trio—plus Madár and Pine—remained aback. So, Harlan set his muddied hands against the riveted crown of the copper apparatus and plucked the cap loose like a cork from a bottle.

"Do forgive if I cannot lift the contents twice from moonrise to moonrise. Better you request help from Guardian Tull in that regard."

As he dusted his hands and stepped away, Harlan invited Gesicht, who rose and peeked at the offering. Inside, packed in snow, sat the removed head of Noeu; whose cheeks still bore the glass pieces Tull set upon him. The air changed and, Harlan gauged, an equal portion of fascination and arousal benefitted Gesicht.

"The head of he who brought mayhem to Ebbe Demesne and to your gracious *half*-sister, Judge Conliffe."

Conliffe rose and, upon seeing Noeu's head, fell unto paleness and stumbled till his posterior found his seat on the bench. This enticed Katch, whose brokenness kept him from rising out of his chair. Even so, if rumors about the Larsonite judge proved true, he might find the gumption to wrestle Gesicht for claim on the grim alms.

"Guardian." Harlan motioned Pine toward the door.

Madár tried to block their exit in perception of his judge's offense but did not impress Harlan as much as he intimidated Pine.

"Afore you go," called out the oppressive, hand-wringing Shelbian advocate whom Madár served, "there is the matter regarding your activity in my territory."

Harlan forced his composure and faced those agitators whom he also agitated.

"To be certain, from this time onward, till this bench declares elsewise, neither Guardian, nor their scion, nor their abettor shall enter the Shelby Territory in any capacity of purpose or service except in direct violation of our ruling authority."

"And, if I might inquire on her behalf, how is Guardian Ozul to serve her fellow Shelbians by her purpose?"

"She will operate from a station along the Jacoby-Shelby border. She is not to trespass, nor is she to see her familial home for the remainder of her service."

Conliffe proved himself the monster that Sondrea claimed and responded now against his half-sibling's meddling and at the expense of one of his daughters. "Because you stuck your nose in my affairs, I will sink my heel against your neck through those who serve you."

Harlan stood as rigid as a statue, minus the trembling of rage.

"The Shelby Territory now banishes all interference from you and your outfit—in scope or form—and will retaliate with boundless fervor and this bench's full endorsement." Judge Conliffe held fire in his eyes and a well-pleased, albeit menacing, sneer on his face. "No longer will Nelson James Tull enjoy the regard of this bench that rules by my order that his purpose be halted with his offenses to be declared throughout the territories—and to his intended shame—as this faultless bench sees fit. Perry Wallace Rudat will resume in his stead with full authority and serve this bench as your equal by this eve's moonrise.

"And expect that I will never allow for Guardian Elragadó's name to be held in an unspotted manner. I will adorn him with shame. I will see that the territories learn how he never recovered from acts done to him—not in protest, I tell you—in the Behemót Woods, and that he sought to harm all Shelbians and Partakers and that he misled those in his charge till he corrupted them with the same poisoned spirit that saw him act as a coward till his end."

The sound of Pine's offended breath and Harlan's growl provoked a smile from the foul advocate.

"Add to this dispute, Guardian Vosburg, and this bench will see every Guardian stripped of their purpose and paraded through these territories as exemplars of our displeasure."

"Guardian Pine." A whisper-like meekness took hold of the new headship, whose reputation of old might have overturned the bench—tactile and symbolic—and made every soul who held authority over him lose control of bowel and bladder. He lost his best friend—whom *honored* souls meant to shame. He lost two Guardians—whom he was purposed to watch over and train. So, in anger's stead, he exhibited humility and patience for Pine's benefit. "We depart now."

But, Conliffe imparted an undue jab. "Keep a closer watch on *this* Larsonite."

TULL & EBBE

Pine received the first scuff mark to his boot when he collided with his stationary and insulted headship. Harlan's ears sank behind his shoulders and with an elbow he batted Pine aside when he approached the bench with a bear's menace till even Conliffe appeared fearful. "When you tire of oppressing those Shelbians whom you cannot rape and have exhausted your daughter in her stained bed, I invite you to find me again. Then we will see who parades whom in their shame."

"Guardian Vosburg . . ." Gesicht spoke as a sort of friend.

"As for that boy whom you, your rotted father, and your half-sister's twisted husband prove so eager to break, I tell you he possesses more spine than the whole of this bench. The Ice Clans who turned from corrupt laws met and determined that Tull has the spirit of the dove upon him." His eyes radiated with tears as he looked Conliffe over. "Only the serpent despises the dove."

Harlan's smile never gleamed so much afore and he captivated Gesicht, who was brushed aside by the hand of curious Katch for blocking the view.

"My heels have crushed the necks of many serpents and will again."

His growl-like whisper went undeciphered by newcomer Pine but whatever words he spoke proved terrifying, for Judge Katch and Mediary Gesicht scurried from their seats. Even the way he prodded the thick-cut slab of snakewood that comprised the tactile bench produced a haunted echo through the chamber; rather like standing inside a resonating bell.

"If you believe, Honored Souls, that other headships of this outfit proved too defiant, I tell you I will make you crave their many eves of governance afore I embrace my end." He then wagged a finger at Gesicht. "Be not like these souls, for I have no dispute with you."

After this, no other spoke. Harlan turned from those who judged him and set a steering hand upon Pine. The pristine-but-for-a-single-scuff new Guardian stepped around Scion Madár and led as the gruff Carpenterian directed him. Neither did Pine look back on their judges; though he would not soon forget his first visit to their chambers.

They ended their unrecorded appearance, of which no offense against Harlan stood, and found the door to keep from spending further time aboard. Harlan nudged the new Larsonite toward an unnamed station at a stop he did not recognize. This was a vulnerability, for Edmond kept him sheltered to the point of uselessness outside their shared territory.

TULL & EBBE

The face of Guardian Arthur George Green proved a beacon of familiarity, though he seemed opposed to stepping away from his collection of horses. Once Harlan's feet met the terrane and his ear departed from the divisive spirits of travelers and judges, the new headship jostled Pine with a hearty pat to his shoulder. No words followed. He then separated Edmond's belongings from the rest whilst he remembered every word spoken against them by Judges Katch and Conliffe, Mediary Gesicht, and Scion Madár with complete accuracy; a feat which made him a most excellent law-writer.

When he sorted not Edmond's alone but also his possessions, he stood aware that neither George nor Pine stirred or spoke. He then counted that he recounted every word aloud. "Such were the words of our judges."

"I believe Olley will regret that he was not present to hear you speak in such ways toward the Shelbian."

"As you say, George!" Harlan howled with laughter and brushed the mud from his hand afore he patted the Westonian's shoulder. Once he saw that brilliant smile, he looked toward Pine's forgettable visage. He then noticed a dusting of a handprint that matched his own and sullied the new Guardian's shoulder. He brushed away the mark with some apology.

"What are your words now?"

In the same manner that Edmond inducted Tull, Olley, George, Asham, and Nita into the outfit, his successor answered, "'We mend, we train, we guard, and we make proud He who made us. If even the breath behind my rules is too difficult for the soul He gave you to bear, I'll give you leave.'"

George looked upon Pine, who did not budge.

"Well answered, Guardian."

"What of Asham? Our friend remains there."

"Hear me, Guardians. Asham has till the last eve that we mourn Edmond—as some, but not all, will mourn him—to find his way from the Shelbians' borders. If he fails, he was not fit to guard. We cannot return for him."

"They"—Pine withdrew his generalization—"Our judges offered no regard for Edmond's sickness."

"Why should they?"

"Judge Katch also—"

"Even unto his end, Edmond refused to address his condition."

TULL & EBBE

Not unlike Tull's ailments, another form of illness afflicted Larsonites more oft than not. By their end, which occurred most by their own hand, they resorted to wicked forms of cruelty, self-mutilation, undue hatred, and a coldness toward hope and forgiveness. Edmond—proud and vain in all his ways—proved coldest toward such suffering, and even toward those who shared his affliction.

"Judge Katch observed his own mother's affliction and bears fresh markings beneath the fingernails that tell of his suffering."

"Larsonites, as you can tell, George, believe the sickness flows upon them from the wickedness that seeps out of the Shelby Territory above their plots." Harlan heard the same tales. "The poison of Shelbian foulness."

Pine nodded in belief. "There is a Reformer. A woman. She keeps an outpost and sees to those who seek help."

"Sister Lois Westmore."

George shivered at the name and caught Pine's eye.

"Edmond was driven from her Corban Outpost, what, George, five—"

"Six."

"Six moons back." He looked over Pine's placidness. "If you are to continue onward with us, you must come to accept the flaw in our characters. Though we traveled with Edmond, though I counted him as my friend, I will not speak against the truth of his virtues or his disgraces."

"I listen, benefactor."

"You will hear much as we go to bury Edmond in a place where he wished his body to rest."

"The three of us and no others?"

Harlan leaned on Cuss. "Your fellow Guardians mend. Even if they were ordered, I do not believe Falk—who renounced Edmond—nor Ozul—who now suffers the shame of banishment—would offer alms of respect for our fallen friend."

"Who tells this to Nelson?"

"He mends at the Scurlock Chamber House."

Tull's friends looked toward Pine.

"All Jacobians tell that Scurlock is the safest of all chamber houses in their territory"—afore any agreed, Pine added—"and sits nearest to the Shelby Territory. Even if he crawled, he would reach their door afore any other in his territory."

TULL & EBBE

"You have an urge to defend him, George? Remember that the Jacobians are a stubborn lot, but they are a noble lot. If any soul comes to harm their Guardian, the breadth of the territory will defend him. His greater obstacle is that he, too, is stubborn and noble."

Pine observed how both laughed. "Meaning?"

"Mightn't he prove too stubborn and too noble to let them defend him?"

"Our friend would lead harm away from others in his mending's stead."

Harlan mounted Cuss with an effortlessness that none of the absent Guardians would believe. Even mild George applauded. Pine mounted Edmond's Gallant, but George held the reins and Harlan kept a hand atop their fallen headship's palled remains.

"I will pass along the name of the chamber house to Olley."

"He will appreciate as much." Harlan chuckled. "Give the same to Ozul."

"He will not appreciate that."

"No, I suspect not." Harlan laughed again. "Have you any misgivings afore we get, sapling?"

"How did that creature's head prove so burdensome?"

Harlan looked toward George, who led them toward the spot where they would leave Edmond. Afore he answered, a chirp of his display plate interrupted. With a motion of his hand, he sent the new Guardian after George and set his focus upon the message he received.

"I BELIEVE YOU CONVINCED THEM WITHOUT DRAWING ATTENTION TO MY CAUSE. I THANK YOU, GUARDIAN, AND STILL INVITE A TIME WHEN WE MIGHT BANTER OVER OUR MANY LAWS."

"As do I, Mediary. First, I must see to an old friend." He then redirected his attentions toward those in his charge. "Locate active beacons and open frequency to authorized devices for Guardians Nita Naomi Ozul and Olley Hendrie Falk. Passcode: Tangle Five-Four, Six-Three Pith."

Aftershock

THIRTY-SEVEN

THE 13TH EVE BENEATH THE MOON OF THE MOTHER'S SONG
THE 107TH WINTER SEASON OF THE ACCESSION
IN THE CARE OF THE HELPER, WHO KEEPS SOULS FROM FRUITLESS WANDERING.

731 SMITHERS STREET
THE WESTON TERRITORY.
ABOVE CHRISMAN SWEETS SHOPPE.

For a soul whose first tooth proved sweet, nearness to a shoppe that specialized in candies and confections proved disastrous. For he who hid the heart's darkness behind the veil of sugary bliss, another sort of disaster visited. That soul lived unaware that another who kept his secret no longer protected his hiding place. As such, Tai'bu Kaas proved an easy foe to locate, and every word spoken of him by Edmond proved reliable.

In point of fact, he who used the Paladin moniker seemed eager to provoke discovery. Around his home and in plain sight through every window stood the relics of his past, appreciated by his eye at each turn. Beyond framed and boastful news clippings that told of the ways he frightened souls and bested Guardians rested the trinkets of victory over the isle's first four defenders. In his time, he took Zeck's dagger, King's copper pendant, Wylie's compass, and Conliffe's pocket watch; the latter of which he kept nearest to his age-sunken lounger that bore the appearance of a third-hand furnishing, as two hardback books propped upright the side missing a wooden leg.

Upon a spindled coatrack rested an aged version of the round-brimmed hat worn by Noeu when he appeared to the elder Guardians. This model, whose stained brim hid sensitive eyes from the light, rested atop a long storm coat marred by a single slice mark upon the lapel that matched Zeck's dagger. Even the solid silver knives carried by Paladin sat tarnished beneath time's breath and discolored blood. Fifty artists drew likenesses of him across three eras, but not one neighbor took notice of the evidence he flaunted.

No indication arose that any regarded or remembered him. Why would they? He was scarred and withered—well beyond the photographs kept in dust-speckled frames on faded walls. His face—his true, scarred, and withered face—brought to mind a dozen forgettable visages minus a peculiar tinge of oxidation near the bony features.

This was no great foe. Rather, he was so common that he went uncounted by those he offended. In this, he disappointed the Archibaldian who sat upon the nemesis's couch and watched him nap. Olley Hendrie Falk kept the heel of his boot against the sunken chest of he who set attackers against the fruit of Count Theodore Reaume Conliffe.

"Awake, wasted shell! Let us see what remains of the soul."

"Might I?" The disembodied voice sounded louder and clearer than Olley's.

He flicked his brow as the richness of Jacobian certainty, mingled with a lilt of Shelbian arrogance, Erorii presumption, and a dash of Archibaldian privilege, warmed the room and stirred the wrinkled soul from slumber. The visitor twisted at the waist and improved the angle by which a small projector lens pinned to the highest pocket of his leather suspenders captured his unaware host's slight frame from head to toe. The Archibaldian ensured a greeting with the leg strength to lift the unmemorable, discolored face of his host. A pair of glazed-over, dull-brass eyes peered back from the greasy pits of his sockets and reflected no light. Even when Olley held up a display plate that featured a mended and radiant countess, Tai'bu Kaas' pupils did not react.

"My father referred to you as the most baffling foe he ever confronted. He was drunk on ginger vermouth at the time and the winter was, well, as Shelbian winters are. I believe I needn't bore you with an introduction, lest you cannot recognize the soul you sought and failed to end."

"Believe what you will." His craggy voice offered no bait and no interest, as proved by an unenthused metallic sigh that made Olley's nose twitch. "I haven't a clue who you or this lout are."

"I cannot tell," Olley volunteered, "for his eyes offer no glimmer, let alone a hint at truthfulness."

"Only an Archibaldian airs his imagination—profitable or elsewise—with such confidence."

"An attack on any member of an advocate's family—or on any Guardian—invites a swift end."

"This is your notion of swiftness?" Tai'bu Kaas hissed like a kettle at the live image of Sondrea and spat upon Olley's leg.

Sondrea preempted violence. "Am I to believe your choice had little to do with my own offense?"

Olley hated to waste a good barb, but did not interrupt the countess. This much caught Paladin's attention. "You take alms from her hand, do you not, poi'kai?"

"Poi'kai." Sondrea recognized the word from the firstkind's tongue. Her father used the same word to antagonize Tull and, afore him, Cameron Lou Fenner. "My father uses that barb."

"I felt no barb."

TULL & EBBE

"Stupid or elsewise." He raised a hand to keep what little light filled the room from his eyes. "Who is your father? You keep speaking of him. Name him now."

Olley thrust at his chest, which did not give, and kept him pinned. "You'll give no further instruction to her . . . or elsewise."

"I am daughter to a magick-wielder. My father—"

The old soul laughed above her honoring of his demand. "A magick-wielder? That pompous deviant, Theo?"

Olley's face contorted in a way that even the Taotáva admired.

"Too bad you have such a weak chin. I could never have such a weak chin." He shook a hand toward the device in Olley's hand a second time. "Zeck's daughter. The doe-eyed soul he coveted. What was her name? Remind me of her name!"

"My mother's name was Maia Espe Zeck."

His head nodded with every syllable. "She was common."

Olley shifted as the hidden lump sighed in tart relief.

"Theo has sent you then. He seeks another arrangement like we shared in yester seasons? Whom does he covet this time? He must be as decrepit as the roots of the entangled forest."

"You say you shared an arrangement?"

"What? Did the buzzard pass without confession? I warned him against such magick! I warned him well!"

"Yes."

"Then, perchance, you and I might enjoy an arrangement?"

Olley felt sickened, and then sickened further.

TULL & EBBE

"Perchance. If you believe in my parentage, tell me of this arrangement. I plead."

"He paid me thirty spans' worth of alms to convince that lot of fools that we were adversaries. Zeck! King!" He motioned toward Olley with a shimmering fingertip. "You must be of Wylie's tree. He was stupid too.

"Conliffe staged every attack. He made them believe his illusions as a way to increase his reputation above theirs, to make that territory of rubes serve him"—he laughed with the steadiness of the water boiler behind his seat—"and to seduce that doe-eyed ti'etö who believed him fearless. Your Maia!"

Caught unaware, and uncertain whether she heard a truthful account or whether her father or Edmond deceived her, Sondrea relied on a soul who was not her most-trusted and beloved. "Guardian Falk . . ."

"*Falk*?" A flare of light shone behind the left iris of Tai'bu Kaas' eye. "I believed you were The Everlasting for a tick."

"He is the bow. I am the saber."

"That chin! That pride! I knew your father!"

Olley tapped at his saber. "Punishment enough, to be certain."

"The seeds of my fellows are not weak—*soft*—like my fellows were soft."

"As your seeds were soft." Olley ignored claims about his father but expressed his most-refined trait: boastfulness. "I saw Ming and Dory at their end. They are no more. Noeu is no more. You are but a withered tree deprived of fruit to spoil."

"I have no seed! Those who called me Father imagined themselves as great as me. I fed from their labor and nourished them at a pace where I remained well-fed and they remained as suckling babes! Had I not, they would have devoured me."

"I s'pose you wish us to consider you a victim in this?"

"I am no victim—but to my own Creator."

"I doubt He ever thinks of you."

TULL & EBBE

"I am not afraid of barbs. I am not the hero, but I am not the foe. I was good, and I was guilty. My path required this much from me." For the first time, he laughed—broken and pitiful, as with no losses uncounted. "Did they see their end like fools? Tell me! Call this my last request."

"They all outlived you."

With that lie told, Olley took his saber and forced the full length of the blade through Tai'bu Kaas' heart, with surprising resistance, then through the chair that kept him upright, but avoided the water boiler. Only once the chill of a departed soul filled the room did he lean toward the misshapen ear.

"I am Olley Hendrie Falk, the third Guardian from the Archibald Territory. I am the grandson of Thesp Silas Hendrie Falk, and the angry son of his angry son and a mother whose name you do not deserve to hear."

"Guardian! This was not our arrangement. And do not speak to me of laws."

"I care not about laws. I care not whether he corrupted Edmond or if your father—or mine—corrupted him. I care not if they even knew his name. More than this end, and he would say we indulged him. Less, and we would shame Nelson in his suffering."

He returned the handheld device to a leather sheath upon his leg, then pulled the saber from a lackluster foe with a sound of metal scraping metal. The vengeful Guardian who lacked proper imagination or curiosity wiped down the iron, oiled both surfaces with a vial from his belt, then buckled his prized weapon into a scabbard that ran two-thirds the length of his leg afore he took his leave from Paladin's nest. He never once offered the slightest hint of remorse nor prayer for the soul of Tai'bu Kaas, whom he took from Yah's plan.

Once out of doors and obscured by the shadow cast by the sweets shoppe, he found a long-limbed, sleek soul perched with utter casualness upon the hood of a rig that the Guardians kept for nondescript travel. Nita wriggled her fingers in greeting and tilted her head enough that her choker gleamed in the remnant of light that outlined the roof of the building he exited.

"I blame you for this, George."

Whether she coerced George for his whereabouts or proved a decent tracker, Nita offered little response whilst she gloated.

"Scion."

"*Guardian.*"

"As you say."

"As should you say."

Olley grasped her meaning. "I haven't any candies."

"I suspect Chief Inspector Fox might wonder about that when he's called to see what's been offered to his purpose"—she pointed toward Tai'bu Kaas' home—"up there."

Olley unbuckled his scabbard and strapped his beloved weapon to the pocketed seatback as if an irreplaceable soul.

Nita crossed her legs and used the momentum to swing around and set her heels upon the tire's contentious tread. "This once you might consider me as more than a Shelbian. He invited me in."

"He is prone to worrisome choices amid women."

She spun on her rump and scrambled across the hood as he rounded the high, blunt end toward the driver's seat. "Ease your stomping, hoof heels! Lest you want the sugar-widened eyes of your many supposed admirers to see you."

"I act within accordance of the laws of our judges."

"Yet, not on their approval. Nor Harlan's." She swung off the side mirror, planted her heels on the running board, and leaned back on the door. "You can agree in charming silence."

Stillness came first and then silence. She approved of his obedience with a smile as thin as the band around her throat. Aware of such expressions, he took hold of the unblocked door latch and nudged the flat slab, which shook Nita's perch and made her leap away. He then used the running board and reached across the bench seat.

"He does make worrisome choices for the sake of certain souls." The side mirror on the passenger's side reflected that she admired his backside afore she seized his overdeveloped shoulder. "We ought to keep him from such mistakes."

"I will not work against Nelson." He flicked away her hand.

"Nor will I."

He sighed in disinterest and removed his coat.

"The countess's brother has warned all Shelbians against showing kindness toward us." She seized hold of an empty sleeve and stopped his action. "This means I must change where I dwell, as must my mother, and as must Nelson's abettor."

"*Half*-brother, and, I have heard his warning." He tugged at the coat and received a slap from the cuff that she released afore he bested her.

"And I have heard of your issues with your family." Her eyes roamed as a clock pendulum whilst he wiped the sleeve as though she sullied the material. "Then you say nothing of concern for the outcast souls from your very outfit?"

"I've no rooms for rent."

"I have many beds to choose from. You needn't worry."

"I haven't an interest in knowing."

"Then are you interested to learn none have identified her?"

He forgot his preening for the chance to lay a barb. "You've your neighbor's crutch for vagueness, Shelbian."

"The rotted husk who gave our friend his new face."

Now Olley showed true interest. "With *your* trinkets."

"As you say, and as you say to the exhaustion of my ears, I *am* a Shelbian. I believe in balance. That husk grieved a soul I admire and made him bleed with what belonged to my hand. Better I see balance in making her suffer the same pain. I cannot do that lest—we—return to my territory. I am told of your uncounted resources."

"You seek alms, then?"

"I seek privileged connections. As you have many."

"Why not ask his abettor? She knows your territory!"

"Her sister serves Chief Inspector Stroud as novitiate."

Olley's eyes glistened as his mind devoured new, usable information. He then glowered when he saw the same glint in her eyes. To his posture he added arrogance, as if a buttress against their mutual regard for Tull.

"Truly! I believed you the sort of friend who might want to retaliate in his name. Others have proven me wrong afore. You're far from the first."

"If I lead you, I'll seek swift repayment, as my time proves most valuable."

"Lead? We work as one."

"I needn't lovers."

"Nor I!"

He twisted and shook the wrinkles from his coat. "Nelson is not given over to violence. What he did was for a reason you could not—"

"He loves the countess."

Olley remained silent.

"You will disappoint him if he learns of"—she pointed again toward Tai'bu Kaas' home—"will you not?"

"I prefer my chances to yours, Shelbian."

"And which of us will the whole of the Shelby Territory end first if they catch us?"

He put on his storm coat and severed the relay of the miniscule projector lens on his shoulder strap.

~

1721 Fresnel Park

The Archibald Territory.

Above the call of Sevier.

"Truly, dear niece! Which of you?"

TULL & EBBE

Sondrea selected an option to erase or replay the reel, watched thrice since the late morn's relay, and chose the latter option, as she now created a new library. Stationed between Mumus Tower and Ebbe Demesne, she set aside her confidential handheld display plate and rose to cross a terrace composed of ornamental copper bones and a composite glass skin that flexed between the heat produced by an array of anthracite kettles stationed around the terrace joists.

She heard every word spoken between her contemptuous half-brother's sly daughter and the Guardian who served the territory where she again resided. His actions against Tai'bu Kaas—justified by every measure of the laws of the judges—offered little comfort against winter's chill and Jacobian judgment. The Second Creation kept ending those members of a rare kind. Had the First Creation proven so aggressive, the scape of Sevier would look different in every way.

"You must survive, Dory. We must prove that there can be peace between us." She then laughed and rubbed the smooth skin between her brows. "O, the way you affect me, Nelson!"

She turned from the view of the port's ceaseless expositions and looked upon the forested Jacoby Territory, which sat on the immediate banks across the Loy River. Past the colorful stacked houses and local industry on Holly Landing, where the mist blanketed the terrane even afore the peak's light faded, she searched for proof of horses grazing and children playing. The air smelled of a coming storm, so her gaze traveled Desard Bridge toward Cheswell Path. This route proved most direct between Fresnel Park and the Scurlock Chamber House where her most beloved Jacobian mended without the aid of recuperative immersion.

"My deeds must prove worthy of your suffering." Her breath fell short. "If your heart is mine, I must do all—even more than seems possible—lest I fail you. I cannot come to you now, but I believe you sense that I am near to your side in imagination and affection; nearer—yes—than I ought to be. Nearer than I can prove."

A voice called from the rooms behind her. "Countess?"

She responded to the soft soul who sought her. "I stand on the terrace."

"Might I prepare a tea or get a blanket for you?"

"I thank you, no. All proves well?"

"Overseers Greer and Sówka proved receptive and agreeable—as you said—but Charles had to threaten to *wallop*—"

"Overseer Forgney."

TULL & EBBE

"As you say. Overseer Guild proved to remain in a certain *Chief Inspector Guild* mood. He will meet with no outsiders now."

Sondrea drew a breath that made the nearest kettle flame stagger. "He and Katch will align. Gwilkoava might join them. Paiva may elect to become their sympathizer."

"I heard tales that the abettor—Koslowski—was counted with the mourners who stood along the roadway in mourning of Guardian Elragadó. Perchance she might serve as a fellow in the Shelby Territory?"

"Her bravery makes her a target. Better she flees from there."

"Overseer Hamer proved most interested in my presentation of alms in your name. I've not met a more interested soul in some time, I can tell you."

"I told you."

"Shall I set an appointment?"

"Let him call on us." Her gaze searched the sky-fires as the richness of color and wonder deepened with the eve's arrival, though she cast another look in the direction of Cheswell Path. "I've other travels in mind for you, dear."

"As you say, Countess."

"For a time, I believe I ought to use the title of Overseer."

She witnessed the agreeable nod of her new succorer's head, though she did not look upon the crème-complexioned, doe-eyed soul. Still, she suspected those eyes took notice of the reel sent by way of Guardian Falk. Whilst those contents more than suggested that her father dusted off the old ruse that he used upon her mother, she felt certain that his scheme had not yet been shown the light. Till such a time, better that she distanced her deeds from Ebbe Demesne and the count.

"The mourners gather soon."

"Charles and I would be honored to stand with you."

Sondrea spoke for her own heart. "For Nelson's sake."

THIRTY-EIGHT

The 14th Morn beneath the Moon of the Mother's Song
The 107th Winter Season of the Accession
In the Care of the Helper, who keeps souls from fruitless wandering.

158 Cheswell Path
The Scurlock Chamber House.
30 parasang west of the Jacoby-Shelby border.

In a decree which cited recklessness, destruction of Shelbian properties, threats against a charitable and dignified Shelbian that came from a tarnished abettor, and Harlan's vileness toward the bench, Judge Dale Marius Conliffe declared his interruption of Tull's purpose too gentle a punishment, but a rebuke that tested his will as a soul who feared the violent Jacobian as much as he loved all Shelbians. The territories believed Tull at fault for the escape of Dory Orlean Sevilla, the burning of Ebbe Demesne, and the emotional scarring of frail Sondrea Ebbe Conliffe, herself a victim of Tull's disobedience toward the bench. Edmond shouldered posthumous blame for Ganix's end and his inability to corral Tull. Hence, whilst Conliffe increased his standing with the Shelbians, the loathed and disobedient Jacobian recovered beyond the loss of his headship and the damage his face sustained.

His refusal to enter a mending chamber cost him. Even his caretaker scoffed at his reasons and called him a fool, in kinder language. None would confuse him for Olley again. From reports, his actions benefitted the countess, though her half-brother declared her too shaken to be taken at her word, thereby undoing her attempt to jar her sibling and their father from the coveted wealth she volunteered to the hurting. Olley's criticism of the Jacobian tenderness notwithstanding, not even he afflicted Conliffe's harshness.

TULL & EBBE

Three lacerations, now sealed with frankincense gum, changed the shape of Tull's face and hairline. His crown, forehead, a portion of his upper lip, and the bridge of his nose bore the marks of ceramic talons. Even if their purposes never collided a second time, he would wear the marks of his Infested attacker till Yah called him home. His left iris, which remained closed and shielded, bore a wound mingled with an assurance that his vision ought to return, though a slighter measure than afore.

Sondrea's half-brother never acknowledged such wounds, for frailty created sympathizers. He recreated facts to construct a trespass upon Ebbe Demesne by the Guardians. All mention of the original orders was withheld too. The Guardians, by Conliffe's pen, trespassed and terrorized the magick-wielder he called father. That same pen supposed Edmond's bias against the Shelbians permitted their offensive abuse of authority; authority that the advocate insisted the bench redetermine afore the thaw.

The outfit stepped on corrupted toes and the corrupt sought to humiliate the secondkind's heroes in the most public forum with the might of the law as their shield. All because they—Tull—supported the count's fairer fruit. To assuage the Jacobian's many offenses, Conliffe fined him the precise sum of one spans' alms; upon which a charitable soul hoped choked and constipated judge and magick-wielder.

Chief Inspector Rusty Waltman Guild and his two prized deputies declared the law and seized Tull's account with utmost swiftness and authority—whilst the Guardian mended beneath complete sedation. They also restricted the bride of Cyril Adair Mumus from obtaining an audience to argue with her cruel half-sibling. As they oft proved, the judges twisted the truth into a weapon that allowed them to rule with power as bloated as the steam bowels on their luxurious tramcar.

As Reformers wept and Believers scurried from the Shelby Territory, inspired Partakers called for the confiscation of wealth and lands from all who served the Triune. With no Guardians to frighten them, their lust for appeasement, excess, and punishment swelled. Some Shelbians called for the disbandment of the outfit. Their Jacobian and Carpenterian neighbors bristled in fear of reprisal and, though they did not betray their Guardians, they did not defend them with reverence either.

When the disgraced Guardian from the Jacoby Territory awoke, he found no arrestors at the foot of his bed. Rather, an abundance of alms and gifts of affection accumulated as word of his suffering spread through those territories that still welcomed the protection that he offered Sondrea, as much as they too shunned

Conliffe's deceit. The strangeness of affection troubled him, as much as the many women who sent the Guardians unmerited gifts that kept him now from self-pity.

Amid handmade wares, pressed flowers, locks of hair, spices, confections, and perfumed trinkets sat a slender, crème-colored box adorned with the blank face of a woman drawn by another's hand. Though rose-hued hair flowed from the right side, the other proved as clean as her watercolor-based jaw and reminded the Guardian of his abettor. He reached for this gift first, but his muddled depth perception bested him, and he knocked over a sachet of Jacobian butter candies in success's stead. The commotion toppled two cards of mourning; the most lavish of which settled with the machine-imprinted message turned toward his eye.

UNCLE TELLS ME I OUGHT TO THANK YOU FOR SAVING MOTHER,
SCARECROW.

"I must've gotten swatted worse than I believed." His voice escaped him as he seized the box, turned over the lid, and found a handwritten message in the same shade as the drawn woman's hair.

May you find the kindness to forgive your shamed abettor. —V.

"I find nothing between us to forgive, my trusted abettor."

Even so, the gift made him curious as to how the package found him. Many accused him of deep slumber, but he doubted he would have slept through a visit. An impression of her lips upon his crown silenced doubt. He plucked a butter candy with his teeth on his return to rest, then held up a black relay disc wrapped in a scrap of silken fabric. The scent of incense on the threads made him smile.

"I know that about you now." He found beside his leg a current-model handheld display plate and set the disc in a recess along the side.

"Hello, boy."

Tull's unmarred eye brimmed with tears as his jaw clenched.

TULL & EBBE

"From the moment we set foot in this profane territory, I have felt Yah's immovable hand upon my trembling shoulder. His finger prods at me. I am weak. Mourn me my three eves, but then you get on with your purpose. I've earned my rest now and I run to that place where I may lay my head evermore.

"Whatever hold our Creator has on you, I do believe I can count on you to carry on the work we've started. I have failed my purpose. Harlan affords me a blind eye, but I know of this cursed place. I know of what you suffered here. Forgive me—I loved she who took you off the countess's breast above all others.

"I believed her lost. I believed her ended when the countess suffered injury to her leg. She was a soul I could not have; a pain you share with me. I speak of she whom our judges had stricken from our annals. Your countess knows her name. I oft believed she ended her for the pain she caused you both. Then my love returned.

"I warn you against faces believed familiar and souls lost from our count, for somehow, some find another path back to us. I am compromised. Better you discover me afore I unravel; but do forgive me for setting such a burden upon you. I do this so you do not become compromised too. I ask not to be remembered, nor forgiven; rather, guard this outfit well.

"Tai'bu Kaas is not Taotáva. He is Seko'tae. Blood like his flows in the veins of those you trust. I tell you this because you've never let me down. Those who serve him have been a thorn in the flesh of the secondkind—and your tree—since the First Creation upended us. No joy comes from compromise. And, if you allow—"

"Edmond, I must"—Ganix's interruption met reciprocal pause when he saw the recorder in his headship's company—"Won't you turn that vile gadget off? I must speak with you!"

A smirk reshaped Edmond's face, then he groaned as he covered the device and stopped the relay.

There ended the last admission of Edmond Anson Elragadó, and the final interaction between two more of Tull's lost elders.

TULL & EBBE

"For you both, I will mourn more than three eves. And, I will celebrate your graciousness, Abettor Koslowski. But, I cannot see she who took me from Ebbe Demesne, my headship. Guide my mind, Yah . . . let me see that face again."

Perchance in restlessness, he counted those who lifted his spirit; which oft improved the workings of his memory. The absence of his fellows—suspended or elsewise—suggested they sought a purpose not meant for the scope of attention he now towed. Perry would be in no mood to talk to him. Likewise, he could not call upon Olley's cousin, Ginger Faye, lest he hint that she worked against the judges on the outfit's behalf. His judge's brother, Larnelle Simon Bliss, offered plenty about the Light; but he and the other Reformers never shared without rebuke.

Carl Alvin Grover wore an unseen tether to his benefactor: Chief Inspector Foster Lyle Stroud. Barbara Adal Snow Dove wore a well-seen tether to her straying husband. His former abettor, Rudolph Arnold Davidson, had kin in the Shelby territory, and Curer Miren Jane Fenner kept too near to her father to rustle amid the aftershock. So, he let his hope travel further east, away from those tied to authority and title, toward those he ought to have shielded in gloom's stead.

In two ticks of the onscreen clock, Jules answered. Her expectant eyes swollen from sleeplessness and emotion roamed from jagged wound to jagged wound. Each time, her posture collapsed, and her breaths proved anguished. Tull set his eye on the ribbon of light affixed to the edge of her pearl-hued crown and awaited her voice. Her lips turned inward. This marked the longest she withheld her greeting in seven winters' time.

"I believe I asked the wrong soul the difference between purple and pearl."

Jules erupted with tears and unrepentant sobbing. Her way, above all other souls, was gentle.

"J. J., don't—"

"Jules, my dove, are you"—Francine entered the view of the lens and what she observed on the family's display plate stopped her—"Nelson? Oooo,"—her eyes too gleamed—"Nelson."

He shut his unmarred eye rather than see the pity upon her face.

"Vic! Nelson has—"

"Nelson?"

TULL & EBBE

If the Guardian heard his given name as many times that winter as he heard in recent moonsets, he would prove weary. He wanted to speak but emotion calmed him, and he turned till his wounds no longer mingled with their attention.

"Say!" Vic spoke with a slow, practiced tongue. "No need for shyness with this lot. We aren't fancy. How bad off are you?"

"I cannot name many places that'll delight in the sight of me for a time."

"Well, we'll just have to come to you then," Francine offered, and rallied her family. "Will we not? These two have worn the floorboards thin since the announced word of what happened."

"Now, w—w—we listen for w—wo—wor—for *news* on that scamp that marked you. Three troupes hunt for her."

"Her?" Tull had not learned that detail about his Infested attacker.

"None told you? They seek to keep her from reaching the mountains."

"I'll not let"—Francine patted Vic's chest—"join the hounds. We grieve for Edmond again this eve."

"But, not Ganix."

"Jules!"

"We don't." She looked toward the display plate's projector lens to see if Tull would scold her. When he did not, she wiped her eyes.

Tull then cited the fallen Shelbian. "'Reassure your Carpenterian dove and her father that I meant them no lasting insult. My ways are upon me and I do enjoy making scatter even the gentlest of souls.' Ganix offered those words without alms."

Vic lowered his head in remorse and his bride consoled him as each parent squeezed Jules. Francine then corralled them. "Did I not tell you that he was too lost in his ways? Still! He proved he could make an apology."

The Jacobian shrugged. "Most of all, he confessed he kept no desire to spend the rest of the moon losing his teeth out the opposite end of him."

"Nelson!"

"I lost count of souls who laughed that he met his end with his end dangled out."

"Victor!"

"I—I best get back down there! Point us in the best direction to you soon?"

"I thank you."

"W—We thank you, Guardian." Vic batted an eye at him, then kissed his daughter's crown. Their interactions soothed him as much as the pain allowed, and

Francine led away her husband so Jules could maintain a hint of privacy. "Soon, we'll see you, Nelson."

When the strain in his eye proved too great to follow their departure, he listened for the sound of the door closing behind them. "I wasn't sure you'd still be home."

"Otto granted me time away from my studies on the promise that he hears from me after you call." She shrugged rather than explain her benefactor's regard for the Jacobian. "I—I—I can't tell what's true."

"About me?"

She bit at her lip, then nodded.

"Those who prove responsible will never profess their blame."

Jules breathed too near to the device and made his eye flutter in confusion when he could not place the source of the sound. "Jules, I ask that you might forgive me if I—or any of the accounts—made you fear-filled."

"I—I—I was scared only"—her voice broke as her eyes followed his bandages—"only that you were hurt."

"I *was* hurt. Now I mend."

"Scurlock is a fine chamber house." Still, the novitiate buried her chin and mouth in her hand and pressed her fingertips against her cheek. Her eyelids concealed the brilliant amethyst hues of her irises, accented with lilts of amber, and forced another tear from between her lashes. "The countess of Ebbe Demesne is even more beautiful when she's wounded."

"The recuperative gels have that affect, though, I cannot say if she will be a countess of embers."

"Why did you not go into a tank, long spine?"

He considered her soul; rather, her heart. "My purpose was to defend her."

She hammered a plank surface with her fist. "Who defended you?"

He adored that heart. Even so, her lacking ferocity made him chuckle.

"Do not laugh at me, Nelson!"

"As you say. The Guardians"—he shook his head, but his peace-filled grin and the light in his eye never faded—"the outfit as a lot, rather, is meant to be broken. To be more puts us above our purpose and takes away from the purposes of those we defend. If I had the chance to go back and undo my burden, I would not go."

"Why?"

TULL & EBBE

He watched her tears fall. "We need you—all the secondkind—to lead brilliant and mighty purposes that we were not created to have."

She shook her head in subtle disagreement; but who would refuse such hopes?

"I was remembering my grandma." He watched with compassion as she wiped tears from her unflawed cheek. "She helped to build Holly's Landing as a soul of as many spans as you."

Jules swept back her tears, but her brow remained heavy with worry.

"Whilst Stuart Wendell Mumus commissioned with extravagance on that side of the Loy, souls on this side struggled to afford supplies. They heaped purpose upon purpose, never slowing, and went without so their blameless kin might eat. Even when they rested, they saw how Mumus boasted his wealth over them."

"Is this going to make me cry again, Nelson?"

"I tell you that he never comprehended *their* wealth. The Jacobians sold almost all they claimed; still, they came together and shared their alms, their food, even their homes, with each other. My grandma oft told that she never felt richer than she felt in that time."

"Afore she met her grandson?"

"Afore she met her grandson. Afore she held her son. She was favored amid the First Creation because of her heart toward the Second Creation."

"Favored how?"

"The Ministers showed her trees that we'd never purposed afore; roots, saps, gums, even the fruits of their vines. Because of the generosity of the Ministers, Jacobians were kept from starving and kept well. They built the port and the first settlement." Tull shrugged the matter away. "Mumus forced enough souls to sell to him later, but not afore those same Jacobians made Grandma their advocate."

"She was the first woman to be called a judge on the isle."

"Judge Juanita Gene James. *My grandma.*"

The proud lilt in his voice made her sigh.

"In that time, those who admired and befriended that fiery soul called her 'J. J.'"

Jules's eyes pooled. After spans and moons of pestering, the Guardian who kept her from her end confessed the reason he called her by that nickname. Now, the nature of her tears changed, and the dignity in her posture lifted her head and straightened her shoulders.

"I need time afore my purpose makes sense to me again."

TULL & EBBE

She nodded in uncertain agreement.

"That's not to say our tether has changed; but *I* am changed."

Her swallow showed her burden to hear him out.

"If I fail to see you for some time, don't believe me uncaring. This has naught to do with you."

"Give me your word."

"My word is yours."

"As you say. I—I—I will miss you, Nelson."

THIRTY-NINE

THE 14TH PEAK BENEATH THE MOON OF THE MOTHER'S SONG

THE 107TH WINTER SEASON OF THE ACCESSION

IN THE CARE OF THE HELPER, WHO KEEPS SOULS FROM FRUITLESS WANDERING.

<u>158 CHESWELL PATH</u>

THE SCURLOCK CHAMBER HOUSE.

WHERE A CONFINED GUARDIAN STIRS.

He who ushered Tull unto the Gyddingford Chamber House and heckled Gloria Bea Greer over unpaid utility fees crossed the Jacoby-Shelby border to further his care for the disgraced Guardian. He also provided updates on the countess, the fire at Ebbe Demesne, and the hearts of the Shelbians against the outfit's remnants. In all, Clifton Lait Keyes proved calming and decent. This explained his apologetic tone as he decided, "I am certain that the ringing will remain permanent."

Tull's many new adornments, including a high-pitched and constant ring in his left ear, changed how he sensed his surroundings. For now, he abandoned his appetite, a partial sense of smell, and the Jacobian steadiness of foothold too. All those who looked upon him spoke only of a single flaw: his choice.

"One eve in the mending chambers would have restored you in full—even better than the Triune made you."

A bruised eye void of humor, a scarred cornea, tears from a newfound sensitivity to light, a perforated upper eyelid, and a segregated brow all swam in pools of discoloration that consumed the better portion of the left side of Tull's face. Infection stayed away. There, the benefits ended. The torn flesh on his crown wept nonstop and the muscle beneath his cheek twitched. Then, the burrowing of a cold tool agitated the numbness that let him forget the heat that coursed through the flesh.

TULL & EBBE

"I haven't a remedy yet." Keyes elsewise made no sudden, jarring moves. "How do you treat your drowning sickness?"

"With locked knees and great caution."

"There are regimens . . . dare I repeat them?"

"No."

Keyes sensed Tull's agitation and exited, as did the technician who carted tools and recorded findings for the former character.

With a balancing cane to aid him till his depth perception returned, their patient let the tap of wood follow the pace that he spoke soothing words to his agitated heart. "'I must keep still.'"

George concocted better remedies than the specialists who managed Tull through grogginess and slumber. What the secondkind's physicians manipulated into powders and ampoules felt too far departed from the firstkind's instruction. So, without counsel or permission, Tull sought what remained of his wardrobe. Though his trousers were tattered and his shirt stained, he still had his trusted boots and a decent pair of suspenders.

An optometrist and local tinkerer sent Tull a gift of protective eyewear with ruby-hued lenses as gratitude for his hand in former times. Though he wore them with his bandages, he felt like a character in a film made by Olley's father or another odd thesp and stripped away the wrappings. He gathered the gifts from his abettor, the butter candies, and a vial of frankincense gum. The rest would be given to others who mended, and the personalized notes sent on to his home; lest kindnesses suffered a halt too.

He exited after too much time wasted on dressing and not falling over, avoided the obvious posts for the staff, and relied on the sturdiness of walls versus the staccato tell of a hardwood cane. Harlan proved he would not leave Tull isolated and set the Jacobian's jilted scion on a post outside the mending area. Even with a limited field of vision, the Guardian recognized the soul who served as his eventual replacement. Ingram Franklin Kemp devoted his full attention to a pleasant technician in Tull's stead. This pleased the injured soul and let him cross the adjacent corridor that led away from the pair unseen.

With his purpose halted, he faced censure from those who minded the judges' dizzying laws and uncounted whims. This was not to say he feared them. If he crossed paths with a soul who held authority there, he could do little more than pelt them with a cane. He still had his reputation, though, and that sufficed for many a soul.

"Guardian Tull?"

One fewer soul than he had hoped. Still, he approached the lesser used of the chamber house's exterior doors and relied on his refusal to acknowledge his own name as a way of dismissing the unrecognized voice. The fact that he could not recall his own scion's voice hindered him. Elsewise, his senses held as well as his legs.

"Guardian Tull!"

He muddled well. Then, the first gasp of wintry air embraced and pulled him out of doors. Aches beneath aches surfaced as a chill set in and made the wounds upon his face pull tighter. The throbbing turned him away from the wind, thus, in that direction he traveled till he found another building that shielded him, too, from the light. From the eastern side of a business that disinterested him more than his escape path, he headed in the direction of the Forbidden Sea, toward the most frequented roadway in the territory of his birth.

"I seek you, Guardian Nelson James Tull!"

Tull sighed and ceased from his next step. From behind, a dash of wooden heels mimicked the wind's briskness. He imagined this would make the next reel of announcements too. In embarrassment's stead, a woman whose scent of fine coronarium powder teased him came alongside the neighboring building with a coyness as soft as that powder, but better spent on tenderer souls.

"Rest easy, Jacobian. I've no intention of dragging you back to your mending area." She took a much-need breath and rested her short legs whilst her opulent gaze followed the line of his wounds.

"There's a meadow to the north filled with butterfly ginger."

"Yes, there is such a meadow."

He braced his shoulder against the cinnamon-hued bricks.

"Guardian Tull, I represent Countess Sondrea Ebbe Conliffe. She wishes an audience with the soul who saved her." She paused that he might look on her and place her; not that the seeing might miss any soul in such a red dress and matching coat. Her lips also matched the fabric, down to the flecks of pink along the lines of her bee-stung expression. Her green irises—hazel near the pupil—appeared jovial, and yet set upon he who froze her out with stern patience. "Do you recognize me?"

Tull's humorlessness showed even through dark lenses and swelling.

TULL & EBBE

"I make no stab"—she erupted with nervous laughter—"no, not *stab*. I'm no *japer*! To be certain! I meant that our paths crossed afore and wondered if you remembered such a time. Truly! As this is going, I fear our previous moment might have been better, for I stayed in utmost silence then."

"I remember."

She fanned her flushed cheeks and throat with both hands. Even though he withheld her name, against the secondkind's common courtesies, she moved onward in her new duties. "Will you travel with me then, Guardian, and not away?"

"I am not a Guardian at present."

Another sigh. Then a calm voice followed. "You are an example of the judges' foolishness—at present. The territories—even some of your neighboring Shelbians—still count you amid our Guardians. For this reason, I call you Guardian Tull."

He weighed her directness and counted every kind word. She was neither a Jacobian nor a Shelbian. "I will travel with you."

"I thank you! Would you prefer I stand to your left or your right?"

He tilted his head toward his right shoulder and she offered him the warmth of a sympathetic grin that ruled her out as an Archibaldian too. "I trust you'll forgive me if I look straight ahead?"

"Your field of vision decreased three-tenths on your left. The eye needs rest. I'm told you've the purest irises of any male born in the northern territories, and I don't imagine a long stay in Sevier if I cause those eyes to dim from the strain. I add, my upbringing in the shadow of well-known elders has taught me not to be offended by those who overlook me.

"This peak might've suffered ruin given I was told not to arrive without you." She hurried her step to keep alongside him but hummed a soft tune till she hemmed together her next remark. "I s'pose I ought to thank you. Imagine my surprise when I learned I accepted duties once offered to you. No regrets?"

"Least on my count of worries." He let her step first through a narrowed passageway and ducked a branch that she passed beneath upright, though she paused and lifted the branch to ensure his safe travel even as her blush flowed. "I thank you."

"I thank my tailor for insisting I take this coat! My attempt to reach so high has made me spill from my dress in what, I can assure you, would be a tremendous embarrassment to both our characters elsewise."

One response dwindled, then another formed. "I believed you worked for—"

TULL & EBBE

"We had a falling out." She laughed at the similar context of two ordeals.

He spoke no more of either spilling or falling.

"Your judge made many uncivil remarks toward his fellows over the contempt you were shown."

"My judge is Ernie Purcell Bliss."

Sondrea's new aide laughed with heartiness that Harlan might envy. "You've no awareness of the many affections you've nurtured in others. That refreshes me! Though, I tell you, my former benefactor had a similar way. He towed no clue of the many offenses he stoked in others."

A second time, and because he might have counted some of the offended as friends, he kept his remarks unspoken.

"Might I hint that you speak to your Judge Bliss and keep him from a reckless, but noble, action?"

"I believe you might."

"Now I thank you. When the countess offered to name me her new succorer, I tell you, I was surprised."

"She has a way of that."

"*She* made clear to me the fact that I was her second choice, as you turned down the offer."

"I was twelve at the time."

"But rooted in your convictions! Though, I believe we are all bettered that you did not go on to become Demolitionist Nelson James Tull either." She smiled when his mouth twisted in confession that also proved her as Sondrea's entrusted succorer.

As they reached an adjoining path, a few locals recognized him and moved aside; some even bowed their heads. Though he imagined looks of terror, they honored him with courtesy. His bright-eyed guide twisted at the waist and waved in gratitude toward them. In a way, Tull found her lightness of spirit as much a balm as the frankincense gum on his wounds, and he appreciated when she patted his arm and steadied him.

"For my first deed as succorer, I delivered a writing to *The Gierig Scribe* that the countess penned. She told of the bravery she observed on Ebbe Demesne and of her favorite Jacobian's heart. In her way, she even made sense of the wondrous."

"Mustn't have been wondrous then."

"Are you a reader?"

"Not as of late."

"You must find trusted eyes who'll read her words to you." She then proved well-informed. "Guardian Green, perchance, or that novitiate from Kanarek."

Tull spun the wooden balancing cane in his hand and set the crown against that prying soul's chin. Her grin held even as she stared up at him. With a confidence that reminded him of her new benefactor, she pushed the cane back into his hand as intended. She then smoothed the lay of her coat.

"You don't choose to be dim, do you? You believe learning of their private choices and struggles is intrusive? Have you ever expressed your regard for her? Is that also indecent?"

"The whole of this banter feels—"

She calmed him with laughter that lacked ridicule. "I meant indecent by your measure to learn the needs and the wishes of those you love. You lost your family at a young age, and that permits a tremendous margin around your detachment, but you cannot thrive alone."

"I am aware."

And, so, she settled on her point. "Her adorableness proves ever increasing, your Jules Baker Shannon. I too know a Jules Baker—Hanna Jules Baker—and a Jules Carrion Keach. What they might achieve with one-tenth of her charm!"

Jules Carrion Baker inspired fourteen names along twelve lines thus far in the secondkind's history. The first judge of the Carpenter Territory inspired as many as he intimidated. Baker shared, too, a history with Beau Itzal Zeck; not that Tull informed the voluble soul. He reasoned that her education exceeded his—for she used the word *japer*—and sought to learn what he could from her. She did not disappoint.

"I had cause to notice your Jules Baker when I visited Otto Meynell Chessy last moon on a preceptive matter. I believe she mimics you with her needling silence, but never have I seen a soul wear pearl-tinged thistle so well." In her nearness, she absorbed the tinge of approval that came with Tull's grin.

"She seldom accepts my flattery since I warned her never to trust the flatterer. And"—he showed pain as he inhaled—"she deserves more than a Guardian's care."

"*Awww.*" She covered her heart with her right hand. "How you've survived all this time by your own sense astonishes me!" She then hooked her arm around his. "Better that I lead you the rest of the way, nimble fawn."

TULL & EBBE

The rest of the way proved nearer than Tull imagined, as he saw afore them the coach that carried Sondrea from the Court of Learning to Ebbe Demesne after Ming's attack. Her driver, Charles Ralph Steinberg, leapt from his perch and removed his cap in the presence of Guardian, first, and lady, second. Charles then embraced Tull with the contagious jovialness of their giggling onlooker.

"May our Creator bless you evermore, fine soul!"

Tull noticed how fast his guide hid herself in the warmth of the coach.

"You were gone in your wits when I brung you here. Truly! I ought to have believed He would not fail us."

Even sedated, he cringed at the driver's grammar. "You?"

"On the orders of Overseer Greer. She believed they would not make a fuss over your mending here, though, after the mess you made at her chamber house, I can't say she would've let their fussing trouble her."

Tull's boyish grin tore at his wounds, still he committed the title of *Overseer* Greer to his mind. Driver Steinberg proved more forgiving than his pat to the Guardian's back, then ushered him toward the doorway of the coach. A faint scent of anthracite heat preceded a burst of warmth and helped Tull's hands as he rubbed away the cold and chose the bench seat opposite of she who walked with him. The way she covered her nose from the scent ruled her out as a Carpenterian or Westonian, from where the secondkind mined anthracite.

"I am impressed."

"You didn't believe I could find my way into the coach?"

"I didn't believe you appreciated the meaning of a japer."

Tull caught a glimpse of her smirk but reclined his head as the warmth mingled with the sedative in his blood and made him drowsy. He trusted that Sondrea would not hire two conniving souls in a row—since she inherited Mim's service—but sensed trouble. Trouble atop drowsiness that exceeded his mind's sifting of words and definitions in exchange for faces and locations. To the best of his mingled abilities, though, he could not recall the new succorer's name or where their paths crossed.

FORTY

<u>1721 Fresnel Park</u>

A once-abandoned tower of lofts.
Upon whose shadow crossed the Loy River.

Fresnel Park reflected light like no other plot along Sevier's northern hem. The place sat derelict fourteen spans, with the ornamental copper and iron skeleton exposed to the elements, since Artisan Merilyn Harris Sundström leapt to her end. Sundström was, to date, the most famous mistress of Master Builder E. E. Hobson due to the uncounted claimed sightings of her apparition throughout every winter since. As such, few souls proved eager to resurrect Hobson's idea.

Like her legacy, Fresnel Park enjoyed completion in the one hundred fifth growing season by Judge Cyril Adair Mumus. He set a glass skin upon the six-storey building as a showcase for his vision of Sevier's future. Ever since, the structure shimmered with all the gas lamps within and reflected the brilliance of the sky-fires above as though a beacon. Who better than a peacock to make a spectacle?

"I remember when first I watched the reel of our celebrated artisan"—the red-lipped succorer hesitated—"as she leapt from this place. My brother forced me to watch knowing that the sight would make me sob."

"I had a similar reaction to entering the Aquarium Exposition for the first time."

"Your honesty calms me." She stepped from the coach and offered her hand to him. "Shall we?"

Whether Tull accepted her help went unacknowledged.

"I read where Patsy Christine Lang paid three hundred gold alms for a loft on the second storey. I tell you, the specters whisked by so oft that she sold at a loss."

"Most—specters—are glints of light from out of doors and the groans of strained tresses met by the imaginations of the eve and changing temperatures."

"Tell that to Patsy. That poor soul was losing her peace by the tick!"

TULL & EBBE

Though the floors were cut from solid slab, occupants kept their privacy from the eyes of passersby to a single room. Given Sondrea's tale of her husband's projection glider investment, the two projects stood to increase the Mumus fortune to a sum that Tull—even whilst clear-minded—could not count.

"As we climb, might I ask how you pinned those creatures? Why broken glass pieces when you're renowned as an archer and feared for your axe?"

"I sacrificed my bow and Harlan took my axe."

"Yes. Are rocks not heavier than glass? Or iron pellets?"

"I tell you the implement was not what trapped them."

"What then?"

"I'emmärtä äksesi si'nun täy äty uskoa."

"I've heard that you speak the tongue of Ministers."

"Not from your benefactor."

"No."

Tull must have swayed more than he measured, for Sondrea's new succorer set her hand against his back and steadied him again till they reached the fourth storey.

"I tell you, this was not meant to be a test for you." Her huff of breath resonated through the stairwell. "I s'pose you prefer we were aboard the hoisted capsules at Mumus Tower."

"I've never set foot within that tower."

"Never?"

He paused afore his next step.

"I've never set foot within the Aquarium Exposition."

"I imagine both sites revel in intolerable pleasantries."

"I rather enjoyed that feeling of breathless uncertainty"—she arose onto the balls of her feet again—"a sensation not unlike what you and Guardian Falk must've felt the time you climbed the Somers Roundabout. Did you not?"

Tull's sense of guilt increased. The soul who led him proved well-informed about his time, yet he could not glean the slightest hint of their prior meeting, her identity, her connection to Otto and Jules, or her bullying brother.

"Or was that tale an invention of some Bel Geddes smear merchant?"

"I warned Olley most would believe him a flaunt. He had to be counted as a soul braver than Cam Fenner." He caught his breath as they reached the sixth storey. "The peacock versus the rooster."

TULL & EBBE

He found her grin awaiting him and then she offered a tilt of her head toward an opaque glass door.

"Here?"

"Our travels delivered us on time." She set her hand against the glass panel of the door and let the sensors that activated the locking mechanisms within identify her. A sweep of light moved as the clock turns and then back again. An image of the woman with shorter, wavier hair and a solemn expression appeared as though a phantom. "Letting pass how you trudge."

Tull read her name beneath her image and smirked; though, given his sedation, he might have displayed a broader response.

"My benefactor awaits you."

He stood the tallest, so the light that swept over them confirmed his identifier beacon first, then an opaque glass door gleamed as the circuits set between dual panes deactivated the lock and slid unto a recessed wall. A loft awaited; built with transparent walls except for a single, small room—three of the visitor's strides in breadth—to Tull's left. An open dwelling area showcased a kitchen along the corridor wall, then flowed against the clock's hand toward a nook meant for studying. Four display plates lined the outer wall, each muted but showing live views from around the isle that failed to dampen the exterior view that enticed the visitor toward a sunken living room.

She who led him now stayed two full strides to his rear, lest she keep him from the details. Two more rooms, situated on either side of the enclosed brick room, sat empty with frosted glass doors half-shut. The nearest to the entry, served as the bath and laundry. The furthest, on the northwest corner, served as the dominant bedroom, complete with a sunken bed, walk-through closet, and dressing area.

Between the bedroom and the four wall-mounted display plates, a set of pristine glass doors stood as ushers unto a terrace. The Jacobian stepped with concentration across lacquered floors as the exposed trellises overhead echoed the strike of his balancing cane. When he stood within reach of them, the terrace doors slid away and a brisk wind entered the loft. From there, he listened to the song of the pylons in the Forbidden Sea but their tune dulled beneath the ringing in his ear.

Anthracite fire in copper kettles stationed atop seven posts that held together a decorative iron hem drew him from the loft. If he strained his good eye, he could see the Somers Roundabout, but preferred the view of the Jacoby Territory. A cloud that matched the color of his irises settled across the northern territory from which he came and narrowed the ribbon of intense light that bled into the loft. Those clouds produced to the breeze that stifled the heat plumes of anthracite kettles and let through a note of clematis terniflora.

"I am relieved you've mended."

"My Guardian's selflessness deserved more from me." Sondrea rested in wait at a table nestled along the northeast wall. "Nelson, please forgive me."

"You have never hurt me."

"O, Nelson. Let kindness be your only lie toward me."

Tull refused his desire to look on her, that he might preserve the last moment afore she saw his new face. He heard the fall of the tails of her coat as she stood without agitating the chair or terrace. She then moved past him with a gentle squeeze of his hand and approached the decorative rail between two anthracite kettles.

"Powerful souls cannot bear to look upon those who bear the truth about their frailties."

The intent of her words escaped him, for he admired the gleam of light that shone against the outline of her frame as she leaned outward against the terrace rail. What drew his eye, then stung as the last ribbon of light gave way to the clouds. He watched the proudness of her shoulders and ignored how the winds turned strands of her hair into a constant distraction. She never seemed burdened by the disappointments or challenges she towed; rather, all challenges burnished her and increased her brilliance.

"Magick-wielders deceive all who are eager to be deceived. Even his daughter forgets her reflection on Ebbe Demesne and in the territory his magick poisoned. I cannot tell if I am a monster. Did I commit a crime against you? Have I paid my debt beneath Cyril's headship? Was all that ruined me a lie crafted by conscripts?"

He did not recognize her use of conscripts in that moment, then both paused as her new succorer loomed nearer.

"The parcel of suits arrived in time for Charles to bring them up."

"Currie upheld his word, did he not?"

"Three appealing ensembles."

"The cold-gray linen with the purple shirt?"

TULL & EBBE

"Along with a dark-blue three-piece that has undercurrents of amber threads and a cocoa-hued tweed with a stark-white, high-collared blouse." She caught Tull's slight head turn. "Shirt. I meant shirt."

"The future of the Guardians should look his best when he appears afore those who believe he steadies the trembling and keeps pure the blameless." Sondrea had changed in character away from the Shelby Territory. The countess proved less hope-filled than she who rescued a blameless soul from the Behemót Woods, and less seductive than she proved toward him till three moonrises ago. Still, she believed each word of praise she ever spoke over him.

"Is this Jacobian about to lose the light?"

"He oft makes such a face." Sondrea turned and saw her beloved Guardian for the first time since he was sent away to mend. Her eyes gleamed with empathy, but her smile bore a fondness she showed no other. She then remembered the ongoing conversation she lobbed around him. "His gold necktie?"

"Accounted. Handsome. And, is he growling? I'll wait in the furthest room."

"I warned her that the necktie would be your final straw."

When the winds intensified, he cradled his ear, then felt her steady him.

"This moment will not be set away and forgotten. Whatever our past, for me, our bond is evermore unchangeable. But, you must mend, my brave defender, and better I confess to you, that from here I must return to my own tower."

The admission bristled him more than the frigid breeze. "This began with you wanting me to prove he had no hand in the attack."

"And you have."

"But you believed him capable."

"I tell you, he poses no threat to me."

He countered in posturing. "There are more jackals on the bench than decent souls. The worst of them took from us our best."

"I have every confidence that Guardians Vosburg and Falk intend to see Guardian Elragadó honored and all responsible birched."

He proved steady as he rose in posture and let her look upon a face that shamed him. "I speak of you alone, Countess."

She reassured him with the calmness of her posture. "My husband slumbers; as he has slumbered since the last eve of our sowing season, and will continue to slumber till our one hundred ninth winter gets."

Though her claim toyed with his muddled gift of discernment, he did recognize that she smiled over the way she took on her grandfather's phrase for the thaw.

"Lest an end find him afore his slumber's end."

He rubbed at a spot on his neck that whiskers irritated. If not her husband, then her father and half-brother conspired against her. If Mumus slept, then no judge stood in her defense.

Her eyes caught the light as she marveled. "You see now why my new succorer is so important, do you not?"

He looked to the place where she who led him stood but found the spot absent. "He who arranged this remains—"

"No. He—*Tai'bu Kaas*—no longer remains. Silas Hendrie Falk Jr. wronged him, too, as I learned a tick afore the Guardian of this territory ended him with his saber."

"You observed as much?"

"Yes."

The Jacobian's pewter irises bore shades of blue monkshood and honey-hued flecks as his new face invited a new expression to his modest collection.

"You fret for me."

"I fear I upended two lines of creatures so your father's son could set a heavier heel against the territory's neck. Against my neck."

"Better you leave him to me. I've more knowledge of his character."

"Then teach me again."

"You are the right hand to the headship and the rightful Guardian of all Jacobians. We will both lose count of the Shelbian judges who followed Dale Marius by the time you lead. There is little more that I need teach you."

"I cannot lead. I am not fit to serve as Mim's replacement."

The countess tapped his chin. "As of this morn, no longer will there be secrets between us. I will repay at once—fourfold—what Dale Marius stole from you. I will see to your every provision, and you to my every whim. I will be she who remains with an open ear in closed chambers for your learning. You will be my observant eye in the fields that hide the truth from me. Together, and aided by my succorer and Charles, and other agents I employ from time to time, I believe we can make this land better for those whom the judges remember only to oppress."

"Am I to become an overseer?"

She offered an amused shake of her head. "Not even my adoration for the fruit of the James, Ellis, Tull, Hobson, Camp, and Nelson trees can advance you above the forty-four lines elder to you in our territory. I am not without kindness, though. If you mend, I will slow my step to let you hobble alongside wherever we go."

"As you say." Even sedated, he understood her sense of humor and looked upon her slow-mended leg.

"I've taken the time to see Blizzard placed in a proper stall—within sight of Ligurus—at my preferred livery in this territory. Charles's son has volunteered to see to both horses in your absence; as alms to you. I believe he prefers those Guardians without a waxed moustache." She looked upon him but withheld her hand. "That verse about a soul finding respect in their home . . ."

He nodded in remembrance.

"The words have stayed with me. You will know respect here."

After his silence loomed, Sondrea's aide spoke up. "Truly, the mixture that eases his pain also slows his ability to connect two points."

She whom he saved tilted her head in fondness for his every way. "For all you've done—for me—this loft is yours to call home. This is amid my alms to you."

"Don't make your time harder for my sake."

Sondrea squeezed two fingers upon his right hand. "Since the first moment you looked on me, a babe with brooding eyes, I've shared my grandfather's *instinct* to shelter you. I've failed you twice—to be certain. Not fighting for you remains my steepest regret. Let me mend my error."

"They would have ended you."

"I believe they did."

The memories of the past mingled with the brute pain he towed. He set his jaw and shut his eyes. As the altitude changed the pitch in his ear and the terrace swayed him, he exhaled and steadied without aide.

"After this eve's moon rises, never again be ashamed to let me see your face. I have you to thank for every moon I see till my end."

Afore he focused, she turned away. As the countess exited his view, her succorer entered; now with a clever smile and an ornery gleam.

"I will wait for you, dear."

TULL & EBBE

She who guided him nodded less out of obedience and more in equal standing, but held her tongue till she gauged Sondrea's whereabouts, then declared her alms to him. "Those in the Creighton Territory who have benefited from your purpose share with our noble friend in this much-belated gift to honor your birth."

He saw that she held a journal of width that proved narrower and a spine broader than other books. The front cover held the shape of a sliver of wood forced against the binding and adorned with frayed silk and small beads.

"The countess considers this work of tremendous value to you. She also passed on the peculiar bookmark; a memento from a journey of hers that began whilst you were called *Scion* Tull. Read the contents of each and understand." She teetered toward his unmarred eye. "You are able to read still, are you not?"

"Are you offering to tell me a tale?"

"Not from these pages."

"You will serve her well."

"She and I are the daughters of monstrous souls. Because I understand her plight, I am tasked—by the countess—to observe her ways and to end her if I see her becoming like her half-brother or her father."

"She believes I cannot remember the eves spent in her care, but I tell you with the certainty of these scars, that she chooses torment over a belief set in her mind by magick—by an intervention of meddlers who sought to spare the advocate of this arrogant territory from the shame of his bride's generosity toward an orphan and her refusal to bow unto them."

She sized him up as if she discerned his truthfulness and integrity. "You'll want well-versed and powerful fellows for what trouble awaits then. Consider this proof that you now have *two* such fellows, and mend well. I suspect that soon I will see you, Guardian Tull."

"Succorer Lael."

Lana Robin Lael let her smile brim as he acknowledged her, then turned to travel with her new benefactor. The daughter of Judge Chester Nicklaus Lael—a rival of Judges Cyril Mumus and Dale Marius Conliffe—never looked back as she took a place alongside the countess of Ebbe Demesne. In turn, the soul who now resided at 1721 Fresnel Park, Tier Six, North Loft, fell short of any remark as well; except that his heart felt a swell of curiosity as the pair departed. After all this time, he still proved slow to anticipate Sondrea's wit as he opened his gift.

TULL & EBBE

The Journal of Lee Arjeta Nelson, a soul who seeks to shine an everlasting light upon creatures called Seko'tae and the conscripts who serve them.
Begun on this Nineteenth Morn beneath the Moon of the Frail Dove in the Eighty-Third Winter of the Accession.

The winter that saw Tull's birth and the start of Sondrea's eleventh winter also marked the time when Tull's beloved grandmother stepped down from the judges' bench in anger. He then turned to the back of the journal and found the date of the closing entry.

The Twenty-Second Peak beneath the Moon of the Reaching Sea in the One Hundred and Third Sowing Season of the Accession.

In that same season, Cameron Lou Fenner sought another purpose in shame, Sondrea hid even from he who saved her from Noeu, and the wounded Jacobian twice ended the same foe for the sake of a stammering keeper's daughter. None of those events brought to mind he who was born to Tull's grandfather's other bride. Even without sedatives or pain, the wounded soul towed no memory of a voice, a face, or a nearness to Lee Arjeta Nelson—who used the words *Seko'tae* and *conscript* long afore his nephew heard them. The gift of his kin in part's journal held answers beyond an heirloom of a family he no longer remembered and Sondrea realized that worth.

The other token—the sliver of wood—creased the right side of his face with wonder. Affixed beneath a hard lacquer coat sat a slip of cotton paper folded once into an oblong shape that displayed two statements side by side versus stacked top to bottom; a writing style accredited to a single soul in all his travels across eighteen lands. The ink faded and the paper withered, but the memory of the words was as fresh to him as the first time he read them five eves ago in the Behemót Woods—this memento from a past journey of Sondrea's.

TULL & EBBE

"'Imagine, imagine!'" He tapped the wooden page-marker to his chin and sighed as he considered the author of a love note intended for him. "Truly, I 'ought to consider what a creepy creature in the shadows might do' when the judge of this territory wakes, J. J."

As he imagined how Sondrea recovered the note that he watched fall unto the shadows with a fumbling Kuusa Si'epä, he recalled the lights beneath the flesh of her leg and the injuries she received on a journey that coincided with his rescue of the love note's author. To this same eve, she had resisted telling him the details of her injury. This time, he pocketed the wooden trinket lest he lose Jules's note a second time. He then closed Lee's journal, tossed aside the balancing cane, and trusted the Helper to navigate him to the furthest point of his new home's terrace.

The wind scrubbed away the sound of the horses but not the pylon song. The coach traveled the roadway and, from his perch, he let his eye map a route to garish Mumus Tower. He then stared down Sevier's structural nemesis as though staring at Cyril Adair Mumus. Sondrea's home to his west, the Jacoby Territory to his north, and between them the ill-fated Forgney Bridge that fell and claimed one-fifth the count of souls who made a home in the Archibald, Gierig, and Jacoby Territories; Patrick James Tull included.

Patrick's son felt overwhelmed with the history and haunting influences that loomed around him. At the same time, he felt somewhat displayed and watched evermore: an outcast in a glass tower. What he might achieve there seemed uncertain. Then, because of a reminder from the Helper, the words of a passage flowed from his heart.

"'Now I'Esh could perform no mighty work there, except that He laid His hands on some sick and healed them. And He marveled because of their unbelief.'"

As he ended his recital of the scripture that Sondrea referenced, he noticed a flutter of motion. At the corners of the terrace, a cluster of Squires gathered as they gathered evermore at the sound of worship or praise. They smiled on him with such sweetness that matching the response arose without contest. There, beneath their provision of warmth that exceeded the anthracite kettles, he felt comforted.

"I am no Healer, and truly I am no Teacher, but I can imagine how a King might have felt blessed and humbled."

As his heart listened for the Helper and the Squires sang a melody of praise that took away the pylon's song, he sensed that another moved around him. Since he delivered Sondrea to the Gyddingford Chamber House and met her friends, Gloria Bea Greer and Clifton Lait Keyes, he felt such comfort. This was gentler than the assured voice that instructed him against Noeu and warmer than the fiery boldness that he associated with Enke'loi. The sensation made him feel cherished, and he sought the shape of that source as the wind blew into the loft.

When no presence appeared, he renewed his admiration for the view of the great sea—the Forbidden Sea—that roared toward the isle's shore and the brilliant, ice-glistening expanse of the Jacoby Territory to the north. This nearness to the territory of his birth produced a sense of gladness that the twisted pylons and the shadow of Mumus Tower could not diminish. Tears formed, despite his smile, and two Squires rushed to pat his back in comfort. As another settled on the bannister, not unlike the way Jules sat beside him on the rafters of the inn, a low hum of a forgotten hymn trickled into the Jacobian's new home.

ʕ | A Season for Gleaning

An Interim

THE 15TH EVE BENEATH THE MOON OF THE MOTHER'S SONG

THE 107TH WINTER SEASON OF THE ACCESSION

IN THE CARE OF THE HELPER, WHO KEEPS SOULS FROM FRUITLESS WANDERING.

191 TAUROG ROADWAY

BENEATH A VEIL OF MAGICK.

IN AN IMMACULATE PARLOR AT EBBE DEMESNE.

She who scarred Tull mended long after she should have recovered from the damage inflicted upon her as recompense for the Guardian's new face. Stripped bare and scrubbed free of the filth that provided her a second skin, she proved far younger than her wickedness suggested. She bore the look of mingled races and a figure primed for inflicting other woes. Though the Wanderers muddled her, remnants of beauty lasted in scarce, overlooked specks.

Seldom had the Squires or Ministers allowed their brethren access to such a vessel. Notorious in their regard for the blameless, they oft gathered those who strayed and tended to them till they corrected the paths of those they corrupted. For whatever reason—as reason differed from purpose—they *let* her suffer beneath the infestation she invited. In this alone, she proved of interest to her mender—her captor.

He who poisoned the Shelby Territory, his fellow Guardians, and the house of Beau Itzal Zeck sat—far from decrepit—eager to unfurl new woes. Magick destroyed the soul of Count Theodore Reaume Conliffe long afore his daughter's first step. Though he forced her to wed a monster of other corruptions, the act illustrated his final deed for another soul afore now. He kept his son and his second bride's cousin near to him and reshaped them into monsters of heartless flesh as he intended with the creature who drew his gaze.

Now, he had others to reshape: The babe given to Sondrea to be called daughter, the many daughters fathered by Dale Marius Conliffe and Saul Ole Ebbe, she who scarred a Guardian, and *more.* As a glazed-over expression added darkness to his false smile, he drummed his fingertips to an approaching heartbeat. Stronger than any other in the parlor, yet brimming with confusion, he sensed a bauble greater than others saw.

Asham, whom Tull bound and the other Guardians ignored, looked to the card-cheating brute who cut him loose and then to the count. The latter welcomed him with a flapping wave of his hand. Because his leg remained twisted from his bindings, the Guardian sidestepped into the parlor on an uncertain gait and with dim interest. Saul Ole Ebbe looked down his nose at his fumbling, but the northern territories' last living elder Guardian paid him the utmost attention.

"Your step is returning." The count wheeled his chair deeper unto the shadows and revealed a defeated soul. "This startling soul found neither the time nor the fighting spirits to cover herself afore you arrived."

Dory Orlean Sevilla—last seen plunged in the frozen millpond on the plot—sat slumped upon the tile floor. Furnished with a blanket, a bowl, and a chained collar woven from throat to four limbs, she reminded Asham of a kept pet. She looked greasy and bruised, which reminded him too of spoiled fruit. Her ruse against the countess failed. By now, all the territories learned of her family's name and failure—and none worried over her.

"Mit látsz, ostoba gyám?"

"Looks to be another bright morn, daughter." Saul Ole Ebbe pounded her proud jaw with a broader fist. "Do not spoil that with your dimness."

"No." The count drew back in his chair. "Not *morn*. What was that—the moon!"

The three souls around him focused their attention, though Dory mopped saliva from her chin across her forearm.

The count's eyes sparkled with delight and his mouth fell open with surprise as he faced his other plaything. "Bright Moon. Yes, yes. This will be the name I give to you—my creation, my daughter—Bright Moon."

As she who mended lifted her head in recognition of her new name, the torn skin fell apart and revealed the lean musculature beneath.

"Loose, loose, loose." He teetered his head from side to side and counted the filthiest creatures that visited his plot—like Katerena's horse. "Lucy! Yes, yes. *Lucy* Bright Moon will be your name."

His lackey applauded, which drew a chuckle from both perverse souls. Asham and Dory remained silent as the former approached the chamber and looked upon the mangled form within.

"Stand away from that glass, poi'kai. We've much work to do. Much work, much work. We must prove well-prepared."

She who changed Tull's face then thrust outward and withdrew into a twisted fetal shape. The veins within her throbbed but offered no outlet. Then, her skin broke open as spiny protrusions pressed from inside her. Bones broke—rock to rubble—and her entire form shook with a violence that made Asham's stomach churn. As he struggled to watch, he heard laughter throughout the room.

"I was beginning to doubt!" Sondrea's cousin declared.

"I told you none can withstand my magick."

"As you say!"

"Look upon her, poi'kai!"

Asham's eyes widened, as though pulled open by unseen fingers, and his head turned to bear witness as the body in the tank contorted in her brokenness. Shapes—unnatural and demonic—rippled her flesh and moved her body through the gel. Her mouth stretched open further than the lips allowed, and then the corners tore till all her teeth appeared and brought to mind Dory's true form. A funnel of violet hue moved through the gel and the glass restraints trembled.

The pane closest to Asham pebbled, struck from the inside by what he soon identified as teeth. An entwined gush of spirits raced from the broken mouth and struck the tooth-embedded glass. Then, a blackened flow poured out of her through natural and forced orifices. A shrill cry arose from out of the gel and the tank shook hard enough to change positions on the floor.

Count Conliffe screamed in an indiscernible tongue that confused and frightened his captive Guardian. The cry rose four octaves till fissures appeared around the embedded teeth. Asham fell to his knee in escape. The cry grew louder still, and the woman sank into the murky pit of her prison. Their captor shouted, and oily forms leapt from the open tank.

Tull & Ebbe

As they took to the air, they erupted unto fire. Some burned with green flame, others with yellow, still others with purple. Each form burned to grit that stung the back of Asham's neck in settling. He slapped away at the sensation, and his palms suffered miniscule puncture marks that bled without pressure.

This rain fell till the tank turned calm. The body within did not—could not—stir. Worse than those wounds that Tull bore, the whole of her face, figure, and stature proved too terrible to look upon. When Asham tried, he vomited. Then, as his ears cleared, he realized that the cry he heard was hers.

"Offer her no granule of sorrow, poi'kai. She is not what she seems."

"What around here is?"

The count and his reeve laughed.

"This amuses you?"

"All amuses me! This leaves me curious; that in our one hundredth sowing season, the Guardian from the Jacoby Territory met his end at Kanarek—and my daughter's heart with him. I tow the distinct memories of such times. I, and the rest of the territories, two distinct memories of his—and my daughter's heart—living still. Tell me how, poi'kai. How does the Jacobian return?"

Asham swallowed and felt the sting of restraints on his flesh. The soreness ran deeper than his loyalty. "He tells us that the Ministers take his soul and travel backward through time—however far Yah chooses—and *rewrites* his soul with both times so he corrects his way."

Dory rolled her eyes and the reeve scoffed, but the count matched and drummed his fingertips together as he spelled out a four-letter name. "I suspected there was another. I had hoped my daughter might . . ."

Asham found the count's sudden softness of interest.

"Tell me, how many times have you felt this *rewrite* happen?"

"I've never felt, but—"

"Still, you believe."

Asham nodded.

"Ever seen him nibble on a cake of cornmeal and honey when no means to make such could be found?"

Asham's eyes searched the shadows above till he nodded. "Seven times or more."

TULL & EBBE

The count laughed at the simplicity and brilliance he saw in Asham. He then saw how Asham admired his creation over the wondrous feats their twisted souls witnessed. "She ruined the Jacobian's face. I am told he failed to end her."

"No. If Nelson wanted her ended, she would be frozen and on a hook."

His host's head wobbled as Saul Ole Ebbe snickered in a way that invited abuse. Then a crooked smile lit the count's wrinkled face. "O, the glorious creatures you'll bring to me!"

"I told you"—the sound of metal striking stone grew louder—"a Creightonian is your truest and safest spy."

Asham stood in welcome silence as the count clapped but Dory retreated in her cage when the source of noise matched the peculiar tracks between the manor and her brother's hiding place in the Behemót Woods. The Guardian then looked upon a face adorned with columns of scar tissue upon her cheek.

"Did I not?"

"I remember your words!" The count faced she whose right leg was replaced at the hip with a mechanical limb that flowed down to a hinged, blade-like foot shaped like a horned-moon. Even Dory peered around Asham's hip for a look as the latest arrival rested her formed hip upon the arm of the magick-wielder's chair and slid her hand around his shoulders.

Asham proved his dull manners as he interrupted a display of their affections. "I have seen you afore. You're—"

"Poi'kai!"

"Yes!" The count's accomplice laughed. "I am she who struck your crown lest you tell of my trespass, who ended Barton Fredrick Ganix to dizzy the Guardians, who drove out the countess's peculiar reeve to make hungry the Kuusa Si'epä, who manipulated Tai'bu Kaas to attract the Taotáva, and who took from the care of our benefactor's daughter a blameless soul who—like me—no longer abides in Yah's purpose. I am she whom your fallen headship once cherished and could not attain, as much as I am she who felled your headship."

"In the flesh!" the count declared. Then, with a drum of fingertips across her limb, clucked his tongue. "As they say."

"The lot of you will help me to feel whole again; a feeling that your fallen headship once promised me, Guardian Gera."

"Why would we help you?" Dory agitated from her confines.

"I can teach you to become what I once was, or I can slit you from throat to belly then set you on fire on my way to find souls with better sense."

Sondrea's ousted succorer simmered as she who created havoc lit her notorious blowtorch. "I sought only a purpose amid your kind."

The count waved a frail hand and rolled nearer toward Lucy Bright Moon's mending chamber. "Come nearer then, my borrowed fruits, and let us speak of how you'll serve me and why these territories will fear you."

TULL & EBBE

SEVEN WINTERS' TIME

THE END

GRIFFIN WRAY

WHAT TROUBLE AWAITS . . .

TULL'S NEW PATH LEADS HIM TO

108 — ANYA THE SEARCHER

WHILST ANOTHER OF SONDREA'S TALES BEGINS IN

100 — EBBE THE OVERSEER

www.ingramcontent.com/pod-product-compliance
Lightning Source LLC
Chambersburg PA
CBHW030541310726
48979CB00010B/1990/J

9780999377611